William F...

THREE FAMOUS :

William Cuthbert Faulkner was bo...
sissippi, the first of four sons of Mur... ...kner (he
later added the "u" to the family name himself). In 1904 the family
moved to the university town of Oxford, Mississippi, where Faulkner
was to spend most of his life. He was named for his great-grandfather
"The Old Colonel," a Civil War veteran who built a railroad, wrote
a bestselling romantic novel called *The White Rose of Memphis*,
became a Mississippi state legislator, and was eventually killed in
what may or may not have been a duel with a disgruntled business
partner. Faulkner identified with this robust and energetic ancestor
and often said that he inherited the "ink stain" from him.

Never fond of school, Faulkner left at the end of football season
his senior year of high school, and began working at his grandfather's
bank. In 1918, after his plans to marry his sweetheart Estelle Oldham
were squashed by their families, he tried to enlist as a pilot in the
U.S. Army but was rejected because he did not meet the height and
weight requirements. He went to Canada, where he pretended to be
an Englishman and joined the RAF training program there.
Although he did not complete his training until after the war ended
and never saw combat, he returned to his hometown in uniform,
boasting of war wounds. He briefly attended the University of Mississippi, where he began to publish his poetry.

After spending a short time living in New York, he again
returned to Oxford, where he worked at the university post office. His
first book, a collection of poetry, *The Marble Faun*, was published at
Faulkner's own expense in 1924. The writer Sherwood Anderson,
whom he met in New Orleans in 1925, encouraged him to try writing
fiction, and his first novel, *Soldier's Pay*, was published in 1926. It was
followed by *Mosquitoes*. His next novel, which he titled *Flags in the
Dust*, was rejected by his publisher and twelve others to whom he
submitted it. It was eventually published in drastically edited form as
Sartoris (the original version was not issued until after his death).
Meanwhile, he was writing *The Sound and the Fury*, which, after

being rejected by one publisher, came out in 1929 and received many ecstatic reviews, although it sold poorly. Yet again, a new novel, *Sanctuary*, was initially rejected by his publisher, this time as "too shocking." While working on the night shift at a power plant, Faulkner wrote what he was determined would be his masterpiece, *As I Lay Dying*. He finished it in about seven weeks, and it was published in 1930, again to generally good reviews and mediocre sales.

In 1929 Faulkner had finally married his childhood sweetheart, Estelle, after her divorce from her first husband. They had a premature daughter, Alabama, who died ten days after birth in 1931; a second daughter, Jill, was born in 1933.

With the eventual publication of his most sensational and violent (as well as, up till then, most successful) novel, *Sanctuary* (1931), Faulkner was invited to write scripts for MGM and Warner Brothers, where he was responsible for much of the dialogue in the film versions of Hemingway's *To Have and Have Not* and Chandler's *The Big Sleep*, and many other films. He continued to write novels and published many stories in the popular magazines. *Light in August* (1932) was his first attempt to address the racial issues of the South, an effort continued in *Absalom, Absalom!* (1936), and *Go Down, Moses* (1942). By 1946, most of Faulkner's novels were out of print in the United States (although they remained well regarded in Europe), and he was seen as a minor, regional writer. But then the influential editor and critic Malcolm Cowley, who had earlier championed Hemingway and Fitzgerald and others of their generation, put together the *Portable Faulkner*, and once again Faulkner's genius was recognized, this time for good. He received the 1949 Nobel Prize for Literature as well as many other awards and accolades, including the National Book Award and the Gold Medal from the American Academy of Arts and Letters and France's Legion of Honor.

In addition to several collections of short fiction, his other novels include *Pylon* (1935), *The Unvanquished* (1938), *The Wild Palms* (1939), *The Hamlet* (1940), *Intruder in the Dust* (1948), *A Fable* (1954), *The Town* (1957), *The Mansion* (1959), and *The Reivers* (1962).

William Faulkner died of a heart attack on July 6, 1962, in Oxford, Mississippi, where he is buried.

BOOKS BY WILLIAM FAULKNER

The Marble Faun (1924)

Soldier's Pay (1926)

Mosquitoes (1927)

Sartoris (1929) [*Flags in the Dust* (1973)]

The Sound and the Fury (1929)

As I Lay Dying (1930)

Sanctuary (1931)

These 13 (1931)

Light in August (1932)

A Green Bough (1933)

Doctor Martino and Other Stories (1934)

Pylon (1935)

Absalom, Absalom! (1936)

The Unvanquished (1938)

The Wild Palms [*If I Forget Thee, Jerusalem*] (1939)

The Hamlet (1940)

Go Down, Moses (1942)

Intruder in the Dust (1948)

Knight's Gambit (1949)

Collected Stories of William Faulkner (1950)

Notes on a Horsethief (1951)

Requiem for a Nun (1954)

A Fable (1954)

Big Woods (1955)

The Town (1957)

The Mansion (1959)

The Reivers (1962)

Uncollected Stories of William Faulkner (1979, Posthumous)

THREE
FAMOUS
SHORT NOVELS

William Faulkner

THREE
FAMOUS
SHORT NOVELS

Spotted Horses

Old Man

The Bear

VINTAGE INTERNATIONAL
Vintage Books
A Division of Random House, Inc.
New York

FIRST VINTAGE INTERNATIONAL EDITION, SEPTEMBER 2011

"Spotted Horses" originally appeared in *The Hamlet*;
"Old Man" originally appeared in *The Wild Palms*; and
"The Bear" originally appeared in *Go Down, Moses*.

The revised texts and the notes for "Spotted Horses" and "Old Man"
are reprinted from *Novels 1936–1940* by William Faulkner, published by
The Library of America, in 1990, by permission.
The revised text and the notes for "The Bear" are reprinted from
Novels 1942–1954 by William Faulkner, published by The Library of America,
in 1994, by permission.

The Library of Congress has cataloged the Modern Library edition as follows:
Faulkner, William.
Three famous short novels / William Faulkner.
p. cm.
1. Mississippi—Social life and customs—Fiction.
PZ3. F272 TJ PS3511.A86
58006368

Vintage ISBN: 978-0-307-94675-1

www.vintagebooks.com

Printed in the United States of America

CONTENTS

PUBLISHER'S NOTE

This edition assembles the texts as corrected by Noel Polk in the Library of America editions of "Spotted Horses" from *The Hamlet* (1990); "Old Man" from *If I Forget Thee, Jerusalem [The Wild Palms]* (1990); and "The Bear" from *Go Down, Moses,* (1994). The copy-text for this edition is the ribbon typescript setting copy at the Alderman Library of the University of Virginia. An editors' note on the corrections by Noel Polk follows the text; the line and page notes were prepared by Joseph Blotner.

Spotted Horses

1

A little while before sundown the men lounging about the gallery of the store saw, coming up the road from the south, a covered wagon drawn by mules and followed by a considerable string of obviously alive objects which in the levelling sun resembled vari-sized and -colored tatters torn at random from large billboards—circus posters, say—attached to the rear of the wagon and inherent with its own separate and collective motion, like the tail of a kite.

"What in the hell is that?" one said.

"It's a circus," Quick said. They began to rise, watching the wagon. Now they could see that the animals behind the wagon were horses. Two men rode in the wagon.

"Hell fire," the first man—his name was Freeman—said. "It's Flem Snopes." They were all standing when the wagon came up and stopped and Snopes got down and approached the steps. He might have departed only this morning. He wore the same cloth cap, the minute bow tie against the white shirt, the same gray trousers. He mounted the steps.

"Howdy, Flem," Quick said. The other looked briefly at all of them and none of them, mounting the steps. "Starting you a circus?"

"Gentlemen," he said. He crossed the gallery; they made way for him. Then they descended the steps and approached the wagon, at the tail of which the horses stood in a restive clump, larger than rabbits and gaudy as parrots and shackled to one another and to the wagon itself with sections of barbed wire. Calico-coated, small-bodied, with delicate legs and pink faces in which their mismatched eyes rolled wild and subdued, they huddled, gaudy motionless and alert, wild as deer, deadly as rattlesnakes, quiet as doves. The men stood at a respectful distance, looking at them. At that moment Jody Varner came through the group, shouldering himself to the front of it.

"Watch yourself, doc," a voice said from the rear. But it was already too late. The nearest animal rose on its hind legs with lightning rapidity and struck twice with its fore feet at Varner's face, faster than a boxer, the movement of its surge against the wire which held it travelling backward among the rest of the band in a wave of thuds and lunges. "Hup, you broom-tailed hay-burning sidewinders," the same voice said. This was the second man who had arrived in the wagon. He was a stranger. He wore a heavy densely black moustache, a wide pale hat. When he thrust himself through and turned to herd them back from the horses they saw, thrust into the hip pockets of his tight jeans pants, the butt of a heavy pearl-handled pistol and a florid carton such as small cakes come in. "Keep away from them, boys," he said. "They've got kind of skittish, they aint been rode in so long."

"Since when have they been rode?" Quick said. The stranger looked at Quick. He had a broad, quite cold, wind-gnawed face and bleak cold eyes. His belly fitted neat and smooth as a peg into the tight trousers.

"I reckon that was when they were rode on the ferry to get across the Mississippi River," Varner said. The stranger looked at him. "My name's Varner," Jody said.

"Hipps," the other said. "Call me Buck." Across the left side of his head, obliterating the tip of that ear, was a savage and recent gash gummed over with a blackish substance like axle-grease. They looked at the scar. Then they watched him remove the carton from his pocket and tilt a gingersnap into his hand and put the gingersnap into his mouth, beneath the moustache.

"You and Flem have some trouble back yonder?" Quick said. The stranger ceased chewing. When he looked directly at anyone, his eyes became like two pieces of flint turned suddenly up in dug earth.

"Back where?" he said.

"Your nigh ear," Quick said.

"Oh," the other said. "That." He touched his ear. "That was my mistake. I was absent-minded one night when I was staking them out. Studying about something else and forgot how long the wire was." He chewed. They looked at his ear. "Happen to any man careless around a horse. Put a little axle-dope on it and you wont notice it tomorrow though. They're pretty lively now, lazing along all day doing nothing. It'll work out of them in a couple of days." He put another gingersnap into his mouth, chewing. "Dont you believe they'll gentle?" No one answered. They looked at the ponies, grave and non-committal. Jody turned and went back into the store. "Them's good, gentle ponies," the stranger said. "Watch now." He put the carton back into his pocket and approached the horses, his hand extended. The nearest one was standing on three legs now. It appeared to be asleep. Its eyelid drooped over the cerulean eye; its head was shaped like an ironing-board. Without even raising the eyelid it flicked its head, the yellow teeth cropped. For an instant it and the man appeared to be inextricable in one violence. Then they became motionless, the stranger's high heels dug into the earth, one hand gripping the animal's nostrils, holding the horse's head wrenched half around while it breathed in hoarse, smothered groans. "See?" the stranger said in a panting voice, the veins standing white and rigid in his neck and along his jaw. "See? All you got to do is handle them a little and work hell out of them for a couple of days. Now look out. Give me room back there." They gave back a little. The stranger gathered himself then sprang away. As he did so, a second horse slashed at his back, severing his vest from collar to hem down the back exactly as the trick swordsman severs a floating veil with one stroke.

"Sho now," Quick said. "But suppose a man dont happen to own a vest."

At that moment Jody Varner, followed by the blacksmith, thrust through them again. "All right, Buck," he said. "Better get them on into the lot. Eck here will help you." The stranger, the severed halves of the vest swinging from either shoulder, mounted to the wagon seat, the blacksmith following.

"Get up, you transmogrified hallucinations of Job and Jezebel," the stranger said. The wagon moved on, the tethered ponies coming gaudily into motion behind it, behind which in turn the men followed at a respectful distance, on up the road and into the lane and so to the lot gate behind Mrs Littlejohn's. Eck got down and opened the gate. The wagon passed through but when the ponies saw the fence the herd surged backward against the wire which attached it to the wagon, standing on its collective hind legs and then trying to turn within itself, so that the wagon moved backward for a few feet until the Texan, cursing, managed to saw the mules about and so lock the wheels. The men following had already fallen rapidly back. "Here, Eck," the Texan said. "Get up here and take the reins." The blacksmith got back in the wagon and took the reins. Then they watched the Texan descend, carrying a looped-up black-snake whip, and go around to the rear of the herd and drive it through the gate, the whip snaking about the harlequin rumps in methodical and pistol-like reports. Then the watchers hurried across Mrs Littlejohn's yard and mounted to the veranda, one end of which overlooked the lot.

"How you reckon he ever got them tied together?" Freeman said.

"I'd a heap rather watch how he aims to turn them loose," Quick said. The Texan had climbed back into the halted wagon. Presently he and Eck both appeared at the rear end of the open hood. The Texan grasped the wire and began to draw the first horse up to the wagon, the animal plunging and surging back against the wire as though trying to hang itself, the contagion passing back through the herd from animal to animal until they were rearing and plunging again against the wire.

"Come on, grab a holt," the Texan said. Eck grasped the wire also. The horses laid back against it, the pink faces tossing above the back-surging mass. "Pull him up, pull him up," the Texan said sharply. "They couldn't get up here in the wagon even if they wanted to." The wagon moved gradually backward until the head of the first horse was snubbed up to the tail-gate. The Texan took a turn of the wire quickly about one of the wagon stakes. "Keep the slack out of it," he said. He vanished and reappeared, almost in the same second, with a pair of heavy wire-cutters. "Hold them like that," he said, and leaped. He vanished, broad hat, flapping vest, wire-cutters and all, into a kaleidoscopic maelstrom of long teeth and wild eyes and slashing feet, from which presently the horses began to burst one by one like partridges flushing, each wearing a necklace of barbed wire. The first one crossed the lot at top speed, on a straight line. It galloped into the fence without any diminution whatever. The wire gave, recovered, and slammed the horse to earth where it lay for a moment, glaring, its legs still galloping in air. It scrambled up without having ceased to gallop and crossed the lot and galloped into the opposite fence and was slammed again to earth. The others were now freed. They whipped and whirled about the lot like dizzy fish in a bowl. It had seemed like a big lot until now, but now the very idea that all that fury and motion should be transpiring inside any one fence was something to be repudiated with contempt, like a mirror trick. From the ultimate dust the stranger, carrying the wire-cutters and his vest completely gone now, emerged. He was not running, he merely moved with a light-poised and watchful celerity, weaving among the calico rushes of the animals, feinting and dodging like a boxer until he reached the gate and crossed the yard and mounted to the veranda. One sleeve of his shirt hung only at one point from his shoulder. He ripped it off and wiped his face with it and threw it away and took out the paper carton and shook a gingersnap into his hand. He was breathing only a little heavily. "Pretty lively now," he said. "But it'll work out of them in a couple of days." The ponies still streaked back and forth through the growing dusk like hysterical fish, but not so violently now.

"What'll you give a man to reduce them odds a little for

you?" Quick said. The Texan looked at him, the eyes bleak, pleasant and hard above the chewing jaw, the heavy moustache. "To take one of them off your hands?" Quick said.

At that moment the little periwinkle-eyed boy came along the veranda, saying, "Papa, papa; where's papa?"

"Who you looking for, sonny?" one said.

"It's Eck's boy," Quick said. "He's still out yonder in the wagon. Helping Mr Buck here." The boy went on to the end of the veranda, in diminutive overalls — a miniature replica of the men themselves.

"Papa," he said. "Papa." The blacksmith was still leaning from the rear of the wagon, still holding the end of the severed wire. The ponies, bunched for the moment, now slid past the wagon, flowing, stringing out again so that they appeared to have doubled in number, rushing on; the hard rapid light patter of unshod hooves came out of the dust. "Mamma says to come on to supper," the boy said.

The moon was almost full then. When supper was over and they had gathered again along the veranda, the alteration was hardly one of visibility even. It was merely a translation from the lapidary-dimensional of day to the treacherous and silver receptivity in which the horses huddled in mazy camouflage, or singly or in pairs rushed, fluid, phantom, and unceasing, to huddle again in mirage-like clumps from which came high abrupt squeals and the vicious thudding of hooves.

Ratliff was among them now. He had returned just before supper. He had not dared take his team into the lot at all. They were now in Bookwright's stable a half mile from the store. "So Flem has come home again," he said. "Well, well, well. Will Varner paid to get him to Texas, so I reckon it aint no more than fair for you fellows to pay the freight on him back." From the lot there came a high thin squeal. One of the animals emerged. It seemed not to gallop but to flow, bodiless, without dimension. Yet there was the rapid light beat of hard hooves on the packed earth.

"He aint said they was his yet," Quick said.

"He aint said they aint neither," Freeman said.

"I see," Ratliff said. "That's what you are holding back on. Until he tells you whether they are his or not. Or maybe you can wait until the auction's over and split up and some can follow Flem and some can follow that Texas fellow and watch to see which one spends the money. But then, when a man's done got trimmed, I dont reckon he cares who's got the money."

"Maybe if Ratliff would leave here tonight, they wouldn't make him buy one of them ponies tomorrow," a third said.

"That's a fact," Ratliff said. "A fellow can dodge a Snopes if he just starts lively enough. In fact, I dont believe he would have to pass more than two folks before he would have another victim intervened betwixt them. You folks aint going to buy them things sho enough, are you?" Nobody answered. They sat on the steps, their backs against the veranda posts, or on the railing itself. Only Ratliff and Quick sat in chairs, so that to them the others were black silhouettes against the dreaming lambence of the moonlight beyond the veranda. The pear tree across the road opposite was now in full and frosty bloom, the twigs and branches springing not outward from the limbs but standing motionless and perpendicular above the horizontal boughs like the separate and upstreaming hair of a drowned woman sleeping upon the uttermost floor of the windless and tideless sea.

"Anse McCallum brought two of them horses back from Texas once," one of the men on the steps said. He did not move to speak. He was not speaking to anyone. "It was a good team. A little light. He worked it for ten years. Light work, it was."

"I mind it," another said. "Anse claimed he traded fourteen rifle cartridges for both of them, didn't he?"

"It was the rifle too, I heard," a third said.

"No, it was just the shells," the first said. "The fellow wanted to swap him four more for the rifle too, but Anse said he never needed them. Cost too much to get six of them back to Mississippi."

"Sho," the second said. "When a man dont have to invest so much into a horse or a team, he dont need to expect so much from it." The three of them were not talking any louder, they were merely talking among themselves, to one another, as if they sat there alone. Ratliff, invisible in the shadow against the wall, made a sound, harsh, sardonic, not loud.

"Ratliff's laughing," a fourth said.

"Dont mind me," Ratliff said. The three speakers had not moved. They did not move now, yet there seemed to gather about the three silhouettes something stubborn, convinced, and passive, like children who have been chidden. A bird, a shadow, fleet and dark and swift, curved across the moonlight, upward into the pear tree and began to sing; a mockingbird.

"First one I've noticed this year," Freeman said.

"You can hear them along Whiteleaf every night," the first man said. "I heard one in February. In that snow. Singing in a gum."

"Gum is the first tree to put out," the third said. "That was why. It made it feel like singing, fixing to put out that way. That was why it taken a gum."

"Gum first to put out?" Quick said. "What about willow?"

"Willow aint a tree," Freeman said. "It's a weed."

"Well, I dont know what it is," the fourth said. "But it aint no weed. Because you can grub up a weed and you are done with it. I been grubbing up a clump of willows outen my spring pasture for fifteen years. They are the same size every year. Only difference is, it's just two or three more trees every time."

"And if I was you," Ratliff said, "that's just exactly where I would be come sunup tomorrow. Which of course you aint going to do. I reckon there aint nothing under the sun or in Frenchman's Bend neither that can keep you folks from giving Flem Snopes and that Texas man your money. But I'd sholy like to know just exactly who I was giving my money to. Seems like Eck here would tell you. Seems like he'd do that for his neighbors, dont it? Besides being Flem's cousin, him and that boy of his, Wallstreet, helped that Texas man tote water for them tonight and Eck's going to help him feed them in the morning too. Why, maybe Eck will be the one that will catch them and lead them up one at a time for you folks to bid on them. Aint that right, Eck?"

The other man sitting on the steps with his back against the post was the blacksmith. "I dont know," he said.

"Boys," Ratliff said, "Eck knows all about them horses. Flem's told him, how much they cost and how much him and that Texas man aim to get for them, make off of them. Come on, Eck. Tell us." The other did not move, sitting on the top step, not quite facing them, sitting there beneath the successive layers of their quiet and intent concentrated listening and waiting.

"I dont know," he said. Ratliff began to laugh. He sat in the chair, laughing while the others sat or lounged upon the steps and the railing, sitting beneath his laughing as Eck had sat beneath their listening and waiting. Ratliff ceased laughing. He rose. He yawned, quite loud.

"All right. You folks can buy them critters if you want to. But me, I'd just as soon buy a tiger or a rattlesnake. And if Flem Snopes offered me either one of them, I would be afraid to touch it for fear it would turn out to be a painted dog or a piece of garden hose when I went up to take possession of it. I bid you one and all goodnight." He entered the house. They did not look after him, though after a while they all shifted a little and looked down into the lot, upon the splotchy, sporadic surge and flow of the horses, from among which from time to time came an abrupt squeal, a thudding blow. In the pear tree the mockingbird's idiot reiteration pulsed and purled.

"Anse McCallum made a good team outen them two of hisn," the first man said. "They was a little light. That was all."

When the sun rose the next morning a wagon and three saddled mules stood in Mrs Littlejohn's lane and six men and Eck Snopes' son were already leaning on the fence, looking at the horses which huddled in a quiet clump before the barn door, watching the men in their turn. A second wagon came up the road and into the lane and stopped, and then there were eight men beside the boy standing at the fence, beyond which the horses stood, their blue-and-brown eyeballs rolling alertly in their gaudy faces. "So this here is the Snopes circus, is it?" one of the newcomers said. He glanced at the faces, then he went to the end of the row and stood beside the blacksmith and the little boy. "Are them Flem's horses?" he said to the blacksmith.

"Eck dont know who them horses belong to anymore than we do," one of the others said. "He knows that Flem come here on the same wagon with them, because he saw him. But that's all."

"And all he will know," a second said. "His own kin will be

the last man in the world to find out anything about Flem Snopes' business."

"No," the first said. "He wouldn't even be that. The first man Flem would tell his business to would be the man that was left after the last man died. Flem Snopes dont even tell himself what he is up to. Not if he was laying in bed with himself in a empty house in the dark of the moon."

"That's a fact," a third said. "Flem would trim Eck or any other of his kin quick as he would us. Aint that right, Eck?"

"I dont know," Eck said. They were watching the horses, which at that moment broke into a high-eared, stiff-kneed swirl and flowed in a patchwork wave across the lot and brought up again, facing the men along the fence, so they did not hear the Texan until he was among them. He wore a new shirt and another vest a little too small for him and he was just putting the paper carton back into his hip pocket.

"Morning, morning," he said. "Come to get an early pick, have you? Want to make me an offer for one or two before the bidding starts and runs the prices up?" They had not looked at the stranger long. They were not looking at him now, but at the horses in the lot, which had lowered their heads, snuffing into the dust.

"I reckon we'll look a while first," one said.

"You are in time to look at them eating breakfast, any-how," the Texan said. "Which is more than they done without they staid up all night." He opened the gate and entered it. At once the horses jerked their heads up, watching him. "Here, Eck," the Texan said over his shoulder, "two or three of you boys help me drive them into the barn." After a moment Eck and two others approached the gate, the little boy at his father's heels, though the other did not see him until he turned to shut the gate.

"You stay out of here," Eck said. "One of them things will snap your head off same as a acorn before you even know it." He shut the gate and went on after the others, whom the Texan had now waved fanwise outward as he approached the horses which now drew into a restive huddle, beginning to mill slightly, watching the men. Mrs Littlejohn came out of the kitchen and crossed the yard to the woodpile, watching the lot. She picked up two or three sticks of wood and paused, watching the lot again. Now there were two more men standing at the fence.

"Come on, come on," the Texan said. "They wont hurt you. They just aint never been in under a roof before."

"I just as lief let them stay out here, if that's what they want to do," Eck said.

"Get yourself a stick—there's a bunch of wagon-stakes against the fence yonder—and when one of them tries to rush you, bust him over the head so he will understand what you mean." One of the men went to the fence and got three of the stakes and returned and distributed them. Mrs Littlejohn, her armful of wood complete now, paused again halfway back to the house, looking into the lot. The little boy was directly behind his father again, though this time the father had not discovered him yet. The men advanced toward the horses, the huddle of which began to break into gaudy units turning inward upon themselves. The Texan was cursing them in a loud steady cheerful voice. "Get in there, you banjo-faced jackrabbits. Dont hurry them, now. Let them take their time. Hi! Get in there. What do you think that barn is—a law-court maybe? Or maybe a church and somebody is going to take up a collection on you?" The animals fell slowly back. Now and then one feinted to break from the huddle, the Texan driving it back each time with skillfully-thrown bits of dirt. Then one at the rear saw the barn door just behind it but before the herd could break the Texan snatched the wagon-stake from Eck and, followed by one of the other men, rushed at the horses and began to lay about the heads and shoulders, choosing by unerring instinct the point animal and striking it first square in the face then on the withers as it turned and then on the rump as it turned further, so that when the break came it was reversed and the entire herd rushed into the long open hallway and brought up against the further wall with a hollow, thunderous sound like that of a collapsing mine-shaft. "Seems to have held all right," the Texan said. He and the other man slammed the half-length doors and looked over them into the tunnel of the barn, at the far end of which the ponies were now a splotchy phantom moiling punctuated by crackings of wooden partitions and the dry reports of hooves which gradually died away. "Yep, it held all right," the Texan said. The other two came to the doors and looked over them. The little boy came up beside his father now, trying to see through a crack, and Eck saw him.

"Didn't I tell you to stay out of here?" Eck said. "Dont you know them things will kill you quicker than you can say scat? You go and get outside of that fence and stay there."

"Why dont you get your paw to buy you one of them, Wall?" one of the men said.

"Me buy one of them things?" Eck said. "When I can go to the river anytime and catch me a snapping turtle or a moccasin for nothing? You go on, now. Get out of here and stay out." The Texan had entered the barn. One of the men closed the doors after him and put the bar up again and over the top of the doors they watched the Texan go on down the hallway, toward the ponies which now huddled like gaudy phantoms in the gloom, quiet now and already beginning to snuff experimentally into the long lipworn trough fastened against the rear wall. The little boy had merely gone around behind his father, to the other side, where he stood peering now through a knot-hole in a plank. The Texan opened a smaller door in the wall and entered it, though almost immediately he reappeared.

"I dont see nothing but shelled corn in here," he said. "Snopes said he would send some hay up here last night."

"Wont they eat corn either?" one of the men said.

"I dont know," the Texan said. "They aint never seen any that I know of. We'll find out in a minute though." He disappeared, though they could still hear him in the crib. Then he emerged once more, carrying a big double-ended feed-basket, and retreated into the gloom where the parti-colored rumps of the horses were now ranged quietly along the feeding-trough. Mrs Littlejohn appeared once more, on the veranda this time, carrying a big brass dinner bell. She raised it to make the first stroke. A small commotion set up among the ponies as the Texan approached but he began to speak to them at once, in a brisk loud unemphatic mixture of cursing and cajolery, disappearing among them. The men at the door heard the dry rattling of the corn-pellets into the trough, a sound broken by a single snort of amazed horror. A plank cracked with a loud report; before their eyes the depths of the hallway dissolved in loud fury, and while they stared over the doors, unable yet to begin to move, the entire interior exploded into mad tossing shapes like a down-rush of flames.

"Hell fire," one of them said. "Jump!" he shouted. The three turned and ran frantically for the wagon, Eck last. Several voices from the fence were now shouting something but Eck did not even hear them until, in the act of scrambling madly at the tail-gate, he looked behind him and saw the little boy still leaning to the knot-hole in the door which in the next instant vanished into matchwood, the knot-hole itself exploding from his eye and leaving him, motionless in the diminutive overalls and still leaning forward a little until he vanished utterly beneath the towering parti-colored wave full of feet and glaring eyes and wild teeth which, overtopping, burst into scattering units, revealing at last the gaping orifice and the little boy still standing in it, unscathed, his eye still leaned to the vanished knot-hole.

"Wall!" Eck roared. The little boy turned and ran for the wagon. The horses were whipping back and forth across the lot, as if while in the barn they had once more doubled their number; two of them rushed up quartering and galloped all over the boy again without touching him as he ran, earnest and diminutive and seemingly without progress, though he reached the wagon at last, from which Eck, his sunburned skin now a sickly white, reached down and snatched the boy into the wagon by the straps of his overalls and slammed him face down across his knees and caught up a coiled hitching-rope from the bed of the wagon.

"Didn't I tell you to get out of here?" Eck said in a shaking voice. "Didn't I tell you?"

"If you're going to whip him, you better whip the rest of us too and then one of us can frail hell out of you," one of the others said.

"Or better still, take the rope and hang that durn fellow yonder," the second said. The Texan was now standing in the wrecked door of the barn, taking the gingersnap carton from his hip pocket. "Before he kills the rest of Frenchman's Bend too."

"You mean Flem Snopes," the first said. The Texan tilted the carton above his other open palm. The horses still rushed and swirled back and forth but they were beginning to slow now, trotting on high, stiff legs, although their eyes were still rolling whitely and various.

"I misdoubted that damn shell corn all along," the Texan said. "But at least they have seen what it looks like. They cant claim they aint got nothing out of this trip." He shook the carton over his open hand. Nothing came out of it. Mrs Littlejohn on the veranda made the first stroke with the dinner bell; at the sound the horses rushed again, the earth of the lot becoming vibrant with the light dry clatter of hooves. The Texan crumpled the carton and threw it aside. "Chuck wagon," he said. There were three more wagons in the lane now and there were twenty or more men at the fence when the Texan, followed by his three assistants and the little boy, passed through the gate. The bright cloudless early sun gleamed upon the pearl butt of the pistol in his hip pocket and upon the bell which Mrs Littlejohn still rang, peremptory, strong, and loud.

When the Texan, picking his teeth with a splintered kitchen match, emerged from the house twenty minutes later, the tethered wagons and riding horses and mules extended from the lot gate to Varner's store, and there were more than fifty men now standing along the fence beside the gate, watching him quietly, a little covertly, as he approached, rolling a little, slightly bowlegged, the high heels of his carved boots printing neatly into the dust. "Morning, gents," he said. "Here, Bud," he said to the little boy, who stood slightly behind him, looking at the protruding butt of the pistol. He took a coin from his pocket and gave it to the boy. "Run to the store and get me a box of gingersnaps." He looked about at the quiet faces, protuberant, sucking his teeth. He rolled the match from one side of his mouth to the other without touching it. "You boys done made your picks, have you? Ready to start her off, hah?" They did not answer. They were not looking at him now. That is, he began to have the feeling that each face had stopped looking at him the second before his gaze reached it. After a moment Freeman said:

"Aint you going to wait for Flem?"

"Why?" the Texan said. Then Freeman stopped looking at him too. There was nothing in Freeman's face either. There was nothing, no alteration, in the Texan's voice. "Eck, you done already picked out yours. So we can start her off when you are ready."

"I reckon not," Eck said. "I wouldn't buy nothing I was afraid to walk up and touch."

"Them little ponies?" the Texan said. "You helped water and feed them. I bet that boy of yours could walk up to any one of them."

"He better not let me catch him," Eck said. The Texan looked about at the quiet faces, his gaze at once abstract and alert, with an impenetrable surface quality like flint, as though the surface were impervious or perhaps there was nothing behind it.

"Them ponies is gentle as a dove, boys. The man that buys them will get the best piece of horseflesh he ever forked or druv for the money. Naturally they got spirit; I aint selling crowbait. Besides, who'd want Texas crowbait anyway, with Mississippi full of it?" His stare was still absent and unwinking; there was no mirth or humor in his voice and there was neither mirth nor humor in the single guffaw which came from the rear of the group. Two wagons were now drawing out of the road at the same time, up to the fence. The men got down from them and tied them to the fence and approached.

"Come up, boys," the Texan said. "You're just in time to buy a good gentle horse cheap."

"How about that one that cut your vest off last night?" a voice said. This time three or four guffawed. The Texan looked toward the sound, bleak and unwinking.

"What about it?" he said. The laughter, if it had been laughter, ceased. The Texan turned to the nearest gatepost and climbed to the top of it, his alternate thighs deliberate and bulging in the tight trousers, the butt of the pistol catching and losing the sun in pearly gleams. Sitting on the post, he looked down at the faces along the fence which were attentive, grave, reserved and not looking at him. "All right," he said. "Who's going to start her off with a bid? Step right up; take your pick and make your bid, and when the last one is sold, walk in that lot and put your rope on the best piece of horseflesh you ever forked or druv for the money. There aint a pony there that aint worth fifteen dollars. Young, sound, good for saddle or work stock, guaranteed to outlast four ordinary horses; you couldn't kill one of them with a axle-tree——" There was a small violent commotion at the rear of the group. The little boy appeared, burrowing among the motionless overalls. He approached the post, the new and unbroken paper carton lifted. The Texan leaned down and took it and tore the end from it and shook three or four of the cakes into the boy's hand, a hand as small and almost as black as that of a coon. He held the carton in his hand while he talked, pointing out the horses with it as he indicated them. "Look at that one with the three stocking feet and the frost-bit ear; watch him now when they pass again. Look at that shoulder-action; that horse is worth twenty dollars of any man's money. Who'll make me a bid on him to start her off?" His voice was harsh,

ready, forensic. Along the fence below him the men stood
with, buttoned close in their overalls, the tobacco-sacks and
worn purses the sparse silver and frayed bills hoarded a coin at
a time in the cracks of chimneys or chinked into the logs of
walls. From time to time the horses broke and rushed with
purposeless violence and huddled again, watching the faces
along the fence with wild mismatched eyes. The lane was full
of wagons now. As the others arrived they would have to stop
in the road beyond it and the occupants came up the lane on
foot. Mrs Littlejohn came out of her kitchen. She crossed the
yard, looking toward the lot gate. There was a blackened wash-
pot set on four bricks in the corner of the yard. She built a fire
beneath the pot and came to the fence and stood there for a
time, her hands on her hips and the smoke from the fire drifting blue and slow behind her. Then she turned and went back
into the house. "Come on, boys," the Texan said. "Who'll
make me a bid?"

"Four bits," a voice said. The Texan did not even glance
toward it.

"Or, if he dont suit you, how about that fiddle-head horse
without no mane to speak of? For a saddle pony, I'd rather
have him than that stocking-foot. I heard somebody say fifty
cents just now. I reckon he meant five dollars, didn't he? Do I
hear five dollars?"

"Four bits for the lot," the same voice said. This time there
were no guffaws. It was the Texan who laughed, harshly, with
only his lower face, as if he were reciting a multiplication
table.

"Fifty cents for the dried mud offen them, he means," he
said. "Who'll give a dollar more for the genuine Texas cockle-
burrs?" Mrs Littlejohn came out of the kitchen, carrying the
sawn half of a wooden hogshead which she set on a stump

beside the smoking pot, and stood with her hands on her hips, looking into the lot for a while without coming to the fence this time. Then she went back into the house. "What's the matter with you boys?" the Texan said. "Here, Eck, you been helping me and you know them horses. How about making me a bid on that wall-eyed one you picked out last night? Here. Wait a minute." He thrust the paper carton into his other hip pocket and swung his feet inward and dropped, cat-light, into the lot. The ponies, huddled, watched him. Then they broke before him and slid stiffly along the fence. He turned them and they whirled and rushed back across the lot; whereupon, as though he had been waiting his chance when they should have turned their backs on him, the Texan began to run too, so that when they reached the opposite side of the lot and turned, slowing to huddle again, he was almost upon them. The earth became thunderous; dust arose, out of which the animals began to burst like flushed quail and into which, with that apparently unflagging faith in his own invulnerability, the Texan rushed. For an instant the watchers could see them in the dust—the pony backed into the angle of the fence and the stable, the man facing it, reaching toward his hip. Then the beast rushed at him in a sort of fatal and hopeless desperation and he struck it between the eyes with the pistol-butt and felled it and leaped onto its prone head. The pony recovered almost at once and pawed itself to its knees and heaved at its prisoned head and fought itself up, dragging the man with it; for an instant in the dust the watchers saw the man free of the earth and in violent lateral motion like a rag attached to the horse's head. Then the Texan's feet came back to earth and the dust blew aside and revealed them, motionless, the Texan's sharp heels braced into the ground, one hand gripping the pony's forelock and the other its nostrils, the long evil muzzle wrung backward over its scarred shoulder while it breathed in labored and hollow groans. Mrs Littlejohn was in the yard again. No one had seen her emerge this time. She carried an armful of clothing and a metal-ridged wash-board and she was standing motionless at the kitchen steps, looking into the lot. Then she moved across the yard, still looking into the lot, and dumped the garments into the tub, still looking into the lot. "Look him over, boys," the Texan panted, turning his own suffused face and the protuberant glare of his eyes toward the fence. "Look him over quick. Them shoulders and——" He had relaxed for an instant apparently. The animal exploded again; again for an instant the Texan was free of the earth, though he was still talking: "—and legs you whoa I'll tear your face right look him over quick boys worth fifteen dollars of let me get a holt of who'll make me a bid whoa you blare-eyed jackrabbit, whoa!" They were moving now—a kaleidoscope of inextricable and incredible violence on the periphery of which the metal clasps of the Texan's suspenders sun-glinted in ceaseless orbit, with terrific slowness across the lot. Then the broad clay-colored hat soared deliberately outward; an instant later the Texan followed it, though still on his feet, and the pony shot free in mad, staglike bounds. The Texan picked up the hat and struck the dust from it against his leg, and returned to the fence and mounted the post again. He was breathing heavily. Still the faces did not look at him as he took the carton from his hip and shook a cake from it and put the cake into his mouth, chewing, breathing harshly. Mrs Littlejohn turned away and began to bail water from the pot into the tub, though after each bucketful she turned her head and looked into the lot again. "Now, boys," the Texan said. "Who says that pony aint worth fifteen dollars? You couldn't buy that much dynamite for just fifteen dollars. There aint one of them cant do a mile in three minutes; turn them into pasture and they will board themselves; work them like hell all day and every time you think about it, lay them over the head with a single-tree and after a couple of days every jackrabbit one of them will be so tame you will have to put them out of the house at night like a cat." He shook another cake from the carton and ate it. "Come on, Eck," he said. "Start her off. How about ten dollars for that horse, Eck?"

"What need I got for a horse I would need a bear-trap to catch?" Eck said.

"Didn't you just see me catch him?"

"I seen you," Eck said. "And I dont want nothing as big as a horse if I got to wrastle with it every time it finds me on the same side of a fence it's on."

"All right," the Texan said. He was still breathing harshly, but now there was nothing of fatigue or breathlessness in it. He shook another cake into his palm and inserted it beneath his moustache. "All right. I want to get this auction started. I aint come here to live, no matter how good a country you folks claim you got. I'm going to give you that horse." For a moment there was no sound, not even that of breathing except the Texan's.

"You going to give it to me?" Eck said.

"Yes. Provided you will start the bidding on the next one." Again there was no sound save the Texan's breathing, and then the clash of Mrs Littlejohn's pail against the rim of the pot.

"I just start the bidding," Eck said. "I dont have to buy it lessen I aint over-topped." Another wagon had come up the lane. It was battered and paintless. One wheel had been repaired by crossed planks bound to the spokes with baling wire and the two underfed mules wore a battered harness patched with bits of cotton rope; the reins were ordinary cotton plow-lines, not new. It contained a woman in a shapeless gray garment and a faded sunbonnet, and a man in faded and patched though clean overalls. There was not room for the wagon to draw out of the lane so the man left it standing where it was and got down and came forward—a thin man, not large, with something about his eyes, something strained and washed-out, at once vague and intense, who shoved into the crowd at the rear, saying,

"What? What's that? Did he give him that horse?"

"All right," the Texan said. "That wall-eyed horse with the scarred neck belongs to you. Now. That one that looks like he's had his head in a flour barrel. What do you say? Ten dollars?"

"Did he give him that horse?" the newcomer said.

"A dollar," Eck said. The Texan's mouth was still open for speech; for an instant his face died so behind the hard eyes.

"A dollar?" he said. "One dollar? Did I actually hear that?"

"Durn it," Eck said. "Two dollars then. But I aint—"

"Wait," the newcomer said. "You, up there on the post." The Texan looked at him. When the others turned, they saw that the woman had left the wagon too, though they had not known she was there since they had not seen the wagon drive up. She came among them behind the man, gaunt in the gray shapeless garment and the sunbonnet, wearing stained canvas gymnasium shoes. She overtook the man but she did not touch him, standing just behind him, her hands rolled before her into the gray dress.

"Henry," she said in a flat voice. The man looked over his shoulder.

"Get back to that wagon," he said.

"Here, missus," the Texan said. "Henry's going to get the bargain of his life in about a minute. Here, boys, let the missus come up close where she can see. Henry's going to pick out that saddle-horse the missus has been wanting. Who says ten——"

"Henry," the woman said. She did not raise her voice. She had not once looked at the Texan. She touched the man's arm. He turned and struck her hand down.

"Get back to that wagon like I told you." The woman stood behind him, her hands rolled again into her dress. She was not looking at anything, speaking to anyone.

"He aint no more despair than to buy one of them things," she said. "And us not but five dollars away from the poor-house, he aint no more despair." The man turned upon her with that curious air of leashed, of dreamlike fury. The others lounged along the fence in attitudes gravely inattentive, almost oblivious. Mrs Littlejohn had been washing for some time now, pumping rhythmically up and down above the wash-board in the sud-foamed tub. She now stood erect again, her soap-raw hands on her hips, looking into the lot.

"Shut your mouth and get back in that wagon," the man said. "Do you want me to take a wagon stake to you?" He turned and looked up at the Texan. "Did you give him that horse?" he said. The Texan was looking at the woman. Then he looked at the man; still watching him, he tilted the paper carton over his open palm. A single cake came out of it.

"Yes," he said.

"Is the fellow that bids in this next horse going to get that first one too?"

"No," the Texan said.

"All right," the other said. "Are you going to give a horse to the man that makes the first bid on the next one?"

"No," the Texan said.

"Then if you were just starting the auction off by giving away a horse, why didn't you wait till we were all here?" The Texan stopped looking at the other. He raised the empty carton and squinted carefully into it, as if it might contain a precious jewel or perhaps a deadly insect. Then he crumpled it and dropped it carefully beside the post on which he sat.

"Eck bids two dollars," he said. "I believe he still thinks he's bidding on them scraps of bob-wire they come here in instead of on one of the horses. But I got to accept it. But are you boys—"

"So Eck's going to get two horses at a dollar a head," the newcomer said. "Three dollars." The woman touched him again. He flung her hand off without turning and she stood again, her hands rolled into her dress across her flat stomach, not looking at anything.

"Misters," she said, "we got chaps in the house that never had shoes last winter. We aint got corn to feed the stock. We got five dollars I earned weaving by firelight after dark. And he aint no more despair."

"Henry bids three dollars," the Texan said. "Raise him a dollar, Eck, and the horse is yours." Beyond the fence the horses rushed suddenly and for no reason and as suddenly stopped, staring at the faces along the fence.

"Henry," the woman said. The man was watching Eck. His stained and broken teeth showed a little beneath his lip. His wrists dangled into fists below the faded sleeves of his shirt too short from many washings.

"Four dollars," Eck said.

"Five dollars!" the husband said, raising one clenched hand. He shouldered himself forward toward the gate-post. The woman did not follow him. She now looked at the Texan for the first time. Her eyes were a washed gray also, as though they had faded too like the dress and the sunbonnet.

"Mister," she said, "if you take that five dollars I earned my chaps a-weaving for one of them things, it'll be a curse on you and yours during all the time of man."

"Five dollars!" the husband shouted. He thrust himself up to the post, his clenched hand on a level with the Texan's knees. He opened it upon a wad of frayed banknotes and silver. "Five dollars! And the man that raises it will have to beat my head off or I'll beat hisn."

"All right," the Texan said. "Five dollars is bid. But dont you shake your hand at me."

At five oclock that afternoon the Texan crumpled the third paper carton and dropped it to the earth beneath him. In the copper slant of the leveling sun which fell also upon the line of limp garments in Mrs Littlejohn's backyard and which cast his shadow and that of the post on which he sat long across the lot where now and then the ponies still rushed in purposeless and tireless surges, the Texan straightened his leg and thrust his hand into his pocket and took out a coin and leaned down to the little boy. His voice was now hoarse, spent. "Here, bud," he said. "Run to the store and get me a box of gingersnaps." The men still stood along the fence, tireless, in their overalls and faded shirts. Flem Snopes was there now, appeared suddenly from nowhere, standing beside the fence with a space the width of three or four men on either side of him, standing there in his small yet definite isolation, chewing tobacco, in the same gray trousers and minute bow tie in which he had departed last summer but in a new cap, gray too like the other, but new, and overlaid with a bright golfer's plaid, looking also at the horses in the lot. All of them save two had been sold for sums ranging from three dollars and a half to eleven and twelve dollars. The purchasers, as they had bid them in, had gathered as though by instinct into a separate group on the other side of the gate, where they stood with their hands lying upon the top strand of the fence, watching with a still more sober intensity the animals which some of them had owned for seven and eight hours now but had not yet laid hands upon. The husband, Henry, stood beside the post on which the Texan sat. The wife had gone back to the wagon, where she sat gray in the gray garment, motionless, looking at nothing still; she might have been something inanimate which he had loaded into the wagon to move it somewhere, waiting now in the wagon until he should be ready to go on again, patient, insensate, timeless.

"I bought a horse and I paid cash for it," he said. His voice was harsh and spent too, the mad look in his eyes had a quality glazed now and even sightless. "And yet you expect me to stand around here till they are all sold before I can get my horse. Well, you can do all the expecting you want. I'm going to take my horse out of there and go home." The Texan looked down at him. The Texan's shirt was blotched with sweat. His big face was cold and still, his voice level.

"Take your horse then." After a moment Henry looked away. He stood with his head bent a little, swallowing from time to time.

"Aint you going to catch him for me?"

"It aint my horse," the Texan said in that flat still voice. After a while Henry raised his head. He did not look at the Texan.

"Who'll help me catch my horse?" he said. Nobody answered. They stood along the fence, looking quietly into the lot where the ponies huddled, already beginning to fade a little where the long shadow of the house lay upon them, deepening. From Mrs Littlejohn's kitchen the smell of frying ham came. A noisy cloud of sparrows swept across the lot and into a chinaberry tree beside the house, and in the high soft vague blue swallows stooped and whirled in erratic indecision, their cries like strings plucked at random. Without looking back, Henry raised his voice: "Bring that ere plow-line." After a time the wife moved. She got down from the wagon and took a coil of new cotton rope from it and approached. The husband took the rope from her and moved toward the gate. The Texan began to descend from the post, stiffly, as Henry put his hand on the latch. "Come on here," he said. The wife had stopped when he took the rope from her. She moved again, obediently, her hands rolled into the dress across her stomach, passing the Texan without looking at him.

"Dont you go in there, missus," he said. She stopped, not looking at him, not looking at anything. The husband opened the gate and entered the lot and turned, holding the gate open but without raising his eyes.

"Come on here," he said.

"Dont you go in there, missus," the Texan said. The wife stood motionless between them, her face almost concealed by the sunbonnet, her hands folded across her stomach.

"I reckon I better," she said. The other men did not look at her at all, at her or Henry either. They stood along the fence, grave and quiet and inattentive, almost bemused. Then the wife passed through the gate; the husband shut it behind them and turned and began to move toward the huddled ponies, the wife following in the gray and shapeless garment within which she moved without inference of locomotion, like something on a moving platform, a float. The horses were watching them. They clotted and blended and shifted among themselves, on the point of breaking though not breaking yet. The husband shouted at them. He began to curse them, advancing, the wife following. Then the huddle broke, the animals moving with high, stiff knees, circling the two people who turned and followed again as the herd flowed and huddled again at the opposite side of the lot.

"There he is," the husband said. "Get him into that corner." The herd divided; the horse which the husband had bought jolted on stiff legs. The wife shouted at it; it spun and poised, plunging, then the husband struck it across the face with the coiled rope and it whirled and slammed into the corner of the fence. "Keep him there now," the husband said. He shook out the rope, advancing. The horse watched him with wild, glaring eyes; it rushed again, straight toward the wife. She shouted at it and waved her arms but it soared past her in a long bound and rushed again into the huddle of its fellows. They followed and hemmed it again into another corner; again the wife failed to stop its rush for freedom and the husband turned and struck her with the coiled rope. "Why didn't you head him?" he said. "Why didn't you?" He struck her again; she did not move, not even to fend the rope with a raised arm. The men along the fence stood quietly, their faces lowered as though brooding upon the earth at their feet. Only Flem Snopes was still watching—if he ever had been looking into the lot at all, standing in his little island of isolation, chewing with his characteristic faint sidewise thrust beneath the new plaid cap.

The Texan said something, not loud, harsh and short. He entered the lot and went to the husband and jerked the uplifted rope from his hand. The husband whirled as though he were about to spring at the Texan, crouched slightly, his knees bent and his arms held slightly away from his sides, though his gaze never mounted higher than the Texan's carved and dusty boots. Then the Texan took the husband by the arm and led him back toward the gate, the wife following, and through the gate which he held open for the woman and then closed. He took a wad of banknotes from his trousers and removed a bill from it and put it into the woman's hand. "Get him into the wagon and get him on home," he said.

"What's that for?" Flem Snopes said. He had approached. He now stood beside the post on which the Texan had been sitting. The Texan did not look at him.

"Thinks he bought one of them ponies," the Texan said. He spoke in a flat still voice, like that of a man after a sharp run. "Get him on away, missus."

"Give him back that money," the husband said, in his lifeless, spent tone. "I bought that horse and I aim to have him if I got to shoot him before I can put a rope on him." The Texan did not even look at him.

"Get him on away from here, missus," he said.

"You take your money and I take my horse," the husband said. He was shaking slowly and steadily now, as though he were cold. His hands open and shut below the frayed cuffs of his shirt. "Give it back to him," he said.

"You dont own no horse of mine," the Texan said. "Get him on home, missus." The husband raised his spent face, his mad glazed eyes. He reached out his hand. The woman held the banknote in her folded hands across her stomach. For a while the husband's shaking hand merely fumbled at it. Then he drew the banknote free.

"It's my horse," he said. "I bought it. These fellows saw me. I paid for it. It's my horse. Here." He turned and extended the banknote toward Snopes. "You got something to do with these horses. I bought one. Here's the money for it. I bought one. Ask him." Snopes took the banknote. The others stood, gravely inattentive, in relaxed attitudes along the fence. The sun had gone now; there was nothing save violet shadow upon them and upon the lot where once more and for no reason the ponies rushed and flowed. At that moment the little boy came up, tireless and indefatigable still, with the new paper carton. The Texan took it, though he did not open it at once. He had dropped the rope and now the husband stooped for it, fumbling at it for some time before he lifted it from the ground. Then he stood with his head bent, his knuckles whitening on the rope. The woman had not moved. Twilight was coming fast now; there was a last mazy swirl of swallows against the high and changing azure. Then the Texan tore the end from the carton and tilted one of the cakes into his hand; he seemed to be watching the hand as it shut slowly upon the cake until a fine powder of snuff-colored dust began to rain from his fingers. He rubbed the hand carefully on his thigh and raised his head and glanced about until he saw the little boy and handed the carton back to him.

"Here, bud," he said. Then he looked at the woman, his voice flat, quiet again. "Mr Snopes will have your money for you tomorrow. Better get him in the wagon and get him on home. He dont own no horse. You can get your money tomorrow from Mr Snopes." The wife turned and went back to the wagon and got into it. No one watched her, nor the husband who still stood, his head bent, passing the rope from one hand to the other. They leaned along the fence, grave and quiet, as though the fence were in another land, another time.

"How many you got left?" Snopes said. The Texan roused; they all seemed to rouse then, returning, listening again.

"Got three now," the Texan said. "Swap all three of them for a buggy or a——"

"It's out in the road," Snopes said, a little shortly, a little

quickly, turning away. "Get your mules." He went on up the
lane. They watched the Texan enter the lot and cross it, the
horses flowing before him but without the old irrational violence, as if they too were spent, vitiated with the long day, and
enter the barn and then emerge, leading the two harnessed
mules. The wagon had been backed under the shed beside
the barn. The Texan entered this and came out a moment
later, carrying a bedding-roll and his coat, and led the mules
back toward the gate, the ponies huddled again and watching
him with their various unmatching eyes, quietly now, as if
they too realised there was not only an armistice between
them at last but that they would never look upon each other
again in both their lives. Someone opened the gate. The
Texan led the mules through it and they followed in a body,
leaving the husband standing beside the closed gate, his head
still bent and the coiled rope in his hand. They passed the
wagon in which the wife sat, her gray garment fading into the
dusk, almost the same color and as still, looking at nothing;
they passed the clothesline with its limp and unwinded drying
garments, walking through the hot vivid smell of ham from
Mrs Littlejohn's kitchen. When they reached the end of the
lane they could see the moon, almost full, tremendous and
pale and still lightless in the sky from which day had not quite
gone. Snopes was standing at the end of the lane beside an
empty buggy. It was the one with the glittering wheels and the
fringed parasol top in which he and Will Varner had used to
drive. The Texan was motionless too, looking at it.

"Well well well," he said. "So this is it."

"If it dont suit you, you can ride one of the mules back to
Texas," Snopes said.

"You bet," the Texan said. "Only I ought to have a powder
puff or at least a mandolin to ride it with." He backed the

mules onto the tongue and lifted the breast-yoke. Two of them came forward and fastened the traces for him. Then they watched him get into the buggy and raise the reins.

"Where you heading for?" one said. "Back to Texas?"

"In this?" the Texan said. "I wouldn't get past the first Texas saloon without starting the vigilance committee. Besides, I aint going to waste all this here lace-trimmed top and these spindle wheels just on Texas. Long as I am this far, I reckon I'll go on a day or two and look-see them northern towns. Washington and New York and Baltimore. What's the short way to New York from here?" They didn't know. But they told him how to reach Jefferson.

"You're already headed right," Freeman said. "Just keep right on up the road past the schoolhouse."

"All right," the Texan said. "Well, remember about busting them ponies over the head now and then until they get used to you. You wont have any trouble with them then." He lifted the reins again. As he did so Snopes stepped forward and got into the buggy.

"I'll ride as far as Varner's with you," he said.

"I didn't know I was going past Varner's," the Texan said.

"You can go to town that way," Snopes said. "Drive on." The Texan shook the reins. Then he said,

"Whoa." He straightened his leg and put his hand into his pocket. "Here, bud," he said to the little boy, "run to the store and— Never mind. I'll stop and get it myself, long as I am going back that way. Well, boys," he said. "Take care of yourselves." He swung the team around. The buggy went on. They looked after it.

"I reckon he aims to kind of come up on Jefferson from behind," Quick said.

"He'll be lighter when he gets there," Freeman said. "He can come up to it easy from any side he wants."

"Yes," Bookwright said. "His pockets wont rattle." They went back to the lot; they passed on through the narrow way between the two lines of patient and motionless wagons, which at the end was completely closed by the one in which the woman sat. The husband was still standing beside the gate with his coiled rope, and now night had completely come. The light itself had not changed so much; if anything, it was brighter but with that other-worldly quality of moonlight, so that when they stood once more looking into the lot, the splotchy bodies of the ponies had a distinctness, almost a brilliance, but without individual shape and without depth—no longer horses, no longer flesh and bone directed by a principle capable of calculated violence, no longer inherent with the capacity to hurt and harm.

"Well, what are we waiting for?" Freeman said. "For them to go to roost?"

"We better all get our ropes first," Quick said. "Get your ropes everybody." Some of them did not have ropes. When they left home that morning, they had not heard about the horses, the auction. They had merely happened through the village by chance and learned of it and stopped.

"Go to the store and get some then," Freeman said.

"The store will be closed now," Quick said.

"No it wont," Freeman said. "If it was closed, Lump Snopes would a been up here." So while the ones who had come prepared got their ropes from the wagons, the others went down to the store. The clerk was just closing it.

"You all aint started catching them yet, have you?" he said. "Good; I was afraid I wouldn't get there in time." He opened the door again and amid the old strong sunless smells of cheese and leather and molasses he measured and cut off sections of plow-line for them and in a body and the clerk in the center and still talking, voluble and unlistened to, they returned up the road. The pear tree before Mrs Littlejohn's was like drowned silver now in the moon. The mockingbird of last night, or another one, was already singing in it, and they now saw, tied to the fence, Ratliff's buckboard and team.

"I thought something was wrong all day," one said. "Ratliff wasn't there to give nobody advice." When they passed down the lane, Mrs Littlejohn was in her backyard, gathering the garments from the clothesline; they could still smell the ham. The others were waiting at the gate, beyond which the ponies, huddled again, were like phantom fish, suspended apparently without legs now in the brilliant treachery of the moon.

"I reckon the best way will be for us all to take and catch them one at a time," Freeman said.

"One at a time," the husband, Henry, said. Apparently he had not moved since the Texan had led his mules through the gate, save to lift his hands to the top of the gate, one of them still clutching the coiled rope. "One at a time," he said. He began to curse in a harsh, spent monotone. "After I've stood around here all day, waiting for that——" He cursed. He began to jerk at the gate, shaking it with spent violence until one of the others slid the latch back and it swung open and Henry entered it, the others following, the little boy pressing close behind his father until Eck became aware of him and turned.

"Here," he said. "Give me that rope. You stay out of here."

"Aw, paw," the boy said.

"No sir. Them things will kill you. They almost done it this morning. You stay out of here."

"But we got two to catch." For a moment Eck stood looking down at the boy.

"That's right," he said. "We got two. But you stay close to me now. And when I holler run, you run. You hear me?"

"Spread out, boys," Freeman said. "Keep them in front of us." They began to advance across the lot in a ragged crescent-shaped line, each one with his rope. The ponies were now at the far side of the lot. One of them snorted; the mass shifted within itself but without breaking. Freeman, glancing back, saw the little boy. "Get that boy out of here," he said.

"I reckon you better," Eck said to the boy. "You go and get in the wagon yonder. You can see us catch them from there." The little boy turned and trotted toward the shed beneath which the wagon stood. The line of men advanced, Henry a little in front.

"Watch them close now," Freeman said. "Maybe we better try to get them into the barn first——" At that moment the huddle broke. It parted and flowed in both directions along the fence. The men at the ends of the line began to run, waving their arms and shouting. "Head them," Freeman said tensely. "Turn them back." They turned them, driving them back upon themselves again; the animals merged and spun in short, huddling rushes, phantom and inextricable. "Hold them now," Freeman said. "Dont let them get by us." The line advanced again. Eck turned; he did not know why—whether a sound, what. The little boy was just behind him again.

"Didn't I tell you to get in that wagon and stay there?" Eck said.

"Watch out, paw!" the boy said. "There he is! There's ourn!" It was the one the Texan had given Eck. "Catch him, paw!"

"Get out of my way," Eck said. "Get back to that wagon."

The line was still advancing. The ponies milled, clotting, forced gradually backward toward the open door of the barn. Henry was still slightly in front, crouched slightly, his thin figure, even in the mazy moonlight, emanating something of that spent fury. The splotchy huddle of animals seemed to be moving before the advancing line of men like a snowball which they might have been pushing before them by some invisible means, gradually nearer and nearer to the black yawn of the barn door. Later it was obvious that the ponies were so intent upon the men that they did not realise the barn was even behind them until they backed into the shadow of it. Then an indescribable sound, a movement desperate and despairing, arose among them; for an instant of static horror men and animals faced one another, then the men whirled and ran before a gaudy vomit of long wild faces and splotched chests which overtook and scattered them and flung them sprawling aside and completely obliterated from sight Henry and the little boy, neither of whom had moved though Henry had flung up both arms, still holding his coiled rope, the herd sweeping on across the lot, to crash through the gate which the last man through it had neglected to close, leaving it slightly ajar, carrying all of the gate save the upright to which the hinges were nailed with them, and so among the teams and wagons which choked the lane, the teams springing and lunging too, snapping hitch-reins and tongues. Then the whole inextricable mass crashed among the wagons and eddied and divided about the one in which the woman sat, and rushed on down the lane and into the road, dividing, one half going one way and one half the other.

The men in the lot, except Henry, got to their feet and ran toward the gate. The little boy once more had not been touched, not even thrown off his feet; for a while his father held him clear of the ground in one hand, shaking him like a rag doll. "Didn't I tell you to stay in that wagon?" Eck cried. "Didn't I tell you?"

"Look out, paw!" the boy chattered out of the violent shaking, "there's ourn! There he goes!" It was the horse the Texan had given them again. It was as if they owned no other, the other one did not exist; as if by some absolute and instantaneous rapport of blood they had relegated to oblivion the one for which they had paid money. They ran to the gate and down the lane where the other men had disappeared. They saw the horse the Texan had given them whirl and dash back and rush through the gate into Mrs Littlejohn's yard and run up the front steps and crash once on the wooden veranda and vanish through the front door. Eck and the boy ran up onto the veranda. A lamp sat on a table just inside the door. In its mellow light they saw the horse fill the long hallway like a pinwheel, gaudy, furious and thunderous. A little further down the hall there was a varnished yellow melodeon. The horse crashed into it; it produced a single note, almost a chord, in bass, resonant and grave, of deep and sober astonishment; the horse with its monstrous and antic shadow whirled again and vanished through another door. It was a bedroom; Ratliff, in his underclothes and one sock and with the other sock in his hand and his back to the door, was leaning out the open window facing the lane, the lot. He looked back over his shoulder. For an instant he and the horse glared at one another. Then he sprang through the window as the horse backed out of the room and into the hall again and whirled and saw Eck and the little boy just entering the front door, Eck still carrying his rope. It whirled again and rushed on down the hall and onto the back porch just as Mrs Littlejohn, carrying an armful of clothes from the line and the wash-board, mounted the steps.

"Get out of here, you son of a bitch," she said. She struck with the wash-board; it divided neatly on the long mad face and the horse whirled and rushed back up the hall, where Eck and the boy now stood.

"Get to hell out of here, Wall!" Eck roared. He dropped to the floor, covering his head with his arms. The boy did not move, and for the third time the horse soared above the unwinking eyes and the unbowed and untouched head and onto the front veranda again just as Ratliff, still carrying the sock, ran around the corner of the house and up the steps. The horse whirled without breaking or pausing. It galloped to the end of the veranda and took the railing and soared out-ward, hobgoblin and floating, in the moon. It landed in the lot still running and crossed the lot and galloped through the wrecked gate and among the overturned wagons and the still intact one in which Henry's wife still sat, and on down the lane and into the road.

A quarter of a mile further on, the road gashed pallid and moony between the moony shadows of the bordering trees, the horse still galloping, galloping its shadow into the dust, the road descending now toward the creek and the bridge. It was of wood, just wide enough for a single vehicle. When the horse reached it, it was occupied by a wagon coming from the opposite direction and drawn by two mules already asleep in the harness and the soporific motion. On the seat were Tull and his wife, in splint chairs in the wagon behind them sat their four daughters, all returning belated from an all-day visit with some of Mrs Tull's kin. The horse neither checked nor swerved. It crashed once on the wooden bridge and rushed between the two mules which waked lunging in opposite directions in the traces, the horse now apparently scrambling along the wagon-tongue itself like a mad squirrel and scrabbling at the end-gate of the wagon with its fore feet as if it intended to climb into the wagon while Tull shouted at it and struck at its face with his whip. The mules were now trying to turn the wagon around in the middle of the bridge. It slewed and tilted, the bridge-rail cracked with a sharp report above the shrieks of the women; the horse scrambled at last across the back of one of the mules and Tull stood up in the wagon and kicked at its face. Then the front end of the wagon rose, flinging Tull, the reins now wrapped several times about his wrist, backward into the wagon bed among the overturned chairs and the exposed stockings and undergarments of his women. The pony scrambled free and crashed again on the wooden planking, galloping again. The wagon lurched again; the mules had finally turned it on the bridge where there was not room for it to turn and were now kicking themselves free of the traces. When they came free, they snatched Tull bodily out of the wagon. He struck the bridge on his face and was dragged for several feet before the wrist-wrapped reins broke. Far up the road now, distancing the frantic mules, the pony faded on. While the five women still shrieked above Tull's unconscious body, Eck and the little boy came up, trotting, Eck still carrying his rope. He was panting. "Which way'd he go?" he said.

In the now empty and moon-drenched lot, his wife and Mrs Littlejohn and Ratliff and Lump Snopes, the clerk, and three other men raised Henry out of the trampled dust and carried him into Mrs Littlejohn's backyard. His face was blanched and stony, his eyes were closed, the weight of his head tautened his throat across the protruding larynx; his teeth glinted dully beneath his lifted lip. They carried him on toward the house, through the dappled shade of the chinaberry trees. Across the dreaming and silver night a faint sound like remote thunder came and ceased. "There's one of them on the creek bridge," one of the men said.

"It's that one of Eck Snopes," another said. "The one that was in the house." Mrs Littlejohn had preceded them into the hall. When they entered with Henry, she had already taken the lamp from the table and she stood beside an open door, holding the lamp high.

"Bring him in here," she said. She entered the room first and set the lamp on the dresser. They followed with clumsy scufflings and pantings and laid Henry on the bed and Mrs Littlejohn came to the bed and stood looking down at Henry's peaceful and bloodless face. "I'll declare," she said. "You men." They had drawn back a little, clumped, shifting from one foot to another, not looking at her nor at his wife either, who stood at the foot of the bed, motionless, her hands folded into her dress. "You all get out of here, V.K.," she said to Ratliff. "Go outside. See if you cant find something else to play with that will kill some more of you."

"All right," Ratliff said. "Come on boys. Aint no more horses to catch in here." They followed him toward the door, on tiptoe, their shoes scuffing, their shadows monstrous on the wall.

"Go get Will Varner," Mrs Littlejohn said. "I reckon you can tell him it's still a mule." They went out; they didn't look back. They tiptoed up the hall and crossed the veranda and descended into the moonlight. Now that they could pay attention to it, the silver air seemed to be filled with faint and sourceless sounds—shouts, thin and distant, again a brief thunder of hooves on a wooden bridge, more shouts faint and thin and earnest and clear as bells; once they even distinguished the words: "Whooey. Head him."

"He went through that house quick," Ratliff said. "He

must have found another woman at home." Then Henry
screamed in the house behind them. They looked back into
the dark hall where a square of light fell through the bedroom
door, listening while the scream sank into a harsh respiration:
"Ah. Ah. Ah" on a rising note about to become screaming
again. "Come on," Ratliff said. "We better get Varner." They
went up the road in a body, treading the moon-blanched dust
in the tremulous April night murmurous with the moving of
sap and the wet bursting of burgeoning leaf and bud and constant with the thin and urgent cries and the brief and fading
bursts of galloping hooves. Varner's house was dark, blank and
without depth in the moonlight. They stood, clumped darkly
in the silver yard and called up at the blank windows until suddenly someone was standing in one of them. It was Flem
Snopes' wife. She was in a white garment; the heavy braided
club of her hair looked almost black against it. She did not
lean out, she merely stood there, full in the moon, apparently
blank-eyed or certainly not looking downward at them—the
heavy gold hair, the mask not tragic and perhaps not even
doomed: just damned, the strong faint lift of breasts beneath
the marblelike fall of the garment; to those below what Brun-
hilde, what Rhinemaiden on what spurious river-rock of
papier-mache, what Helen returned to what topless and
shoddy Argos, waiting for no one. "Evening, Mrs Snopes,"
Ratliff said. "We want Uncle Will. Henry Armstid is hurt at
Mrs Littlejohn's." She vanished from the window. They
waited in the moonlight, listening to the faint remote shouts
and cries, until Varner emerged, sooner than they had actually
expected, hunching into his coat and buttoning his trousers
over the tail of his nightshirt, his suspenders still dangling in
twin loops below the coat. He was carrying the battered bag
which contained the plumber-like tools with which he

drenched and wormed and blistered and floated or drew the teeth of horses and mules; he came down the steps, lean and loosejointed, his shrewd ruthless head cocked a little as he listened also to the faint bell-like cries and shouts with which the silver air was full.

"Are they still trying to catch them rabbits?" he said.

"All of them except Henry Armstid," Ratliff said. "He caught his."

"Hah," Varner said. "That you, V.K.? How many did you buy?"

"I was too late," Ratliff said. "I never got back in time."

"Hah," Varner said. They moved on to the gate and into the road again. "Well, it's a good bright cool night for running them." The moon was now high overhead, a pearled and mazy yawn in the soft sky, the ultimate ends of which rolled onward, whorl on whorl, beyond the pale stars and by pale stars surrounded. They walked in a close clump, tramping their shadows into the road's mild dust, blotting the shadows of the burgeoning trees which soared, trunk branch and twig against the pale sky, delicate and finely thinned. They passed the dark store. Then the pear tree came in sight. It rose in mazed and silver immobility like exploding snow; the mockingbird still sang in it. "Look at that tree," Varner said. "It ought to make this year, sho."

"Corn'll make this year too," one said.

"A moon like this is good for every growing thing outen earth," Varner said. "I mind when me and Mrs Varner was expecting Eula. Already had a mess of children and maybe we ought to quit then. But I wanted some more gals. Others had done married and moved away, and a passel of boys, soon as they get big enough to be worth anything, they aint got time to work. Got to set around store and talk. But a gal will stay home and work until she does get married. So there was a old woman told my mammy once that if a woman showed her belly to the full moon after she had done caught, it would be a gal. So Mrs Varner taken and laid every night with the moon on her nekid belly, until it fulled and after. I could lay my ear to her belly and hear Eula kicking and scrouging like all get-out, feeling the moon."

"You mean it actually worked sho enough, Uncle Will?" the other said.

"Hah," Varner said. "You might try it. You get enough women showing their nekid bellies to the moon or the sun either or even just to your hand fumbling around often enough and more than likely after a while there will be something in it you can lay your ear and listen to, provided something come up and you aint got away by that time. Hah, V.K.?" Someone guffawed.

"Dont ask me," Ratliff said. "I cant even get nowhere in time to buy a cheap horse." Two or three guffawed this time. Then they began to hear Henry's respirations from the house: "Ah. Ah. Ah" and they ceased abruptly, as if they had not been aware of their closeness to it. Varner walked on in front, lean, shambling, yet moving quite rapidly, though his head was still slanted with listening as the faint, urgent, indomitable cries murmured in the silver lambence, sourceless, at times almost musical, like fading bell-notes; again there was a brief rapid thunder of hooves on wooden planking.

"There's another one on the creek bridge," one said.

"They are going to come out even on them things, after all," Varner said. "They'll get the money back in exercise and relaxation. You take a man that aint got no other relaxation all year long except dodging mule-dung up and down a field furrow. And a night like this one, when a man aint old enough yet to lay still and sleep, and yet he aint young enough anymore to be tomcatting in and out of other folks' back windows, something like this is good for him. It'll make him sleep tomorrow night anyhow, provided he gets back home by then. If we had just knowed about this in time, we could have trained up a pack of horse-dogs. Then we could have held one of these field trials."

"That's one way to look at it, I reckon," Ratliff said. "In fact, it might be a considerable comfort to Bookwright and Quick and Freeman and Eck Snopes and them other new horse-owners if that side of it could be brought to their attention, because the chances are aint none of them thought to look at it in that light yet. Probably there aint a one of them that believes now there's any cure a-tall for that Texas disease Flem Snopes and that Dead-eye Dick brought here."

"Hah," Varner said. He opened Mrs Littlejohn's gate. The dim light still fell outward across the hall from the bedroom door; beyond it, Armstid was saying "Ah. Ah. Ah" steadily. "There's a pill for every ill but the last one."

"Even if there was always time to take it," Ratliff said.

"Hah," Varner said again. He glanced back at Ratliff for an instant, pausing. But the little hard bright eyes were invisible now; it was only the bushy overhang of the brows which seemed to concentrate downward toward him in writhen immobility, not frowning but with a sort of fierce risibility. "Even if there was time to take it. Breathing is a sight-draft dated yesterday."

At nine o'clock on the second morning after that, five men were sitting or squatting along the gallery of the store. The sixth was Ratliff. He was standing up, and talking: "Maybe there wasn't but one of them things in Mrs Littlejohn's house that night, like Eck says. But it was the biggest drove of just one horse I ever seen. It was in my room and it was on the front porch and I could hear Mrs Littlejohn hitting it over the head with that wash-board in the backyard all at the same time. And still it was missing everybody everytime. I reckon that's what that Texas man meant by calling them bargains: that a man would need to be powerful unlucky to ever get close enough to one of them to get hurt." They laughed, all except Eck himself. He and the little boy were eating. When they mounted the steps, Eck had gone on into the store and emerged with a paper sack, from which he took a segment of cheese and with his pocket knife divided it carefully into two exact halves and gave one to the boy and took a handful of crackers from the sack and gave them to the boy, and now they squatted against the wall, side by side and, save for the difference in size, identical, eating.

"I wonder what that horse thought Ratliff was," one said. He held a spray of peach bloom between his teeth. It bore four blossoms like miniature ballet skirts of pink tulle. "Jumping out windows and running in doors in his shirttail? I wonder how many Ratliffs that horse thought he saw."

"I dont know," Ratliff said. "But if he saw just half as many of me as I saw of him, he was sholy surrounded. Every time I turned my head, that thing was just running over me or just swirling to run back over that boy again. And that boy there, he stayed right under it one time to my certain knowledge for a full one-and-one-half minutes without ducking his head or even batting his eyes. Yes sir, when I looked around and seen that varmint in the door behind me blaring its eyes at me, I'd a made sho Flem Snopes had brought a tiger back from Texas except I knowed that couldn't no just one tiger completely fill a entire room." They laughed again, quietly. Lump Snopes, the clerk, sitting in the only chair tilted back against the door-facing and partly blocking the entrance, cackled suddenly.

"If Flem had knowed how quick you fellows was going to snap them horses up, he'd a probably brought some tigers," he said. "Monkeys too."

"So they was Flem's horses," Ratliff said. The laughter stopped. The other three had open knives in their hands, with which they had been trimming idly at chips and slivers of wood. Now they sat apparently absorbed in the delicate and almost tedious movements of the knife-blades. The clerk had looked quickly up and found Ratliff watching him. His constant expression of incorrigible and mirthful disbelief had left him now; only the empty wrinkles of it remained about his mouth and eyes.

"Has Flem ever said they was?" he said. "But you town fellows are smarter than us country folks. Likely you done already read Flem's mind." But Ratliff was not looking at him now.

"And I reckon we'd a bought them," he said. He stood above them again, easy, intelligent, perhaps a little sombre but still perfectly impenetrable. "Eck here, for instance. With a wife and family to support. He owns two of them, though to be sho he never had to pay money for but one. I heard folks chasing them things up until midnight last night, but Eck and that boy aint been home a-tall in two days." They laughed again, except Eck. He pared off a bite of cheese and speared it on the knife-point and put it into his mouth.

"Eck caught one of hisn," the second man said.

"That so?" Ratliff said. "Which one was it, Eck? The one he give you or the one you bought?"

"The one he give me," Eck said, chewing.

"Well, well," Ratliff said. "I hadn't heard about that. But Eck's still one horse short. And the one he had to pay money for. Which is pure proof enough that them horses wasn't Flem's because wouldn't no man ever give his own blood kin something he couldn't even catch." They laughed again, but they stopped when the clerk spoke. There was no mirth in his voice at all.

"Listen," he said. "All right. We done all admitted you are too smart for anybody to get ahead of. You never bought no horse from Flem or nobody else, so maybe it aint none of your business and maybe you better just leave it at that."

"Sholy," Ratliff said. "It's done already been left at that two nights ago. The fellow that forgot to shut that lot gate done that. With the exception of Eck's horse. And we know that wasn't Flem's, because that horse was give to Eck for nothing."

"There's others besides Eck that aint got back home yet," the man with the peach spray said. "Bookwright and Quick are still chasing theirs. They was reported three miles west of Burtsboro Old Town at eight oclock last night. They aint got close enough to it yet to tell which one it belongs to."

"Sholy," Ratliff said. "The only new horse-owner in this country that could a been found without bloodhounds since whoever it was left that gate open two nights ago, is Henry Armstid. He's laying right there in Mrs Littlejohn's bedroom where he can watch the lot so that any time the one he bought happens to run back into it, all he's got to do is to holler at his wife to run out with the rope and catch it——" He ceased, though he said, "Morning, Flem," so immediately afterward and with no change whatever in tone, that the pause was not even discernible. With the exception of the clerk, who sprang up, vacated the chair with a sort of servile alacrity, and Eck and the little boy who continued to eat, they watched above their stilled hands as Snopes in the gray trousers and the minute tie and the new cap with its bright overplaid mounted the steps. He was chewing; he already carried a piece of white pine board; he jerked his head at them, looking at nobody, and took the vacated chair and opened his knife and began to whittle. The clerk now leaned in the opposite side of the door, rubbing his back against the facing. The expression of merry and invincible disbelief had returned to his face, with a quality watchful and secret.

"You're just in time," he said. "Ratliff here seems to be in a considerable sweat about who actually owned them horses." Snopes drew his knife-blade neatly along the board, the neat, surgeon-like sliver curling before it. The others were whittling again, looking carefully at nothing, except Eck and the boy, who were still eating, and the clerk rubbing his back against the door-facing and watching Snopes with that secret and alert intensity. "Maybe you could put his mind at rest." Snopes turned his head slightly and spat, across the gallery and the steps and into the dust beyond them. He drew the knife back and began another curling sliver.

"He was there too," Snopes said. "He knows as much as anybody else." This time the clerk guffawed, chortling, his features gathering toward the center of his face as though plucked there by a hand. He slapped his leg, cackling.

"You might as well to quit," he said. "You cant beat him."

"I reckon not," Ratliff said. He stood above them, not looking at any of them, his gaze fixed apparently on the empty road beyond Mrs Littlejohn's house, impenetrable, brooding even. A hulking, half-grown boy in overalls too small for him appeared suddenly from nowhere in particular. He stood for a while in the road, just beyond spitting-range of the gallery, with that air of having come from nowhere in particular and of not knowing where he would go next when he should move again and of not being troubled by that fact. He was looking at nothing, certainly not toward the gallery, and no one on the gallery so much as looked at him except the little boy, who now watched the boy in the road, his periwinkle eyes grave and steady above the bitten cracker in his halted hand. The boy in the road moved on, thickly undulant in the tight overalls, and vanished beyond the corner of the store, the round head and the unwinking eyes of the little boy on the gallery turning steadily to watch him out of sight. Then the little boy bit the cracker again, chewing. "Of course there's Mrs Tull," Ratliff said. "But that's Eck she's going to sue for damaging Tull against that bridge. And as for Henry Armstid——"

"If a man aint got gumption enough to protect himself, it's his own look-out," the clerk said.

"Sholy," Ratliff said, still in that dreamy, abstracted tone, actually speaking over his shoulder even. "And Henry Armstid, that's all right because from what I hear of the conversation that taken place, Henry had already stopped owning that horse he thought was his before that Texas man left. And as for that broke leg, that wont put him out none because his wife can make his crop." The clerk had ceased to rub his back against the door. He watched the back of Ratliff's head, unwinking too, sober and intent; he glanced at Snopes who, chewing, was watching another sliver curl away from the advancing knife-blade, then he watched the back of Ratliff's head again.

"It wont be the first time she has made their crop," the man with the peach spray said. Ratliff glanced at him.

"You ought to know. This wont be the first time I ever saw you in their field, doing plowing Henry never got around to. How many days have you already given them this year?" The man with the peach spray removed it and spat carefully and put the spray back between his teeth.

"She can run a furrow straight as I can," the second said.

"They're unlucky," the third said. "When you are unlucky, it dont matter much what you do."

"Sholy," Ratliff said. "I've heard laziness called bad luck so much that maybe it is."

"He aint lazy," the third said. "When their mule died three or four years ago, him and her broke their land working time about in the traces with the other mule. They aint lazy."

"So that's all right," Ratliff said, gazing up the empty road again. "Likely she will begin right away to finish the plowing; that oldest gal is pretty near big enough to work with a mule, aint she? or at least to hold the plow steady while Mrs Armstid helps the mule?" He glanced again toward the man with the peach spray as though for an answer, but he was not looking at the other and he went on talking without any pause. The clerk stood with his rump and back pressed against the door-facing as if he had paused in the act of scratching, watching Ratliff quite hard now, unwinking. If Ratliff had looked at Flem Snopes, he would have seen nothing below the down-slanted peak of the cap save the steady motion of his jaws. Another sliver was curling with neat deliberation before the moving knife. "Plenty of time now because all she's got to do after she finishes washing Mrs Littlejohn's dishes and sweeping out the house to pay hers and Henry's board, is to go out home and milk and cook up enough vittles to last the children until tomorrow and feed them and get the littlest ones to sleep and wait outside the door until that biggest gal gets the bar up and gets into bed herself with the axe—"

"The axe?" the man with the peach spray said.

"She takes it to bed with her. She's just twelve, and what

with this country still more or less full of them uncaught horses that never belonged to Flem Snopes, likely she feels maybe she cant swing a mere wash-board like Mrs Littlejohn can.—and then come back and wash up the supper dishes. And after that, not nothing to do until morning except to stay close enough where Henry can call her until it's light enough to chop the wood to cook breakfast and then help Mrs Little-john wash the dishes and make the beds and sweep while watching the road. Because likely any time now Flem Snopes will get back from wherever he has been since the auction, which of course is to town naturally to see about his cousin that's got into a little legal trouble, and so get that five dollars. 'Only maybe he wont give it back to me,' she says, and maybe that's what Mrs Littlejohn thought too, because she never said nothing. I could hear her—"

"And where did you happen to be during all this?" the clerk said.

"Listening," Ratliff said. He glanced back at the clerk, then he was looking away again, almost standing with his back to them. "—could hear her dumping the dishes into the pan like she was throwing them at it. 'Do you reckon he will give it back to me?' Mrs Armstid says. 'That Texas man give it to him and said he would. All the folks there saw him give Mr Snopes the money and heard him say I could get it from Mr Snopes tomorrow.' Mrs Littlejohn was washing the dishes now, wash-ing them like a man would, like they was made out of iron. 'No,' she says. 'But asking him wont do no hurt.'—'If he wouldn't give it back, it aint no use to ask,' Mrs Armstid says.—'Suit yourself,' Mrs Littlejohn says. 'It's your money.' Then I couldn't hear nothing but the dishes for a while. 'Do you reckon he might give it back to me?' Mrs Armstid says. 'That Texas man said he would. They all heard him say it.'—

'Then go and ask him for it,' Mrs Littlejohn says. Then I couldn't hear nothing but the dishes again. 'He wont give it back to me,' Mrs Armstid says. — 'All right,' Mrs Littlejohn says. 'Dont ask him, then.' Then I just heard the dishes. They would have two pans, both washing. 'You dont reckon he would, do you?' Mrs Armstid says. Mrs Littlejohn never said nothing. It sounded like she was throwing the dishes at one another. 'Maybe I better go and talk to Henry,' Mrs Armstid says. — 'I would,' Mrs Littlejohn says. And I be dog if it didn't sound exactly like she had two plates in her hands, beating them together like these here brass bucket-lids in a band. 'Then Henry can buy another five-dollar horse with it. Maybe he'll buy one next time that will out and out kill him. If I just thought he would, I'd give him back that money, myself.' — 'I reckon I better talk to him first,' Mrs Armstid says. And then it sounded just like Mrs Littlejohn taken up the dishes and pans and all and throwed the whole business at the cook-stove—" Ratliff ceased. Behind him the clerk was hissing "Psst! Psst! Flem. Flem!" Then he stopped, and all of them watched Mrs Armstid approach and mount the steps, gaunt in the shapeless gray garment, the stained tennis shoes hissing faintly on the boards. She came among them and stood, facing Snopes but not looking at anyone, her hands rolled into her apron.

"He said that day he wouldn't sell Henry that horse," she said in a flat toneless voice. "He said you had the money and I could get it from you." Snopes raised his head and turned it slightly again and spat neatly past the woman, across the gallery and into the road.

"He took all the money with him when he left," he said. Motionless, the gray garment hanging in rigid, almost formal folds like drapery in bronze, Mrs Armstid appeared to be watching something near Snopes' feet, as though she had not

heard him, or as if she had quitted her body as soon as she finished speaking and although her body, hearing, had received
the words, they would have no life nor meaning until she
returned. The clerk was rubbing his back steadily against the
door-facing again, watching her. The little boy was watching
her too with his unwinking ineffable gaze, but nobody else
was. The man with the peach spray removed it and spat and
put the twig back into his mouth.

"He said Henry hadn't bought no horse," she said. "He
said I could get the money from you."

"I reckon he forgot it," Snopes said. "He took all the
money away with him when he left." He watched her a
moment longer, then he trimmed again at the stick. The clerk
rubbed his back gently against the door, watching her. After a
time Mrs Armstid raised her head and looked up the road
where it went on, mild with spring dust, past Mrs Littlejohn's,
beginning to rise, on past the not-yet-bloomed (that would be
in June) locust grove across the way, on past the schoolhouse,
the weathered roof of which, rising beyond an orchard of
peach and pear trees, resembled a hive swarmed about by a
cloud of pink-and-white bees, ascending, mounting toward
the crest of the hill where the church stood among its sparse
gleam of marble headstones in the sombre cedar grove where
during the long afternoons of summer the constant mourning
doves called back and forth. She moved; once more the rubber soles hissed on the gnawed boards.

"I reckon it's about time to get dinner started," she said.

"How's Henry this morning, Mrs Armstid?" Ratliff said.
She looked at him, pausing, the blank eyes waking for an
instant.

"He's resting, I thank you kindly," she said. Then the eyes
died again and she moved again. Snopes rose from the chair,

closing his knife with his thumb and brushing a litter of minute shavings from his lap.

"Wait a minute," he said. Mrs Armstid paused again, half-turning, though still not looking at Snopes nor at any of them. Because she cant possibly actually believe it, Ratliff told himself. Anymore than I do. Snopes entered the store, the clerk, motionless again, his back and rump pressed against the door-facing as though waiting to start rubbing again, watched him enter, his head turning as the other passed him like the head of an owl, the little eyes blinking rapidly now. Jody Varner came up the road on his horse. He did not pass but instead turned in beside the store, toward the mulberry tree behind it where he was in the habit of hitching his horse. A wagon came up the road, creaking past. The man driving it lifted his hand; one or two of the men on the gallery lifted theirs in response. The wagon went on. Mrs Armstid looked after it. Snopes came out of the door, carrying a small striped paper bag and approached Mrs Armstid. "Here," he said. Her hand turned just enough to receive it. "A little sweetening for the chaps," he said. His other hand was already in his pocket, and as he turned back to the chair, he drew something from his pocket and handed it to the clerk, who took it. It was a five-cent piece. He sat down in the chair and tilted it back against the door again. He now had the knife in his hand again, already open. He turned his head slightly and spat again, neatly past the gray garment, into the road. The little boy was watching the sack in Mrs Armstid's hand. Then she seemed to discover it also, rous-ing.

"You're right kind," she said. She rolled the sack into the apron, the little boy's unwinking gaze fixed upon the lump her hands made beneath the cloth. She moved again. "I reckon I better get on and help with dinner," she said. She descended the steps, though as soon as she reached the level earth and began to retreat, the gray folds of the garment once more lost all inference and intimation of locomotion, so that she seemed to progress without motion like a figure on a retreating and diminishing float; a gray and blasted tree-trunk moving, somehow intact and upright, upon an unhurried flood. The clerk in the doorway cackled suddenly, explosively, chortling. He slapped his thigh.

"By God," he said, "you cant beat him."

Jody Varner, entering the store from the rear, paused in midstride like a pointing bird-dog. Then, on tiptoe, in complete silence and with astonishing speed, he darted behind the counter and sped up the gloomy tunnel, at the end of which a hulking, bear-shaped figure stooped, its entire head and shoulders wedged into the glass case which contained the needles and thread and snuff and tobacco and the stale gaudy candy. He snatched the boy savagely and viciously out; the boy gave a choked cry and struggled flabbily, cramming a final handful of something into his mouth, chewing. But he ceased to struggle almost at once and became slack and inert save for his jaws. Varner dragged him around the counter as the clerk entered, seemed to bounce suddenly into the store with a sort of alert concern. "You, Saint Elmo!" he said.

"Aint I told you and told you to keep him out of here?" Varner demanded, shaking the boy. "He's damn near eaten that candy-case clean. Stand up!" The boy hung like a half-filled sack from Varner's hand, chewing with a kind of fatalistic desperation, the eyes shut tight in the vast flaccid colorless face, the ears moving steadily and faintly to the chewing. Save for the jaw and the ears, he appeared to have gone to sleep chewing.

"You, Saint Elmo!" the clerk said. "Stand up!" The boy

assumed his own weight, though he did not open his eyes yet nor cease to chew. Varner released him. "Git on home," the clerk said. The boy turned obediently to re-enter the store. Varner jerked him about again.

"Not that way," he said. The boy crossed the gallery and descended the steps, the tight overalls undulant and reluctant across his flabby thighs. Before he reached the ground, his hand rose from his pocket to his mouth; again his ears moved faintly to the motion of chewing.

"He's worse than a rat, aint he?" the clerk said.

"Rat, hell," Varner said, breathing harshly. "He's worse than a goat. First thing I know, he'll graze on back and work through that lace leather and them hame-strings and lap-links and ring-bolts and eat me and you and him all three clean out the back door. And then be damned if I wouldn't be afraid to turn my back for fear he would cross the road and start in on the gin and the blacksmith shop. Now you mind what I say. If I catch him hanging around here one more time, I'm going to set a bear-trap for him." He went out onto the gallery, the clerk following. "Morning, gentlemen," he said.

"Who's that one, Jody?" Ratliff said. Save for the clerk in the background, they were the only two standing, and now, in juxtaposition, you could see the resemblance between them— a resemblance intangible, indefinite, not in figure, speech, dress, intelligence; certainly not in morals. Yet it was there, but with this bridgeless difference, this hallmark of his fate upon him: he would become an old man; Ratliff, too: but an old man who at about sixty-five would be caught and married by a creature not yet seventeen probably, who would for the rest of his life continue to take revenge upon him for her whole sex; Ratliff, never. The boy was moving without haste up the road. His hand rose again from his pocket to his mouth.

"That boy of I.O.'s," Varner said. "By God, I've done everything but put out poison for him."

"What?" Ratliff said. He glanced quickly about at the faces; for an instant there was in his own not only bewilderment but something almost like terror. "I thought—the other day you fellows told me—You said it was a woman, a young woman with a baby—Here now," he said. "Wait."

"This here's another one," Varner said. "I wish to hell he couldn't walk. Well, Eck, I hear you caught one of your horses."

"That's right," Eck said. He and the little boy had finished the crackers and cheese and he had sat for some time now, holding the empty bag.

"It was the one he give you, wasn't it?" Varner said.

"That's right," Eck said.

"Give the other one to me, paw," the little boy said.

"What happened?" Varner said.

"He broke his neck," Eck said.

"I know," Varner said. "But how?" Eck did not move. Watching him, they could almost see him visibly gathering and arranging words, speech. Varner, looking down at him, began to laugh steadily and harshly, sucking his teeth. "I'll tell you what happened. Eck and that boy finally run it into that blind lane of Freeman's, after a chase of about twenty-four hours. They figured it couldn't possibly climb them eight-foot fences of Freeman's so him and the boy tied their rope across the end of the lane, about three feet off the ground. And sho enough, soon as the horse come to the end of the lane and seen Freeman's barn, it whirled just like Eck figured it would and come helling back up that lane like a scared hen-hawk. It probably never even seen the rope at all. Mrs Freeman was watching from where she had run up onto the porch. She said that when it hit that rope, it looked just like one of these here great big Christmas pinwheels. But the one you bought got clean away, didn't it?"

"That's right," Eck said. "I never had time to see which way the other one went."

"Give him to me, paw," the little boy said.

"You wait till we catch him," Eck said. "We'll see about it then."

That afternoon Ratliff sat in the halted buckboard in front of Bookwright's gate. Bookwright stood in the road beside it. "You were wrong," Bookwright said. "He come back."

"He come back," Ratliff said. "I misjudged his . . . nerve aint the word I want, and sholy lack of it aint. But I wasn't wrong."

"Nonsense," Bookwright said. "He was gone all day yesterday. Nobody saw him going to town or coming back, but that's bound to be where he was at. Aint no man, I dont care if his name is Snopes, going to let his own blood kin rot in jail."

"He wont be in jail long. Court is next month, and after they send him to Parchman, he can stay out doors again. He will even go back to farming, plowing. Of course it wont be his cotton, but then he never did make enough out of his own cotton to quite pay him for staying alive."

"Nonsense," Bookwright said. "I dont believe it. Flem aint going to let him go to the penitentiary."

"Yes," Ratliff said. "Because Flem Snopes has got to cancel all them loose-flying notes that turns up here and there every now and then. He's going to discharge at least some of them notes for good and all." They looked at one another—Ratliff grave and easy in the blue shirt, Bookwright sober too, blackbrowed, intent.

"I thought you said you and him burned them notes."

"I said we burned two notes that Mink Snopes gave me. Do you think that any Snopes is going to put all of anything on one piece of paper that can be destroyed by one match? Do you think there is any Snopes that dont know that?"

"Oh," Bookwright said. "Hah," he said, with no mirth. "I reckon you gave Henry Armstid back his five dollars too." Then Ratliff looked away. His face changed—something fleeting, quizzical, but not smiling, his eyes did not smile; it was gone.

"I could have," he said. "But I didn't. I might have if I could just been sho he would buy something this time that would sho enough kill him, like Mrs Littlejohn said. Besides, I wasn't protecting a Snopes from Snopeses; I wasn't even protecting a people from a Snopes. I was protecting something that wasn't even a people, that wasn't nothing but something that dont want nothing but to walk and feel the sun and wouldn't know how to hurt no man even if it would and wouldn't want to even if it could, just like I wouldn't stand by and see you steal a meat-bone from a dog. I never made them Snopeses and I never made the folks that cant wait to bare their backsides to them. I could do more, but I wont. I wont, I tell you!"

"All right," Bookwright said. "Hook your drag up; it aint nothing but a hill. I said it's all right."

2

The two actions of Armstid pl. vs. Snopes, and Tull pl. vs. Eckrum Snopes (and anyone else named Snopes or Varner either which Tull's irate wife could contrive to involve, as the village well knew) were accorded a change of venue by mutual agreement and arrangement among the litigants. Three of the parties did, that is, because Flem Snopes flatly refused to recognise the existence of the suit against himself, stating once and without heat and first turning his head slightly aside to spit, "They wasn't none of my horses," then fell to whittling again while the baffled and helpless bailiff stood before the tilted chair with the papers he was trying to serve.

"What a opportunity for that Snopes family lawyer this would a been," Ratliff said when told about it. "What's his name? that quick-fatherer, the Moses with his mouth full of mottoes and his coat-tail full of them already halfgrown retroactive sons? I dont understand yet how a man that has to spend as much time as I do being constantly reminded of them folks, still cant keep the names straight. I.O. That he never had time to wait. This here would be probably the one tried case in his whole legal existence where he wouldn't be bothered with no narrow-ideaed client trying to make him stop talking, and the squire presiding himself would be the only man in company with authority to tell him to shut up."

So neither did the Varner surrey nor Ratliff's buckboard make one among the wagons, the buggies, and the saddled horses and mules which moved out of the village on that May Saturday morning, to converge upon Whiteleaf store eight miles away, coming not only from Frenchman's Bend but from other directions too since by that time, what Ratliff had called "that Texas sickness," that spotted corruption of frantic and uncatchable horses, had spread as far as twenty and thirty miles. So by the time the Frenchman's Bend people began to arrive, there were two dozen wagons, the teams reversed and eased of harness and tied to the rear wheels in order to pass the day, and twice that many saddled animals already standing about the locust grove beside the store and the site of the hearing had already been transferred from the store to an adjacent shed where in the fall cotton would be stored. But by nine oclock it was seen that even the shed would not hold them all, so the palladium was moved again, from the shed to the grove itself. The horses and mules and wagons were cleared from it; the single chair, the gnawed table bearing a thick bible which had the appearance of loving and constant use of a piece of old and perfectly-kept machinery and an almanac and a copy of Mississippi Reports dated 1881 and bearing along its opening edge a single thread-thin line of soilure as if during all the time of his possession its owner (or user) had opened it at only one page though that quite often, were fetched from the shed to the grove; a wagon and four men were dispatched and returned presently from the church a mile away with four wooden pews for the litigants and their clansmen and witnesses; behind these in turn the spectators stood—the men, the women, the children, sober, attentive, and neat, not in their Sunday clothes to be sure, but in the clean working garments donned that morning for the Saturday's diversion of sitting about the country stores or trips into the county seat, and in which they would return to the field on Monday morning and would wear all that week until Friday night came round again. The Justice of the Peace was a neat, small, plump old man resembling a tender caricature of all grandfathers who ever breathed, in a beautifully laundered though collarless white shirt with immaculate starch-gleaming cuffs and bosom, and steel-framed spectacles and neat, faintly curling white hair. He sat behind the table and looked at them—at the gray woman in the gray sunbonnet and dress, her clasped and motionless hands on her lap resembling a gnarl of pallid and drowned roots from a drained swamp; at Tull in his faded but absolutely clean shirt and the overalls which his women-folks not only kept immaculately washed but starched and ironed also, and not creased through the legs but flat across them from seam to seam, so that on each Saturday morning they resembled the short pants of a small boy, and the sedate and innocent blue of his eyes above the month-old cornsilk beard which concealed most of his abraded face and which gave him an air of incredible and paradoxical dissoluteness, not as though at last and without warning he had appeared in the sight of his fellowmen in his true character, but as if an old Italian portrait of a child saint had been defaced by a vicious and idle boy; at Mrs Tull, a strong, full-bosomed though slightly dumpy woman with an expression of grim and seething outrage which the elapsed four weeks had apparently neither increased nor diminished but had merely set, an outrage which curiously and almost at once began to give the impression of being directed not at any Snopes or at any other man in particular but at all men, all males, and of which Tull himself was not at all the victim but the subject, who sat on one side of her husband while the biggest of the four daughters sat on the other as if they (or Mrs Tull at least) were not so much convinced that Tull might leap up and flee, as determined that he would not; and at Eck and the little boy, identical save for size, and Lump the clerk in a gray cap which someone actually recognised as being the one which Flem Snopes had worn when he went to Texas last year, who between spells of rapid blinking would sit staring at the Justice with the lidless intensity of a rat—and into the lens-distorted and irisless old-man's eyes of the Justice there grew an expression not only of amazement and bewilderment but, as in Ratliff's eyes while he stood on the store gallery four weeks ago, something very like terror.

"This—" he said. "I didn't expect—I didn't look to see——.

I'm going to pray," he said. "I aint going to pray aloud. But I hope—" He looked at them. "I wish. . . . Maybe some of you all anyway had better do the same." He bowed his head. They watched him, quiet and grave, while he sat motionless behind the table, the light morning wind moving faintly in his thin hair and the shadow-stipple of windy leaves gliding and flowing across the starched bulge of bosom and the gleaming bone-buttoned cuffs, as rigid and almost as large as sections of six-inch stovepipe, at his joined hands. He raised his head. "Armstid against Snopes," he said. Mrs Armstid spoke. She did not move, she looked at nothing, her hands clasped in her lap, speaking in that flat, toneless and hopeless voice:

"That Texas man said——"

"Wait," the Justice said. He looked about at the faces, the blurred eyes fleeing behind the thick lenses. "Where is the defendant? I dont see him."

"He wouldn't come," the bailiff said.

"Wouldn't come?" the Justice said. "Didn't you serve the papers on him?"

"He wouldn't take them," the bailiff said. "He said—"

"Then he is in contempt!" the Justice cried.

"What for?" Lump Snopes said. "Aint nobody proved yet they was his horses." The Justice looked at him.

"Are you representing the defendant?" he said. Snopes blinked at him for a moment.

"What's that mean?" he said. "That you aim for me to pay
— think you can clap onto him?"
            ' himself," the Justice said. "Dont
            ainst him for that reason, even if
            nt enough?"
            ng," Snopes said. "It dont take no
            ur mind is——"

"Shut up, Snopes," the bailiff said. "If you aint in this case, you keep out of it." He turned back to the Justice. "What you want me to do: go over to the Bend and fetch Snopes here anyway? I reckon I can do it."

"No," the Justice said. "Wait." He looked about at the sober faces again with that bafflement, that dread. "Does anybody here know for sho who them horses belonged to? Anybody?" They looked back at him, sober, attentive—at the neat immaculate old man sitting with his hands locked together on the table before him to still the trembling. "All right, Mrs Armstid," he said. "Tell the court what happened." She told it, unmoving, in the flat, inflectionless voice, looking at nothing, while they listened quietly, coming to the end and ceasing without even any fall of voice, as though the tale mattered nothing and came to nothing. The Justice was looking down at his hands. When she ceased, he looked up at her. "But you haven't showed yet that Snopes owned the horses. The one you want to sue is that Texas man. And he's gone. If you got a judgment against him, you couldn't collect the money. Dont you see?"

"Mr Snopes brought him here," Mrs Armstid said. "Likely that Texas man wouldn't have knowed where Frenchman's Bend was if Mr Snopes hadn't showed him."

"But it was the Texas man that sold the horses and collected the money for them." The Justice looked about again at the faces. "Is that right? You, Bookwright, is that what happened?"

"Yes," Bookwright said. The Justice looked at Mrs Armstid again, with that pity and grief. As the morning increased th wind had risen, so that from time to time gusts of it ran thr̶ the branches overhead, bringing a faint snow of petals,·

turely bloomed as the spring itself had condensed with spend-
thrift speed after the hard winter, and the heavy and drowsing
scent of them, about the motionless heads.

"He give Mr Snopes Henry's money. He said Henry
hadn't bought no horse. He said I could get the money from
Mr Snopes tomorrow."

"And you have witnesses that saw and heard him?"

"Yes, sir. The other men that was there saw him give Mr
Snopes the money and say that I could get it—"

"And you asked Snopes for the money?"

"Yes, sir. He said that Texas man taken it away with him
when he left. But I would. . . ." She ceased again, perhaps
looking down at her hands also. Certainly she was not looking
at anyone.

"Yes?" the Justice said. "You would what?"

"I would know them five dollars. I earned them myself,
weaving at night after Henry and the chaps was asleep. Some
of the ladies in Jefferson would save up string and such and
give it to me and I would weave things and sell them. I earned
that money a little at a time and I would know it when I saw it
because I would take the can outen the chimney and count it
now and then while it was making up to enough to buy my
chaps some shoes for next winter. I would know it if I was to
see it again. If Mr Snopes would just let—"

"Suppose there was somebody seen Flem give that money
back to that Texas fellow," Lump Snopes said suddenly.

"Did anybody here see that?" the Justice said.

"Yes," Snopes said, harshly and violently. "Eck here did."
He looked at Eck. "Go on. Tell him." The Justice looked at
Eck; the four Tull girls turned their heads as one head and
looked at him, and Mrs Tull leaned forward to look past her

husband, her face cold, furious, and contemptuous, and those standing shifted to look past one another's heads at Eck sitting motionless on the bench.

"Did you see Snopes give Armstid's money back to the Texas man, Eck?" the Justice said. Still Eck did not answer nor move. Lump Snopes made a gross violent sound through the side of his mouth.

"By God, I aint afraid to say it if Eck is. I seen him do it."

"Will you swear that as testimony?" Snopes looked at the Justice. He did not blink now.

"So you wont take my word," he said.

"I want the truth," the Justice said. "If I cant find that, I got to have sworn evidence of what I will have to accept as truth." He lifted the bible from the two other books.

"All right," the bailiff said. "Step up here." Snopes rose from the bench and approached. They watched him, though now there was no shifting nor craning, no movement at all among the faces, the still eyes. Snopes at the table looked back at them once, his gaze traversing swiftly the crescent-shaped rank; he looked at the Justice again. The bailiff grasped the bible, though the Justice did not release it yet.

"You are ready to swear you saw Snopes give that Texas man back the money he took from Henry Armstid for that horse?" he said.

"I said I was, didn't I?" Snopes said. The Justice released the bible.

"Swear him," he said.

"Put your left hand on the Book raise your right hand you solemnly swear and affirm—" the bailiff said rapidly. But Snopes had already done so, his left hand clapped onto the extended bible and the other hand raised and his head turned away as once more his gaze went rapidly along the circle of expressionless and intent faces, saying in that harsh and snarling voice:

"Yes. I saw Flem Snopes give back to that Texas man whatever money Henry Armstid or anybody else thinks Henry Armstid or anybody else paid Flem for any of them horses. Does that suit you?"

"Yes," the Justice said. Then there was no movement, no sound anywhere among them. The bailiff placed the bible quietly on the table beside the Justice's locked hands, and there was no movement save the flow and recover of the windy shadows and the drift of the locust petals. Then Mrs Armstid rose; she stood once more (or still) looking at nothing, her hands clasped across her middle.

"I reckon I can go now, cant I?" she said.

"Yes," the Justice said, rousing. "Unless you would like—"

"I better get started," she said. "It's a right far piece." She had not come in the wagon, but on one of the gaunt and underfed mules. One of the men followed her across the grove and untied the mule for her and led it up to a wagon, from one hub of which she mounted. Then they looked at the Justice again. He sat behind the table, his hands still joined before him, though his head was not bowed now. Yet he did not move until the bailiff leaned and spoke to him, when he roused, came suddenly awake without starting, as an old man wakes from an old man's light sleep. He removed his hands from the table and, looking down, he spoke exactly as if he were reading from a paper:

"Tull against Snopes. Assault and—"

"Yes!" Mrs Tull said. "I'm going to say a word before you start." She leaned, looking past Tull at Lump Snopes again. "If you think you are going to lie and perjure Flem and Eck Snopes out of—"

"Now, mamma," Tull said. Now she spoke to Tull, without changing her position or her tone or even any break or pause in her speech:

"Dont you say hush to me! You'll let Eck Snopes or Flem Snopes or that whole Varner tribe snatch you out of the wagon and beat you half to death against a wooden bridge. But when it comes to suing them for your just rights and a punishment, oh no. Because that wouldn't be neighborly. What's neighborly got to do with you lying flat on your back in the middle of planting time while we pick splinters out of your face?" By this time the bailiff was shouting,

"Order! Order! This here's a law court!" Mrs Tull ceased. She sat back, breathing hard, staring at the Justice, who sat and spoke again as if he were reading aloud:

"—assault and battery on the person of Vernon Tull, through the agency and instrument of one horse, unnamed, belonging to Eckrum Snopes. Evidence of physical detriment and suffering, defendant himself. Witnesses, Mrs Tull and daughters—"

"Eck Snopes saw it too," Mrs Tull said, though with less violence now. "He was there. He got there in plenty of time to see it. Let him deny it. Let him look me in the face and deny it if he—"

"If you please, ma'am," the Justice said. He said it so quietly that Mrs Tull hushed and became quite calm, almost a rational and composed being. "The injury to your husband aint disputed. And the agency of the horse aint disputed. The law says that when a man owns a creature which he knows to be dangerous and if that creature is restrained and restricted from the public commons by a pen or enclosure capable of restraining and restricting it, if a man enter that pen or enclosure, whether he knows the creature in it is dangerous or not dangerous, then that man has committed trespass and the owner of that creature is not liable. But if that creature known to him to be dangerous ceases to be restrained by that suitable pen or enclosure, either by accident or design and either with or without the owner's knowledge, then that owner is liable. That's the law. All necessary now is to establish first, the ownership of the horse, and second, that the horse was a dangerous creature within the definition of the law as provided."

"Hah," Mrs Tull said. She said it exactly as Bookwright would have. "Dangerous. Ask Vernon Tull. Ask Henry Armstid if them things was pets."

"If you please, ma'am," the Justice said. He was looking at Eck. "What is the defendant's position? Denial of ownership?"

"What?" Eck said.

"Was that your horse that ran over Mr Tull?"

"Yes," Eck said. "It was mine. How much do I have to p——"

"Hah," Mrs Tull said again. "Denial of ownership. When there were at least forty men—fools too, or they wouldn't have been there. But even a fool's word is good about what he saw and heard.—at least forty men heard that Texas murderer give that horse to Eck Snopes. Not sell it to him, mind; give it to him."

"What?" the Justice said. "Gave it to him?"

"Yes," Eck said. "He give it to me. I'm sorry Tull happened to be using that bridge too at the same time. How much do I——"

"Wait," the Justice said. "What did you give him? a note? a swap of some kind?"

"No," Eck said. "He just pointed to it in the lot and told me it belonged to me."

"And he didn't give you a bill of sale or a deed or anything in writing?"

"I reckon he never had time," Eck said. "And after Lon Quick forgot and left that gate open, never nobody had time to do no writing even if we had a thought of it."

"What's all this?" Mrs Tull said. "Eck Snopes has just told you he owned that horse. And if you wont take his word, there were forty men standing at that gate all day long doing nothing, that heard that murdering card-playing whiskey-drinking antichrist—" This time the Justice raised one hand, in its enormous pristine cuff, toward her. He did not look at her.

"Wait," he said. "Then what did he do?" he said to Eck. "Just lead the horse up and put the rope in your hand?"

"No," Eck said. "Him nor nobody else never got no ropes on none of them. He just pointed to the horse in the lot and said it was mine and auctioned off the rest of them and got into the buggy and said goodbye and druv off. And we got our ropes and went into the lot, only Lon Quick forgot to shut the gate. I'm sorry it made Tull's mules snatch him outen the wagon. How much do I owe him?" Then he stopped, because the Justice was no longer looking at him and, as he realised a moment later, no longer listening either. Instead, he was sitting back in the chair, actually leaning back in it for the first time, his head bent slightly and his hands resting on the table before him, the fingers lightly overlapped. They watched him quietly for almost a half-minute before anyone realised that he was looking quietly and steadily at Mrs Tull.

"Well, Mrs Tull," he said, "by your own testimony, Eck never owned that horse."

"What?" Mrs Tull said. It was not loud at all. "What did you say?"

"In the law, ownership cant be conferred or invested by

word-of-mouth. It must be established either by recorded or authentic document, or by possession or occupation. By your testimony and his both, he never gave that Texas man anything in exchange for that horse, and by his testimony the Texas man never gave him any paper to prove he owned it, and by his testimony and by what I know myself from these last four weeks, nobody yet has ever laid hand or rope either on any one of them. So that horse never came into Eck's possession at all. That Texas man could have given that same horse to a dozen other men standing around that gate that day, without even needing to tell Eck he had done it; and Eck himself could have transferred all his title and equity in it to Mr Tull right there while Mr Tull was lying unconscious on that bridge just by thinking it to himself, and Mr Tull's title would be just as legal as Eck's."

"So I get nothing," Mrs Tull said. Her voice was still calm, quiet, though probably no one but Tull realised that it was too calm and quiet. "My team is made to run away by a wild spotted mad-dog, my wagon is wrecked; my husband is jerked out of it and knocked unconscious and unable to work for a whole week with less than half of our seed in the ground, and I get nothing."

"Wait," the Justice said. "The law—"

"The law," Mrs Tull said. She stood suddenly up—a short, broad, strong woman, balanced on the balls of her planted feet.

"Now, mamma," Tull said.

"Yes, ma'am," the Justice said. "Your damages are fixed by statute. The law says that when a suit for damages is brought against the owner of an animal which has committed damage or injury, if the owner of the animal either cant or wont assume liability, the injured or damaged party shall find recompense in the body of the animal. And since Eck Snopes never owned that horse at all, and since you just heard a case here this morning that failed to prove that Flem Snopes had any equity in any of them, that horse still belongs to that Texas man. Or did belong. Because now that horse that made your team run away and snatch your husband out of the wagon, belongs to you and Mr Tull."

"Now, mamma!" Tull said. He rose quickly. But Mrs Tull was still quiet, only quite rigid and breathing hard, until Tull spoke. Then she turned on him, not screaming: shouting; presently the bailiff was banging the table-top with his hand-polished hickory cane and roaring "Order! Order!" while the neat old man, thrust backward in his chair as though about to dodge and trembling with an old man's palsy, looked on with amazed unbelief.

"The horse!" Mrs Tull shouted. "We see it for five seconds, while it is climbing into the wagon with us and then out again. Then it's gone, God dont know where and thank the Lord He dont! And the mules gone with it and the wagon wrecked and you laying there on the bridge with your face full of kindling-wood and bleeding like a hog and dead for all we knew. And he gives us the horse! Dont you hush me! Get on to that wagon, fool that would sit there behind a pair of young mules with the reins tied around his wrist! Get on to that wagon, all of you!"

"I cant stand no more!" the old Justice cried. "I wont! This court's adjourned! Adjourned!"

There was another trial then. It began on the following Monday and most of those same faces watched it too, in the county court house in Jefferson when the prisoner entered between two officers and looking hardly larger than a child, in a suit of brand-new overalls, thin, almost frail-looking, the sombre violent face thin in repose and pallid from the eight months in jail, and was arraigned and then plead by the counsel appointed him by the Court—a young man graduated only last June from the State University's law school and admitted to the Bar, who did what he could and overdid what he could not, zealous and, for all practical purposes and results, ignored, having exhausted all his challenges before the State had made one and in despite of which seeing himself faced by an authenticated jury in almost record time as if the State, the public, all rational mankind, possessed an inexhaustible pool of interchangeable faces and names all cradling one identical conviction and intention, so that his very challenges could have been discharged for him by the janitor who opened the court-room, by merely counting off the first members of the panel corresponding to that number. And, if the defendant's counsel had had any detachment and objectivity left at all by then, he probably realised soon that it was not his client but himself who was embattled with that jury. Because his client was paying no attention whatever to what was going on. He did not seem to be interested in watching and listening to it as someone else's trial. He sat where they had placed him, manacled to one of the officers, small, in the new iron-hard board-stiff overalls, the back of his head toward the Bar and what was going on there and his upper body shifting constantly until they realised that he was trying to watch the rear of the room, the doors and who entered them. He had to be spoken to twice before he stood up and plead and continued to stand, his back completely turned to the Court now, his face sombre, thin, curiously urgent and quite calm and with something else in it which was not even just hope but was actual faith, looking not at his wife who sat on the bench just behind him but out into the crowded room, among the ranked and intent

faces some of which, most of which, he knew, until the officer
he was handcuffed to pulled him down again. And he sat that
way through the rest of the brief and record day-and-a-quarter
of his trial, the small, neatly-combed, vicious and ironlike
incorrigible head turning and craning constantly to see backward past the bulk of the two officers, watching the entrance
while his attorney did what he could, talked himself frantic
and at last voiceless before the grave impassivity of the jury
which resembled a conclave of grown men self-delegated with
the necessity (though for a definitely specified and limited
time) of listening to prattle of a licensed child. And still the
client listened to none of it, watching constantly the rear of
the room while toward the end of the first day the faith went
out of his face, leaving only the hope, and at the beginning of
the second day the hope was gone too and there was only the
urgency, the grim and intractable sombreness, while still he
watched the door. The State finished in mid-morning of the
second day. The jury was out twenty minutes and returned
with a ballot of murder in the second degree; the prisoner
stood again and was sentenced by the Court to be transported
to the State Penal Farm and there remain until he died. But
he was not listening to that either; he had not only turned his
back to the Court to look out into the crowded room, he was
speaking himself even before the Judge had ceased, continuing to speak even while the Judge hammered the desk with his
gavel and the two officers and three bailiffs converged upon
the prisoner as he struggled, flinging them back and for a short
time actually successful, staring out into the room. "Flem
Snopes!" he said. "Flem Snopes! Is Flem Snopes in this
room? Tell that son of a bitch——"

Old Man

O nce (it was in Mississippi, in May, in the flood year 1927) there were two convicts. One of them was about twenty-five, tall, lean, flat-stomached, with a sunburned face and Indian-black hair and pale, china-colored outraged eyes—an outrage directed not at the men who had foiled his crime, not even at the lawyers and judges who had sent him here, but at the writers, the uncorporeal names attached to the stories, the paper novels—the Diamond Dicks and Jesse Jameses and such—whom he believed had led him into his present predicament through their own ignorance and gullibility regarding the medium in which they dealt and took money for, in accepting information on which they placed the stamp of verisimilitude and authenticity (this so much the more criminal since there was no sworn notarised statement attached and hence so much the quicker would the information be accepted by one who expected the same unspoken good faith, demanding, asking, expecting no certification, which he extended along with the dime or fifteen cents to pay for it) and retailed for money and which on actual application proved to be impractical and (to the convict) criminally false; there would be times when he would halt his mule and plow in midfurrow (there is no walled penitentiary in Mississippi; it is a cotton plantation which the convicts work under the rifles and shotguns of guards and trusties) and muse with a kind of enraged impotence, fumbling among the rubbish left him by his one and only experience with courts and law, fumbling until the meaningless and verbose shibboleth took form at last (himself seeking justice at the same blind fount where he had met justice and been hurled back and down): using the mails to defraud: who felt that he had been defrauded by the third class mail system not of crass and stupid money which he did not particularly want anyway, but of liberty and honor and pride.

He was in for fifteen years (he had arrived shortly after his nineteenth birthday) for attempted train robbery. He had laid his plans in advance, he had followed his printed (and false) authority to the letter; he had saved the paper-backs for two years, reading and rereading them, memorising them, comparing and weighing story and method against story and method, taking the good from each and discarding the dross as his workable plan emerged, keeping his mind open to make the subtle last-minute changes, without haste and without impatience, as the newer pamphlets appeared on their appointed days as a conscientious dressmaker makes the subtle alterations in a court presentation costume as the newer bulletins appear. And then when the day came, he did not even have a chance to go through the coaches and collect the watches and the rings, the brooches and the hidden money-belts, because he had been captured as soon as he entered the express car where the safe and the gold would be. He had shot no one because the pistol which they took away from him was not that kind of a pistol although it was loaded; later he admitted to the District Attorney that he had got it, as well as the

dark lantern in which a candle burned and the black handkerchief to wear over the face, by peddling among his pine-
hill neighbors subscriptions to the *Detectives' Gazette*. So now
from time to time (he had ample leisure for it) he mused with
that raging impotence because there was something else he
could not tell them at the trial, did not know how to tell them.
It was not the money he had wanted. It was not riches, not the
crass loot; that would have been merely a bangle to wear upon
the breast of his pride like the Olympic runner's amateur
medal—a symbol, a badge to show that he too was the best at
his chosen gambit in the living and fluid world of his time. So
that at times as he trod the richly shearing black earth behind
his plow or with a hoe thinned the sprouting cotton and corn
or lay on his sullen back in his bunk after supper, he cursed in
a harsh steady unrepetitive stream, not at the living men who
had put him where he was but at what he did not even know
were pen-names, did not even know were not actual men but
merely the designations of shades who had written about
shades.

The second convict was short and plump. Almost hairless,
he was quite white. He looked like something exposed to light
by turning over rotting logs or planks and he too carried
(though not in his eyes like the first convict) a sense of burning and impotent outrage. So it did not show on him and
hence none knew it was there. But then nobody knew very
much about him, including the people who had sent him
here. His outrage was directed at no printed word but at the
paradoxical fact that he had been forced to come here of his
own free choice and will. He had been forced to choose
between the Mississippi State penal farm and the Federal Penitentiary at Atlanta, and the fact that he, who resembled a hairless and pallid slug, had chosen the out-of-doors and the

sunlight was merely another manifestation of the close-guarded and solitary enigma of his character, as something recognisable roils momentarily into view from beneath stagnant and opaque water, then sinks again. None of his fellow prisoners knew what his crime had been, save that he was in for a hundred and ninety-nine years—this incredible and impossible period of punishment or restraint itself carrying a vicious and fabulous quality which indicated that his reason for being here was such that the very men, the paladins and pillars of justice and equity who had sent him here had during that moment become blind apostles not of mere justice but of all human decency, blind instruments not of equity but of all human outrage and vengeance, acting in a savage personal concert, judge lawyer and jury, which certainly abrogated justice and possibly even law. Possibly only the Federal and State's attorneys knew what the crime actually was. There had been a woman in it and a stolen automobile transported across a state line, a filling station robbed and the attendant shot to death. There had been a second man in the car at the time and anyone could have looked once at the convict (as the two attorneys did) and known he would not even have had the synthetic courage of alcohol to pull trigger on anyone. But he and the woman and the stolen car had been captured while the second man, doubtless the actual murderer, had escaped, so that, brought to bay at last in the State's Attorney's office, harried, dishevelled and snarling, the two grimly implacable and viciously gleeful attorneys in his front and the now raging woman held by two policemen in the anteroom in his rear, he was given his choice. He could be tried in Federal Court under the Mann Act and for the automobile, that is, by electing to pass through the anteroom where the woman raged he could take his chances on the lesser crime in Federal Court, or by accepting a sentence for manslaughter in the State Court he would be permitted to quit the room by a back entrance, without having to pass the woman. He had chosen; he stood at the Bar and heard a judge (who looked down at him as if the District Attorney actually had turned over a rotten plank with his toe and exposed him) sentence him to a hundred and ninety-nine years at the State Farm. Thus (he had ample leisure too; they had tried to teach him to plow and had failed, they had put him in the blacksmith shop and the foreman trusty himself had asked to have him removed: so that now, in a long apron like a woman, he cooked and swept and dusted in the deputy wardens' barracks) he too mused at times with that sense of impotence and outrage though it did not show on him as on the first convict since he leaned on no halted broom to do it and so none knew it was there.

It was this second convict who, toward the end of April, began to read aloud to the others from the daily newspapers when, chained ankle to ankle and herded by armed guards, they had come up from the fields and had eaten supper and were gathered in the bunkhouse. It was the Memphis newspaper which the deputy wardens had read at breakfast; the convict read aloud from it to his companions who could have had but little active interest in the outside world, some of whom could not have read it for themselves at all and did not even know where the Ohio and Missouri river basins were, some of whom had never even seen the Mississippi river although for past periods ranging from a few days to ten and twenty and thirty years (and for future periods ranging from a few months to life) they had plowed and planted and eaten and slept beneath the shadow of the levee itself, knowing only that there was water beyond it from hearsay and because now and then they heard the whistles of steamboats from beyond it, and during the last week or so had seen the stacks and pilot houses moving along the sky sixty feet above their heads.

But they listened, and soon even those who like the taller convict had probably never before seen more water than a horse pond would hold knew what thirty feet on a river gauge at Cairo or Memphis meant and could (and did) talk glibly of sandboils. Perhaps what actually moved them were the accounts of the conscripted levee gangs, mixed blacks and whites working in double shifts against the steadily rising water; stories of men, even though they were negroes, being forced like themselves to do work for which they received no other pay than coarse food and a place in a mudfloored tent to sleep on—stories, pictures, which emerged from the shorter convict's reading voice: the mudsplashed white men with the inevitable shotguns, the antlike lines of negroes carrying sand-bags, slipping and crawling up the steep face of the revetment to hurl their futile ammuntion into the face of a flood and return for more. Or perhaps it was more than this. Perhaps they watched the approach of the disaster with that same amazed and incredulous hope of the slaves—the lions and bears and elephants, the grooms and bathmen and pas-trycooks—who watched the mounting flames of Rome from Ahenobarbus' gardens. But listen they did and presently it was May and the warden's newspaper began to talk in headlines two inches tall—those black staccato slashes of ink which, it would almost seem, even the illiterate should be able to read: *Crest Passes Memphis at Midnight. 4000 Homeless in White River Basin. Governor Calls out National Guard Martial Law Declared in Following Counties. Red Cross Train with Secretary Hoover Leaves Washington Tonight;* then, three evenings later (It had been raining all day—not the vivid brief thunderous downpours of April and May, but the slow steady gray rain of November and December before a cold north wind. The men had not gone to the fields at all during the day, and the very second-hand optimism of the almost twenty-four-hour old news seemed to contain its own refutation.): *Crest Now Below Memphis. 22,000 Refugees Safe at Vicksburg. Army Engineers Say Levees Will Hold.*

"I reckon that means it will bust tonight," one convict said.

"Well, maybe this rain will hold on until the water gets here," a second said. They all agreed to this because what they meant, the living unspoken thought among them, was that if the weather cleared, even though the levees broke and the flood moved in upon the Farm itself, they would have to return to the fields and work, which they would have had to do. There was nothing paradoxical in this, although they could not have expressed the reason for it which they instinctively perceived: that the land they farmed and the substance they produced from it belonged neither to them who worked it nor to those who forced them at guns' point to do so, that as far as either—convicts or guards—were concerned, it could have been pebbles they put into the ground and papier-mache cotton- and corn-sprouts which they thinned. So it was that, what between the sudden wild hoping and the idle day and the evening's headlines, they were sleeping restlessly beneath the sound of the rain on the tin roof when at midnight the sudden glare of the electric bulbs and the guards' voices waked them and they heard the throbbing of the waiting trucks.

"Turn out of there!" the deputy shouted. He was fully dressed—rubber boots, slicker, and shotgun. "The levee went out at Mound's Landing an hour ago. Get up out of it!"

When the belated and streaming dawn broke the two convicts, along with twenty others, were in a truck. A trusty drove, two armed guards sat in the cab with him. Inside the high, stall-like topless body the convicts stood, packed like matches in an upright box or like the pencil-shaped ranks of cordite in a shell, shackled by the ankles to a single chain which wove among the motionless feet and swaying legs and a clutter of picks and shovels among which they stood, and was rivetted by both ends to the steel body of the truck.

Then and without warning they saw the flood about which the plump convict had been reading and they listening for two weeks or more. The road ran south. It was built on a raised levee, known locally as a dump, about eight feet above the flat surrounding land, bordered on both sides by the barrow pits from which the earth of the levee had been excavated. These barrow pits had held water all winter from the fall rains, not to speak of the rain of yesterday, but now they saw that the pit on either side of the road had vanished and instead there lay a flat still sheet of brown water which extended into the fields beyond the pits, ravelled out into long motionless shreds in the bottom of the plow furrows and gleaming faintly in the gray light like the bars of a prone and enormous grating. And then (the truck was moving at good speed) as they watched quietly (they had not been talking much anyway but now they were all silent and quite grave, shifting and craning as one to look soberly off to the west side of the road) the crests of the furrows vanished too and they now looked at a single perfectly flat and motionless steel-colored sheet in which the telephone poles and the straight hedgerows which marked section lines seemed to be fixed and rigid as though set in concrete.

It was perfectly motionless, perfectly flat. It looked, not innocent, but bland. It looked almost demure. It looked as if you could walk on it. It looked so still that they did not realise it possessed motion until they came to the first bridge. There was a ditch under the bridge, a small stream, but ditch and stream were both invisible now, indicated only by the rows of cypress and bramble which marked its course. Here they both saw and heard movement—the slow profound eastward and upstream ("It's running backward," one convict said quietly.) set of the still rigid surface, from beneath which came a deep faint subaquean rumble which (though none in the truck could have made the comparison) sounded like a subway train passing far beneath the street and which inferred a terrific and secret speed. It was as if the water itself were in three strata, separate and distinct, the bland and unhurried surface bearing a frothy scum and a miniature flotsam of twigs and screening as though by vicious calculation the rush and fury of the flood itself, and beneath this in turn the original stream, trickle, murmuring along in the opposite direction, following undisturbed and unaware its appointed course and serving its Lilliputian end, like a thread of ants between the rails on which an express train passes, they (the ants) as unaware of the power and fury as if it were a cyclone crossing Saturn.

Now there was water on both sides of the road and now, as if once they had become aware of movement in the water the water seemed to have given over deception and concealment, they seemed to be able to watch it rising up the flanks of the dump; trees which a few miles back had stood on tall trunks above the water now seemed to burst from the surface at the level of the lower branches like decorative shrubs on barbered lawns. The truck passed a negro cabin. The water was up to the window ledges. A woman clutching two children squatted on the ridgepole, a man and a halfgrown youth, standing waist-deep, were hoisting a squealing pig onto the slanting roof of a barn, on the ridgepole of which sat a row of chickens and a turkey. Near the barn was a haystack on which a cow stood tied by a rope to the center pole and bawling steadily; a yelling negro boy on a saddleless mule which he flogged steadily, his legs clutching the mule's barrel and his body leaned to the drag of a rope attached to a second mule, approached the haystack, splashing and floundering. The woman on the housetop began to shriek at the passing truck, her voice carrying faint and melodious across the brown water, becoming fainter and fainter as the truck passed and went on, ceasing at last, whether because of distance or because she had stopped screaming those in the truck did not know.

Then the road vanished. There was no perceptible slant to it yet it had slipped abruptly beneath the brown surface with no ripple, no ridgy demarcation, like a flat thin blade slipped obliquely into flesh by a delicate hand, annealed into the water without disturbance, as if it had existed so for years, had been built that way. The truck stopped. The trusty descended from the cab and came back and dragged two shovels from among their feet, the blades clashing against the serpentining of the chain about their ankles. "What is it?" one said. "What are you fixing to do?" The trusty didn't answer. He returned to the cab, from which one of the guards had descended, without his shotgun. He and the trusty, both in hip boots and each carrying a shovel, advanced into the water, gingerly, probing and feeling ahead with the shovel handles. The same convict spoke again. He was a middle-aged man with a wild thatch of iron-gray hair and a slightly mad face. "What the hell are they doing?" he said. Again nobody answered him. The truck moved, on into the water, behind the guard and the trusty, beginning to push ahead of itself a thick slow viscid ridge of chocolate water. Then the gray-haired convict began to scream. "God damn it, unlock the chain!" He began to struggle, thrashing violently about him, striking at the men nearest him until he reached the cab, the roof of which he now hammered on with his fists, screaming. "God damn it, unlock us! Unlock us! Son of a bitch!" he screamed, addressing no one. "They're going to drown us! Unlock the chain!" But for all the answer he got the men within radius of his voice might have been dead. The truck crawled on, the guard and the trusty feeling out the road ahead with the reversed shovels, the second guard at the wheel, the twenty-two convicts packed like sardines into the truck bed and padlocked by the ankles to the body of the truck itself. They crossed another bridge—two delicate and paradoxical iron railings slanting out of the water, travelling parallel to it for a distance, then slanting down into it again with an outrageous quality almost significant yet apparently meaningless like something in a dream not quite nightmare. The truck crawled on.

Along toward noon they came to a town, their destination. The streets were paved; now the wheels of the truck made a sound like tearing silk. Moving faster now, the guard and the trusty in the cab again, the truck even had a slight bone in its teeth, its bow-wave spreading beyond the submerged sidewalks and across the adjacent lawns, lapping against the stoops and porches of houses where people stood among piles of furniture. They passed through the business district; a man in hip boots emerged knee-deep in water from a store, dragging a flat-bottomed skiff containing a steel safe.

At last they reached the railroad. It crossed the street at right angles, cutting the town in two. It was on a dump, a levee, also, eight or ten feet above the town itself; the street ran blankly into it and turned at right angles beside a cotton compress and a loading platform on stilts at the level of a freight car door. On this platform was a khaki army tent and a uniformed National Guard sentry with a rifle and bandolier.

The truck turned and crawled out of the water and up the ramp which cotton wagons used and where trucks and private cars filled with household goods came and unloaded onto the platform. They were unlocked from the chain in the truck and shackled ankle to ankle in pairs they mounted the platform and into an apparently inextricable jumble of beds and trunks, gas and electric stoves, radios and tables and chairs and framed pictures which a chain of negroes under the eye of an unshaven white man in muddy corduroy and hip boots carried piece by piece into the compress, at the door of which another guardsman stood with his rifle, they (the convicts) not stopping here but herded on by the two guards with their shotguns, into the dim and cavernous building where among the piled heterogeneous furniture the ends of cotton bales and the mirrors on dressers and sideboards gleamed with an identical mute and unreflecting concentration of pallid light.

They passed on through, onto the loading platform where the army tent and the first sentry were. They waited here. Nobody told them for what nor why. While the two guards talked with the sentry before the tent the convicts sat in a line along the edge of the platform like buzzards on a fence, their shackled feet dangling above the brown motionless flood out of which the railroad embankment rose, pristine and intact, in a kind of paradoxical denial and repudiation of change and portent, not talking, just looking quietly across the track to where the other half of the amputated town seemed to float, house shrub and tree, ordered and pageant-like and without motion, upon the limitless liquid plain beneath the thick gray sky.

After a while the other four trucks from the Farm arrived. They came up, bunched closely, radiator to tail light, with their four separate sounds of tearing silk and vanished beyond the compress. Presently the ones on the platform heard the feet, the mute clashing of the shackles, the first truckload emerged from the compress, the second, the third; there were more than a hundred of them now in their bed-ticking overalls and jumpers and fifteen or twenty guards with rifles and shotguns. The first lot rose and they mingled, paired, twinned by their clanking and clashing umbilicals; then it began to rain, a slow steady gray drizzle like November instead of May. Yet not one of them made any move toward the open door of the compress. They did not even look toward it, with longing or hope or without it. If they thought at all, they doubtless knew that the available space in it would be needed for furniture, even if it were not already filled. Or perhaps they knew that, even if there were room in it, it would not be for them, not that the guards would wish them to get wet but that the guards would not think about getting them out of the rain. So they just stopped talking and with their jumper collars turned up and shackled in braces like dogs at a field trial they stood, immobile, patient, almost ruminant, their backs turned to the rain as sheep and cattle do.

After another while they became aware that the number of soldiers had increased to a dozen or more, warm and dry beneath rubberised ponchos, there was an officer with a pistol at his belt, then and without making any move toward it, they began to smell food and, turning to look, saw an army field kitchen set up just inside the compress door. But they made no move, they waited until they were herded into line, they inched forward, their heads lowered and patient in the rain, and received each a bowl of stew, a mug of coffee, two slices of bread. They ate this in the rain. They did not sit down because the platform was wet, they squatted on their heels as country men do, hunching forward trying to shield the bowls and mugs into which nevertheless the rain splashed steadily as into miniature ponds and soaked, invisible and soundless, into the bread.

After they had stood on the platform for three hours, a train came for them. Those nearest the edge saw it, watched it—a passenger coach apparently running under its own power and trailing a cloud of smoke from no visible stack, a cloud which did not rise but instead shifted slowly and heavily aside and lay upon the surface of the aqueous earth with a quality at once weightless and completely spent. It came up and stopped, a single old fashioned open-ended wooden car coupled to the nose of a pushing switch engine considerably smaller. They were herded into it, crowding forward to the other end where there was a small cast iron stove. There was no fire in it, nevertheless they crowded about it—the cold and voiceless lump of iron stained with fading tobacco and hovered about by the ghosts of a thousand Sunday excursions to Memphis or Moorhead and return—the peanuts, the bananas, the soiled garments of infants—huddling, shoving for places near it. "Come on, come on," one of the guards shouted. "Sit down, now." At last three of the guards, laying aside their guns, came among them and broke up the huddle, driving them back and into seats.

There were not enough seats for all. The others stood in the aisle, they stood braced, they heard the air hiss out of the released brakes, the engine whistled four blasts, the car came into motion with a snapping jerk; the platform, the compress fled violently as the train seemed to transpose from immobility to full speed with that same quality of unreality with which it had appeared, running backward now though with the engine in front where before it had moved forward but with the engine behind.

When the railroad in its turn ran beneath the surface of the water, the convicts did not even know it. They felt the train stop, they heard the engine blow a long blast which wailed away unechoed across the waste, wild and forlorn, and they were not even curious; they sat or stood behind the rain-streaming windows as the train crawled on again, feeling its way as the truck had while the brown water swirled between the trucks and among the spokes of the driving wheels and lapped in cloudy steam against the dragging fire-filled belly of the engine; again it blew four short harsh blasts filled with the wild triumph and defiance yet also with repudiation and even farewell, as if the articulated steel itself knew it did not dare stop and would not be able to return. Two hours later in the twilight they saw through the streaming windows a burning plantation house. Juxtaposed to nowhere and neighbored by nothing it stood, a clear steady pyre-like flame rigidly fleeing its own reflection, burning in the dusk above the watery desolation with a quality paradoxical, outrageous and bizarre.

Sometime after dark the train stopped. The convicts did not know where they were. They did not ask. They would no more have thought of asking where they were than they would have asked why and what for. They couldn't even see, since the car was unlighted and the windows fogged on the outside by rain and on the inside by the engendered heat of the packed bodies. All they could see was a milky and sourceless flick and glare of flashlights. They could hear shouts and commands, then the guards inside the car began to shout; they were herded to their feet and toward the exit, the ankle chains clashing and clanking. They descended into a fierce hissing of steam, through ragged wisps of it blowing past the car. Laid-to alongside the train and resembling a train itself was a thick blunt motor launch to which was attached a string of skiffs and flat boats. There were more soldiers; the flashlights played on the rifle barrels and bandolier buckles and flicked and glinted on the ankle chains of the convicts as they stepped gingerly down into knee-deep water and entered the boats; now car and engine both vanished completely in steam as the crew began dumping the fire from the firebox.

After another hour they began to see lights ahead—a faint wavering row of red pin-pricks extending along the horizon and apparently hanging low in the sky. But it took almost another hour to reach them while the convicts squatted in the skiffs, huddled into the soaked garments (they no longer felt the rain anymore at all as separate drops) and watched the lights draw nearer and nearer until at last the crest of the levee defined itself; now they could discern a row of army tents stretching along it and people squatting about the fires, the wavering reflections from which, stretching across the water, revealed an involved mass of other skiffs tied against the flank of the levee which now stood high and dark overhead. Flashlights glared and winked along the base, among the tethered skiffs; the launch, silent now, drifted in.

When they reached the top of the levee they could see the long line of khaki tents, interspersed with fires about which people—men, women and children, negroes and white—crouched or stood among shapeless bales of clothing, their heads turning, their eyeballs glinting in the firelight as they looked quietly at the striped garments and the chains; further down the levee, huddled together too though untethered, was a drove of mules and two or three cows. Then the taller convict became conscious of another sound. He did not begin to hear it all at once, he suddenly became aware that he had been hearing it all the time, a sound so much beyond all his experience and his powers of assimilation that up to this point he had been as oblivious of it as an ant or a flea might be of the sound of the avalanche on which it rides; he had been travelling upon water since early afternoon and for seven years now he had run his plow and harrow and planter within the very shadow of the levee on which he now stood, but this profound deep whisper which came from the further side of it he did not at once recognise. He stopped. The line of convicts behind jolted into him like a line of freight cars stopping, with an iron clashing like cars. "Get on!" a guard shouted.

"What's that?" the convict said. A negro man squatting before the nearest fire answered him:

"Dat's him. Dat's de Ole Man."

"The old man?" the convict said.

"Get on! Get on up there!" the guard shouted. They went on; they passed another huddle of mules, the eyeballs rolling too, the long morose faces turning into and out of the firelight; they passed them and reached a section of empty tents, the light pup tents of a military campaign, made to hold two men. The guards herded the convicts into them, three brace of shackled men to each tent.

They crawled in on all fours, like dogs into cramped kennels, and settled down. Presently the tent became warm from their bodies. Then they became quiet and then all of them could hear it, they lay listening to the bass whisper deep, strong and powerful. "The old man?" the train-robber convict said.

"Yah," another said. "He dont have to brag."

At dawn the guards waked them by kicking the soles of the projecting feet. Opposite the muddy landing and the huddle of skiffs an army field kitchen was set up, already they could smell the coffee. But the taller convict at least, even though he had had but one meal yesterday and that at noon in the rain, did not move at once toward the food. Instead and for the first time he looked at the River within whose shadow he had spent the last seven years of his life but had never seen before; he stood in quiet and amazed surmise and looked at the rigid steel-colored surface not broken into waves but merely slightly undulant. It stretched from the levee on which he stood, further than he could see—a slowly and heavily roiling choco-late-frothy expanse broken only by a thin line a mile away as fragile in appearance as a single hair, which after a moment he recognised. *It's another levee* he thought quietly. *That's what we look like from there. That's what I am standing on looks like from there.* He was prodded from the rear; a guard's voice carried forward: "Go on! Go on! You'll have plenty of time to look at that!"

They received the same stew and coffee and bread as the day before, they squatted again with their bowls and mugs as yesterday, though it was not raining yet. During the night an intact wooden barn had floated up. It now lay jammed by the current against the levee while a crowd of negroes swarmed over it, ripping off the shingles and planks and carrying them up the bank; eating steadily and without haste, the taller con-vict watched the barn dissolve rapidly down to the very water-line exactly as a dead fly vanished beneath the moiling industry of a swarm of ants.

They finished eating. Then it began to rain again, as upon a signal, while they stood or squatted in their harsh garments

which had not dried out during the night but had merely
become slightly warmer than the air. Presently they were
haled to their feet and told off into two groups, one of which
was armed from a stack of mud-clogged picks and shovels
nearby, and marched away up the levee. A little later the
motor launch with its train of skiffs came up across what was,
fifteen feet beneath its keel, probably a cotton field, the skiffs
loaded to the gunwales with negroes and a scattering of white
people nursing bundles on their laps. When the engine shut
off the faint plinking of a guitar came across the water. The
skiffs warped in and unloaded; the convicts watched the men
and women and children struggle up the muddy slope, carrying heavy towsacks and bundles wrapped in quilts. The sound
of the guitar had not ceased and now the convicts saw him—a
young, black, lean-hipped man, the guitar slung by a piece of
cotton plow line about his neck. He mounted the levee, still
picking it. He carried nothing else, no food, no change of
clothes, not even a coat.

The taller convict was so busy watching this that he did
not hear the guard until the guard stood directly beside him
shouting his name. "Wake up!" the guard shouted. "Can you
fellows paddle a boat?"

"Paddle a boat where?" the taller convict said.

"In the water," the guard said. "Where in hell do you
think?"

"I aint going to paddle no boat nowhere out yonder," the
tall convict said, jerking his head toward the invisible river
beyond the levee behind him.

"No, it's on this side," the guard said. He stooped swiftly
and unlocked the chain which joined the tall convict and the
plump hairless one. "It's just down the road a piece." He rose.
The two convicts followed him down to the boats. "Follow

them telephone poles until you come to a filling station. You can tell it, the roof is still above water. It's on a bayou and you can tell the bayou because the tops of the trees are sticking up. Follow the bayou until you come to a cypress snag with a woman in it. Pick her up and then cut straight back west until you come to a cotton house with a fellow sitting on the ridge-pole—" He turned, looking at the two convicts, who stood perfectly still, looking first at the skiff and then at the water with intense sobriety. "Well? What are you waiting for?"

"I cant row a boat," the plump convict said.

"Then it's high time you learned," the guard said. "Get in."

The tall convict shoved the other forward. "Get in," he said. "That water aint going to hurt you. Aint nobody going to make you take a bath."

As, the plump one in the bow and the other in the stern, they shoved away from the levee, they saw other pairs being unshackled and manning the other skiffs. "I wonder how many more of them fellows are seeing this much water for the first time in their lives too," the tall convict said. The other did not answer. He knelt in the bottom of the skiff, pecking gingerly at the water now and then with his paddle. The very shape of his thick soft back seemed to wear that expression of wary and tense concern.

Sometime after midnight a rescue boat filled to the guard rail with homeless men and women and children docked at Vicksburg. It was a steamer, shallow of draft; all day long it had poked up and down cypress- and gum-choked bayous and across cotton fields (where at times instead of swimming it waded) gathering its sorry cargo from the tops of houses and barns and even out of trees, and now it warped into that mushroom city of the forlorn and despairing where kerosene flares smoked in the drizzle and hurriedly-strung electrics glared upon the bayonets of martial policemen and the red cross brassards of doctors and nurses and canteen-workers. The bluff overhead was almost solid with tents, yet still there were more people than shelter for them; they sat or lay, single and by whole families, under what shelter they could find or sometimes under the rain itself, in the little death of profound exhaustion while the doctors and the nurses and the soldiers stepped over and around and among them.

Among the first to disembark was one of the penitentiary deputy wardens, followed closely by the plump convict and another white man—a small man with a gaunt unshaven wan face still wearing an expression of incredulous outrage. The deputy warden seemed to know exactly where he wished to go. Followed closely by his two companions he threaded his way swiftly among the piled furniture and the sleeping bodies and stood presently in a fiercely lighted and hastily established temporary office, almost a military post of command in fact, where the Warden of the Penitentiary sat with two army officers wearing majors' leaves. The deputy warden spoke without preamble. "We lost a man," he said. He called the tall convict's name.

"Lost him?" the Warden said.

"Yah. Drowned." Without turning his head he spoke to the plump convict. "Tell him," he said.

"He was the one that said he could row a boat," the plump convict said. "I never. I told him myself—" he indicated the deputy warden with a jerk of his head "—I couldn't. So when we got to the bayou—"

"What's this?" the Warden said.

"The launch brought word in," the deputy warden said. "Woman in a cypress snag on the bayou, then this fellow—"

he indicated the third man; the Warden and the two officers looked at the third man "—on a cotton house. Never had room in the launch to pick them up. Go on."

"So we come to where the bayou was," the plump convict continued in a voice perfectly flat, without any inflection whatever. "Then the boat got away from him. I dont know what happened. I was just sitting there because he was so positive he could row a boat. I never saw any current. Just all of a sudden the boat whirled clean around and begun to run fast backward like it was hitched to a train and it whirled around again and I happened to look up and there was a limb right over my head and I grabbed it just in time and that boat was snatched out from under me like you'd snatch off a sock and I saw it one time more upside down and that fellow that said he knew all about rowing holding to it with one hand and still holding the paddle in the other—" He ceased. There was no dying fall to his voice, it just ceased and the convict stood looking quietly at a half-full quart of whiskey sitting on the table.

"How do you know he's drowned?" the Warden said to the deputy. "How do you know he didn't just see his chance to escape, and took it?"

"Escape where?" the other said. "The whole Delta's flooded. There's fifteen foot of water for fifty miles, clean back to the hills. And that boat was upside down."

"That fellow's drowned," the plump convict said. "You dont need to worry about him. He's got his pardon; it wont cramp nobody's hand signing it, neither."

"And nobody else saw him?" the Warden said. "What about the woman in the tree?"

"I dont know," the deputy said. "I aint found her yet. I reckon some other boat picked her up. But this is the fellow on the cotton house."

Again the Warden and the two officers looked at the third man, at the gaunt, unshaven wild face in which an old terror, an old blending of fear and impotence and rage still lingered. "He never came for you?" the Warden said. "You never saw him?"

"Never nobody came for me," the refugee said. He began to tremble though at first he spoke quietly enough. "I set there on that sonabitching cotton house, expecting hit to go any minute, I saw that launch and them boats come up and they never had no room for me. Full of bastard niggers and one of them setting there playing a guitar but there wasn't no room for me. A guitar!" he cried; now he began to scream, trembling, slavering, his face twitching and jerking. "Room for a bastard nigger guitar but not for me—"

"Steady now," the Warden said. "Steady now."

"Give him a drink," one of the officers said. The Warden poured the drink. The deputy handed it to the refugee, who took the glass in both jerking hands and tried to raise it to his mouth. They watched him for perhaps twenty seconds, then the deputy took the glass from him and held it to his lips while he gulped, though even then a thin trickle ran from each corner of his mouth, into the stubble on his chin.

"So we picked him and—" the deputy called the plump convict's name now "—both up just before dark and come on in. But that other fellow is gone."

"Yes," the Warden said. "Well. Here I haven't lost a prisoner in ten years, and now, like this—I'm sending you back to the Farm tomorrow. Have his family notified, and his discharge papers filled out at once."

"All right," the deputy said. "And listen, chief. He wasn't a bad fellow and maybe he never had no business in that boat. Only he did say he could paddle one. Listen. Suppose I write on his discharge, Drowned while trying to save lives in the great flood of nineteen twenty-seven, and send it down for the Governor to sign it. It will be something nice for his folks to have, to hang on the wall when neighbors come in or something. Maybe they will even give his folks a cash bonus because after all they sent him to the Farm to raise cotton, not to fool around in a boat in a flood."

"All right," the Warden said. "I'll see about it. The main thing is to get his name off the books as dead before some politician tries to collect his food allowance."

"All right," the deputy said. He turned and herded his companions out. In the drizzling darkness again he said to the plump convict: "Well, your partner beat you. He's free. He's done served his time out but you've got a right far piece to go yet."

"Yah," the plump convict said. "Free. He can have it."

As the short convict had testified, the tall one, when he returned to the surface, still retained what the short one called the oar. He clung to it, not instinctively against the time when he would be back inside the boat and would need it, because for a time he did not believe he would ever regain the skiff or anything else that would support him, but because he did not have time to think about turning it loose. Things had moved too fast for him. He had not been warned, he had felt the first snatching tug of the current, he had seen the skiff begin to spin and his companion vanish violently upward like in a translation out of Isaiah, then he himself was in the water, struggling against the drag of the paddle which he did not know he still held each time he fought back to the surface and grasped at the spinning skiff which at one instant was ten feet away and the next poised above his head as though about to brain him, until at last he grasped the stern, the drag of his body becoming a rudder to the skiff, the two of them, man and boat and with the paddle perpendicular above them like a jackstaff, vanishing from the view of the short convict (who had vanished from that of the tall one with the same celerity though in a vertical direction) like a tableau snatched offstage intact with violent and incredible speed.

He was now in the channel of a slough, a bayou, in which until today no current had run probably since the old subterranean outrage which had created the country. There was plenty of current in it now though; from his trough behind the stern he seemed to see the trees and sky rushing past with vertiginous speed, looking down at him between the gouts of cold yellow in. lugubrious and mournful amazement. But they were fixed and secure in something; he thought of that, he remembered in an instant of despairing rage the firm earth fixed and founded strong and cemented fast and stable forever by the generations of laborious sweat, somewhere beneath him, beyond the reach of his feet, when, and again without warning, the stern of the skiff struck him a stunning blow across the bridge of his nose. The instinct which had caused him to cling to it now caused him to fling the paddle into the boat in order to grasp the gunwale with both hands just as the skiff pivoted and spun away again. With both hands free he now dragged himself over the stern and lay prone on his face, streaming with blood and water and panting, not with exhaustion but with that furious rage which is terror's aftermath.

But he had to get up at once because he believed he had come much faster (and so further) than he had. So he rose, out of the watery scarlet puddle in which he had lain, streaming, the soaked denim heavy as iron on his limbs, the black hair plastered to his skull, the blood-infused water streaking his jumper, and dragged his forearm gingerly and hurriedly across his lower face and glanced at it then grasped the paddle and began to try to swing the skiff back upstream. It did not even occur to him that he did not know where his companion was, in which tree among all which he had passed or might pass. He did not even speculate on that for the reason that he knew so incontestably that the other was upstream from him, and after his recent experience the mere connotation of the term upstream carried a sense of such violence and force and speed that the conception of it as other than a straight line was something which the intelligence, reason, simply refused to harbor, like the notion of a rifle bullet the width of a cotton field.

The bow began to swing back upstream. It turned readily, it outpaced the aghast and outraged instant in which he realised it was swinging far too easily, it had swung on over the arc and lay broadside to the current and began again that vicious spinning while he sat, his teeth bared in his bloody streaming face while his spent arms flailed the impotent paddle at the water, that innocent-appearing medium which at one time had held him in iron-like and shifting convolutions like an anaconda yet which now seemed to offer no more resistance to the thrust of his urge and need than so much air, like air: the boat which had threatened him and at last actually struck him in the face with the shocking violence of a mule's hoof now seemed to poise weightless upon it like a thistle bloom, spinning like a wind vane while he flailed at the water and thought of, envisioned, his companion safe inactive and at ease in the tree with nothing to do but wait, musing with impotent and terrified fury upon that arbitrariness of human affairs which had abrogated to the one the secure tree and to the other the hysterical and unmanageable boat for the very reason that it knew that he alone of the two of them would make any attempt to return and rescue his companion.

The skiff had paid off and now ran with the current again. It seemed again to spring from immobility into incredible speed, and he thought he must already be miles away from where his companion had quitted him, though actually he had merely described a big circle since getting back into the skiff and the object (a clump of cypress trees choked by float-ing logs and debris) which the skiff was now about to strike was the same one it had careened into before when the stern had struck him. He didn't know this because he had not yet ever looked higher than the bow of the boat. He didn't look higher now, he just saw that he was going to strike; he seemed to feel run through the very insentient fabric of the skiff a cur-rent of eager gleeful vicious incorrigible wilfulness; and he who had never ceased to flail at the bland treacherous water with what he had believed to be the limit of his strength now from somewhere, some ultimate absolute reserve, produced a final measure of endurance, will to endure which adum-brated mere muscle and nerves, continuing to flail the paddle right up to the instant of striking, completing one last reach thrust and recover out of pure desperate reflex, as a man slip-ping on ice reaches for his hat and money-pocket, as the skiff struck and hurled him once more flat on his face in the bot-tom of it.

This time he did not get up at once. He lay flat on his face, slightly spread-eagled and in an attitude almost peaceful, a kind of abject meditation. He would have to get up sometime, he knew that, just as all life consists of having to get up sooner or later and then having to lie down again sooner or later after a while. And he was not exactly exhausted and he was not particularly without hope and he did not especially dread getting up. It merely seemed to him that he had accidentally been caught in a situation in which time and environment, not himself, was mesmerised; he was being toyed with by a current of water going nowhere, beneath a day which would wane toward no evening; when it was done with him it would spew him back into the comparatively safe world he had been snatched violently out of and in the meantime it did not much matter just what he did or did not do. So he lay on his face, now not only feeling but hearing the strong quiet rustling of the current on the underside of the planks, for a while longer. Then he raised his head and this time touched his palm gingerly to his face and looked at the blood again, then he sat up onto his heels and leaning over the gunwale he pinched his nostrils between thumb and finger and expelled a gout of blood and was in the act of wiping his fingers on his thigh when a voice slightly above his line of sight said quietly, "It taken you a while," and he who up to this moment had had neither reason nor time to raise his eyes higher than the bows looked up and saw, sitting in a tree and looking at him, a woman. She was not ten feet away. She sat on the lowest limb of one of the trees holding the jam he had grounded on, in a calico wrapper and an army private's tunic and a sunbonnet, a woman whom he did not even bother to examine since that first startled glance had been ample to reveal to him all the generations of her life and background, who could have been his sister if he had a sister, his wife if he had not entered the penitentiary at an age scarcely out of adolescence and some years younger than that at which even his prolific and monogamous kind married—a woman who sat clutching the trunk of the tree, her stockingless feet in a pair of man's unlaced brogans less than a yard from the water, who was very probably somebody's sister and quite certainly (or certainly should have been) somebody's wife, though this too he had entered the penitentiary too young to have had more than mere theoretical female experience to discover yet. "I thought for a minute you wasn't aiming to come back."

"Come back?"

"After the first time. After you run into this brush pile the first time and got into the boat and went on." He looked about, touching his face tenderly again; it could very well be the same place where the boat had hit him in the face.

"Yah," he said. "I'm here now though."

"Could you maybe get the boat a little closer? I taken a right sharp strain getting up here; maybe I better. . . ." He was not listening; he had just discovered that the paddle was gone; this time when the skiff hurled him forward he had flung the paddle not into it but beyond it. "It's right there in them brush tops," the woman said. "You can get it. Here. Catch a holt of this." It was a grapevine. It had grown up into the tree and the flood had torn the roots loose. She had taken a turn with it about her upper body; she now loosed it and swung it out until he could grasp it. Holding to the end of the vine he warped the skiff around the end of the jam, picking up the paddle, and warped the skiff on beneath the limb and held it and now he watched her move, gather herself heavily and carefully to descend—that heaviness which was not painful but just excruciatingly careful, that profound and almost lethargic awkwardness which added nothing to the sum of that first aghast amazement which had served already for the cata-falque of invincible dream since even in durance he had con-tinued (and even with the old avidity, even though they had caused his downfall) to consume the impossible pulp-printed fables carefully censored and as carefully smuggled into the penitentiary; and who to say what Helen, what living Garbo, he had not dreamed of rescuing from what craggy pinnacle or dragoned keep when he and his companion embarked in the skiff. He watched her, he made no further effort to help her beyond holding the skiff savagely steady while she lowered herself from the limb—the entire body, the deformed swell of belly bulging the calico, suspended by its arms, thinking *And this is what I get. This, out of all the female meat that walks, is what I have to be caught in a runaway boat with.*

"Where's that cottonhouse?" he said.

"Cottonhouse?"

"With that fellow on it. The other one."

"I dont know. It's a right smart of cottonhouses around here. With folks on them too, I reckon." She was examining him. "You're bloody as a hog," she said. "You look like a convict."

"Yah," he said, snarled. "I feel like I done already been hung. Well, I got to pick up my pardner and then find that cottonhouse." He cast off. That is, he released his hold on the vine. That was all he had to do, for even while the bow of the skiff hung high on the log jam and even while he held it by the vine in the comparatively dead water behind the jam, he felt steadily and constantly the whisper, the strong purring power of the water just one inch beyond the frail planks on which he squatted and which, as soon as he released the vine, took charge of the skiff not with one powerful clutch but in a series of touches light, tentative, and catlike; he realised now that he had entertained a sort of foundationless hope that the added weight might make the skiff more controllable. During the first moment or two he had a wild (and still foundationless) belief that it had; he had got the head upstream and managed to hold it so by terrific exertion continued even after he discovered that they were travelling straight enough but stern-first and continued somehow even after the bow began to wear away and swing: the old irresistible movement which he knew well by now, too well to fight against it, so that he let the bow swing on downstream with the hope of utilising the skiff's own momentum to bring it through the full circle and so upstream again, the skiff travelling broadside then bow-first then broad-side again, diagonally across the channel, toward the other wall of submerged trees; it began to flee beneath him with ter-rific speed, they were in an eddy but did not know it, he had no time to draw conclusions or even wonder; he crouched, his teeth bared in his blood-caked and swollen face, his lungs bursting, flailing at the water while the trees stooped hugely down at him. The skiff struck, spun, struck again; the woman half lay in the bow, clutching the gunwales, as if she were try-ing to crouch behind her own pregnancy; he banged now not at the water but at the living sapblooded wood with the pad-dle, his desire now not to go anywhere, reach any destination, but just to keep the skiff from beating itself to fragments against the tree trunks. Then something exploded, this time against the back of his head, and stooping trees and dizzy water, the woman's face and all, fled together and vanished in bright soundless flash and glare.

An hour later the skiff came slowly up an old logging road and so out of the bottom, the forest, and into (or onto) a cot-tonfield—a gray and limitless desolation now free of turmoil, broken only by a thin line of telephone poles like a wading millipede. The woman was now paddling, steadily and delib-erately, with that curious lethargic care, while the convict squatted, his head between his knees, trying to stanch the fresh and apparently inexhaustible flow of blood from his nose with handsfull of water. The woman ceased paddling, the skiff drifted on, slowing, while she looked about. "We're done out," she said.

The convict raised his head and also looked about. "Out where?"

"I thought maybe you might know."

"I dont even know where I used to be. Even if I knowed which way was north, I wouldn't know if that was where I wanted to go." He cupped another handfull of water to his face and lowered his hand and regarded the resulting crimson marbling on his palm, not with dejection, not with concern, but with a kind of sardonic and vicious bemusement. The woman watched the back of his head.

"We got to get somewhere."

"Dont I know it? A fellow on a cottonhouse. Another in a tree. And now that thing in your lap."

"It wasn't due yet. Maybe it was having to climb that tree quick yesterday, and having to set in it all night. I'm doing the best I can. But we better get somewhere soon."

"Yah," the convict said. "I thought I wanted to get somewhere too and I aint had no luck at it. You pick out a place to get to now and we'll try yours. Gimme that oar." The woman passed him the paddle. The boat was a double-ender; he had only to turn around.

"Which way you fixing to go?" the woman said.

"Never you mind that. You just keep on holding on." He began to paddle, on across the cottonfield. It began to rain again, though not hard at first. "Yah," he said. "Ask the boat. I been in it since breakfast and I aint never knowed, where I aimed to go or where I was going either."

That was about one oclock. Toward the end of the afternoon the skiff (they were in a channel of some sort again, they had been in it for some time; they had got into it before they knew it and too late to get out again, granted there had been any reason to get out, as, to the convict anyway, there was certainly none and the fact that their speed had increased again was reason enough to stay in it) shot out upon a broad expanse of debris-filled water which the convict recognised as a river and, from its size, the Yazoo River though it was little enough he had seen of this country which he had not quitted for so much as one single day in the last seven years of his life. What he did not know was that it was now running backward. So as soon as the drift of the skiff indicated the set of the current, he began to paddle in that direction which he believed to be downstream, where he knew there were towns—Yazoo City, and as a last resort, Vicksburg, if his luck was that bad; if not, smaller towns whose names he did not know but where there would be people, houses, something, anything he might reach and surrender his charge to and turn his back on her forever, on all pregnant and female life forever and return to that monastic existence of shotguns and shackles where he would be secure from it. Now, with the imminence of habitations, release from her, he did not even hate her. When he looked upon the swelling and unmanageable body before him it seemed to him that it was not the woman at all but rather a separate demanding threatening inert yet living mass of which both he and she were equally victims; thinking, as he had been for the last three or four hours, of that minute's—nay, second's—aberration of eye or hand which would suffice to precipitate her into the water to be dragged down to death by that senseless millstone which in its turn would not even have to feel agony, he no longer felt any glow of revenge toward her as its custodian, he felt sorry for her as he would for the living timber in a barn which had to be burned to rid itself of vermin.

He paddled on, helping the current, steadily and strongly, with a calculated husbandry of effort, toward what he believed was downstream, towns, people, something to stand upon, while from time to time the woman raised herself to bail the accumulated rain from the skiff. It was raining steadily now though still not hard, still without passion, the sky, the day itself dissolving without grief; the skiff moved in a nimbus, an aura of gray gauze which merged almost without demarcation with the roiling spittle-frothed debris-choked water. Now the day, the light, definitely began to end and the convict permitted himself an extra notch or two of effort because it suddenly seemed to him that the speed of the skiff had lessened. This was actually the case though the convict did not know it. He merely took it as a phenomenon of the increasing obfuscation, or at most as a result of the long day's continuous effort with no food complicated by the ebbing and fluxing phases of anxiety and impotent rage at his absolutely gratuitous predicament. So he stepped up his stroke a beat or so, not from alarm but on the contrary, since he too had received that lift from the mere presence of a known stream, a river known by its ineradicable name to generations of men who had been drawn to live beside it as man always has been drawn to dwell beside water, even before he had a name for water and fire, drawn to the living water, the course of his destiny and his actual physical appearance rigidly coerced and postulated by it. So he was not alarmed. He paddled on, upstream without knowing it, unaware that all the water which for forty hours now had been pouring through the levee break to the north was somewhere ahead of him, on its way back to the River.

It was full dark now. That is, night had completely come, the gray dissolving sky had vanished, yet as though in perverse ratio surface visibility had sharpened, as though the light which the rain of the afternoon had washed out of the air had gathered upon the water as the rain itself had done, so that the yellow flood spread on before him now with a quality almost phosphorescent, right up to the instant where vision ceased. The darkness in fact had its advantages; he could now stop seeing the rain. He and his garments had been wet for more than twenty-four hours now so he had long since stopped feeling it, and now that he could no longer see it either it had in a certain sense ceased for him. Also, he now had to make no effort even not to see the swell of his passenger's belly. So he was paddling on, strongly and steadily, not alarmed and not concerned but just exasperated because he had not yet begun to see any reflection on the clouds which would indicate the city or cities which he believed he was approaching but which were actually now miles behind him, when he heard a sound. He did not know what it was because he had never heard it before and he would never be expected to hear such again since it is not given to every man to hear such at all and to none to hear it more than once in his life. And he was not alarmed now either because there was not time, for although the visibility ahead, for all its clarity, did not extend very far, yet in the next instant to the hearing he was also seeing something such as he had never seen before. This was that the sharp line where the phosphorescent water met the darkness was now about ten feet higher than it had been an instant before and that it was curled forward upon itself like a sheet of dough being rolled out for a pudding. It reared, stooping; the crest of it swirled like the mane of a galloping horse and, phosphorescent too, fretted and flickered like fire. And while the woman huddled in the bow, aware or not aware the convict did not know which, he (the convict), his swollen and blood-streaked face gaped in an expression of aghast and incredulous amazement, continued to paddle directly into it. Again he simply had not had time to order his rhythm-hypnotised muscles to cease. He continued to paddle though the skiff had ceased to move forward at all but seemed to be hanging in space while the paddle still reached thrust recovered and reached again; now instead of space the skiff became abruptly surrounded by a welter of fleeing debris—planks, small buildings, the bodies of drowned yet antic animals, entire trees leaping and diving like porpoises above which the skiff seemed to hover in weightless and airy indecision like a bird above a fleeing countryside, undecided where to light or whether to light at all, while the convict squatted in it still going through the motions of paddling, waiting for an opportunity to scream. He never found it. For an instant the skiff seemed to stand erect on its stern and then shoot scrabbling and scrambling up the curling wall of water like a cat, and soared on above the licking crest itself and hung cradled into the high actual air in the limbs of a tree, from which bower of new-leafed boughs and branches the convict, like a bird in its nest and still waiting his chance to scream and still going through the motions of paddling though he no longer even had the paddle now, looked down upon a world turned to furious motion and in incredible retrograde.

Sometime about midnight, accompanied by a rolling cannonade of thunder and lightning like a battery going into action, as though some forty hours' constipation of the elements, the firmament itself, were discharging in clapping and glaring salute to the ultimate acquiescence to desperate and furious motion, and still leading its charging welter of dead cows and mules and outhouses and cabins and hencoops, the skiff passed Vicksburg. The convict didn't know it. He wasn't looking high enough above the water, who still squatted, clutching the gunwales and glaring at the yellow turmoil about him out of which entire trees, the sharp gables of houses, the long mournful heads of mules which he fended off with a splintered length of plank snatched from he knew not where in passing (and which seemed to glare reproach-fully back at him with sightless eyes, in limber-lipped and incredulous amazement) rolled up and then down again, the skiff now travelling forward now sideways now sternward, sometimes in the water, sometimes riding for yards upon the roofs of houses and trees and even upon the backs of the mules as though even in death they were not to escape that burden-bearing doom with which their eunuch race was cursed. But he didn't see Vicksburg; the skiff, travelling at express speed, was in a seething gut between soaring and dizzy banks with a glare of light above them but he did not see it, he saw the flotsam ahead of him divide violently and begin to climb upon itself, mounting, and he was sucked through the resulting gap too fast to recognise it as the trestling of a railroad bridge; for a horrible moment the skiff seemed to hang in sta-tic indecision before the looming flank of a steamboat as though undecided whether to climb over it or dive under it, then a hard icy wind filled with the smell and taste and sense of wet and boundless desolation blew upon him; the skiff made one long bounding lunge as the convict's native state, in a final paroxysm, regurgitated him onto the wild bosom of the Father of Waters.

This is how he told about it seven weeks later, sitting in new bedticking garments, shaved and with his hair cut again, on his bunk in the barracks:

During the next three or four hours after the thunder and lightning had spent itself the skiff ran in pitch streaming darkness upon a roiling expanse which, even if he could have seen, apparently had no boundaries. Wild and invisible, it tossed and heaved about and beneath the boat, ridged with dirty phosphorescent foam and filled with a debris of destruction—objects nameless and enormous and invisible which struck and slashed at the skiff and whirled on. He did not know he was now upon the River. At that time he would have refused to believe it, even if he had known. Yesterday he had known he was in a channel by the regularity of the spacing between the bordering trees. Now, since even by daylight he could have seen no boundaries, the last place under the sun (or the streaming sky rather) he would have suspected himself to be would have been a river; if he had pondered at all about his present whereabouts, about the geography beneath him, he would merely have taken himself to be travelling at dizzy and inexplicable speed above the largest cottonfield in the world; if he who yesterday had known he was in a river, had accepted that fact in good faith and earnest, then had seen that river turn without warning and rush back upon him with furious and deadly intent like a frenzied stallion in a lane,—if he had suspected for one second that the wild and limitless expanse on which he now found himself was a river, consciousness would simply have refused; he would have fainted.

When daylight—a gray and ragged dawn filled with driving scud between icy rain-squalls—came and he could see again, he knew he was in no cottonfield. He knew that the wild water on which the skiff tossed and fled flowed above no soil tamely trod by man, behind the straining and surging buttocks of a mule. That was when it occurred to him that its present condition was no phenomenon of a decade, but that the intervening years during which it consented to bear upon its placid and sleepy bosom the frail mechanicals of man's clumsy contriving was the phenomenon and this the norm and the river was now doing what it liked to do, had waited patiently the ten years in order to do, as a mule will work for you ten years for the privilege of kicking you once. And he also learned something else about fear too, something he had even failed to discover on that other occasion when he was really afraid—that three or four seconds of that night in his youth while he looked down the twice-flashing pistol barrel of the terrified mail clerk before the clerk could be persuaded that his (the convict's) pistol would not shoot: that if you just held on long enough a time would come in fear after which it would no longer be agony at all but merely a kind of horrible outrageous itching, as after you have been burned bad.

He did not have to paddle now, he just steered (who had been without food for twenty-four hours now and without any sleep to speak of for fifty) while the skiff sped on across that boiling desolation where he had long since begun to not dare believe he could possibly be where he could not doubt he was, trying with his fragment of splintered plank merely to keep the skiff intact and afloat among the houses and trees and dead animals (the entire towns, stores residences parks and farmyards, which leaped and played about him like fish), not trying to reach any destination, just trying to keep the skiff afloat until he did. He wanted so little. He wanted nothing for himself. He just wanted to get rid of the woman, the belly, and he was trying to do that in the right way, not for himself, but for her. He could have put her back into another tree at any time——

"Or you could have jumped out of the boat and let her and it drown," the plump convict said. "Then they could have give you the ten years for escaping and then hung you for the murder and charged the boat to your folks."

"Yah," the tall convict said.—But he had not done that. He wanted to do it the right way, find somebody, anybody he could surrender her to, something solid he could set her down on and then jump back into the river, if that would please anyone. That was all he wanted—just to come to something, anything. That didn't seem like a great deal to ask. And he couldn't do it. He told how the skiff fled on—

"Didn't you pass nobody?" the plump convict said. "No steamboat, nothing?"

"I dont know," the tall one said.—while he tried merely to keep it afloat, until the darkness thinned and lifted and revealed—

"Darkness?" the plump convict said. "I thought you said it was already daylight."

"Yah," the tall one said. He was rolling a cigarette, pouring the tobacco carefully from a new sack, into the creased paper. "This was another one. They had several while I was gone."—the skiff to be moving still rapidly up a winding corridor bordered by drowned trees which the convict recognised again to be a river running again in the direction that, until two days ago, had been upstream. He was not exactly warned through instinct that this one, like that of two days ago, was in reverse. He would not say that he now believed himself to be in the same river, though he would not have been surprised to find that he did believe this, existing now, as he did and had and apparently was to continue for an unnamed period, in a state in which he was toy and pawn on a vicious and inflammable geography. He merely realised that he was in a river again, with all the subsequent inferences of a comprehensible, even if not familiar, portion of the earth's surface. Now he

believed that all he had to do would be to paddle far enough
and he would come to something horizontal and above water
even if not dry and perhaps even populated; and, if fast
enough, in time, and that his only other crying urgency was to
refrain from looking at the woman who, as vision, the incontrovertible and apparently inescapable presence of his passenger, returned with dawn, had ceased to be a human being and
(you could add twenty-four more hours to the first twenty-four
and the first fifty now, even counting the hen. It was dead,
drowned, caught by one wing under a shingle on a roof which
had rolled momentarily up beside the skiff yesterday and he
had eaten some of it raw though the woman would not) had
become instead one single inert monstrous sentient womb
from which, he now believed, if he could only turn his gaze
away and keep it away, would disappear, and if he could only
keep his gaze from pausing again at the spot it had occupied,
would not return. That's what he was doing this time when he
discovered the wave was coming.

He didn't know how he discovered it was coming back. He
heard no sound, it was nothing felt nor seen. He did not even
believe that finding the skiff to be now in slack water—that is,
that the motion of the current which, whether right or wrong,
had at least been horizontal, had now stopped that and
assumed a vertical direction—was sufficient to warn him. Perhaps it was just an invincible and almost fanatic faith in the
inventiveness and innate viciousness of that medium on
which his destiny was now cast, apparently forever; a sudden
conviction far beyond either horror or surprise that now was
none too soon for it to prepare to do whatever it was it
intended doing. So he whirled the skiff, spun it on its heel like
a running horse, whereupon, reversed, he could not even distinguish the very channel he had come up. He did not know

whether he simply could not see it or if it had vanished some time ago and he not aware at the time; whether the river had become lost in a drowned world or if the world had become drowned in one limitless river. So now he could not tell if he were running directly before the wave or quartering across its line of charge; all he could do was keep that sense of swiftly accumulating ferocity behind him and paddle as fast as his spent and now numb muscles could be driven, and try not to look at the woman, to wrench his gaze from her and keep it away until he reached something flat and above water. So, gaunt, hollow-eyed, striving and wrenching almost physically at his eyes as if they were two of those suction-tipped rubber arrows shot from the toy gun of a child, his spent muscles obeying not will now but that attenuation beyond mere exhaustion which, mesmeric, can continue easier than cease, he once more drove the skiff full tilt into something it could not pass and, once more hurled violently forward onto his hands and knees, crouching, he glared with his wild swollen face up at the man with the shotgun and said in a harsh, croaking voice: "Vicksburg? Where's Vicksburg?"

Even when he tried to tell it, even after the seven weeks and he safe, secure, rivetted warranted and doubly guaranteed by the ten years they had added to his sentence for attempted escape, something of the old hysteric incredulous outrage came back into his face, his voice, his speech. He never did even get on the other boat. He told how he clung to a strake (it was a dirty unpainted shanty boat with a drunken rake of tin stove pipe, it had been moving when he struck it and apparently it had not even changed course even though the three people on it must have been watching him all the while—a second man, barefoot and with matted hair and beard also at the steering sweep, and then—he did not know how long—a

woman leaning in the door, in a filthy assortment of men's garments, watching him too with the same cold speculation)
being dragged violently along, trying to state and explain his
simple (and to him at least) reasonable desire and need;
telling it, trying to tell it, he could feel again the old unforgettable affronting like an ague fit as he watched the abortive
tobacco rain steadily and faintly from between his shaking
hands and then the paper itself part with a thin dry snapping
report:

"Burn my clothes?" the convict cried. "Burn them?"

"How in hell do you expect to escape in them billboards?"
the man with the shotgun said. He (the convict) tried to tell
it, tried to explain as he had tried to explain not to the three
people on the boat alone but to the entire circumambience —
desolate water and forlorn trees and sky — not for justification
because he needed none and knew that his hearers, the other
convicts, required none from him, but rather as, on the point
of exhaustion, he might have picked dreamily and incredu-
lously at a suffocation. He told the man with the gun how he
and his partner had been given the boat and told to pick up a
man and a woman, how he had lost his partner and failed to
find the man, and now all in the world he wanted was something flat to leave the woman on until he could find an officer,
a sheriff. He thought of home, the place where he had lived
almost since childhood, his friends of years whose ways he
knew and who knew his ways, the familiar fields where he did
work he had learned to do well and to like, the mules with
characters he knew and respected as he knew and respected
the characters of certain men; he thought of the barracks at
night, with screens against the bugs in summer and good
stoves in winter and someone to supply the fuel and the food
too; the Sunday ball games and the picture shows — things

which, with the exception of the ball games, he had never known before. But most of all, his own character (Two years ago they had offered to make a trusty of him. He would no longer need to plow or feed stock, he would only follow those who did with a loaded gun, but he declined. "I reckon I'll stick to plowing," he said, absolutely without humor. "I done already tried to use a gun one time too many.") his good name, his responsibility not only toward those who were responsible toward him but to himself, his own honor in the doing of what was asked of him, his pride in being able to do it, no matter what it was. He thought of this and listened to the man with the gun talking about escape and it seemed to him that, hanging there, being dragged violently along (it was here he said that he first noticed the goats' beards of moss in the trees, though it could have been there for several days so far as he knew. It just happened that he first noticed it here.) that he would simply burst.

"Cant you get it into your head that the last thing I want to do is run away?" he cried. "You can set there with that gun and watch me; I give you fair lief. All I want is to put this woman—"

"And I told you she could come aboard," the man with the gun said in his level voice. "But there aint no room on no boat of mine for nobody hunting a sheriff in no kind of clothes, let alone a penitentiary suit."

"When he steps aboard, knock him in the head with the gun barrel," the man at the sweep said. "He's drunk."

"He aint coming aboard," the man with the gun said. "He's crazy."

Then the woman spoke. She didn't move, leaning in the door, in a pair of faded and patched and filthy overalls like the two men: "Give them some grub and tell them to get out of here." She moved, she crossed the deck and looked down at the convict's companion with her cold sullen face. "How much more time have you got?"

"It wasn't due till next month," the woman in the boat said. "But I—" The woman in overalls turned to the man with the gun.

"Give them some grub," she said. But the man with the gun was still looking down at the woman in the boat.

"Come on," he said to the convict. "Put her aboard, and beat it."

"And what'll happen to you," the woman in overalls said, "when you try to turn her over to an officer. When you lay alongside a sheriff and the sheriff asks you who you are?" Still the man with the gun didn't even look at her. He hardly even shifted the gun across his arm as he struck the woman across the face with the back of his other hand, hard. "You son of a bitch," she said. Still the man with the gun did not even look at her.

"Well?" he said to the convict.

"Dont you see I cant?" the convict cried. "Cant you see that?"

Now, he said, he gave up. He was doomed. That is, he knew now that he had been doomed from the very start never to get rid of her, just as the ones who sent him out with the skiff knew that he never would actually give up; when he recognised one of the objects which the woman in overalls was hurling into the skiff to be a can of condensed milk, he believed it to be a presage, gratuitous and irrevocable as a death-notice over the telegraph, that he was not even to find a flat stationary surface in time for the child to be born on it. So he told how he held the skiff alongside the shanty boat while the first tentative toying of the second wave made up beneath him, while the woman in overalls passed back and forth between house and rail, flinging the food—the hunk of salt meat, the ragged and filthy quilt, the scorched lumps of cold bread which she poured into the skiff from a heaped dishpan like so much garbage—while he clung to the strake against the mounting pull of the current, the new wave which for the moment he had forgotten because he was still trying to state the incredible simplicity of his desire and need until the man with the gun (the only one of the three who wore shoes) began to stamp at his hands, he snatching his hands away one at a time to avoid the heavy shoes then grasping the rail again until the man with the gun kicked at his face, he flinging himself sideways to avoid the shoe and so breaking his hold on the rail, his weight canting the skiff off at a tangent on the increasing current so that it began to leave the shanty boat behind and he paddling again now, violently, as a man hurries toward the precipice for which he knows at last he is doomed, looking back at the other boat, the three faces sullen derisive and grim and rapidly diminishing across the wideing water and at last, apoplectic, suffocating with the intolerable fact not that he had been refused but that he had been refused so little, had wanted so little, asked for so little, yet there had been demanded of him in return the one price out of all breath which (they must have known) if he could have paid it, he would not have been where he was, asking what he asked, raising the paddle and shaking it and screaming curses back at them even after the shotgun flashed and the charge went scuttering past along the water to one side.

So he hung there, he said, shaking the paddle and howling, when suddenly he remembered that other wave, the second wall of water full of houses and dead mules building up behind him back in the swamp. So he quit yelling then and went back to paddling. He was not trying to outrun it. He just knew from experience that when it overtook him, he would have to travel in the same direction it was moving in anyway, whether he wanted to or not, and when it did overtake him, he would begin to move too fast to stop, no matter what places he might come to where he could leave the woman, land her in time. Time: that was his itch now, so his only chance was to stay ahead of it as long as he could and hope to reach something before it struck. So he went on, driving the skiff with muscles which had been too tired so long they had quit feeling it, as when a man has had bad luck for so long that he ceases to believe it is even bad, let alone luck. Even when he ate—the scorched lumps the size of baseballs and the weight and durability of cannel coal even after having lain in the skiff's bilge where the shanty boat woman had thrown them— the ironlike lead-heavy objects which no man would have called bread outside of the crusted and scorched pan in which they had cooked—it was with one hand, begrudging even that from the paddle.

He tried to tell that too—that day while the skiff fled on among the bearded trees while every now and then small quiet tentative exploratory feelers would come up from the wave behind and toy for a moment at the skiff, light and curious, then go on with a faint hissing sighing, almost a chuckling, sound, the skiff going on, driving on with nothing to see but trees and water and solitude: until after a while it no longer seemed to him that he was trying to put space and distance behind him or shorten space and distance ahead but that both he and the wave were now hanging suspended simultaneous and unprogressing in pure time, upon a dreamy desolation in which he paddled on not from any hope even to reach anything at all but merely to keep intact what little of distance the length of the skiff provided between himself and the inert and inescapable mass of female meat before him; then night and the skiff rushing on, fast since any speed over anything unknown and invisible is too fast, with nothing before him and behind him the outrageous idea of a volume of moving water toppling forward, its crest frothed and shredded like fangs, and then dawn again (another of those dreamlike alterations day to dark then back to day again with that quality truncated anachronic and unreal as the waxing and waning of lights in a theatre scene) and the skiff emerging now with the woman no longer supine beneath the shrunken soaked private's coat but sitting bolt upright, gripping the gunwales with both hands, her eyes closed and her lower lip caught between her teeth and he driving the splintered board furiously now, glaring at her out of his wild swollen sleepless face and crying, croaking, "Hold on! For God's sake hold on!"

"I'm trying to," she said. "But hurry! Hurry!" He told it, the unbelievable: hurry, hasten: the man falling from a cliff being told to catch onto something and save himself; the very telling of it emerging shadowy and burlesque, ludicrous comic and mad, from the ague of unbearable forgetting with a quality more dreamily furious than any fable behind proscenium lights:

He was in a basin now— "A basin?" the plump convict said. "That's what you wash in."

"All right," the tall one said, harshly, above his hands. "I did." With a supreme effort he stilled them long enough to release the two bits of cigarette paper and watched them waft in light fluttering indecision to the floor between his feet, holding his hands motionless even for a moment longer.—a basin, a broad peaceful yellow sea which had an abruptly and curiously ordered air, giving him, even at that moment, the

impression that it was accustomed to water even if not total
submersion; he even remembered the name of it, told to him
two or three weeks later by someone: Atchafalaya—

"Louisiana?" the plump convict said. "You mean you
were clean out of Mississippi? Hell fire." He stared at the tall
one. "Shucks," he said. "That aint but just across from Vicksburg."

"They never named any Vicksburg across from where I
was," the tall one said. "It was Baton Rouge they named." And
now he began to talk about a town, a little neat white portrait
town nestling among enormous very green trees, appearing
suddenly in the telling as it probably appeared in actuality,
abrupt and airy and miragelike and incredibly serene before
him behind a scattering of boats moored to a line of freight
cars standing flush to the doors in water. And now he tried to
tell that too: how he stood waist-deep in water for a moment
looking back and down at the skiff in which the woman half
lay, her eyes still closed, her knuckles white on the gunwales
and a tiny thread of blood creeping down her chin from her
chewed lip, and he looking down at her in a kind of furious
desperation.

"How far will I have to walk?" she said.

"I dont know, I tell you!" he cried. "But it's land somewhere yonder! It's land, houses."

"If I try to move, it wont even be born inside a boat," she
said. "You'll have to get closer."

"Yes," he cried, wild, desperate, incredulous. "Wait. I'll go
and surrender, then they will have—" He didn't finish, wait to
finish; he told that too: himself splashing, stumbling, trying to
run, sobbing and gasping; now he saw it—another loading
platform standing above the yellow flood, the khaki figures on
it as before, identical, the same; he said how the intervening

days since that first innocent morning telescoped, vanished as
if they had never been, the two contiguous succeeding
instants (succeeding? simultaneous) and he transported across
no intervening space but merely turned in his own footsteps,
plunging, splashing, his arms raised, croaking harshly. He
heard the startled shout, "There's one of them!," the command, the clash of equipment, the alarmed cry: "There he
goes! There he goes!"

"Yes!" he cried, running, plunging, "here I am! Here!
Here!" running on, into the first scattered volley, stopping
among the bullets, waving his arms, shrieking, "I want to surrender! I want to surrender!" watching not in terror but in
amazed and absolutely unbearable outrage as a squatting
clump of the khaki figures parted and he saw the machine
gun, the blunt thick muzzle slant and drop and probe toward
him and he still screaming in his hoarse crow's voice, "I want
to surrender! Cant you hear me?," continuing to scream even
as he whirled and plunged splashing, ducking, went completely under and heard the bullets going thuck-thuck-thuck
on the water above him and he scrabbling still on the bottom,
still trying to scream even before he regained his feet and still
all submerged save his plunging unmistakable buttocks, the
outraged screaming bubbling from his mouth and about his
face since he merely wanted to surrender. Then he was comparatively screened, out of range, though not for long. That is
(he didn't tell how nor where) there was a moment in which
he paused, breathed for a second before running again, the
course back to the skiff open for the time being though he
could still hear the shouts behind him and now and then a
shot, and he panting, sobbing, a long savage tear in the flesh of
one hand, got when and how he did not know, and he wasting
precious breath, speaking to no one now anymore than the

scream of the dying rabbit is addressed to any mortal ear but
rather an indictment of all breath and its folly and suffering, its
infinite capacity for folly and pain, which seems to be its only
immortality: "All in the world I want is just to surrender."

He returned to the skiff and got in and took up his splintered plank. And now when he told this, despite the fury of
element which climaxed it, it (the telling) became quite simple; he now even creased another cigarette paper between fingers which did not tremble at all and filled the paper from the
tobacco sack without spilling a flake, as though he had passed
from the machine gun's barrage into a bourne beyond any
more amazement: so that the subsequent part of his narrative
seemed to reach his listeners as though from beyond a sheet of
slightly milky though still transparent glass, as something not
heard but seen—a series of shadows, edgeless yet distinct, and
smoothly flowing, logical and unfrantic and making no
sound: They were in the skiff, in the center of the broad placid
trough which had no boundaries and down which the tiny forlorn skiff flew to the irresistible coercion of a current going
once more he knew not where, the neat small liveoak-
bowered towns unattainable and miragelike and apparently
attached to nothing upon the airy and unchanging horizon.
He did not believe them, they did not matter, he was doomed;
they were less than the figments of smoke or of delirium, and
he driving his unceasing paddle without destination or even
hope now, looking now and then at the woman sitting with
her knees drawn up and locked and her entire body one terrific clench while the threads of bloody saliva crept from her
teeth-clenched lower lip. He was going nowhere and fleeing
from nothing, he merely continued to paddle because he had
paddled so long now that he believed if he stopped his muscles would scream in agony. So when it happened he was not

surprised. He heard the sound which he knew well (he had heard it but once before, true enough, but no man needed hear it but once) and he had been expecting it; he looked back, still driving the paddle, and saw it, curled, crested with its strawlike flotsam of trees and debris and dead beasts and he glared over his shoulder at it for a full minute out of that attenuation far beyond the point of outragement where even suffering, the capability of being further affronted, had ceased, from which he now contemplated with savage and invulnerable curiosity the further extent to which his now anesthetised nerves could bear, what next could be invented for them to bear, until the wave actually began to rear above his head into its thunderous climax. Then only did he turn his head. His stroke did not falter, it neither slowed nor increased; still paddling with that spent hypnotic steadiness, he saw the swimming deer. He did not know what it was nor that he had altered the skiff's course to follow it, he just watched the swimming head before him as the wave boiled down and the skiff rose bodily in the old familiar fashion on a welter of tossing trees and houses and bridges and fences, he still paddling even while the paddle found no purchase save air and still paddled even as he and the deer shot forward side by side at arm's length, he watching the deer now, watching the deer begin to rise out of the water bodily until it was actually running along upon the surface, rising still, soaring clear of the water altogether, vanishing upward in a dying crescendo of splashings and snapping branches, its damp scut flashing upward, the entire animal vanishing upward as smoke vanishes. And now the skiff struck and canted and he was out of it too, standing knee-deep, springing out and falling to his knees, scrambling up, glaring after the vanished deer. "Land!" he croaked. "Land! Hold on! Just hold on!" He caught the woman beneath the arms, dragging her out of the boat, plunging and panting after the vanished deer. Now earth actually appeared—an acclivity smooth and swift and steep, bizarre solid and unbelievable; an Indian mound, and he plunging at the muddy slope, slipping back, the woman struggling in his muddy hands.

"Let me down!" she cried. "Let me down!" But he held her, panting, sobbing, and rushed again at the muddy slope; he had almost reached the flat crest with his now violently unmanageable burden when a stick under his foot gathered itself with thick convulsive speed. *It was a snake* he thought as his feet fled beneath him and with the indubitable last of his strength he half pushed and half flung the woman up the bank as he shot feet first and face down back into that medium upon which he had lived for more days and nights than he could remember and from which he himself had never completely emerged, as if his own failed and spent flesh were attempting to carry out his furious unflagging will for severance at any price, even that of drowning, from the burden with which, unwitting and without choice, he had been doomed. Later it seemed to him that he had carried back beneath the surface with him the sound of the infant's first mewling cry.

When the woman asked him if he had a knife, standing there in the streaming bedticking garments which had got him shot at, the second time by a machine gun, on the two occasions when he had seen any human life after leaving the levee four days ago, the convict felt exactly as he had in the fleeing skiff when the woman suggested that they had better hurry. He felt the same outrageous affronting of a condition purely moral, the same raging impotence to find any answer to it; so that, standing above her, spent suffocating and inarticulate, it was a full minute before he comprehended that she was now crying, "The can! The can in the boat!" He did not anticipate what she could want with it, he did not even wonder nor stop to ask. He turned running; this time he thought *It's another moccasin* as the thick body truncated in that awkward reflex which had nothing of alarm in it but only alertness, he not even shifting his stride though he knew his running foot would fall within a yard of the flat head. The bow of the skiff was well up the slope now where the wave had set it and there was another snake just crawling over the stern into it and as he stooped for the bailing can he saw something else swimming toward the mound, he didn't know what—a head, a face at the apex of a vee of ripples. He snatched up the can; by pure juxtaposition of it and water he scooped it full, already turning. He saw the deer again, or another one. That is, he saw a deer—a side glance, the light smoke-colored phantom in a cypress vista then gone, vanished, he not pausing to look after it, galloping back to the woman and kneeling with the can to her lips until she told him better.

It had contained a pint of beans or tomatoes, something, hermetically sealed and opened by four blows of an axe heel, the metal flap turned back, the jagged edges razor-sharp. She told him how, and he used this in lieu of a knife, he removed one of his shoelaces and cut it in two with the sharp tin. Then she wanted warm water—"If I just had a little hot water," she said in a weak serene voice without particular hope, only when he thought of matches it was again a good deal like when she had asked him if he had a knife, until she fumbled in the pocket of the shrunken tunic (it had a darker double vee on one cuff and a darker blotch on one shoulder where service stripes and a divisional emblem had been ripped off but this meant nothing to him) and produced a matchbox contrived by telescoping two shotgun shells. So he drew her back a little from the water and went to hunt wood dry enough to burn, thinking this time *It's just another snake* only, he said, he should have thought *ten thousand other snakes*: and now he knew it was not the same deer because he saw three at one time, does or bucks he did not know which since they were all antlerless in May and besides he had never seen one of any kind anywhere before except on a Christmas card; and then the rabbit, drowned, dead anyway, already torn open, the bird, the hawk, standing upon it—the erected crest, the hard vicious patrician nose, the intolerant omnivorous yellow eye—and he kicking at it, kicking it lurching and broad-winged into the actual air.

When he returned with the wood and the dead rabbit the baby, wrapped in the tunic, lay wedged between two cypress-knees and the woman was not in sight, though while the convict knelt in the mud, blowing and nursing his meagre flame, she came slowly and weakly from the direction of the water. Then, the water heated at last and there produced from somewhere he was never to know, she herself perhaps never to know until the need comes, no woman perhaps ever to know, only no woman will even wonder, that square of something somewhere between sackcloth and silk;—squatting, his own wet garments steaming in the fire's heat, he watched her bathe the child with a savage curiosity and interest that became amazed unbelief, so that at last he stood above them both, looking down at the tiny terra cotta colored creature resem-bling nothing, and thought *And this is all. This is what severed me violently from all I ever knew and did not wish to leave and*

cast me upon a medium I was born to fear, to fetch up at last in
a place I never saw before and where I do not even know where
I am.

Then he returned to the water and refilled the bailing
can. It was drawing toward sunset now (or what would have
been sunset save for the high prevailing overcast) of this day
whose beginning he could not even remember; when he
returned to where the fire burned in the interlaced gloom of
the cypresses, even after this short absence, evening had definitely come, as though darkness too had taken refuge upon
that quarter-acre mound, that earthen ark out of Genesis, that
dim wet cypress-choked life-teeming constricted desolation
in what direction and how far from what and where he had no
more idea than of the day of the month, and had now with the
setting of the sun crept forth again to spread upon the waters.
He stewed the rabbit in sections while the fire burned redder
and redder in the darkness where the shy wild eyes of small
animals—once the tall mild almost plate-sized stare of one of
the deer—glowed and vanished and glowed again, the broth
hot and rank after the four days; he seemed to hear the roar of
his own saliva as he watched the woman sip the first canful.
Then he drank too, they ate the other fragments which had
been charring and scorching on willow twigs; it was full night
now. "You and him better sleep in the boat," the convict said.
"We want to get an early start tomorrow." He shoved the bow
of the skiff off the land so it would lie level, he lengthened the
painter with a piece of grapevine and returned to the fire and
tied the grapevine about his wrist and lay down. It was mud he
lay upon, but it was solid underneath, it was earth, it did not
move; if you fell upon it you broke your bones against its
incontrovertible passivity sometimes but it did not accept you
substanceless and enveloping and suffocating, down and

down and down; it was hard at times to drive a plow through, it sent you spent, weary, and cursing its light-long insatiable demands back to your bunk at sunset at times but it did not snatch you violently out of all familiar knowing and sweep you thrall and impotent for days against any returning. *I dont know where I am and I dont reckon I know the way back to where I want to go* he thought. *But at least the boat has stopped long enough to give me a chance to turn it around*

He waked at dawn, the light faint, the sky jonquil-colored; the day would be fine. The fire had burned out; on the opposite side of the cold ashes lay three snakes motionless and parallel as underscoring, and in the swiftly making light others seemed to materialise: earth which an instant before had been mere earth broke up into motionless coils and loops, branches which a moment before had been mere branches now become immobile ophidian festoons even as the convict stood thinking about food, about something hot before they started. But he decided against this, against wasting this much time, since there still remained in the skiff quite a few of the rocklike objects which the shanty woman had flung into it, besides (thinking this) no matter how fast nor successfully he hunted, he would never be able to lay up enough food to get them back to where they wanted to go. So he returned to the skiff, paying himself back to it by his vine-spliced painter, back to the water on which a low mist thick as cotton batting (though apparently not very tall, deep) lay, into which the stern of the skiff was already beginning to disappear although it lay with its prow almost touching the mound. The woman waked, stirred. "We fixing to start now?" she said.

"Yah," the convict said. "You aint aiming to have another one this morning, are you?" He got in and shoved the skiff clear of the land, which immediately began to dissolve into the mist. "Hand me the oar," he said over his shoulder, not turning yet.

"The oar?"

He turned his head. "The oar. You're laying on it." But she was not, and for an instant during which the mound, the island continued to fade slowly into the mist which seemed to enclose the skiff in weightless and impalpable wool like a precious or fragile bauble or jewel, the convict squatted not in dismay but in that frantic and astonished outrage of a man who, having just escaped a falling safe, is struck by the following two-ounce paper weight which was sitting on it: this the more unbearable because he knew that never in his life had he less time to give way to it. Because he did not hesitate. Grasping the grapevine end he sprang into the water, vanishing in the violent action of climbing and reappeared still climbing and (who had never learned to swim) plunged and threshed on toward the almost-vanished mound, moving through the water then upon it as the deer had done yesterday and scrabbled up the muddy slope and lay gasping and panting, still clutching the grapevine end.

Now the first thing he did was to choose what he believed to be the most suitable tree (for an instant in which he knew he was insane he thought of trying to saw it down with the flange of the bailing can) and build a fire against the butt of it. Then he went to seek food. He spent the next six days seeking it while the tree burned through and fell and burned through again at the proper length and he nursing little constant cunning flames along the flanks of the log to make it paddle-shaped, nursing them at night too while the woman and baby (it was eating, nursing now, he turning his back or even retiring into the woods each time she prepared to open the faded tunic) slept in the skiff. He learned to watch for stooping hawks and so found more rabbits and twice possums; they ate some drowned fish which gave them both a rash and then a violent flux and one snake which the woman thought was turtle and which did them no harm, and one night it rained and he got up and dragged brush, shaking the snakes (he no longer thought *It aint nothing but another moccasin,* he just stepped aside for them as they, when there was time, telescoped sullenly aside for him) out of it with the old former feeling of personal invulnerability and built a shelter and the rain stopped at once and did not recommence and the woman went back to the skiff.

Then one night—the slow tedious charring log was almost a paddle now—one night and he was in bed, in his bed in the bunkhouse and it was cold, he was trying to pull the covers up only his mule wouldn't let him, prodding and bumping heavily at him, trying to get into the narrow bed with him and now the bed was cold too and wet and he was trying to get out of it only the mule would not let him, holding him by his belt in its teeth, jerking and bumping him back into the cold wet bed and, leaning, gave him a long swipe across the face with its cold limber musculated tongue and he waked to no fire, no coal even beneath where the almost-finished paddle had been charring and something else prolonged and coldly limber passed swiftly across his body where he lay in four inches of water while the nose of the skiff alternately tugged at the grapevine tied about his waist and bumped and shoved him back into the water again. Then something else came up and began to nudge at his ankle (the log, the oar, it was) even as he groped frantically for the skiff, hearing the swift rustling going to and fro inside the hull as the woman began to thrash about and scream. "Rats!" she cried. "It's full of rats!"

"Lay still!" he cried. "It's just snakes. Cant you hold still long enough for me to find the boat?" Then he found it, he got into it with the unfinished paddle; again the thick muscular body convulsed under his foot; it did not strike; he would not have cared, glaring astern where he could see a little—the faint outer luminosity of the open water. He poled toward it, thrusting aside the snake-looped branches, the bottom of the skiff resounding faintly to thick solid plops, the woman shrieking steadily. Then the skiff was clear of the trees, the mound, and now he could feel the bodies whipping about his ankles and hear the rasp of them as they went over the gunwale. He drew the log in and scooped it forward along the bottom of the boat and up and out; against the pallid water he could see three more of them in lashing convolutions before they vanished. "Shut up!" he cried. "Hush! I wish I was a snake so I could get out too!"

When once more the pale and heatless wafer disc of the early sun stared down at the skiff (whether they were moving or not the convict did not know) in its nimbus of fine cotton batting, the convict was hearing again that sound which he had heard twice before and would never forget—that sound of deliberate and irresistible and monstrously disturbed water. But this time he could not tell from what direction it came. It seemed to be everywhere, waxing and fading; it was like a phantom behind the mist, at one instant miles away, the next on the point of overwhelming the skiff within the next second; suddenly in the instant he would believe (his whole weary body would spring and scream) that he was about to drive the skiff point-blank into it and with the unfinished paddle of the color and texture of sooty bricks, like something gnawed out of an old chimney by beavers and weighing twenty-five pounds, he would whirl the skiff frantically and find the sound dead ahead of him again. Then something bellowed tremendously above his head, he heard human voices, a bell jangled and the sound ceased and the mist vanished like when you draw your hand across a frosted pane, and the skiff now lay upon a sunny glitter of brown water flank to flank with, and about thirty yards away from, a steamboat. The decks were crowded and packed with men women and children sitting or standing beside and among a homely conglomeration of hurried furniture, who looked mournfully and silently down into the skiff while the convict and the man with a megaphone in the pilot house talked to each other in alternate puny shouts and roars above the chuffing of the reversed engines:

"What in hell are you trying to do? Commit suicide?"

"Which is the way to Vicksburg?"

"Vicksburg? Vicksburg? Lay alongside and come aboard."

"Will you take the boat too?"

"Boat? Boat?" Now the megaphone cursed, the roaring waves of blasphemy and biological supposition empty cavernous and bodiless in turn, as if the water, the air, the mist had spoken it, roaring the words then taking them back to itself and no harm done, no scar, no insult left anywhere. "If I took aboard every floating sardine can you sonabitchin mushrats want me to I wouldn't even have room forrard for a leadsman. Come aboard! Do you expect me to hang here on stern engines till hell freezes?"

"I aint coming without the boat," the convict said. Now another voice spoke, so calm and mild and sensible that for a moment it sounded more foreign and out of place than even the megaphone's bellowing and bodiless profanity:

"Where is it you are trying to go?"

"I aint trying," the convict said. "I'm going. Parchman." The man who had spoken last turned and appeared to con-

verse with a third man in the pilot house. Then he looked
down at the skiff again.

"Carnarvon?"

"What?" the convict said. "Parchman?"

"All right. We're going that way. We'll put you off where
you can get home. Come aboard."

"The boat too?"

"Yes yes. Come along. We're burning coal just to talk to
you." So the convict came alongside then and watched them
help the woman and baby over the rail and he came aboard
himself, though he still held to the end of the vine-spliced
painter until the skiff was hoisted onto the boiler deck. "My
God," the man, the gentle one, said, "is that what you have
been using for a paddle?"

"Yah," the convict said. "I lost the plank."

"The plank," the mild man (the convict told how he
seemed to whisper it), "the plank. Well. Come along and get
something to eat. Your boat is all right now."

"I reckon I'll wait here," the convict said. Because now, he
told them, he began to notice for the first time that the other
people, the other refugees who crowded the deck, who had
gathered in a quiet circle about the upturned skiff on which
he and the woman sat, the grapevine painter wrapped several
times about his wrist and clutched in his hand, staring at him
and the woman with queer hot mournful intensity, were not
white people—

"You mean niggers?" the plump convict said.

"No. Not Americans."

"Not Americans? You was clean out of *America* even?"

"I dont know," the tall one said. "They called it
Atchafalaya."—because after a while he said "What?" to the
man and the man did it again, gobble-gobble—

"Gobble-gobble?" the plump convict said.

"That's the way they talked," the tall one said. "Gobble-gobble, whang, caw-caw-to-to."—and he sat there and watched them gobbling at one another and then looking at him again, then they fell back and the mild man (he wore a Red Cross brassard) entered, followed by a waiter with a tray of food. The mild man carried two glasses of whiskey.

"Drink this," the mild man said. "This will warm you." The woman took hers and drank it but the convict told how he looked at his and thought *I aint tasted whiskey in seven years.* He had not tasted it but once before that; it was at the still itself back in a pine hollow; he was seventeen, he had gone there with four companions, two of whom were grown men, one of twenty-two or -three, the other about forty; he remembered it. That is, he remembered perhaps a third of that evening—a fierce turmoil in the hell-colored firelight, the shock and shock of blows about his head (and likewise of his own fists on other hard bone), then the waking to a splitting and blinding sun in a place, a cowshed, he had never seen before and which later turned out to be twenty miles from his home. He said he thought of this and he looked about at the faces watching him and he said,

"I reckon not."

"Come, come," the mild man said. "Drink it."

"I dont want it."

"Nonsense," the mild man said. "I'm a doctor. Here. Then you can eat." So he took the glass and even then he hesitated but again the mild man said, "Come along, down with it; you're still holding us up" in that voice still calm and sensible but a little sharp too—the voice of a man who could keep calm and affable because he wasn't used to being crossed—and he drank the whiskey and even in the second between the sweet full fire in his belly and when it began to happen he was trying to say, "I tried to tell you! I tried to!" But it was too late now in the pallid sun-glare of the tenth day of terror and hopelessness and despair and impotence and rage and outrage and it was himself and the mule, his mule (they had let him name it—John Henry) which no man save he had plowed for five years now and whose ways and habits he knew and respected and who knew his ways and habits so well that each of them could anticipate the other's very movements and intentions; it was himself and the mule, the little gobbling faces flying before them, the familiar hard skull-bones shocking against his fists, his voice shouting, "Come on, John Henry! Plow them down! Gobble them down, boy!" even as the bright hot red wave turned back, meeting it joyously, happily, lifted, poised, then hurling through space, triumphant and yelling, then again the old shocking blow at the back of his head: he lay on the deck, flat on his back and pinned arm and leg and cold sober again, his nostrils gushing again, the mild man stooping over him with behind the thin rimless glasses the coldest eyes the convict had ever seen—eyes which the convict said were not looking at him but at the gushing blood with nothing in the world in them but complete impersonal interest.

"Good man," the mild man said. "Plenty of life in the old carcass yet, eh? Plenty of good red blood too. Anyone ever suggest to you that you were hemophilic?" ("What?" the plump convict said. "Hemophilic? You know what that means?" The tall convict had his cigarette going now, his body jackknifed backward into the coffinlike space between the upper and lower bunks, lean, clean, motionless, the blue smoke wreathing across his lean dark aquiline shaven face. "That's a calf that's a bull and a cow at the same time."

"No it aint," a third convict said. "It's a calf or a colt that aint neither one."

"Hell fire," the plump one said. "He's got to be one or the other to keep from drownding." He had never ceased to look at the tall one in the bunk; now he spoke to him again: "You let him call you that?") The tall one had done so. He did not answer the doctor (this was where he stopped thinking of him as the mild man) at all. He could not move either, though he felt fine, he felt better than he had in ten days. So they helped him to his feet and steadied him over and lowered him onto the upturned skiff beside the woman, where he sat bent forward, elbows on knees in the immemorial attitude, watching his own bright crimson staining the mud-trodden deck, until the doctor's clean clipped hand appeared under his nose with a phial.

"Smell," the doctor said. "Deep." The convict inhaled, the sharp ammoniac sensation burned up his nostrils and into his throat. "Again," the doctor said. The convict inhaled obediently. This time he choked and spat a gout of blood, his nose now had no more feeling than a toenail, other than it felt about the size of a ten-inch shovel, and as cold.

"I ask you to excuse me," he said. "I never meant—"

"Why?" the doctor said. "You put up as pretty a scrap against forty or fifty men as I ever saw. You lasted a good two seconds. Now you can eat something. Or do you think that will send you haywire again?"

They both ate, sitting on the skiff, the gobbling faces no longer watching them now, the convict gnawing slowly and painfully at the thick sandwich, hunched, his face laid sideways to the food and parallel to the earth as a dog chews; the steamboat went on. At noon there were bowls of hot soup and bread and more coffee; they ate this too, sitting side by side on the skiff, the grapevine still wrapped about the convict's wrist. The baby waked and nursed and slept again and they talked quietly:

"Was it Parchman he said he was going to take us?"

"That's where I told him I wanted to go."

"It never sounded exactly like Parchman to me. It sounded like he said something else." The convict had thought that too. He had been thinking about that fairly soberly ever since they boarded the steamboat and soberly indeed ever since he had remarked the nature of the other passengers, those men and women definitely a little shorter than he and with skin a little different in pigmentation from any sunburn, even though the eyes were sometimes blue or gray, who talked to one another in a tongue he had never heard before and who apparently did not understand his own, people the like of whom he had never seen about Parchman nor anywhere else and whom he did not believe were going there or beyond there either. But after his hill-billy country fashion and kind he would not ask, because to his raising asking information was asking a favor and you did not ask favors of strangers; if they offered them perhaps you accepted and you expressed gratitude almost tediously recapitulant, but you did not ask. So he would watch and wait, as he had done before, and do or try to do to the best of his ability what the best of his judgment dictated.

So he waited, and in midafternoon the steamboat chuffed and thrust through a willow-choked gorge and emerged from it, and now the convict knew it was the River. He could believe it now—the tremendous reach yellow and sleepy in the afternoon—("Because it's too big," he told them soberly. "Aint no flood in the world big enough to make it do more than stand a little higher so it can look back and see just where the flea is, just exactly where to scratch. It's the little ones, the little piddling creeks that run backward one day and forward the next and come busting down on a man full of dead mules and hen houses.")—and the steamboat moving up this now (*like a ant crossing a plate* the convict thought, sitting beside the woman on the upturned skiff, the baby nursing again, apparently looking too out across the water where, a mile away on either hand, the twin lines of levee resembled parallel unbroken floating thread) and then it was nearing sunset and he began to hear, to notice, the voices of the doctor and of the man who had first bawled at him through the megaphone now bawling again from the pilot house overhead:

"Stop? Stop? Am I running a street car?"

"Stop for the novelty then," the doctor's pleasant voice said. "I dont know how many trips back and forth you have made in yonder nor how many of what you call mushrats you have fetched out. But this is the first time you ever had two people—no, three—who not only knew the name of some place they wished to go to but were actually trying to go there." So the convict waited while the sun slanted more and more and the steamboat-ant crawled steadily on across its vacant and gigantic plate turning more and more to copper. But he did not ask, he just waited. *Maybe it was Carrollton he said* he thought. *It begun with a C.* But he did not believe that either. He did not know where he was, but he did know that this was not anywhere near the Carrollton he remembered from that day seven years ago when, shackled wrist to wrist with the deputy sheriff, he had passed through it on the train—the slow spaced repeated shattering banging of trucks where two railroads crossed, a random scattering of white houses tranquil among trees on green hills lush with summer, a pointing spire, the finger of the hand of God. But there was no river there. *And you aint never close to this river without knowing it* he thought. *I dont care who you are nor where you have been all your life.* Then the head of the steamboat began to swing across the stream, its shadow swinging too, travelling long before it across the water, toward the vacant ridge of willow-massed earth empty of all life. There was nothing there at all, the convict could not even see either earth or water beyond it; it was as though the steamboat were about to crash slowly through the thin low frail willow barrier and embark into space, or lacking this, slow and back and fill and disembark him into space, granted it was about to disembark him, granted this was that place which was not near Parchman and was not Carrollton either, even though it did begin with c. Then he turned his head and saw the doctor stooping over the woman, pushing the baby's eyelid up with his forefinger, peering at it.

"Who else was there when he came?" the doctor said.

"Nobody," the convict said.

"Did it all yourselves, eh?"

"Yes," the convict said. Now the doctor stood up and looked at the convict.

"This is Carnarvon," he said.

"Carnarvon?" the convict said. "That aint—" Then he stopped, ceased. And now he told about that—the intent eyes as dispassionate as ice behind the rimless glasses, the clipped quick-tempered face that was not accustomed to being crossed or lied to either. ("Yes," the plump convict said. "That's what I was aiming to ask. Them clothes. Anybody would know them. How if this doctor was as smart as you claim he was—"

"I had slept in them for ten nights, mostly in the mud," the tall one said. "I had been rowing since midnight with that sapling oar I had tried to burn out that I never had time to scrape the soot off. But it's being scared and worried and then scared and then worried again in clothes for days and days and days that changes the way they look. I dont mean just your pants." He did not laugh. "Your face too. That doctor knowed."

"All right," the plump one said. "Go on.")

"I know it," the doctor said. "I discovered that while you were lying on the deck yonder sobering up again. Now dont lie to me. I dont like lying. This boat is going to New Orleans."

"No," the convict said immediately, quietly, with absolute finality. He could hear them again—the thuck-thuck-thuck on the water where an instant before he had been. But he was not thinking of the bullets. He had forgotten them, forgiven them. He was thinking of himself crouching, sobbing, panting before running again—the voice, the indictment, the cry of final and irrevocable repudiation of the old primal faithless Manipulator of all the lust and folly and injustice: *All in the world I wanted was just to surrender;* thinking of it, remembering it but without heat now, without passion now and briefer than an epitaph: *No. I tried that once. They shot at me.*

"So you dont want to go to New Orleans. And you didn't exactly plan to go to Carnarvon. But you will take Carnarvon in preference to New Orleans." The convict said nothing. The doctor looked at him, the magnified pupils like the heads of two bridge nails. "What were you in for? Hit him harder than you thought, eh?"

"No. I tried to rob a train."

"Say that again." The convict said it again. "Well? Go on. You dont say that in the year 1927 and just stop, man." So the convict told it, dispassionately too—about the magazines, the pistol which would not shoot, the mask and the dark lantern in which no draft had been arranged to keep the candle burning so that it died almost with the match but even then left the metal too hot to carry, won with subscriptions. *Only it aint my eyes or my mouth either he's watching* he thought. *It's like he is watching the way my hair grows on my head.* "I see," the doctor said. "But something went wrong. But you've had plenty of time to think about it since. To decide what was wrong, what you failed to do."

"Yes," the convict said. "I've thought about it a right smart since."

"So next time you are not going to make that mistake."

"I dont know," the convict said. "There aint going to be a next time."

"Why? If you know what you did wrong, they wont catch you next time."

The convict looked at the doctor steadily. They looked at each other steadily; the two sets of eyes were not so different after all. "I reckon I see what you mean," the convict said presently. "I was eighteen then. I'm twenty-five now."

"Oh," the doctor said. Now (the convict tried to tell it) the doctor did not move, he just simply quit looking at the convict. He produced a pack of cheap cigarettes from his coat. "Smoke?" he said.

"I wouldn't care for none," the convict said.

"Quite," the doctor said in that affable clipped voice. He put the cigarettes away. "There has been conferred upon my race (the Medical race) also the power to bind and to loose, if not by Jehovah perhaps, certainly by the American Medical Association—on which incidentally, in this day of Our Lord, I would put my money, at any odds, at any amount, at any time. I dont know just how far out of bounds I am on this specific occasion but I think we'll put it to the touch." He cupped his hands to his mouth, toward the pilot house overhead. "Captain!" he shouted. "We'll put these three passengers ashore here." He turned to the convict again. "Yes," he said, "I think I shall let your native state lick its own vomit. Here." Again his hand emerged from his pocket, this time with a bill in it.

"No," the convict said.

"Come, come; I dont like to be disputed either."

"No," the convict said. "I aint got any way to pay it back."

"Did I ask you to pay it back?"

"No," the convict said. "I never asked to borrow it either."

So once more he stood on dry land, who had already been toyed with twice by that risible and concentrated power of water, once more than should have fallen to the lot of any one man, any one lifetime, yet for whom there was reserved still another unbelievable recapitulation, he and the woman standing on the empty levee, the sleeping child wrapped in the faded tunic and the grapevine painter still wrapped about the convict's wrist, watching the steamboat back away and turn and once more crawl onward up the platter-like reach of vacant water burnished more and more to copper, its trailing smoke roiling in slow copper-edged gouts, thinning out along the water, fading, stinking away across the vast serene desolation, the boat growing smaller and smaller until it did not seem to crawl at all but to hang stationary in the airy substanceless sunset, dissolving into nothing like a pellet of floating mud.

Then he turned and for the first time looked about him, behind him, recoiling, not through fear but through pure reflex and not physically but the soul, the spirit, that profound sober alert attentiveness of the hillman who will not ask anything of strangers, not even information, thinking quietly *No. This aint Carrollton neither.* Because he now looked down the almost perpendicular landward slope of the levee through sixty feet of absolute space, upon a surface, a terrain flat as a waffle and of the color of a waffle or perhaps of the summer coat of a claybank horse and possessing that same piled density of a rug or peltry, spreading away without undulation yet with that curious appearance of imponderable solidity like fluid, broken here and there by thick humps of arsenical green which nevertheless still seemed to possess no height and by writhen veins of the color of ink which he began to suspect to be actual water but with judgment reserved, with judgment still reserved even when presently he was walking in it. That's what he said, told: So they went on. He didn't tell how he got the skiff singlehanded up the revetment and across the crown and down the opposite sixty-foot drop, he just said he went on, in a swirling cloud of mosquitoes like hot cinders, thrusting and plunging through the saw-edged grass which grew taller than his head and which whipped back at his arms and face like limber knives, dragging by the vine-spliced painter the skiff in which the woman sat, slogging and stumbling knee-deep in something less of earth than water, along one of those black winding channels less of water than earth: and then (he was in the skiff too now, paddling with the charred log, what footing there had been having given away beneath him without warning thirty minutes ago, leaving only the air-filled bubble of his jumper-back ballooning lightly on the twilit water until he rose to the surface and scrambled into the skiff) the house, the cabin a little larger than a horse-box, of cypress boards and an iron roof, rising on ten-foot stilts slender as spiders' legs, like a shabby and death-stricken (and probably poisonous) wading creature which had got that far into that flat waste and died with nothing anywhere in reach or sight to lie down upon, a pirogue tied to the foot of a crude ladder, a man standing in the open door holding a lantern (it was that dark now) above his head, gobbling down at them.

He told it—of the next eight or nine or ten days, he did not remember which, while the four of them—himself and the woman and baby and the little wiry man with rotting teeth and soft wild bright eyes like a rat or a chipmunk, whose language neither of them could understand—lived in the room and a half. He did not tell it that way, just as he apparently did not consider it worth the breath to tell how he had got the hundred-and-sixty-pound skiff singlehanded up and across and down the sixty-foot levee. He just said, "After a while we come to a house and we stayed there eight or nine days then they blew up the levee with dynamite so we had to leave." That was all. But he remembered it, but quietly now, with the cigar now, the good one the Warden had given him (though not lighted yet) in his peaceful and steadfast hand, remembering that first morning when he waked on the thin pallet beside his host (the woman and baby had the one bed) with the fierce sun already latticed through the warped rough planking of the wall, and stood on the ricketty porch looking out upon that flat fecund waste neither earth nor water, where even the senses doubted which was which, which rich and massy air and which mazy and impalpable vegetation, and thought quietly *He must do something here to eat and live. But I dont know what. And until I can go on again, until I can find where I am and how to pass that town without them seeing me I will have to help him do it so we can eat and live too, and I dont know what.* And he had a change of clothing too, almost at once on that first morning, not telling any more than he had about the skiff and the levee how he had begged borrowed or bought from the man whom he had not laid eyes on twelve hours ago and with whom on the day he saw him for the last time he still could exchange no word, the pair of dungaree pants which even the Cajan had discarded as no longer wearable, filthy, buttonless, the legs slashed and frayed into fringe like that on an 1890 hammock, in which he stood naked from the waist up and holding out to her the mud-caked and soot-stained jumper and overall when the woman waked on that first morning in the crude bunk nailed into one corner and filled with dried grass, saying, "Wash them. Good. I want all them stains out. All of them."

"But the jumper," she said. "Aint he got ere old shirt too? That sun and them mosquitoes—" But he did not even answer, and she said no more either, though when he and the Cajan returned at dark the garments were clean, stained a little still with the old mud and soot, but clean, resembling again what they were supposed to resemble as (his arms and back already a fiery red which would be blisters by tomorrow) he spread the garments out and examined them and then rolled them up carefully in a six-months-old New Orleans paper and thrust the bundle behind a rafter, where it remained while day followed day and the blisters on his back broke and suppu-rated and he would sit with his face expressionless as a wooden mask beneath the sweat while the Cajan doped his back with something on a filthy rag from a filthy saucer, she still saying nothing since she too doubtless knew what his reason was, not from that rapport of the wedded conferred upon her by the two weeks during which they had jointly suffered all the crises emotional social economic and even moral which do not always occur even in the ordinary fifty married years (the old married: you have seen them, the electroplate reproductions, the thousand identical coupled faces with only a collarless stud or a fichu out of Louisa Alcott to denote the sex, looking

in pairs like the winning braces of dogs after a field trial out
from among the packed columns of disaster and alarm and
baseless assurance and hope and incredible insensitivity and
insulation from tomorrow propped by a thousand morning
sugar bowls or coffee urns; or singly, rocking on porches or sitting in the sun beneath the tobacco-stained porticoes of a
thousand county courthouses, as though with the death of the
other having inherited a sort of rejuvenescence, immortality;
relict, they take a new lease on breath and seem to live forever,
as though that flesh which the old ceremony or ritual had
morally purified and made legally one had actually become so
with long tedious habit and he or she who entered the ground
first took all of it with him or her, leaving only the old perma-
nent enduring bone, free and tramelless)—not because of this
but because she too had stemmed at some point from the
same dim hill-bred Abraham.

So the bundle remained behind the rafter and day followed day while he and his partner (he was in partnership now
with his host, hunting alligators on shares, on the halvers he
called it— "Halvers?" the plump convict said. "How could
you make a business agreement with a man you claim you
couldn't even talk to?"

"I never had to talk to him," the tall one said. "Money aint
got but one language.") departed at dawn each day, at first
together in the pirogue but later singly, the one in the pirogue
and the other in the skiff, the one with the battered and pitted
rifle, the other with the knife and a piece of knotted rope and
a lightwood club the size and weight and shape of a
Thuringian mace, stalking their pleistocene nightmares up
and down the secret inky channels which writhed the flat
brass-colored land. He remembered that too: that first morning when turning in the sunrise from the ricketty platform he

saw the hide nailed drying to the wall and stopped dead, looking at it quietly, thinking quietly and soberly *So that's it. That's
what he does in order to eat and live* knowing it was a hide, a
skin, but from what animal, by association, ratiocination or
even memory of any picture out of his dead youth, he did not
know but knowing that it was the reason, the explanation, for
the little lost spider-legged house (which had already begun
to die, to rot from the legs upward almost before the roof
was nailed on) set in that teeming and myriad desolation,
enclosed and lost within the furious embrace of flowing mare
earth and stallion sun, divining through pure rapport of kind
for kind, hill-billy and bayou-rat, the two one and identical
because of the same grudged dispensation and niggard fate of
hard and unceasing travail not to gain future security, a balance in bank or even in a buried soda can for slothful and easy
old age, but just permission to endure and endure to buy air to
feel and sun to drink for each's little while, thinking (the convict) *Well, anyway I am going to find out what it is sooner than
I expected to* and did so, re-entered the house where the
woman was just waking in the one sorry built-in straw-filled
bunk which the Cajan had surrendered to her, and ate the
breakfast (the rice, a semi-liquid mess violent with pepper and
mostly fish considerably high, the chicory-thickened coffee)
and shirtless followed the little scuttling bobbing bright-eyed
rotten-toothed man down the crude ladder and into the
pirogue. He had never seen a pirogue either and he believed
that it would not remain upright—not that it was light and
precariously balanced with its open side upward but that there
was inherent in the wood, the very log, some dynamic and
unsleeping natural law, almost will, which its present position
outraged and violated—yet accepting this too as he had the
fact that that hide had belonged to something larger than any

calf or hog and that anything which looked like that on the
outside would be more than likely to have teeth and claws too,
accepting this, squatting in the pirogue, clutching both gunwales, rigidly immobile as though he had an egg filled with
nitroglycerin in his mouth and scarcely breathing, thinking *If
that's it, then I can do it too and even if he cant tell me how I
reckon I can watch him and find out.* And he did this too, he
remembered it, quietly even yet, thinking *I thought that was
how to do it and I reckon I would still think that even if I had it
to do again now for the first time*—the brazen day already
fierce upon his naked back, the crooked channel like a
voluted thread of ink, the pirogue moving steadily to the paddle which both entered and left the water without a sound;
then the sudden cessation of the paddle behind him and the
fierce hissing gobble of the Cajan at his back and he squatting
bate-breathed and with that intense immobility of complete
sobriety of a blind man listening while the frail wooden shell
stole on at the dying apex of its own parted water. Afterward he
remembered the rifle too—the rust-pitted single-shot weapon
with a clumsily wired stock and a muzzle you could have
driven a whisky cork into, which the Cajan had brought into
the boat—but not now; now he just squatted, crouched,
immobile, breathing with infinitesimal care, his sober unceasing gaze going here and there constantly as he thought *What?
What? I not only dont know what I am looking for, I dont even
know where to look for it.* Then he felt the motion of the
pirogue as the Cajan moved and then the tense gobbling hissing actually, hot rapid and repressed, against his neck and ear,
and glancing downward saw projecting between his own arm
and body from behind the Cajan's hand holding the knife,
and glaring up again saw the flat thick spit of mud which as he
looked at it divided and became a thick mud-colored log

which in turn seemed, still immobile, to leap suddenly against his retinae in three—no, four—dimensions: volume, solidity, shape, and another: not fear but pure and intense speculation and he looking at the scaled motionless shape, thinking not *It looks dangerous* but *It looks big* thinking *Well maybe a mule standing in a lot looks big to a man that never walked up to one with a halter before* thinking *Only if he could just tell me what to do it would save time*, the pirogue drawing nearer now, creeping now, with no ripple now even and it seemed to him that he could even hear his companion's held breath and he taking the knife from the other's hand now and not even thinking this since it was too fast, a flash; it was not a surrender, not a resignation, it was too calm, it was a part of him, he had drunk it with his mother's milk and lived with it all his life: *After all a man cant only do what he has to do, with what he has to do it with, with what he has learned, to the best of his judgment. And I reckon a hog is still a hog, no matter what it looks like. So here goes* sitting still for an instant longer until the bow of the pirogue grounded lighter than the falling of a leaf and stepped out of it and paused just for one instant while the words *It does look big* stood for just a second, unemphatic and trivial, somewhere where some fragment of his attention could see them and vanished, and stooped straddling, the knife driving even as he grasped the near foreleg, this all in the same instant when the lashing tail struck him a terrific blow upon the back. But the knife was home, he knew that even on his back in the mud, the weight of the thrashing beast longwise upon him, its ridged back clutched to his stomach, his arm about its throat, the hissing head clamped against his jaw, the furious tail lashing and flailing, the knife in his other hand probing for the life and finding it, the hot fierce gush: and now sitting beside the profound up-bellied carcass, his head again between his knees in the old attitude while his own blood freshened the other which drenched him, thinking *It's my durn nose again.*

So he sat there, his head, his streaming face, bowed between his knees in an attitude not of dejection but profoundly bemused, contemplative while the shrill voice of the Cajan seemed to buzz at him from an enormous distance; after a time he even looked up at the antic wiry figure bouncing hysterically about him, the face wild and grimacing, the voice gobbling and high; while the convict, holding his face carefully slanted so the blood would run free, looked at him with the cold intentness of a curator or custodian paused before one of his own glass cases, the Cajan threw up the rifle, cried "Boom-boom-boom!" flung it down and in pantomime re-enacted the recent scene then whirled his hands again, crying "Magnifique! Magnifique! Cent d'argent! mille d'argent! Tout l'argent sous le ciel de Dieu!" But the convict was already looking down again, cupping the coffee-colored water to his face, watching the constant bright carmine marble it, thinking *It's a little late to be telling me that now* and not even thinking this long because presently they were in the pirogue again, the convict squatting again with that unbreathing rigidity as though he were trying by holding his breath to decrease his very weight, the bloody skin in the bows before him and he looking at it, thinking *And I cant even ask him how much my half will be.*

But this not for long either, because as he was to tell the plump convict later, money has but one language. He remembered that too (they were at home now, the skin spread on the platform, where for the woman's benefit now the Cajan once more went through the pantomime—the gun which was not used, the hand-to-hand battle; for the second time the invisible alligator was slain amid cries, the victor rose and found this time that not even the woman was watching him. She was looking at the once more swollen and inflamed face of the convict. "You mean it kicked you right in the face?" she said.

"Nah," the convict said harshly, savagely. "It never had to. I done seem to got to where if that boy was to shoot me in the tail with a bean blower my nose would bleed.")—remembered that too but he did not try to tell it. Perhaps he could not have—how two people who could not even talk to one another made an agreement which both not only understood but which each knew the other would hold true and protect (perhaps for this reason) better than any written and witnessed contract. They even discussed and agreed somehow that they should hunt separately, each in his own vessel, to double the chances of finding prey. But this was easy: the convict could almost understand the words in which the Cajan said, "You do not need me and the rifle; we will only hinder you, be in your way." And more than this, they even agreed about the second rifle: that there was someone, it did not matter who— friend, neighbor, perhaps one in business in that line—from whom they could rent a second rifle; in their two patois, the one bastard English, the other bastard French—the one volatile, with his wild bright eyes and his voluble mouth full of stumps of teeth, the other sober, almost grim, swollen-faced and with his naked back blistered and scoriated like so much beef—they discussed this, squatting on either side of the pegged-out hide like two members of a corporation facing each other across a mahogany board table, and decided against it, the convict deciding: "I reckon not," he said. "I reckon if I had knowed enough to wait to start out with a gun, I still would. But since I done already started out without one,

I dont reckon I'll change." Because it was a question of the
money in terms of time, days. (Strange to say, that was the one
thing which the Cajan could not tell him: how much the half
would be. But the convict knew it was half.) He had so little of
them. He would have to move on soon, thinking (the convict)
All this durn foolishness will stop soon and I can get on back
and then suddenly he found that he was thinking *Will have to
get on back* and he became quite still and looked about at the
rich strange desert which surrounded him, in which he was
temporarily lost in peace and hope and into which the last
seven years had sunk like so many trivial pebbles into a pool,
leaving no ripple, and he thought quietly, with a kind of
bemused amazement *Yes. I reckon I had done forgot how good
making money was. Being let to make it.*

So he used no gun, his the knotted rope and the Thuringian mace, and each morning he and the Cajan took their
separate ways in the two boats to comb and creep the secret
channels about the lost land from (or out of) which now
and then still other pint-sized dark men appeared gobbling,
abruptly and as though by magic from nowhere, in other hol-
lowed logs, to follow quietly and watch him at his single combats—men named Tine and Toto and Theodule, who were
not much larger than and looked a good deal like the muskrats
which the Cajan (the host did this too, supplied the kitchen
too, he expressed this too like the rifle business, in his own
tongue, the convict comprehending this too as though it had
been English: "Do not concern yourself about food, O Her-
cules. Catch alligators; I will supply the pot.") took now and
then from traps as you take a shoat pig at need from a pen, and
varied the eternal rice and fish (the convict did tell this: how at
night, in the cabin, the door and one sashless window bat-
tened against mosquitoes—a form, a ritual, as empty as cross-

ing the fingers or knocking on wood—sitting beside the bug-swirled lantern on the plank table in a temperature close to blood heat he would look down at the swimming segment of meat on his sweating plate and think *It must be Theodule. He was the fat one.*)—day following day, unemphatic and identical, each like the one before and the one which would follow while his theoretical half of a sum to be reckoned in pennies, dollars, or tens of dollars he did not know mounted—the mornings when he set forth to find waiting for him like the *matador* his *aficionados* the small clump of constant and deferential pirogues, the hard noons when ringed half about by little motionless shells he fought his solitary combats, the evenings, the return, the pirogues departing one by one into inlets and passages which during the first few days he could not even distinguish, then the platform in the twilight where before the static woman and the usually nursing infant and the one or two bloody hides of the day's take the Cajan would perform his ritualistic victorious pantomime before the two growing rows of knifemarks in one of the boards of the wall; then the nights when, the woman and child in the single bunk and the Cajan already snoring on the pallet and the reeking lantern set close, he (the convict) would sit on his naked heels, sweating steadily, his face worn and calm, immersed and indomitable, his bowed back raw and savage as beef beneath the suppurant old blisters and the fierce welts of tails, and scrape and chip at the charred sapling which was almost a paddle now, pausing now and then to raise his head while the cloud of mosquitoes about it whined and whirled, to stare at the wall before him until after a while the crude boards themselves must have dissolved away and let his blank unseeing gaze go on and on unhampered, through the rich oblivious darkness, beyond it even perhaps, even perhaps beyond the

seven wasted years during which, so he had just realised, he
had been permitted to toil but not to work. Then he would
retire himself, he would take a last look at the rolled bundle
behind the rafter and blow out the lantern and lie down as he
was beside his snoring partner, to lie sweating (on his stomach, he could not bear the touch of anything to his back) in
the whining ovenlike darkness filled with the forlorn bellowing of alligators, thinking not *They never gave me time to learn*
but *I had forgot how good it is to work.*

Then on the tenth day it happened. It happened for the
third time. At first he refused to believe it, not that he felt that
now he had served out and discharged his apprenticeship to
mischance, had with the birth of the child reached and
crossed the crest of his Golgotha and would now be, possibly
not permitted so much as ignored, to descend the opposite
slope freewheeling. That was not his feeling at all. What he
declined to accept was the fact that a power, a force such as
that which had been consistent enough to concentrate upon
him with deadly undeviation for weeks, should with all the
wealth of cosmic violence and disaster to draw from, have
been so barren of invention and imagination, so lacking in
pride of artistry and craftmanship, as to repeat itself twice.
Once he had accepted, twice he even forgave, but three times
he simply declined to believe, particularly when he was at last
persuaded to realise that this third time was to be instigated
not by the blind potency of volume and motion but by human
direction and hands: that now the cosmic joker, foiled twice,
had stooped in its vindictive concentration to the employing
of dynamite.

He did not tell that. Doubtless he did not know himself
how it happened, what was happening. But he doubtless
remembered it (but quietly above the thick rich-colored pris-

tine cigar in his clean steady hand) what he knew, divined of it. It would be evening, the ninth evening, he and the woman on either side of their host's empty place at the evening meal, he hearing the voices from without but not ceasing to eat, still chewing steadily, because it would be the same as though he were seeing them anyway—the two or three or four pirogues floating on the dark water beneath the platform on which the host stood, the voices gobbling and jabbering, incomprehensible and filled not with alarm and not exactly with rage or even perhaps absolute surprise but rather just cacophony like those of disturbed marsh fowl, he (the convict) not ceasing to chew but just looking up quietly and maybe without a great deal of interrogation or surprise too as the Cajan burst in and stood before them, wild-faced, glaring, his blackened teeth gaped against the inky orifice of his distended mouth, watching (the convict) while the Cajan went through his violent pantomime of violent evacuation, ejection, scooping something invisible into his arms and hurling it out and downward and in the instant of completing the gesture changing from instigator to victim of that which he had set into pantomimic motion, clasping his head and, bowed over and not otherwise moving, seeming to be swept on and away before it, crying "Boom! Boom! Boom!," the convict watching him, his jaw not chewing now, though for just that moment, thinking *What? What is it he is trying to tell me?* thinking (this a flash too, since he could not have expressed this, and hence did not even know that he had ever thought it) that though his life had been cast here, circumscribed by this environment, accepted by this environment and accepting it in turn (and he had done well here—this quietly, soberly indeed, if he had been able to phrase it, think it instead of merely knowing it—better than he had ever done, who had not even known until now how good

work, making money, could be) yet it was not his life, he still
and would ever be no more than the water bug upon the surface of the pond, the plumbless and lurking depths of which
he would never know, his only actual contact with it being the
instants when on lonely and glaring mudspits under the piti-
less sun and amphitheatred by his motionless and rivetted
semicircle of watching pirogues, he accepted the gambit
which he had not elected, entered the lashing radius of the
armed tail and beat at the thrashing and hissing head with his
lightwood club, or this failing, embraced without hesitation
the armored body itself with the frail web of flesh and bone in
which he walked and lived and sought the raging life with an
eight-inch knifeblade.

So he and the woman merely watched the Cajan as he
acted out the whole charade of eviction—the little wiry man
gesticulant and wild, his hysterical shadow leaping and falling
upon the rough wall as he went through the pantomime of
abandoning the cabin, gathering in pantomime his meagre
belongings from the walls and corners—objects which no
other man would want and only some power or force like
blind water or earthquake or fire would ever dispossess him of,
the woman watching too, her mouth slightly open upon a
mass of chewed food, on her face an expression of placid
astonishment, saying, "What? What's he saying?"

"I dont know," the convict said. "But I reckon if it's something we ought to know we will find it out when it's ready for
us to." Because he was not alarmed, though by now he had
read the other's meaning plainly enough. *He's fixing to leave*
he thought *He's telling me to leave too*—this later, after they
had quitted the table and the Cajan and the woman had gone
to bed and the Cajan had risen from the pallet and
approached the convict and once more went through the pan-

tomime of abandoning the cabin, this time as one repeats a speech which may have been misunderstood, tediously, carefully repetitional as to a child, seeming to hold the convict with one hand while he gestured, talked, with the other, gesturing as though in single syllables, the convict (squatting, the knife open and the almost-finished paddle across his lap) watching, nodding his head, even speaking in English: "Yah; sure. You bet. I got you."—trimming again at the paddle but no faster, with no more haste than on any other night, serene in his belief that when the time came for him to know whatever it was, that would take care of itself, having already and without even knowing it, even before the possibility, the question, ever arose, declined, refused to accept even the thought of moving also, thinking about the hides, thinking *If there was just someway he could tell me where to carry my share to get the money* but thinking this only for an instant between two delicate strokes of the blade because almost at once he thought *I reckon as long as I can catch them I wont have no big trouble finding whoever it is that will buy them.*

So the next morning he helped the Cajan load his few belongings—the pitted rifle, a small bundle of clothing (again they traded, who could not even converse with one another, this time the few cooking vessels by definite allocation, and something embracing and abstractional which included the stove, the crude bunk, the house or its occupancy— something—in exchange for one alligator hide) a few rusty traps—into the pirogue, then, squatting and as two children divide sticks they divided the hides, separating them into two piles, one-for-me-and-one-for-you, two-for-me-and-two-for-you, and the Cajan loaded his share and shoved away from the platform and paused again, though this time he only put the paddle down, gathered something invisibly into his two hands

and flung it violently upward, crying "Boom? Boom?" on a rising inflection, nodding violently to the half-naked and savagely scoriated man on the platform who stared with a sort of
grim equability back at him and said, "Sure. Boom. Boom."
Then the Cajan went on. He did not look back. They watched
him, already paddling rapidly, or the woman did; the convict
had already turned.

"Maybe he was trying to tell us to leave too," she said.

"Yah," the convict said. "I thought of that last night. Hand
me the paddle." She fetched it to him—the sapling, the one
he had been trimming at nightly, not quite finished yet though
one more evening would do it (he had been using a spare one
of the Cajan's. The other had offered to let him keep it, to
include it perhaps with the stove and the bunk and the cabin's
freehold, but the convict had declined. Perhaps he had com-
puted it by volume against so much alligator hide, this
weighed against one more evening with the tedious and careful blade.) and he departed too with his knotted rope and
mace, in the opposite direction, as though not only not con-
tent with refusing to quit the place he had been warned
against, he must establish and affirm the irrevocable finality of
his refusal by penetrating even further and deeper into it. And
then and without warning the high fierce drowsing of his solitude gathered itself and struck at him.

He could not have told this if he had tried—this not yet
midmorning and he going on, alone for the first time, no
pirogue emerging anywhere to fall in behind him, but he had
not expected this anyway, he knew that the others would have
departed too; it was not this, it was his very solitude, his desolation which was now his alone and in full since he had
elected to remain; the sudden cessation of the paddle, the skiff
shooting on for a moment yet while he thought *What? What?*

then *No. No. No.* as the silence and solitude and emptiness roared down upon him in a jeering bellow: and now reversed, the skiff spun violently on its heel, he the betrayed driving furiously back toward the platform where he knew it was already too late, that citadel where the very crux and dear breath of his life—the being allowed to work and earn money, that right and privilege which he believed he had earned to himself unaided, asking no favor of anyone or anything save the right to be let alone to pit his will and strength against the sauric Protagonist of a land, a region, which he had not asked to be projected into—was being threatened, driving the home-made paddle in grim fury, coming in sight of the platform at last and seeing the motor launch lying alongside it with no surprise at all but actually with a kind of pleasure as though at a visible justification of his outrage and fear, the privilege of saying *I told you so* to his own affronting, driving on toward it in a dreamlike state in which there seemed to be no progress at all, in which, unimpeded and suffocating, he strove dreamily with a weightless oar, with muscles without strength or resiliency, at a medium without resistance, seeming to watch the skiff creep infinitesimally across the sunny water and up to the platform while a man in the launch (there were five of them in all) gobbled at him in that same tongue he had been hearing constantly now for ten days and still knew no word of, just as a second man, followed by the woman carrying the baby and dressed again for departure in the faded tunic and the sunbonnet, emerged from the house, carrying (the man carried several other things but the convict saw nothing else) the paper-wrapped bundle which the convict had put behind the rafter ten days ago and no other hand had touched since, he (the convict) on the platform too now, holding the skiff's painter in one hand and the bludgeon-like paddle in the other, contriving to speak to the woman at last in a voice dreamy and suffocating and incredibly calm: "Take it away from him and carry it back into the house."

"So you can talk English, can you?" the man in the launch said. "Why didn't you come out like they told you to last night?"

"Out?" the convict said. Again he even looked, glared, at the man in the launch, contriving even again to control his voice: "I aint got time to take trips. I'm busy," already turning to the woman again, his mouth already open to repeat as the dreamy buzzing voice of the man came to him and he turning once more, in a terrific and absolutely unbearable exasperation, crying, "Flood? What flood? Hell a mile, it's done passed me twice months ago! It's gone! What flood?" and then (he did not think this in actual words either but he knew it, suffered that flashing insight into his own character or destiny: how there was a peculiar quality of repetitiveness about his present fate, how not only the almost seminal crises recurred with a certain monotony, but the very physical circumstances followed a stupidly unimaginative pattern) the man in the launch said "Take him" and he was on his feet for a few minutes yet, lashing and striking in panting fury, then once more on his back on hard unyielding planks while the four men swarmed over him in a fierce wave of hard bones and panting curses and at last the thin dry vicious snapping of handcuffs.

"Damn it, are you mad?" the man in the launch said. "Cant you understand they are going to dynamite that levee at noon today?—Come on," he said to the others. "Get him aboard. Let's get out of here."

"I want my hides and boat," the convict said.

"Damn your hides," the man in the launch said. "If they dont get that levee blowed pretty soon you can hunt plenty more of them on the capitol steps at Baton Rouge. And this is all the boat you will need and you can say your prayers about it."

"I aint going without my boat," the convict said. He said it calmly and with complete finality, so calm, so final that for almost a minute nobody answered him, they just stood looking quietly down at him as he lay, half-naked, blistered and scarred, helpless and manacled hand and foot, on his back, delivering his ultimatum in a voice peaceful and quiet as that in which you talk to your bedfellow before going to sleep. Then the man in the launch moved; he spat quietly over the side and said in a voice as calm and quiet as the convict's:

"All right. Bring his boat." They helped the woman, carrying the baby and the paper-wrapped parcel, into the launch. Then they helped the convict to his feet and into the launch too, the shackles on his wrists and ankles clashing. "I'd unlock you if you'd promise to behave yourself," the man said. The convict did not answer this at all, he said,

"I want to hold the rope."

"The rope?"

"Yes," the convict said. "The rope." So they lowered him into the stern and gave him the end of the painter after it had passed the towing cleat, and they went on. The convict did not look back. But then, he did not look forward either, he lay half sprawled, his shackled legs before him, the end of the skiff's painter in one shackled hand. The launch made two other stops; when the hazy wafer of the intolerable sun began to stand once more directly overhead there were fifteen people in the launch; and then the convict, sprawled and motionless, saw the flat brazen land begin to rise and become a greenish-black mass of swamp, bearded and convoluted, this in turn stopping short off and there spread before him an expanse of

water embraced by a blue dissolution of shore line and glittering thinly under the noon, larger than he had ever seen
before, the sound of the launch's engine ceasing, the hull sliding on behind its fading bow-wave. "What are you doing?" the
leader said.

"It's noon," the helmsman said. "I thought we might hear
the dynamite." So they all listened, the launch lost of all forward motion, rocking slightly, the glitter-broken small waves
slapping and whispering at the hull, but no sound, no tremble
even, came anywhere under the fierce hazy sky; the long
moment gathered itself and turned on and noon was past. "All
right," the leader said. "Let's go." The engine started again,
the hull began to gather speed. The leader came aft and
stooped over the convict, key in hand. "I guess you'll have to
behave now, whether you want to or not," he said, unlocking
the manacles. "Wont you?"

"Yes," the convict said. They went on; after a time the
shore vanished completely and a little sea got up. The convict
was free now but he lay as before, the end of the skiff's painter
in his hand, bent now with three or four turns about his wrist;
he turned his head now and then to look back at the towing
skiff as it slewed and bounced in the launch's wake; now and
then he even looked out over the lake, the eyes alone moving,
the face grave and expressionless, thinking *This is a greater
immensity of water, of waste and desolation, than I have ever
seen before*; perhaps not; thinking three or four hours later, the
shoreline raised again and broken into a clutter of sailing
sloops and power cruisers, *These are more boats than I believed
existed, a maritime race of which I also had no cognizance* or
perhaps not thinking it but just watching as the launch
opened the shored gut of the ship canal, the low smoke of the
city beyond it, then a wharf, the launch slowing in; a quiet

crowd of people watching with that same forlorn passivity he had seen before and whose race he did recognise even though he had not seen Vicksburg when he passed it—the brand, the unmistakable hallmark of the violently homeless, he more so than any, who would have permitted no man to call him one of them.

"All right," the leader said to him. "Here you are."

"The boat," the convict said.

"You've got it. What do you want me to do—give you a receipt for it?"

"No," the convict said. "I just want the boat."

"Take it. Only you ought to have a bookstrap or something to carry it in." ("Carry it in?" the plump convict said. "Carry it where? Where would you have to carry it?")

He (the tall one) told that: how he and the woman disembarked and how one of the men helped him haul the skiff up out of the water and how he stood there with the end of the painter wrapped around his wrist and the man bustled up, saying, "All right. Next load! Next load!" and how he told this man too about the boat and the man cried, "Boat? Boat?" and how he (the convict) went with them when they carried the skiff over and racked, berthed, it with the others and how he lined himself up by a coca cola sign and the arch of a draw bridge so he could find the skiff again quick when he returned, and how he and the woman (he carrying the paper-wrapped parcel) were herded into a truck and after a while the truck began to run in traffic, between close houses, then there was a big building, an armory—

"Armory?" the plump one said. "You mean a jail."

"No. It was a kind of warehouse, with people with bundles laying on the floor." And how he thought maybe his partner might be there and how he even looked about for the Cajan while waiting for a chance to get back to the door again, where the soldier was and how he got back to the door at last, the woman behind him and his chest actually against the dropped rifle.

"Gwan, gwan," the soldier said. "Get back. They'll give you some clothes in a minute. You cant walk around the streets that way. And something to eat too. Maybe your kinfolks will come for you by that time." And he told that too: how the woman said,

"Maybe if you told him you had some kinfolks here he would let us out." And how he did not; he could not have expressed this either, it too deep, too ingrained; he had never yet had to think it into words through all the long generations of himself—his hill-man's sober and jealous respect not for truth but for the power, the strength, of lying—not to be niggard with lying but rather to use it with respect and even care, delicate quick and strong, like a fine and fatal blade. And how they fetched him clothes—a blue jumper and overalls, and then food too (a brisk starched young woman saying "But the baby must be bathed, cleaned. It will die if you dont" and the woman saying "Yessum. He might holler some, he aint never been bathed before. But he's a good baby") and now it was night, the unshaded bulbs harsh and savage and forlorn above the snorers and he rising, gripping the woman awake, and then the window. He told that: how there were doors in plenty, leading he did not know where, but he had a hard time finding a window they could use but he found one at last, he carrying the parcel and the baby too while he climbed through first—"You ought to tore up a sheet and slid down it," the plump convict said. But he needed no sheet, there were cobbles under his feet now, in the rich darkness. The city was there too but he had not seen it yet and would not—the low

constant glare; Bienville had stood there too, it had been the
figment of an emasculate also calling himself Napoleon but
no more, Andrew Jackson had found it one step from Pennsylvania Avenue. But the convict found it considerably further
than one step back to the ship canal and the skiff, the coca
cola sign dim now, the draw bridge arching spidery against the
jonquil sky at dawn: nor did he tell, anymore than about
the sixty-foot levee, how he got the skiff back into the water.
The lake was behind him now; there was but one direction he
could go. When he saw the River again he knew it at once. He
should have; it was now ineradicably a part of his past, his life;
it would be a part of what he would bequeath, if that were in
store for him. But four weeks later it would look different from
what it did now and did: he (the old man) had recovered from
his debauch, back in banks again, the Old Man, rimpling
placidly toward the sea, brown and rich as chocolate between
levees whose inner faces were wrinkled as though in a frozen
and aghast amazement, crowned with the rich green of summer in the willows; beyond them, sixty feet below, slick mules
squatted against the broad pull of middle-busters in the rich-
ened soil which would not need to be planted, which would
need only to be shown a cotton seed to sprout and make; there
would be the symmetric miles of strong stalks by July, purple
bloom in August, in September the black fields snowed over,
spilled, the middles dragged smooth by the long sacks, the
long black limber hands plucking, the hot air filled with the
whine of gins, the September air then but now June air heavy
with locust and (the towns) the smell of new paint and the
sour smell of the paste which holds wall paper—the towns,
the villages, the little lost wood landings on stilts on the inner
face of the levee, the lower storeys bright and rank under the
new paint and paper and even the marks on spile and post and

tree of May's raging water-height fading beneath each bright silver gust of summer's loud and inconstant rain; there was a store at the levee's lip, a few saddled and rope-bridled mules in the sleepy dust, a few dogs, a handful of negroes sitting on the steps beneath the chewing tobacco and malaria medicine signs, and three white men, one of them a deputy sheriff canvassing for votes to beat his superior (who had given him his job) in the August primary, all pausing to watch the skiff emerge from the glitter-glare of the afternoon water and approach and land, a woman carrying a child stepping out, then a man, a tall man who, approaching, proved to be dressed in a faded but recently-washed and quite clean suit of penitentiary clothing, stopping in the dust where the mules dozed and watching with pale cold humorless eyes while the deputy sheriff was still making toward his armpit that gesture which everyone present realised was to have produced a pistol in one flashing motion for a considerable time while still nothing came of it. It was apparently enough for the newcomer, however.

"You a officer?" he said.

"You damn right I am," the deputy said. "Just let me get this damn gun—"

"All right," the other said. "Yonder's your boat, and here's the woman. But I never did find that bastard on the cottonhouse."

One of the Governor's young men arrived at the Penitentiary the next morning. That is, he was fairly young (he would not see thirty again though without doubt he did not want to, there being that about him which indicated a character which

never had and never would want anything it did not, or was
not about to, possess), a Phi Beta Kappa out of an eastern university, a colonel on the Governor's staff who did not buy it
with a campaign contribution, who had stood in his negligent
eastern-cut clothes and his arched nose and lazy contemptuous eyes on the galleries of any number of little lost backwoods
stores and told his stories and received the guffaws of his over-
alled and spitting hearers and with the same look in his eyes
fondled infants named in memory of the last administration
and in honor (or hope) of the next, and (it was said of him and
doubtless not true) by lazy accident the behinds of some who
were not infants any longer though still not old enough to
vote. He was in the Warden's office with a briefcase, and
presently the deputy warden of the levee was there too. He
would have been sent for presently though not yet, but he
came anyhow, without knocking, with his hat on, calling the
Governor's young man loudly by a nickname and striking him
with a flat hand on the back and lifted one thigh to the Warden's desk, almost between the Warden and the caller, the
emissary. Or the vizier with the command, the knotted cord,
as began to appear immediately.

"Well," the Governor's young man said, "you've played
the devil, haven't you?" The Warden had a cigar. He had
offered the caller one. It had been refused, though presently,
while the Warden looked at the back of his neck with hard
immobility even a little grim, the deputy leaned and reached
back and opened the desk drawer and took one.

"Seems straight enough to me," the Warden said. "He got
swept away against his will. He came back as soon as he could
and surrendered."

"He even brought that damn boat back," the deputy said.
"If he'd a throwed the boat away he could a walked back in

three days. But no sir. He's got to bring the boat back. 'Here's
your boat and here's the woman but I never found no bastard
on no cottonhouse.' " He slapped his knee, guffawing. "Them
convicts. A mule's got twice as much sense."

"A mule's got twice as much sense as anything except a
rat," the emissary said in his pleasant voice. "But that's not the
trouble."

"What is the trouble?" the Warden said.

"This man is dead."

"Hell fire, he aint dead," the deputy said. "He's up yonder
in that bunkhouse right now, lying his head off probly. I'll take
you up there and you can see him." The Warden was looking
at the deputy.

"Look," he said. "Bledsoe was trying to tell me something
about that Kate mule's leg. You better go up to the stable
and—"

"I done tended to it," the deputy said. He didn't even look
at the Warden. He was watching, talking to, the emissary. "No
sir. He aint—"

"But he has received an official discharge as being dead.
Not a pardon nor a parole either: a discharge. He's either
dead, or free. In either case he doesn't belong here." Now both
the Warden and the deputy looked at the emissary, the
deputy's mouth open a little, the cigar poised in his hand to
have its tip bitten off. The emissary spoke pleasantly, extremely
distinctly: "On a report of death forwarded to the Governor
by the Warden of the Penitentiary." The deputy closed his
mouth, though otherwise he didn't move. "On the official evidence of the officer delegated at the time to the charge and
returning of the body of the prisoner to the Penitentiary." Now
the deputy put the cigar into his mouth and got slowly off the
desk, the cigar rolling across his lip as he spoke:

"So that's it. I'm to be it, am I?" He laughed shortly, a stage laugh, two notes. "When I done been right three times running through three separate administrations? That's on a book somewhere too. Somebody in Jackson can find that too. And if they cant, I can show——"

"Three administrations?" the emissary said. "Well, well. That's pretty good."

"You damn right it's good," the deputy said. "The woods are full of folks that didn't." The Warden was again watching the back of the deputy's neck.

"Look," he said. "Why dont you step up to my house and get that bottle of whiskey out of the sideboard and bring it down here?"

"All right," the deputy said. "But I think we better settle this first. I'll tell you what we'll do——"

"We can settle it quicker with a drink or two," the Warden said. "You better step on up to your place and get a coat so the bottle—"

"That'll take too long," the deputy said. "I wont need no coat." He moved to the door, where he stopped and turned. "I'll tell you what to do. Just call twelve men in here and tell him it's a jury—he never seen but one before and he wont know no better—and try him over for robbing that train. Hamp can be the judge."

"You cant try a man twice for the same crime," the emissary said. "He might know that even if he doesn't know a jury when he sees one."

"Look," the Warden said.

"All right. Just call it a new train robbery. Tell him it happened yesterday, tell him he robbed another train while he was gone and just forgot it. He couldn't help himself. Besides, he wont care. He'd just as lief be here as out. He wouldn't have nowhere to go if he was out. None of them do. Turn one loose and be damned if he aint right back here by Christmas like it was a reunion or something, for doing the very same thing they caught him at before." He guffawed again. "Them convicts."

"Look," the Warden said. "While you're there, why dont you open the bottle and see if the liquor's any good. Take a drink or two. Give yourself time to feel it. If it's not good, no use in bringing it."

"O.K.," the deputy said. He went out this time.

"Couldn't you lock the door?" the emissary said. The Warden squirmed faintly. That is, he shifted his position in his chair.

"After all, he's right," he said. "He's guessed right three times now. And he's kin to all the folks in Pittman county except the niggers."

"Maybe we can work fast then." The emissary opened the briefcase and took out a sheaf of papers. "So there you are," he said.

"There what are?"

"He escaped."

"But he came back voluntarily and surrendered."

"But he escaped."

"All right," the Warden said. "He escaped. Then what?" Now the emissary said Look. That is, he said,

"Listen. I'm on per diem. That's tax-payers, votes. And if there's any possible chance for it to occur to anyone to hold an investigation about this, there'll be ten senators and twenty-five representatives here on a special train maybe. On per diem. And it will be mighty hard to keep some of them from going back to Jackson by way of Memphis or New Orleans— on per diem."

"All right," the Warden said. "What does he say to do?"

"This. The man left here in charge of one specific officer. But he was delivered back here by a different one."

"But he surren—" This time the Warden stopped of his own accord. He looked, stared almost, at the emissary. "All right. Go on."

"In specific charge of an appointed and delegated officer, who returned here and reported that the body of the prisoner was no longer in his possession; that, in fact, he did not know where the prisoner was. That's correct, isn't it?" The Warden said nothing. "Isn't that correct?" the emissary said, pleasantly, insistently.

"But you cant do that to him. I tell you he's kin to half the—"

"That's taken care of. The Chief has made a place for him on the highway patrol."

"Hell," the Warden said. "He cant ride a motorcycle. I dont even let him try to drive a truck."

"He wont have to. Surely an amazed and grateful state can supply the man who guessed right three times in succession in Mississippi general elections with a car to ride in and somebody to run it if necessary. He wont even have to stay in it all the time. Just so he's near enough so when an inspector sees the car and stops and blows the horn of it he can hear it and come out."

"I still dont like it," the Warden said.

"Neither do I. Your man could have saved all of this if he had just gone on and drowned himself, as he seems to have led everybody to believe he had. But he didn't. And the Chief says do. Can you think of anything better?" The Warden sighed.

"No," he said.

"All right." The emissary opened the papers and uncapped a pen and began to write. "Attempted escape from the Penitentiary, ten years' additional sentence," he said. "Deputy Warden Buckworth transferred to Highway Patrol. Call it for meritorious service even if you want to. It wont matter now. Done?"

"Done," the Warden said.

"Then suppose you send for him. Get it over with." So the Warden sent for the tall convict and he arrived presently, saturnine and grave, in his new bed-ticking, his jowls blue and close under the sunburn, his hair recently cut and neatly parted and smelling faintly of the prison barber's (the barber was in for life, for murdering his wife, still a barber) pomade. The Warden called him by name.

"You had bad luck, didn't you." The convict said nothing. "They are going to have to add ten years to your time."

"All right," the convict said.

"It's hard luck. I'm sorry."

"All right," the convict said. "If that's the rule." So they gave him the ten years more and the Warden gave him the cigar and now he sat, jackknifed backward into the space between the upper and lower bunks, the unlighted cigar in his hand while the plump convict and four others listened to him. Or questioned him, that is, since it was all done, finished, now and he was safe again so maybe it wasn't even worth talking about anymore.

"All right," the plump one said. "So you come back into the River. Then what?"

"Nothing. I rowed."

"Wasn't it pretty hard rowing coming back?"

"The water was still high. It was running pretty hard still. I never made much speed for the first week or two. After that it

got better." Then, suddenly and quietly, something—the inar-
ticulateness, the innate and inherited reluctance for speech,
dissolved and he found himself, listened to himself, telling it
quietly, the words coming not fast but easily to the tongue as
he required them: How he paddled on (he found out by trying
it that he could make better speed, if you could call it speed,
next the bank—this after he had been carried suddenly and
violently out to midstream before he could prevent it and
found himself, the skiff, travelling back toward the region
from which he had just escaped and he spent the better part of
the morning getting back inshore and up to the canal again
from which he had emerged at dawn) until night came and
they tied up to the bank and ate some of the food he had
secreted in his jumper before leaving the armory in New
Orleans and the woman and the infant slept in the boat as
usual and when daylight came they went on and tied up again
that night too and the next day the food gave out and he came
to a landing, a town, he didn't notice the name of it, and he
got a job. It was a cane farm—

"Cane?" one of the other convicts said. "What does anybody want to raise cane for? You cut cane. You have to fight it
where I come from. You burn it just to get shut of it."

"It was sorghum," the tall convict said.

"Sorghum?" another said. "A whole farm just raising
sorghum? *Sorghum?* What did they do with it?" The tall one
didn't know. He didn't ask, he just came up the levee and
there was a truck waiting full of niggers and a white man
said, "You there. Can you run a shovel plow?" and the convict said Yes and the man said, "Jump in then" and the convict
said, "Only I've got a—"

"Yes," the plump one said. "That's what I been aiming to

ask. What did—" The tall convict's face was grave, his voice was calm, just a little short:

"They had tents for the folks to live in. They were behind." The plump one blinked at him.

"Did they think she was your wife?"

"I dont know. I reckon so." The plump one blinked at him.

"Wasn't she your wife? Just from time to time kind of, you might say?" The tall one didn't answer this at all. After a moment he raised the cigar and appeared to examine a loosening of the wrapper because after another moment he licked the cigar carefully near the end. "All right," the plump one said. "Then what?" So he worked there four days. He didn't like it. Maybe that was why: that he too could not quite put credence in that much of what he believed to be sorghum. So when they told him it was Saturday and paid him and the white man told him about somebody who was going to Baton Rouge the next day in a motor boat, he went to see the man and took the six dollars he had earned and bought food with it and tied the skiff behind the motor boat and went to Baton Rouge. It didn't take long and even after they left the motor boat at Baton Rouge and he was paddling again it seemed to the convict that the River was lower and the current not so fast, so hard, so they made fair speed, tying up to the bank at night among the willows, the woman and baby sleeping in the skiff as of old. Then the food gave out again. This time it was a wood landing, the wood stacked and waiting, a wagon and team being unladen of another load. The men with the wagon told him about the sawmill and helped him drag the skiff up the levee; they wanted to leave it there but he would not so they loaded it onto the wagon too and he and the woman got on the wagon too and they went to the sawmill. They gave them one room in a house to live in here. They paid two dollars a day and furnish. The work was hard. He liked it. He stayed there eight days.

"If you liked it so well, why did you quit?" the plump one said. The tall convict examined the cigar again, holding it up where the light fell upon the rich chocolate-colored flank.

"I got in trouble," he said.

"What trouble?"

"Woman. It was a fellow's wife."

"You mean you had been toting one piece up and down the country day and night for over a month, and now the first time you have a chance to stop and catch your breath almost you got to get in trouble over another one?" The tall convict had thought of that. He remembered it: how there were times, seconds, at first when if it had not been for the baby he might have, might have tried. But they were just seconds because in the next instant his whole being would seem to flee the very idea in a kind of savage and horrified revulsion; he would find himself looking from a distance at this millstone which the force and power of blind and risible Motion had fastened upon him, thinking, saying aloud actually, with harsh and savage outrage even though it had been two years since he had had a woman and that a nameless and not young negress, a casual, a straggler whom he had caught more or less by chance on one of the fifth-Sunday visiting days, the man— husband or sweetheart—whom she had come to see having been shot by a trusty a week or so previous and she had not heard about it: "She aint even no good to me for that."

"But you got this one, didn't you?" the plump convict said.

"Yah," the tall one said. The plump one blinked at him.

"Was it good?"

"It's all good," one of the others said. "Well? Go on. How many more did you have on the way back? Sometimes when a fellow starts getting it it looks like he just cant miss even if—" That was all, the convict told them. They left the sawmill fast, he had no time to buy food until they reached the next landing. There he spent the whole sixteen dollars he had earned and they went on. The River was lower now, there was no doubt of it, and sixteen dollars' worth looked like a lot of food and he thought maybe it would do, would be enough. But maybe there was more current in the River still than it looked like. But this time it was Mississippi, it was cotton; the plow handles felt right to his palms again, the strain and squat of the slick buttocks against the middle buster's blade was what he knew, even though they paid but a dollar a day here. But that did it. He told it: they told him it was Saturday again and paid him and he told about it—night, a smoked lantern in a disc of worn and barren earth as smooth as silver, a circle of crouching figures, the importunate murmurs and ejaculations, the meagre piles of worn bills beneath the crouching knees, the dotted cubes clicking and scuttering in the dust; that did it. "How much did you win?" the second convict said.

"Enough," the tall one said.

"But how much?"

"Enough," the tall one said. It was enough exactly; he gave it all to the man who owned the second motor boat (he would not need food now), he and the woman in the launch now and the skiff towing behind, the woman with the baby and the paper-wrapped parcel beneath his peaceful hand, on his lap; almost at once he recognised, not Vicksburg because he had never seen Vicksburg, but the trestle beneath which on his roaring wave of trees and houses and dead animals he had shot, accompanied by thunder and lightning, a month and three weeks ago; he looked at it once without heat, even without interest as the launch went on. But now he began to watch the bank, the levee. He didn't know how he would know but he knew he would, and then it was early afternoon and sure enough the moment came and he said to the launch owner: "I reckon this will do."

"Here?" the launch owner said. "This dont look like any-where to me."

"I reckon this is it," the convict said. So the launch put inshore, the engine ceased, it drifted up and lay against the levee and the owner cast the skiff loose.

"You better let me take you on until we come to something," he said. "That was what I promised."

"I reckon this will do," the convict said. So they got out and he stood with the grapevine painter in his hand while the launch purred again and drew away, already curving; he did not watch it. He laid the bundle down and made the painter fast to a willow root and picked up the bundle and turned. He said no word, he mounted the levee, passing the mark, the tide-line of the old raging, dry now and lined, traversed by shallow and empty cracks like foolish and deprecatory senile grins, and entered a willow clump and removed the overalls and shirt they had given him in New Orleans and dropped them without even looking to see where they fell and opened the parcel and took out the other, the known, the desired, faded a little, stained and worn, but clean, recognisable, and put them on and returned to the skiff and took up the paddle. The woman was already in it.

The plump convict stood blinking at him. "So you come back," he said. "Well well." Now they all watched the tall con-vict as he bit the end from the cigar neatly and with complete deliberation and spat it out and licked the bite smooth and damp and took a match from his pocket and examined the match for a moment as though to be sure it was a good one, worthy of the cigar perhaps, and raked it up his thigh with the same deliberation—a motion almost too slow to set fire to it, it would seem—and held it until the flame burned clear and free of sulphur, then put it to the cigar. The plump one watched him, blinking rapidly and steadily. "And they give you ten years more for running. That's bad. A fellow can get used to what they give him at first, to start off with, I dont care how much it is, even a hundred and ninety-nine years. But ten more years. Ten years more, on top of that. When you never expected it. Ten more years to have to do without no society, no female companionship—" He blinked steadily at the tall convict. But he (the tall convict) had thought of that too. He had had a sweetheart. That is, he had gone to church singings and picnics with her—a girl a year or so younger than he, short-legged, with ripe breasts and a heavy mouth and dull eyes like ripe muscadines, who owned a baking powder can almost full of ear-rings and brooches and rings bought (or presented at suggestion) from ten-cent stores. Presently he had divulged his plan to her, and there were times later when, musing, the thought occurred to him that possibly if it had not been for her he would not actually have attempted it—this a mere feeling, unworded, since he could not have phrased this either: that who to know what Capone's uncandled bridehood she might not have dreamed to be her destiny and fate, what fast car filled with authentic colored glass and machine guns, running traffic lights. But that was all past and done when the notion first occurred to him, and in the third month of his incarceration she came to see him. She wore ear-rings and a bracelet or so which he had never seen before and it never became quite clear how she had got that far from home, and she cried violently for the first three minutes though presently (and without his ever knowing either exactly how they had got separated or how she had made the acquaintance) he saw her in animated conversation with one of the guards. But she kissed him before she left that evening and said she would return the first chance she got, clinging to him, sweating a little, smelling of scent and soft young female flesh, slightly pneumatic. But she didn't come back though he continued to write to her, and seven months later he got an answer. It was a postcard, a colored lithograph of a Birmingham hotel, a childish X inked heavily across one window, the heavy writing on the reverse slanted and primer-like too: *This is where were honnymonning at. Your friend* (Mrs) *Vernon Waldrip*

The plump convict stood blinking at the tall one, rapidly and steadily. "Yes sir," he said. "It's them ten more years that hurt. Ten more years to do without a woman, no woman a tall that a fellow wants—" He blinked steadily and rapidly, watching the tall one. The other did not move, jackknifed backward between the two bunks, grave and clean, the cigar burning smoothly and richly in his clean steady hand, the smoke wreathing upward across his face saturnine, humorless, and calm. "Ten more years—"

"Women, shit," the tall convict said.

The Bear

I

There was a man and a dog too this time. Two beasts, counting Old Ben, the bear, and two men, counting Boon Hogganbeck, in whom some of the same blood ran which ran in Sam Fathers, even though Boon's was a plebeian strain of it and only Sam and Old Ben and the mongrel Lion were taintless and incorruptible.

He was sixteen. For six years now he had been a man's hunter. For six years now he had heard the best of all talking. It was of the wilderness, the big woods, bigger and older than any recorded document: —of white man fatuous enough to believe he had bought any fragment of it, of Indian ruthless enough to pretend that any fragment of it had been his to convey; bigger than Major de Spain and the scrap he pretended to, knowing better; older than old Thomas Sutpen of whom Major de Spain had had it and who knew better; older even than old Ikkemotubbe, the Chickasaw chief, of whom old Sutpen had had it and who knew better in his turn. It was of the men, not white nor black nor red but men, hunters, with the will and hardihood to endure and the humility and skill to survive, and the dogs and the bear and deer juxtaposed and reliefed against it, ordered and compelled by and within the wilderness in the ancient and unremitting contest according to the ancient and immitigable rules which voided all regrets and brooked no quarter;—the best game of all, the best of all breathing and forever the best of all listening, the voices quiet and weighty and deliberate for retrospection and recollection and exactitude among the concrete trophies—the racked guns and the heads and skins—in the libraries of town houses or the offices of plantation houses or (and best of all) in the camps themselves where the intact and still-warm meat yet hung, the men who had slain it sitting before the burning logs on hearths when there were houses and hearths or about the smoky blazing of piled wood in front of stretched tarpaulins when there were not. There was always a bottle present, so that it would seem to him that those fine fierce instants of heart and brain and courage and wiliness and speed were concentrated and distilled into that brown liquor which not women, not boys and children, but only hunters drank, drinking not of the blood they spilled but some condensation of the wild immortal spirit, drinking it moderately, humbly even, not with the pagan's base and baseless hope of acquiring thereby the virtues of cunning and strength and speed but in salute to them. Thus it seemed to him on this December morning not only natural but actually fitting that this should have begun with whisky.

He realised later that it had begun long before that. It had already begun on that day when he first wrote his age in two ciphers and his cousin McCaslin brought him for the first time to the camp, the big woods, to earn for himself from the wilderness the name and state of hunter provided he in his turn were humble and enduring enough. He had already inherited then, without ever having seen it, the big old bear with one trap-ruined foot that in an area almost a hundred miles square had earned for himself a name, a definite designation like a living man:—the long legend of corn-cribs broken down and rifled, of shoats and grown pigs and even calves carried bodily into the woods and devoured and traps and deadfalls overthrown and dogs mangled and slain and shotgun and even rifle shots delivered at point-blank range yet with no more effect than so many peas blown through a tube by a child—a corridor of wreckage and destruction beginning back before the boy was born, through which sped, not fast but rather with the ruthless and irresistible deliberation of a locomotive, the shaggy tremendous shape. It ran in his knowledge before he ever saw it. It loomed and towered in his dreams before he even saw the unaxed woods where it left its crooked print, shaggy, tremendous, red-eyed, not malevolent but just big, too big for the dogs which tried to bay it, for the horses which tried to ride it down, for the men and the bullets they fired into it; too big for the very country which was its constricting scope. It was as if the boy had already divined what his senses and intellect had not encompassed yet: that doomed wilderness whose edges were being constantly and punily gnawed at by men with plows and axes who feared it because it was wilderness, men myriad and nameless even to one another in the land where the old bear had earned a name, and through which ran not even a mortal beast but an anachronism indomitable and invincible out of an old dead time, a phantom, epitome and apotheosis of the old wild life which the little puny humans swarmed and hacked at in a fury of abhorrence and fear like pygmies about the ankles of a drowsing elephant;—the old bear, solitary, indomitable, and alone; widowered childless and absolved of mortality—old Priam reft of his old wife and outlived all his sons.

Still a child, with three years then two years then one year yet before he too could make one of them, each November he would watch the wagon containing the dogs and the bedding and food and guns and his cousin McCaslin and Tennie's Jim and Sam Fathers too until Sam moved to the camp to live, depart for the Big Bottom, the big woods. To him, they were going not to hunt bear and deer but to keep yearly rendezvous with the bear which they did not even intend to kill. Two weeks later they would return, with no trophy, no skin. He had not expected it. He had not even feared that it might be in the wagon this time with the other skins and heads. He did not even tell himself that in three years or two years or one year more he would be present and that it might even be his gun. He believed that only after he had served his apprenticeship in the woods which would prove him worthy to be a hunter, would he even be permitted to distinguish the crooked print, and that even then for two November weeks he would merely make another minor one, along with his cousin and Major de Spain and General Compson and Walter Ewell and Boon and the dogs which feared to bay it and the shotguns and rifles which failed even to bleed it, in the yearly pageant-rite of the old bear's furious immortality.

His day came at last. In the surrey with his cousin and Major de Spain and General Compson he saw the wilderness through a slow drizzle of November rain just above the ice point as it seemed to him later he always saw it or at least always remembered it—the tall and endless wall of dense November woods under the dissolving afternoon and the year's death, sombre, impenetrable (he could not even discern yet how, at what point they could possibly hope to enter it

even though he knew that Sam Fathers was waiting there with
the wagon), the surrey moving through the skeleton stalks of
cotton and corn in the last of open country, the last trace of
man's puny gnawing at the immemorial flank, until, dwarfed
by that perspective into an almost ridiculous diminishment,
the surrey itself seemed to have ceased to move (this too to be
completed later, years later, after he had grown to a man and
had seen the sea) as a solitary small boat hangs in lonely
immobility, merely tossing up and down, in the infinite waste
of the ocean while the water and then the apparently impenetrable land which it nears without appreciable progress,
swings slowly and opens the widening inlet which is the
anchorage. He entered it. Sam was waiting, wrapped in a quilt
on the wagon seat behind the patient and steaming mules. He
entered his novitiate to the true wilderness with Sam beside
him as he had begun his apprenticeship in miniature to man-
hood after the rabbits and such with Sam beside him, the two
of them wrapped in the damp, warm, negro-rank quilt while
the wilderness closed behind his entrance as it had opened
momentarily to accept him, opening before his advancement
as it closed behind his progress, no fixed path the wagon followed but a channel nonexistent ten yards ahead of it and
ceasing to exist ten yards after it had passed, the wagon pro-
gressing not by its own volition but by attrition of their intact
yet fluid circumambience, drowsing, earless, almost lightless.

It seemed to him that at the age of ten he was witnessing
his own birth. It was not even strange to him. He had experienced it all before, and not merely in dreams. He saw the
camp—a paintless six-room bungalow set on piles above the
spring high-water—and he knew already how it was going to
look. He helped in the rapid orderly disorder of their estab-
lishment in it and even his motions were familiar to him, fore-

known. Then for two weeks he ate the coarse rapid food—the shapeless sour bread, the wild strange meat, venison and bear and turkey and coon which he had never tasted before—which men ate, cooked by men who were hunters first and cooks afterward; he slept in harsh sheetless blankets as hunters slept. Each morning the gray of dawn found him and Sam Fathers on the stand, the crossing, which had been allotted him. It was the poorest one, the most barren. He had expected that; he had not dared yet to hope even to himself that he would even hear the running dogs this first time. But he did hear them. It was on the third morning—a murmur, sourceless, almost indistinguishable, yet he knew what it was although he had never before heard that many dogs running at once, the murmur swelling into separate and distinct voices until he could call the five dogs which his cousin owned from among the others. "Now," Sam said, "slant your gun up a little and draw back the hammers and then stand still."

But it was not for him, not yet. The humility was there; he had learned that. And he could learn the patience. He was only ten, only one week. The instant had passed. It seemed to him that he could actually see the deer, the buck, smoke-colored, elongated with speed, vanished, the woods, the gray solitude still ringing even when the voices of the dogs had died away; from far away across the sombre woods and the gray half-liquid morning there came two shots. "Now let your hammers down," Sam said.

He did so. "You knew it too," he said.

"Yes," Sam said. "I want you to learn how to do when you didn't shoot. It's after the chance for the bear or the deer has done already come and gone that men and dogs get killed."

"Anyway, it wasn't him," the boy said. "It wasn't even a bear. It was just a deer."

"Yes," Sam said, "it was just a deer."

Then one morning, it was in the second week, he heard the dogs again. This time before Sam even spoke he readied the too-long, too-heavy, man-size gun as Sam had taught him, even though this time he knew the dogs and the deer were coming less close than ever, hardly within hearing even. They didn't sound like any running dogs he had ever heard before even. Then he found that Sam, who had taught him first of all to cock the gun and take position where he could see best in all directions and then never to move again, had himself moved up beside him. "There," he said. "Listen." The boy listened, to no ringing chorus strong and fast on a free scent but a moiling yapping an octave too high and with something more than indecision and even abjectness in it which he could not yet recognise, reluctant, not even moving very fast, taking a long time to pass out of hearing, leaving even then in the air that echo of thin and almost human hysteria, abject, almost humanly grieving, with this time nothing ahead of it, no sense of a fleeing unseen smoke-colored shape. He could hear Sam breathing at his shoulder. He saw the arched curve of the old man's inhaling nostrils.

"It's Old Ben!" he cried, whispering.

Sam didn't move save for the slow gradual turning of his head as the voices faded on and the faint steady rapid arch and collapse of his nostrils. "Hah," he said. "Not even running. Walking."

"But up here!" the boy cried. "Way up here!"

"He do it every year," Sam said. "Once. Ash and Boon say he comes up here to run the other little bears away. Tell them to get to hell out of here and stay out until the hunters are gone. Maybe." The boy no longer heard anything at all, yet still Sam's head continued to turn gradually and steadily until the back of it was toward him. Then it turned back and looked down at him—the same face, grave, familiar, expressionless until it smiled, the same old man's eyes from which as he watched there faded slowly a quality darkly and fiercely lambent, passionate and proud. "He dont care no more for bears than he does for dogs or men neither. He come to see who's here, who's new in camp this year, whether he can shoot or not, can stay or not. Whether we got the dog yet that can bay and hold him until a man gets there with a gun. Because he's the head bear. He's the man." It faded, was gone; again they were the eyes as he had known them all his life. "He'll let them follow him to the river. Then he'll send them home. We might as well go too; see how they look when they get back to camp."

The dogs were there first, ten of them huddled back under the kitchen, himself and Sam squatting to peer back into the obscurity where they crouched, quiet, the eyes rolling and luminous, vanishing, and no sound, only that effluvium which the boy could not quite place yet, of something more than dog, stronger than dog and not just animal, just beast even. Because there had been nothing in front of the abject and painful yapping except the solitude, the wilderness, so that when the eleventh hound got back about mid-afternoon and he and Tennie's Jim held the passive and still trembling bitch while Sam daubed her tattered ear and raked shoulder with turpentine and axle-grease, it was still no living creature but only the wilderness which, leaning for a moment, had patted lightly once her temerity. "Just like a man," Sam said. "Just like folks. Put off as long as she could having to be brave, knowing all the time that sooner or later she would have to be brave once so she could keep on calling herself a dog, and knowing beforehand what was going to happen when she done it."

He did not know just when Sam left. He only knew that he was gone. For the next three mornings he rose and ate breakfast and Sam was not waiting for him. He went to his stand alone; he found it without help now and stood on it as Sam had taught him. On the third morning he heard the dogs again, running strong and free on a true scent again, and he readied the gun as he had learned to do and heard the hunt sweep past on since he was not ready yet, had not deserved other yet in just one short period of two weeks as compared to all the long life which he had already dedicated to the wilderness with patience and humility; he heard the shot again, one shot, the single clapping report of Walter Ewell's rifle. By now he could not only find his stand and then return to camp without guidance, by using the compass his cousin had given him he reached Walter waiting beside the buck and the moiling of dogs over the cast entrails before any of the others except Major de Spain and Tennie's Jim on the horses, even before Uncle Ash arrived with the one-eyed wagon-mule which did not mind the smell of blood or even, so they said, of bear.

It was not Uncle Ash on the mule. It was Sam, returned. And Sam was waiting when he finished his dinner and, himself on the one-eyed mule and Sam on the other one of the wagon team, they rode for more than three hours through the rapid shortening sunless afternoon, following no path, no trail even that he could discern, into a section of country he had never seen before. Then he understood why Sam had made him ride the one-eyed mule which would not spook at the smell of blood, of wild animals. The other one, the sound one, stopped short and tried to whirl and bolt even as Sam got down, jerking and wrenching at the rein while Sam held it, coaxing it forward with his voice since he did not dare risk hitching it, drawing it forward while the boy dismounted from the marred one which would stand. Then, standing beside Sam in the thick great gloom of ancient woods and the winter's dying afternoon, he looked quietly down at the rotted log scored and gutted with claw-marks and, in the wet earth beside it, the print of the enormous warped two-toed foot. Now he knew what he had heard in the hounds' voices in the woods that morning and what he had smelled when he peered under the kitchen where they huddled. It was in him too, a little different because they were brute beasts and he was not, but only a little different—an eagerness, passive; an abjectness, a sense of his own fragility and impotence against the timeless woods, yet without doubt or dread; a flavor like brass in the sudden run of saliva in his mouth, a hard sharp constriction either in his brain or his stomach, he could not tell which and it did not matter; he knew only that for the first time he realised that the bear which had run in his listening and loomed in his dreams since before he could remember and which therefore must have existed in the listening and the dreams of his cousin and Major de Spain and even old General Compson before they began to remember in their turn, was a mortal animal and that they had departed for the camp each November with no actual intention of slaying it, not because it could not be slain but because so far they had no actual hope of being able to. "It will be tomorrow," he said.

"You mean we will try tomorrow," Sam said. "We aint got the dog yet."

"We've got eleven," he said. "They ran him Monday."

"And you heard them," Sam said. "Saw them too. We aint got the dog yet. It wont take but one. But he aint there. Maybe he aint nowhere. The only other way will be for him to run by accident over somebody that had a gun and knowed how to shoot it."

"That wouldn't be me," the boy said. "It would be Walter or Major or——"

"It might," Sam said. "You watch close tomorrow. Because he's smart. That's how come he has lived this long. If he gets hemmed up and has got to pick out somebody to run over, he will pick out you."

"How?" he said. "How will he know. . . ." He ceased. "You mean he already knows me, that I aint never been to the big bottom before, aint had time to find out yet whether I . . ." He ceased again, staring at Sam; he said humbly, not even amazed: "It was me he was watching. I dont reckon he did need to come but once."

"You watch tomorrow," Sam said. "I reckon we better start back. It'll be long after dark now before we get to camp."

The next morning they started three hours earlier than they had ever done. Even Uncle Ash went, the cook, who called himself by profession a camp cook and who did little else save cook for Major de Spain's hunting and camping parties, yet who had been marked by the wilderness from simple juxtaposition to it until he responded as they all did, even the boy who until two weeks ago had never even seen the wilderness, to a hound's ripped ear and shoulder and the print of a crooked foot in a patch of wet earth. They rode. It was too far to walk: the boy and Sam and Uncle Ash in the wagon with the dogs, his cousin and Major de Spain and General Compson and Boon and Walter and Tennie's Jim riding double on the horses; again the first gray light found him, as on that first morning two weeks ago, on the stand where Sam had placed and left him. With the gun which was too big for him, the breech-loader which did not even belong to him but to Major de Spain and which he had fired only once, at a stump on the first day to learn the recoil and how to reload it with the paper shells, he stood against a big gum tree beside a little bayou whose black still water crept without motion out of a cane-brake, across a small clearing and into the cane again, where, invisible, a bird, the big woodpecker called Lord-to-God by negroes, clattered at a dead trunk. It was a stand like any other stand, dissimilar only in incidentals to the one where he had stood each morning for two weeks; a territory new to him yet no less familiar than that other one which after two weeks he had come to believe he knew a little—the same solitude, the same loneliness through which frail and timorous man had merely passed without altering it, leaving no mark nor scar, which looked exactly as it must have looked when the first ancestor of Sam Fathers' Chickasaw predecessors crept into it and looked about him, club or stone axe or bone arrow drawn and ready, different only because, squatting at the edge of the kitchen, he had smelled the dogs huddled and cringing beneath it and saw the raked ear and side of the bitch that, as Sam had said, had to be brave once in order to keep on calling herself a dog, and saw yesterday in the earth beside the gutted log, the print of the living foot. He heard no dogs at all. He never did certainly hear them. He only heard the drumming of the woodpecker stop short off, and knew that the bear was looking at him. He never saw it. He did not know whether it was facing him from the cane or behind him. He did not move, holding the useless gun which he knew now he would never fire at it, now or ever, tasting in his saliva that taint of brass which he had smelled in the huddled dogs when he peered under the kitchen.

Then it was gone. As abruptly as it had stopped, the woodpecker's dry hammering set up again, and after a while he believed he even heard the dogs—a murmur, scarce a sound even, which he had probably been hearing for a time, perhaps a minute or two, before he remarked it, drifting into hearing and then out again, dying away. They came nowhere near him. If it was dogs he heard, he could not have sworn to it; if it was a bear they ran, it was another bear. It was Sam himself who emerged from the cane and crossed the bayou, the injured bitch following at heel as a bird dog is taught to walk. She came and crouched against his leg, trembling. "I didn't see him," he said. "I didn't, Sam."

"I know it," Sam said. "He done the looking. You didn't hear him neither, did you?"

"No," the boy said. "I——"

"He's smart," Sam said. "Too smart." Again the boy saw in his eyes that quality of dark and brooding lambence as Sam looked down at the bitch trembling faintly and steadily against the boy's leg. From her raked shoulder a few drops of fresh blood clung like bright berries. "Too big. We aint got the dog yet. But maybe some day."

Because there would be a next time, after and after. He was only ten. It seemed to him that he could see them, the two of them, shadowy in the limbo from which time emerged and became time: the old bear absolved of mortality and himself who shared a little of it. Because he recognised now what he had smelled in the huddled dogs and tasted in his own saliva, recognised fear as a boy, a youth, recognises the existence of love and passion and experience which is his heritage but not yet his patrimony, from entering by chance the presence or perhaps even merely the bedroom of a woman who has loved and been loved by many men. *So I will have to see him*, he thought, without dread or even hope. *I will have to look at him.* So it was in June of the next summer. They were at the camp again, celebrating Major de Spain's and General Compson's birthdays. Although the one had been born in September and the other in the depth of winter and almost thirty years earlier, each June the two of them and McCaslin and Boon and Walter Ewell (and the boy too from now on) spent two weeks at the camp, fishing and shooting squirrels and turkey and running coons and wildcats with the dogs at night. That is, Boon and the negroes (and the boy too now) fished and shot squirrels and ran the coons and cats, because the proven hunters, not only Major de Spain and old General Compson (who spent those two weeks sitting in a rocking chair before a tremendous iron pot of Brunswick stew, stirring and tasting, with Uncle Ash to quarrel with about how he was making it and Tennie's Jim to pour whisky into the tin dipper from which he drank it) but even McCaslin and Walter Ewell who were still young enough, scorned such other than shooting the wild gobblers with pistols for wagers or to test their marksmanship.

That is, his cousin McCaslin and the others thought he was hunting squirrels. Until the third evening he believed that Sam Fathers thought so too. Each morning he would leave the camp right after breakfast. He had his own gun now, a new breech-loader, a Christmas gift; he would own and shoot it for almost seventy years, through two new pairs of barrels and locks and one new stock, until all that remained of the original gun was the silver-inlaid triggerguard with his and McCaslin's engraved names and the date in 1878. He found the tree beside the little bayou where he had stood that morning. Using the compass he ranged from that point; he was teaching himself to be better than a fair woodsman without even knowing he was doing it. On the third day he even found the gutted log where he had first seen the print. It was almost completely crumbled now, healing with unbelievable speed, a passionate and almost visible relinquishment, back into the earth from which the tree had grown. He ranged the summer woods now, green with gloom, if anything actually dimmer than they had been in November's gray dissolution, where even at noon the sun fell only in windless dappling upon the earth which never completely dried and which crawled with snakes—moccasins and watersnakes and rattlers, themselves the color of the dappled gloom so that he would not always see them until they moved; returning to camp later and later and later, first day, second day, passing in the twilight of the third evening the little log pen enclosing the log barn where Sam was putting up the stock for the night. "You aint looked right yet," Sam said.

He stopped. For a moment he didn't answer. Then he said peacefully, in a peaceful rushing burst, as when a boy's miniature dam in a little brook gives way: "All right. Yes. But how? I went to the bayou. I even found that log again. I——"

"I reckon that was all right. Likely he's been watching you. You never saw his foot?"

"I . . ." the boy said. "I didn't . . . I never thought . . ."

"It's the gun," Sam said. He stood beside the fence, motionless, the old man, son of a negro slave and a Chickasaw chief, in the battered and faded overalls and the frayed five-cent straw hat which had been the badge of the negro's slavery and was now the regalia of his freedom. The camp—the clearing, the house, the barn and its tiny lot with which Major de Spain in his turn had scratched punily and evanescently at the wilderness—faded in the dusk, back into the immemorial darkness of the woods. *The gun*, the boy thought. *The gun.* "You will have to choose," Sam said.

He left the next morning before light, without breakfast, long before Uncle Ash would wake in his quilts on the kitchen floor and start the fire. He had only the compass and a stick for the snakes. He could go almost a mile before he would need to see the compass. He sat on a log, the invisible compass in his hand, while the secret nightsounds which had ceased at his movements, scurried again and then fell still for good and the owls ceased and gave over to the waking day birds and there was light in the gray wet woods and he could see the compass. He went fast yet still quietly, becoming steadily better and better as a woodsman without yet having time to realise it; he jumped a doe and a fawn, walked them out of the bed, close enough to see them—the crash of undergrowth, the white scut, the fawn scudding along behind her, faster than he had known it could have run. He was hunting right, upwind, as Sam had taught him, but that didn't matter now. He had left the gun; by his own will and relinquishment he had accepted not a gambit, not a choice, but a condition in which not only the bear's heretofore inviolable anonymity but all the ancient rules and balances of hunter and hunted had been abrogated. He would not even be afraid, not even in the moment when the fear would take him completely: blood, skin, bowels, bones, memory from the long time before it even became his memory—all save that thin clear quenchless lucidity which alone differed him from this bear and from all the other bears and bucks he would follow during almost seventy years, to which Sam had said: "Be scared. You cant help that. But dont be afraid. Aint nothing in the woods going to hurt you if you dont corner it or it dont smell that you are afraid. A bear or a deer has got to be scared of a coward the same as a brave man has got to be."

By noon he was far beyond the crossing on the little bayou, farther into the new and alien country than he had ever been, travelling now not only by the compass but by the old, heavy, biscuit-thick silver watch which had been his father's. He had left the camp nine hours ago; nine hours from now, dark would already have been an hour old. He stopped, for the first time since he had risen from the log when he could see the compass face at last, and looked about, mopping his sweating face on his sleeve. He had already relinquished, of his will, because of his need, in humility and peace and without regret, yet apparently that had not been enough, the leaving of the gun was not enough. He stood for a moment— a child, alien and lost in the green and soaring gloom of the markless wilderness. Then he relinquished completely to it. It was the watch and the compass. He was still tainted. He removed the linked chain of the one and the looped thong of the other from his overalls and hung them on a bush and leaned the stick beside them and entered it.

When he realised he was lost, he did as Sam had coached and drilled him: made a cast to cross his backtrack. He had not been going very fast for the last two or three hours, and he had gone even less fast since he left the compass and watch on the bush. So he went slower still now, since the tree could not be very far; in fact, he found it before he really expected to and turned and went to it. But there was no bush beneath it, no compass nor watch, so he did next as Sam had coached and drilled him: made this next circle in the opposite direction and much larger, so that the pattern of the two of them would bisect his track somewhere, but crossing no trace nor mark anywhere of his feet or any feet, and now he was going faster though still not panicked, his heart beating a little more rapidly but strong and steady enough, and this time it was not even the tree because there was a down log beside it which he had never seen before and beyond the log a little swamp, a seepage of moisture somewhere between earth and water, and he did what Sam had coached and drilled him as the next and the last, seeing as he sat down on the log the crooked print, the warped indentation in the wet ground which while he looked at it continued to fill with water until it was level full and the water began to overflow and the sides of the print began to dissolve away. Even as he looked up he saw the next one, and, moving, the one beyond it; moving, not hurrying, running, but merely keeping pace with them as they appeared before him as though they were being shaped out of thin air just one constant pace short of where he would lose them forever and be lost forever himself, tireless, eager, without doubt or dread, panting a little above the strong rapid little hammer of his heart, emerging suddenly into a little glade and the wilderness coalesced. It rushed, soundless, and solidified—the tree, the bush, the compass and the watch glinting where a ray of sunlight touched them. Then he saw the bear. It did not emerge, appear: it was just there, immobile, fixed in the green and windless noon's hot dappling, not as big as he had dreamed it but as big as he had expected, bigger, dimensionless against the dappled obscurity, looking at him. Then it moved. It crossed the glade without haste, walking for an instant into the sun's full glare and out of it, and stopped again and looked back at him across one shoulder. Then it was gone. It didn't walk into the woods. It faded, sank back into the wilderness without motion as he had watched a fish, a huge old bass, sink back into the dark depths of its pool and vanish without even any movement of its fins.

2

So he should have hated and feared Lion. He was thirteen then. He had killed his buck and Sam Fathers had marked his face with the hot blood, and in the next November he killed a bear. But before that accolade he had become as competent in the woods as many grown men with the same experience. By now he was a better woodsman than most grown men with more. There was no territory within twenty-five miles of the camp that he did not know—bayou, ridge, landmark trees and path; he could have led anyone direct to any spot in it and brought him back. He knew game trails that even Sam Fathers had never seen; in the third fall he found a buck's bedding-place by himself and unbeknown to his cousin he borrowed Walter Ewell's rifle and lay in wait for the buck at dawn and killed it when it walked back to the bed as Sam had told him how the old Chickasaw fathers did.

By now he knew the old bear's footprint better than he did his own, and not only the crooked one. He could see any one of the three sound prints and distinguish it at once from any other, and not only because of its size. There were other bears within that fifty miles which left tracks almost as large, or at least so near that the one would have appeared larger only by juxtaposition. It was more than that. If Sam Fathers had been his mentor and the backyard rabbits and squirrels his kinder-garten, then the wilderness the old bear ran was his college and the old male bear itself, so long unwifed and childless as to have become its own ungendered progenitor, was his alma mater.

He could find the crooked print now whenever he

wished, ten miles or five miles or sometimes closer than that, to the camp. Twice while on stand during the next three years he heard the dogs strike its trail and once even jump it by chance, the voices high, abject, almost human in their hysteria. Once, still-hunting with Walter Ewell's rifle, he saw it cross a long corridor of down timber where a tornado had passed. It rushed through rather than across the tangle of trunks and branches as a locomotive would, faster than he had ever believed it could have moved, almost as fast as a deer even because the deer would have spent most of that distance in the air; he realised then why it would take a dog not only of abnormal courage but size and speed too ever to bring it to bay. He had a little dog at home, a mongrel, of the sort called fyce by negroes, a ratter, itself not much bigger than a rat and possessing that sort of courage which had long since stopped being bravery and had become foolhardiness. He brought it with him one June and, timing them as if they were meeting an appointment with another human being, himself carrying the fyce with a sack over its head and Sam Fathers with a brace of the hounds on a rope leash, they lay downwind of the trail and actually ambushed the bear. They were so close that it turned at bay although he realised later this might have been from surprise and amazement at the shrill and frantic uproar of the fyce. It turned at bay against the trunk of a big cypress, on its hind feet; it seemed to the boy that it would never stop rising, taller and taller, and even the two hounds seemed to have taken a kind of desperate and despairing courage from the fyce. Then he realised that the fyce was actually not going to stop. He flung the gun down and ran. When he overtook and grasped the shrill, frantically pinwheeling little dog, it seemed to him that he was directly under the bear. He could smell it, strong and hot and rank. Sprawling, he looked up where it loomed and towered over him like a thunderclap. It was quite familiar, until he remembered: this was the way he had used to dream about it.

Then it was gone. He didn't see it go. He knelt, holding the frantic fyce with both hands, hearing the abased wailing of the two hounds drawing further and further away, until Sam came up, carrying the gun. He laid it quietly down beside the boy and stood looking down at him. "You've done seed him twice now, with a gun in your hands," he said. "This time you couldn't have missed him."

The boy rose. He still held the fyce. Even in his arms it continued to yap frantically, surging and straining toward the fading sound of the hounds like a collection of live-wire springs. The boy was panting a little. "Neither could you," he said. "You had the gun. Why didn't you shoot him?"

Sam didn't seem to have heard. He put out his hand and touched the little dog in the boy's arms which still yapped and strained even though the two hounds were out of hearing now. "He's done gone," Sam said. "You can slack off and rest now, until next time." He stroked the little dog until it began to grow quiet under his hand. "You's almost the one we wants," he said. "You just aint big enough. We aint got that one yet. He will need to be just a little bigger than smart, and a little braver than either." He withdrew his hand from the fyce's head and stood looking into the woods where the bear and the hounds had vanished. "Somebody is going to, some day."

"I know it," the boy said. "That's why it must be one of us. So it wont be until the last day. When even he dont want it to last any longer."

So he should have hated and feared Lion. It was in the fourth summer, the fourth time he had made one in the cele-

bration of Major de Spain's and General Compson's birthday.
In the early spring Major de Spain's mare had foaled a horse
colt. One evening when Sam brought the horses and mules
up to stable them for the night, the colt was missing and it was
all he could do to get the frantic mare into the lot. He had
thought at first to let the mare lead him back to where she had
become separated from the foal. But she would not do it. She
would not even feint toward any particular part of the woods
or even in any particular direction. She merely ran, as if she
couldn't see, still frantic with terror. She whirled and ran at
Sam once, as if to attack him in some ultimate desperation, as
if she could not for the moment realise that he was a man and
a long-familiar one. He got her into the lot at last. It was too
dark by that time to back-track her, to unravel the erratic
course she had doubtless pursued.

He came to the house and told Major de Spain. It was an
animal, of course, a big one, and the colt was dead now, wherever it was. They all knew that. "It's a panther," General
Compson said at once. "The same one. That doe and fawn
last March." Sam had sent Major de Spain word of it when
Boon Hogganbeck came to the camp on a routine visit to see
how the stock had wintered—the doe's throat torn out, and
the beast had run down the helpless fawn and killed it too.

"Sam never did say that was a panther," Major de Spain
said. Sam said nothing now, standing behind Major de Spain
where they sat at supper, inscrutable, as if he were just waiting
for them to stop talking so he could go home. He didn't even
seem to be looking at anything. "A panther might jump a doe,
and he wouldn't have much trouble catching the fawn afterward. But no panther would have jumped that colt with the
dam right there with it. It was Old Ben," Major de Spain said.
"I'm disappointed in him. He has broken the rules. I didn't

think he would have done that. He has killed mine and McCaslin's dogs, but that was all right. We gambled the dogs against him; we gave each other warning. But now he has come into my house and destroyed my property, out of season too. He broke the rules. It was Old Ben, Sam." Still Sam said nothing, standing there until Major de Spain should stop talking. "We'll back-track her tomorrow and see," Major de Spain said.

Sam departed. He would not live in the camp; he had built himself a little hut something like Joe Baker's, only stouter, tighter, on the bayou a quarter-mile away, and a stout log crib where he stored a little corn for the shoat he raised each year. The next morning he was waiting when they waked. He had already found the colt. They did not even wait for breakfast. It was not far, not five hundred yards from the stable—the three-months' colt lying on its side, its throat torn out and the entrails and one ham partly eaten. It lay not as if it had been dropped but as if it had been struck and hurled, and no cat-mark, no claw-mark where a panther would have gripped it while finding its throat. They read the tracks where the frantic mare had circled and at last rushed in with that same ultimate desperation with which she had whirled on Sam Fathers yesterday evening, and the long tracks of dead and terrified running and those of the beast which had not even rushed at her when she advanced but had merely walked three or four paces toward her until she broke, and General Compson said, "Good God, what a wolf!"

Still Sam said nothing. The boy watched him while the men knelt, measuring the tracks. There was something in Sam's face now. It was neither exultation nor joy nor hope. Later, a man, the boy realised what it had been, and that Sam had known all the time what had made the tracks and what had torn the throat out of the doe in the spring and killed the fawn. It had been foreknowledge in Sam's face that morning. *And he was glad,* he told himself. *He was old. He had no children, no people, none of his blood anywhere above earth that he would ever meet again. And even if he were to, he could not have touched it, spoken to it, because for seventy years now he had had to be a negro. It was almost over now and he was glad.*

They returned to camp and had breakfast and came back with guns and the hounds. Afterward the boy realised that they also should have known then what killed the colt as well as Sam Fathers did. But that was neither the first nor the last time he had seen men rationalise from and even act upon their misconceptions. After Boon, standing astride the colt, had whipped the dogs away from it with his belt, they snuffed at the tracks. One of them, a young dog hound without judgment yet, bayed once, and they ran for a few feet on what seemed to be a trail. Then they stopped, looking back at the men, eager enough, not baffled, merely questioning, as if they were asking "Now what?" Then they rushed back to the colt, where Boon, still astride it, slashed at them with the belt.

"I never knew a trail to get cold that quick," General Compson said.

"Maybe a single wolf big enough to kill a colt with the dam right there beside it dont leave scent," Major de Spain said.

"Maybe it was a hant," Walter Ewell said. He looked at Tennie's Jim. "Hah, Jim?"

Because the hounds would not run it, Major de Spain had Sam hunt out and find the tracks a hundred yards farther on and they put the dogs on it again and again the young one bayed and not one of them realised then that the hound was not baying like a dog striking game but was merely bellowing like a country dog whose yard has been invaded. General Compson spoke to the boy and Boon and Tennie's Jim: to the squirrel hunters. "You boys keep the dogs with you this morning. He's probably hanging around somewhere, waiting to get his breakfast off the colt. You might strike him."

But they did not. The boy remembered how Sam stood watching them as they went into the woods with the leashed hounds—the Indian face in which he had never seen anything until it smiled, except that faint arching of the nostrils on that first morning when the hounds had found Old Ben. They took the hounds with them on the next day, though when they reached the place where they hoped to strike a fresh trail, the carcass of the colt was gone. Then on the third morning Sam was waiting again, this time until they had finished breakfast. He said, "Come." He led them to his house, his little hut, to the corn-crib beyond it. He had removed the corn and had made a deadfall of the door, baiting it with the colt's carcass; peering between the logs, they saw an animal almost the color of a gun or pistol barrel, what little time they had to examine its color or shape. It was not crouched nor even standing. It was in motion, in the air, coming toward them—a heavy body crashing with tremendous force against the door so that the thick door jumped and clattered in its frame, the animal, whatever it was, hurling itself against the door again seemingly before it could have touched the floor and got a new purchase to spring from. "Come away," Sam said, "fore he break his neck." Even when they retreated the heavy and measured crashes continued, the stout door jumping and clattering each time, and still no sound from the beast itself—no snarl, no cry.

"What in hell's name is it?" Major de Spain said.

"It's a dog," Sam said, his nostrils arching and collapsing

faintly and steadily and that faint, fierce milkiness in his eyes again as on that first morning when the hounds had struck the old bear. "It's the dog."

"*The* dog?" Major de Spain said.

"That's gonter hold Old Ben."

"Dog the devil," Major de Spain said. "I'd rather have Old Ben himself in my pack than that brute. Shoot him."

"No," Sam said.

"You'll never tame him. How do you ever expect to make an animal like that afraid of you?"

"I dont want him tame," Sam said; again the boy watched his nostrils and the fierce milky light in his eyes. "But I almost rather he be tame than scared, of me or any man or any thing. But he wont be neither, of nothing."

"Then what are you going to do with it?"

"You can watch," Sam said.

Each morning through the second week they would go to Sam's crib. He had removed a few shingles from the roof and had put a rope on the colt's carcass and had drawn it out when the trap fell. Each morning they would watch him lower a pail of water into the crib while the dog hurled itself tirelessly against the door and dropped back and leaped again. It never made any sound and there was nothing frenzied in the act but only a cold and grim indomitable determination. Toward the end of the week it stopped jumping at the door. Yet it had not weakened appreciably and it was not as if it had rationalised the fact that the door was not going to give. It was as if for that time it simply disdained to jump any longer. It was not down. None of them had ever seen it down. It stood, and they could see it now—part mastiff, something of Airedale and something of a dozen other strains probably, better than thirty inches at the shoulders and weighing as they guessed almost ninety pounds, with cold yellow eyes and a tremendous chest and over all that strange color like a blued gun-barrel.

Then the two weeks were up. They prepared to break camp. The boy begged to remain and his cousin let him. He moved into the little hut with Sam Fathers. Each morning he watched Sam lower the pail of water into the crib. By the end of that week the dog was down. It would rise and half stagger, half crawl to the water and drink and collapse again. One morning it could not even reach the water, could not raise its forequarters even from the floor. Sam took a short stick and prepared to enter the crib. "Wait," the boy said. "Let me get the gun——"

"No," Sam said. "He cant move now." Nor could it. It lay on its side while Sam touched it, its head and the gaunted body, the dog lying motionless, the yellow eyes open. They were not fierce and there was nothing of petty malevolence in them, but a cold and almost impersonal malignance like some natural force. It was not even looking at Sam nor at the boy peering at it between the logs.

Sam began to feed it again. The first time he had to raise its head so it could lap the broth. That night he left a bowl of broth containing lumps of meat where the dog could reach it. The next morning the bowl was empty and the dog was lying on its belly, its head up, the cold yellow eyes watching the door as Sam entered, no change whatever in the cold yellow eyes and still no sound from it even when it sprang, its aim and co-ordination still bad from weakness so that Sam had time to strike it down with the stick and leap from the crib and slam the door as the dog, still without having had time to get its feet under it to jump again seemingly, hurled itself against the door as if the two weeks of starving had never been.

At noon that day someone came whooping through the

woods from the direction of the camp. It was Boon. He came and looked for a while between the logs, at the tremendous dog lying again on its belly, its head up, the yellow eyes blinking sleepily at nothing: the indomitable and unbroken spirit. "What we better do," Boon said, "is to let that son of a bitch go and catch Old Ben and run him on the dog." He turned to the boy his weather-reddened and beetling face. "Get your traps together. Cass says for you to come on home. You been in here fooling with that horse-eating varmint long enough."

Boon had a borrowed mule at the camp; the buggy was waiting at the edge of the bottom. He was at home that night. He told McCaslin about it. "Sam's going to starve him again until he can go in and touch him. Then he will feed him again. Then he will starve him again, if he has to."

"But why?" McCaslin said. "What for? Even Sam will never tame that brute."

"We dont want him tame. We want him like he is. We just want him to find out at last that the only way he can get out of that crib and stay out of it is to do what Sam or somebody tells him to do. He's the dog that's going to stop Old Ben and hold him. We've already named him. His name is Lion."

Then November came at last. They returned to the camp. With General Compson and Major de Spain and his cousin and Walter and Boon he stood in the yard among the guns and bedding and boxes of food and watched Sam Fathers and Lion come up the lane from the lot—the Indian, the old man in battered overalls and rubber boots and a worn sheepskin coat and a hat which had belonged to the boy's father; the tremendous dog pacing gravely beside him. The hounds rushed out to meet them and stopped, except the young one which still had but little of judgment. It ran up to Lion, fawning. Lion didn't snap at it. He didn't even pause. He struck it rolling and yelping for five or six feet with a blow of one paw as a bear would have done and came on into the yard and stood, blinking sleepily at nothing, looking at no one, while Boon said, "Jesus. Jesus.—Will he let me touch him?"

"You can touch him," Sam said. "He dont care. He dont care about nothing or nobody."

The boy watched that too. He watched it for the next two years from that moment when Boon touched Lion's head and then knelt beside him, feeling the bones and muscles, the power. It was as if Lion were a woman—or perhaps Boon was the woman. That was more like it—the big, grave, sleepy-seeming dog which, as Sam Fathers said, cared about no man and no thing; and the violent, insensitive, hard-faced man with his touch of remote Indian blood and the mind almost of a child. He watched Boon take over Lion's feeding from Sam and Uncle Ash both. He would see Boon squatting in the cold rain beside the kitchen while Lion ate. Because Lion neither slept nor ate with the other dogs though none of them knew where he did sleep until in the second November, thinking until then that Lion slept in his kennel beside Sam Fathers' hut, when the boy's cousin McCaslin said something about it to Sam by sheer chance and Sam told him. And that night the boy and Major de Spain and McCaslin with a lamp entered the back room where Boon slept—the little, tight, airless room rank with the smell of Boon's unwashed body and his wet hunting-clothes—where Boon, snoring on his back, choked and waked and Lion raised his head beside him and looked back at them from his cold, slumbrous yellow eyes.

"Damn it, Boon," McCaslin said. "Get that dog out of here. He's got to run Old Ben tomorrow morning. How in hell do you expect him to smell anything fainter than a skunk after breathing you all night?"

"The way I smell aint hurt my nose none that I ever noticed," Boon said.

"It wouldn't matter if it had," Major de Spain said. "We're not depending on you to trail a bear. Put him outside. Put him under the house with the other dogs."

Boon began to get up. "He'll kill the first one that happens to yawn or sneeze in his face or touches him."

"I reckon not," Major de Spain said. "None of them are going to risk yawning in his face or touching him either, even asleep. Put him outside. I want his nose right tomorrow. Old Ben fooled him last year. I dont think he will do it again."

Boon put on his shoes without lacing them; in his long soiled underwear, his hair still tousled from sleep, he and Lion went out. The others returned to the front room and the poker game where McCaslin's and Major de Spain's hands waited for them on the table. After a while McCaslin said, "Do you want me to go back and look again?"

"No," Major de Spain said. "I call," he said to Walter Ewell. He spoke to McCaslin again. "If you do, dont tell me. I am beginning to see the first sign of my increasing age: I dont like to know that my orders have been disobeyed, even when I knew when I gave them that they would be. —A small pair," he said to Walter Ewell.

"How small?" Walter said.

"Very small," Major de Spain said.

And the boy, lying beneath his piled quilts and blankets waiting for sleep, knew likewise that Lion was already back in Boon's bed, for the rest of that night and the next one and during all the nights of the next November and the next one. He thought then: *I wonder what Sam thinks. He could have Lion with him, even if Boon is a white man. He could ask Major or*

McCaslin either. *And more than that. It was Sam's hand that
touched Lion first and Lion knows it.* Then he became a man
and he knew that too. It had been all right. That was the way it
should have been. Sam was the chief, the prince; Boon, the
plebeian, was his huntsman. Boon should have nursed the
dogs.

On the first morning that Lion led the pack after Old Ben,
seven strangers appeared in the camp. They were swampers:
gaunt, malaria-ridden men appearing from nowhere, who ran
trap-lines for coons or perhaps farmed little patches of cotton
and corn along the edge of the bottom, in clothes but little
better than Sam Fathers' and nowhere near as good as Tennie's Jim's, with worn shotguns and rifles, already squatting
patiently in the cold drizzle in the side yard when day broke.
They had a spokesman; afterward Sam Fathers told Major de
Spain how all during the past summer and fall they had
drifted into the camp singly or in pairs and threes, to look quietly at Lion for a while and then go away: "Mawnin, Major.
We heerd you was aimin to put that ere blue dawg on that old
two-toed bear this mawnin. We figgered we'd come up and
watch, if you dont mind. We wont do no shooting, lessen he
runs over us."

"You are welcome," Major de Spain said. "You are welcome to shoot. He's more your bear than ours."

"I reckon that aint no lie. I done fed him enough cawn to
have a sheer in him. Not to mention a shoat three years ago."

"I reckon I got a sheer too," another said. "Only it aint in
the bear." Major de Spain looked at him. He was chewing
tobacco. He spat. "Hit was a heifer calf. Nice un too. Last year.
When I finally found her, I reckon she looked about like that
colt of yourn looked last June."

"Oh," Major de Spain said. "Be welcome. If you see game in front of my dogs, shoot it."

Nobody shot Old Ben that day. No man saw him. The dogs jumped him within a hundred yards of the glade where the boy had seen him that day in the summer of his eleventh year. The boy was less than a quarter-mile away. He heard the jump but he could distinguish no voice among the dogs that he did not know and therefore would be Lion's, and he thought, believed, that Lion was not among them. Even the fact that they were going much faster than he had ever heard them run behind Old Ben before and that the high thin note of hysteria was missing now from their voices was not enough to disabuse him. He didn't comprehend until that night, when Sam told him that Lion would never cry on a trail. "He gonter growl when he catches Old Ben's throat," Sam said. "But he aint gonter never holler, no more than he ever done when he was jumping at that two-inch door. It's that blue dog in him. What you call it?"

"Airedale," the boy said.

Lion was there; the jump was just too close to the river. When Boon returned with Lion about eleven that night, he swore that Lion had stopped Old Ben once but that the hounds would not go in and Old Ben broke away and took to the river and swam for miles down it and he and Lion went down one bank for about ten miles and crossed and came up the other but it had begun to get dark before they struck any trail where Old Ben had come up out of the water, unless he was still in the water when he passed the ford where they crossed. Then he fell to cursing the hounds and ate the supper Uncle Ash had saved for him and went off to bed and after a while the boy opened the door of the little stale room thunderous with snoring and the great grave dog raised its head

from Boon's pillow and blinked at him for a moment and lowered its head again.

When the next November came and the last day, the day
on which it was now becoming traditional to save for Old Ben,
there were more than a dozen strangers waiting. They were
not all swampers this time. Some of them were townsmen,
from other county seats like Jefferson, who had heard about
Lion and Old Ben and had come to watch the great blue dog
keep his yearly rendezvous with the old two-toed bear. Some
of them didn't even have guns and the hunting-clothes and
boots they wore had been on a store shelf yesterday.

This time Lion jumped Old Ben more than five miles
from the river and bayed and held him and this time the
hounds went in, in a sort of desperate emulation. The boy
heard them; he was that near. He heard Boon whooping; he
heard the two shots when General Compson delivered both
barrels, one containing five buckshot, the other a single ball,
into the bear from as close as he could force his almost
unmanageable horse. He heard the dogs when the bear broke
free again. He was running now; panting, stumbling, his lungs
bursting, he reached the place where General Compson had
fired and where Old Ben had killed two of the hounds. He saw
the blood from General Compson's shots, but he could go no
further. He stopped, leaning against a tree for his breathing to
ease and his heart to slow, hearing the sound of the dogs as it
faded on and died away.

In camp that night—they had as guests five of the still terrified strangers in new hunting coats and boots who had been
lost all day until Sam Fathers went out and got them—he
heard the rest of it: how Lion had stopped and held the bear
again but only the one-eyed mule which did not mind the
smell of wild blood would approach and Boon was riding the

mule and Boon had never been known to hit anything. He shot at the bear five times with his pump gun, touching nothing, and Old Ben killed another hound and broke free once more and reached the river and was gone. Again Boon and Lion hunted as far down one bank as they dared. Too far; they crossed in the first of dusk and dark overtook them within a mile. And this time Lion found the broken trail, the blood perhaps, in the darkness where Old Ben had come up out of the water, but Boon had him on a rope, luckily, and he got down from the mule and fought Lion hand-to-hand until he got him back to camp. This time Boon didn't even curse. He stood in the door, muddy, spent, his huge gargoyle's face tragic and still amazed. "I missed him," he said. "I was in twenty-five feet of him and I missed him five times."

"But we have drawn blood," Major de Spain said. "General Compson drew blood. We have never done that before."

"But I missed him," Boon said. "I missed him five times. With Lion looking right at me."

"Never mind," Major de Spain said. "It was a damned fine race. And we drew blood. Next year we'll let General Compson or Walter ride Katie, and we'll get him."

Then McCaslin said, "Where is Lion, Boon?"

"I left him at Sam's," Boon said. He was already turning away. "I aint fit to sleep with him."

So he should have hated and feared Lion. Yet he did not. It seemed to him that there was a fatality in it. It seemed to him that something, he didn't know what, was beginning; had already begun. It was like the last act on a set stage. It was the beginning of the end of something, he didn't know what except that he would not grieve. He would be humble and proud that he had been found worthy to be a part of it too or even just to see it too.

3

It was December. It was the coldest December he had ever remembered. They had been in camp four days over two weeks, waiting for the weather to soften so that Lion and Old Ben could run their yearly race. Then they would break camp and go home. Because of these unforeseen additional days which they had had to pass waiting on the weather, with nothing to do but play poker, the whisky had given out and he and Boon were being sent to Memphis with a suitcase and a note from Major de Spain to Mr Semmes, the distiller, to get more. That is, Major de Spain and McCaslin were sending Boon to get the whisky and sending him to see that Boon got back with it or most of it or at least some of it.

Tennie's Jim waked him at three. He dressed rapidly, shivering, not so much from the cold because a fresh fire already boomed and roared on the hearth, but in that dead winter hour when the blood and the heart are slow and sleep is incomplete. He crossed the gap between house and kitchen, the gap of iron earth beneath the brilliant and rigid night where dawn would not begin for three hours yet, tasting, tongue palate and to the very bottom of his lungs the searing dark, and entered the kitchen, the lamplit warmth where the stove glowed, fogging the windows, and where Boon already sat at the table at breakfast, hunched over his plate, almost in his plate, his working jaws blue with stubble and his face innocent of water and his coarse, horse-mane hair innocent of comb—the quarter Indian, grandson of a Chickasaw squaw, who on occasion resented with his hard and furious fists the intimation of one single drop of alien blood and on others, usually after whisky, affirmed with the same fists and the same

fury that his father had been the full-blood Chickasaw and
even a chief and that even his mother had been only half
white. He was four inches over six feet; he had the mind of a
child, the heart of a horse, and little hard shoe-button eyes
without depth or meanness or generosity or viciousness or
gentleness or anything else, in the ugliest face the boy had
ever seen. It looked like somebody had found a walnut a little
larger than a football and with a machinist's hammer had
shaped features into it and then painted it, mostly red; not
Indian red but a fine bright ruddy color which whisky might
have had something to do with but which was mostly just
happy and violent out-of-doors, the wrinkles in it not the
residue of the forty years it had survived but from squinting
into the sun or into the gloom of canebrakes where game had
run, baked into it by the camp fires before which he had lain
trying to sleep on the cold November or December ground
while waiting for daylight so he could rise and hunt again, as
though time were merely something he walked through as he
did through air, aging him no more than air did. He was brave,
faithful, improvident and unreliable; he had neither profession job nor trade and owned one vice and one virtue: whisky,
and that absolute and unquestioning fidelity to Major de
Spain and the boy's cousin McCaslin. "Sometimes I'd call
them both virtues," Major de Spain said once. "Or both
vices," McCaslin said.

He ate his breakfast, hearing the dogs under the kitchen,
wakened by the smell of frying meat or perhaps by the feet
overhead. He heard Lion once, short and peremptory, as the
best hunter in any camp has only to speak once to all save the
fools, and none other of Major de Spain's and McCaslin's
dogs were Lion's equal in size and strength and perhaps even

in courage, but they were not fools; Old Ben had killed the last fool among them last year.

Tennie's Jim came in as they finished. The wagon was outside. Ash decided he would drive them over to the log-line where they would flag the outbound log-train and let Tennie's Jim wash the dishes. The boy knew why. It would not be the first time he had listened to old Ash badgering Boon.

It was cold. The wagon wheels banged and clattered on the frozen ground; the sky was fixed and brilliant. He was not shivering, he was shaking, slow and steady and hard, the food he had just eaten still warm and solid inside him while his outside shook slow and steady around it as though his stomach floated loose. "They wont run this morning," he said. "No dog will have any nose today."

"Cep Lion," Ash said. "Lion dont need no nose. All he need is a bear." He had wrapped his feet in towsacks and he had a quilt from his pallet bed on the kitchen floor drawn over his head and wrapped around him until in the thin brilliant starlight he looked like nothing at all that the boy had ever seen before. "He run a bear through a thousand-acre ice-house. Catch him too. Them other dogs dont matter because they aint going to keep up with Lion nohow, long as he got a bear in front of him."

"What's wrong with the other dogs?" Boon said. "What the hell do you know about it anyway? This is the first time you've had your tail out of that kitchen since we got here except to chop a little wood."

"Aint nothing wrong with them," Ash said. "And long as it's left up to them, aint nothing going to be. I just wish I had knowed all my life how to take care of my health good as them hounds knows."

"Well, they aint going to run this morning," Boon said. His voice was harsh and positive. "Major promised they wouldn't until me and Ike get back."

"Weather gonter break today. Gonter soft up. Rain by night." Then Ash laughed, chuckled, somewhere inside the quilt which concealed even his face. "Hum up here, mules!" he said, jerking the reins so that the mules leaped forward and snatched the lurching and banging wagon for several feet before they slowed again into their quick, short-paced, rapid plodding. "Sides, I like to know why Major need to wait on you. It's Lion he aiming to use. I aint never heard tell of you bringing no bear nor no other kind of meat into this camp."

Now Boon's going to curse Ash or maybe even hit him, the boy thought. But Boon never did, never had; the boy knew he never would even though four years ago Boon had shot five times with a borrowed pistol at a negro on the street in Jefferson, with the same result as when he had shot five times at Old Ben last fall. "By God," Boon said, "he aint going to put Lion or no other dog on nothing until I get back tonight. Because he promised me. Whip up them mules and keep them whipped up. Do you want me to freeze to death?"

They reached the log-line and built a fire. After a while the log-train came up out of the woods under the paling east and Boon flagged it. Then in the warm caboose the boy slept again while Boon and the conductor and brakeman talked about Lion and Old Ben as people later would talk about Sullivan and Kilrain and, later still, about Dempsey and Tunney. Dozing, swaying as the springless caboose lurched and clattered, he would hear them still talking, about the shoats and calves Old Ben had killed and the cribs he had rifled and the traps and deadfalls he had wrecked and the lead he probably carried under his hide—Old Ben, the two-toed bear in a land

where bears with trap-ruined feet had been called Two-Toe or
Three-Toe or Cripple-Foot for fifty years, only Old Ben was an
extra bear (the head bear, General Compson called him) and
so had earned a name such as a human man could have worn
and not been sorry.

They reached Hoke's at sunup. They emerged from the
warm caboose in their hunting clothes, the muddy boots and
stained khaki and Boon's blue unshaven jowls. But that was all
right. Hoke's was a sawmill and commissary and two stores and
a loading-chute on a sidetrack from the main line, and all the
men in it wore boots and khaki too. Presently the Memphis
train came. Boon bought three packages of popcorn-and-
molasses and a bottle of beer from the news butch and the boy
went to sleep again to the sound of his chewing.

But in Memphis it was not all right. It was as if the high
buildings and the hard pavements, the fine carriages and the
horse cars and the men in starched collars and neckties made
their boots and khaki look a little rougher and a little muddier
and made Boon's beard look worse and more unshaven and
his face look more and more like he should never have
brought it out of the woods at all or at least out of reach of
Major de Spain or McCaslin or someone who knew it and
could have said, "Dont be afraid. He wont hurt you." He
walked through the station, on the slick floor, his face moving
as he worked the popcorn out of his teeth with his tongue, his
legs spraddled and stiff in the hips as if he were walking on
buttered glass, and that blue stubble on his face like the filings
from a new gun-barrel. They passed the first saloon. Even
through the closed doors the boy could seem to smell the saw-
dust and the reek of old drink. Boon began to cough. He
coughed for something less than a minute. "Damn this cold,"
he said. "I'd sure like to know where I got it."

"Back there in the station," the boy said.

Boon had started to cough again. He stopped. He looked at the boy. "What?" he said.

"You never had it when we left camp nor on the train either." Boon looked at him, blinking. Then he stopped blinking. He didn't cough again. He said quietly:

"Lend me a dollar. Come on. You've got it. If you ever had one, you've still got it. I dont mean you are tight with your money because you aint. You just dont never seem to ever think of nothing you want. When I was sixteen a dollar bill melted off of me before I even had time to read the name of the bank that issued it." He said quietly: "Let me have a dollar, Ike."

"You promised Major. You promised McCaslin. Not till we get back to camp."

"All right," Boon said in that quiet and patient voice. "What can I do on just one dollar? You aint going to lend me another."

"You're damn right I aint," the boy said, his voice quiet too, cold with rage which was not at Boon, remembering: Boon snoring in a hard chair in the kitchen so he could watch the clock and wake him and McCaslin and drive them the seventeen miles in to Jefferson to catch the train to Memphis; the wild, never-bridled Texas paint pony which he had persuaded McCaslin to let him buy and which he and Boon had bought at auction for four dollars and seventy-five cents and fetched home wired between two gentle old mares with pieces of barbed wire and which had never even seen shelled corn before and didn't even know what it was unless the grains were bugs maybe and at last (he was ten and Boon had been ten all his life) Boon said the pony was gentled and with a towsack over its head and four negroes to hold it they backed it into an

old two-wheeled cart and hooked up the gear and he and
Boon got up and Boon said, "All right, boys. Let him go" and
one of the negroes—it was Tennie's Jim—snatched the towsack off and leaped for his life and they lost the first wheel
against a post of the open gate only at that moment Boon
caught him by the scruff of the neck and flung him into the
roadside ditch so he only saw the rest of it in fragments: the
other wheel as it slammed through the side gate and crossed
the back yard and leaped up onto the gallery and scraps of the
cart here and there along the road and Boon vanishing rapidly
on his stomach in the leaping and spurting dust and still holding the reins until they broke too and two days later they
finally caught the pony seven miles away still wearing the
hames and the headstall of the bridle around its neck like a
duchess with two necklaces at one time. He gave Boon the
dollar.

"All right," Boon said. "Come on in out of the cold."

"I aint cold," he said.

"You can have some lemonade."

"I dont want any lemonade."

The door closed behind him. The sun was well up now. It
was a brilliant day, though Ash had said it would rain before
night. Already it was warmer; they could run tomorrow. He
felt the old lift of the heart, as pristine as ever, as on the first
day; he would never lose it, no matter how old in hunting and
pursuit: the best, the best of all breathing, the humility and the
pride. He must stop thinking about it. Already it seemed to
him that he was running, back to the station, to the tracks
themselves: the first train going south; he must stop thinking
about it. The street was busy. He watched the big Norman
draft horses, the Percherons; the trim carriages from which the
men in the fine overcoats and the ladies rosy in furs descended

and entered the station. (They were still next door to it but one.) Twenty years ago his father had ridden into Memphis as a member of Colonel Sartoris' horse in Forrest's command, up Main street and (the tale told) into the lobby of the Gayoso Hotel where the Yankee officers sat in the leather chairs spitting into the tall bright cuspidors and then out again, scot-free——

The door opened behind him. Boon was wiping his mouth on the back of his hand. "All right," he said. "Let's go tend to it and get the hell out of here."

They went and had the suitcase packed. He never knew where or when Boon got the other bottle. Doubtless Mr Semmes gave it to him. When they reached Hoke's again at sundown, it was empty. They could get a return train to Hoke's in two hours; they went straight back to the station as Major de Spain and then McCaslin had told Boon to do and then ordered him to do and had sent the boy along to see that he did. Boon took the first drink from his bottle in the wash room. A man in a uniform cap came to tell him he couldn't drink there and looked at Boon's face once and said nothing. The next time he was pouring into his water glass beneath the edge of a table in the restaurant when the manager (she was a woman) did tell him he couldn't drink there and he went back to the washroom. He had been telling the negro waiter and all the other people in the restaurant who couldn't help but hear him and who had never heard of Lion and didn't want to, about Lion and Old Ben. Then he happened to think of the zoo. He had found out that there was another train to Hoke's at three oclock and so they would spend the time at the zoo and take the three oclock train until he came back from the washroom for the third time. Then they would take the first train back to camp, get Lion and come back to the zoo where, he said, the bears were fed on ice cream and lady fingers and he would match Lion against them all.

So they missed the first train, the one they were supposed to take, but he got Boon onto the three oclock train and they were all right again, with Boon not even going to the wash-room now but drinking in the aisle and talking about Lion and the men he buttonholed no more daring to tell Boon he couldn't drink there than the man in the station had dared.

When they reached Hoke's at sundown, Boon was asleep. The boy waked him at last and got him and the suitcase off the train and he even persuaded him to eat some supper at the sawmill commissary. So he was all right when they got in the caboose of the log-train to go back into the woods, with the sun going down red and the sky already overcast and the ground would not freeze tonight. It was the boy who slept now, sitting behind the ruby stove while the springless caboose jumped and clattered and Boon and the brakeman and the conductor talked about Lion and Old Ben because they knew what Boon was talking about because this was home. "Overcast and already thawing," Boon said. "Lion will get him tomorrow."

It would have to be Lion, or somebody. It would not be Boon. He had never hit anything bigger than a squirrel that anybody ever knew, except the negro woman that day when he was shooting at the negro man. He was a big negro and not ten feet away but Boon shot five times with the pistol he had borrowed from Major de Spain's negro coachman and the negro he was shooting at outed with a dollar-and-a-half mail-order pistol and would have burned Boon down with it only it never went off, it just went snicksnicksnicksnicksnick five times and Boon still blasting away and he broke a plate-glass window that cost McCaslin forty-five dollars and hit a negro woman who happened to be passing in the leg only Major de

Spain paid for that; he and McCaslin cut cards, the plate-glass window against the negro woman's leg. And the first day on stand this year, the first morning in camp, the buck ran right over Boon; he heard Boon's old pump gun go whow. whow. whow. whow. whow. and then his voice: "God damn, here he comes! Head him! Head him!" and when he got there the buck's tracks and the five exploded shells were not twenty paces apart.

There were five guests in camp that night, from Jefferson: Mr Bayard Sartoris and his son and General Compson's son and two others. And the next morning he looked out the window, into the gray thin drizzle of daybreak which Ash had predicted, and there they were, standing and squatting beneath the thin rain, almost two dozen of them who had fed Old Ben corn and shoats and even calves for ten years, in their worn hats and hunting coats and overalls which any town negro would have thrown away or burned and only the rubber boots strong and sound, and the worn and blueless guns and some even without guns. While they ate breakfast a dozen more arrived, mounted and on foot: loggers from the camp thirteen miles below and sawmill men from Hoke's and the only gun among them that one which the log-train conductor carried: so that when they went into the woods this morning Major de Spain led a party almost as strong, excepting that some of them were not armed, as some he had led in the last darkening days of '64 and '65. The little yard would not hold them. They overflowed it, into the lane where Major de Spain sat his mare while Ash in his dirty apron thrust the greasy cartridges into his carbine and passed it up to him and the great grave blue dog stood at his stirrup not as a dog stands but as a horse stands, blinking his sleepy topaz eyes at nothing, deaf even to the yelling of the hounds which Boon and Tennie's Jim held on leash.

"We'll put General Compson on Katie this morning," Major de Spain said. "He drew blood last year; if he'd had a mule then that would have stood, he would have——"

"No," General Compson said. "I'm too old to go helling through the woods on a mule or a horse or anything else any more. Besides, I had my chance last year and missed it. I'm going on a stand this morning. I'm going to let that boy ride Katie."

"No, wait," McCaslin said. "Ike's got the rest of his life to hunt bears in. Let somebody else——"

"No," General Compson said. "I want Ike to ride Katie. He's already a better woodsman than you or me either and in another ten years he'll be as good as Walter."

At first he couldn't believe it, not until Major de Spain spoke to him. Then he was up, on the one-eyed mule which would not spook at wild blood, looking down at the dog motionless at Major de Spain's stirrup, looking in the gray streaming light bigger than a calf, bigger than he knew it actually was—the big head, the chest almost as big as his own, the blue hide beneath which the muscles flinched or quivered to no touch since the heart which drove blood to them loved no man and no thing, standing as a horse stands yet different from a horse which infers only weight and speed while Lion inferred not only courage and all else that went to make up the will and desire to pursue and kill, but endurance, the will and desire to endure beyond all imaginable limits of flesh in order to overtake and slay. Then the dog looked at him. It moved its head and looked at him across the trivial uproar of the hounds, out of the yellow eyes as depthless as Boon's, as free as Boon's of meanness or generosity or gentleness or viciousness. They were just cold and sleepy. Then it blinked, and he knew it was not looking at him and never had been, without even bothering to turn its head away.

That morning he heard the first cry. Lion had already vanished while Sam and Tennie's Jim were putting saddles on the mule and horse which had drawn the wagon and he watched the hounds as they crossed and cast, snuffing and whimpering, until they too disappeared. Then he and Major de Spain and Sam and Tennie's Jim rode after them and heard the first cry out of the wet and thawing woods not two hundred yards ahead, high, with that abject, almost human quality he had come to know, and the other hounds joining in until the gloomed woods rang and clamored. They rode then. It seemed to him that he could actually see the big blue dog boring on, silent, and the bear too: the thick, locomotive-like shape which he had seen that day four years ago crossing the blow-down, crashing on ahead of the dogs faster than he had believed it could have moved, drawing away even from the running mules. He heard a shotgun, once. The woods had opened, they were going fast, the clamor faint and fading on ahead; they passed the man who had fired—a swamper, a pointing arm, a gaunt face, the small black orifice of his yelling studded with rotten teeth.

He heard the changed note in the hounds' uproar and two hundred yards ahead he saw them. The bear had turned. He saw Lion drive in without pausing and saw the bear strike him aside and lunge into the yelling hounds and kill one of them almost in its tracks and whirl and run again. Then they were in a streaming tide of dogs. He heard Major de Spain and Tennie's Jim shouting and the pistol sound of Tennie's Jim's leather thong as he tried to turn them. Then he and Sam

Fathers were riding alone. One of the hounds had kept on with Lion though. He recognised its voice. It was the young hound which even a year ago had had no judgment and which, by the lights of the other hounds anyway, still had none. *Maybe that's what courage is,* he thought. "Right," Sam said behind him. "Right. We got to turn him from the river if we can."

Now they were in cane: a brake. He knew the path through it as well as Sam did. They came out of the undergrowth and struck the entrance almost exactly. It would traverse the brake and come out onto a high open ridge above the river. He heard the flat clap of Walter Ewell's rifle, then two more. "No," Sam said. "I can hear the hound. Go on."

They emerged from the narrow roofless tunnel of snapping and hissing cane, still galloping, onto the open ridge below which the thick yellow river, reflectionless in the gray and streaming light, seemed not to move. Now he could hear the hound too. It was not running. The cry was a high frantic yapping and Boon was running along the edge of the bluff, his old gun leaping and jouncing against his back on its sling made of a piece of cotton plowline. He whirled and ran up to them, wild-faced, and flung himself onto the mule behind the boy. "That damn boat!" he cried. "It's on the other side! He went straight across! Lion was too close to him! That little hound too! Lion was so close I couldn't shoot! Go on!" he cried, beating his heels into the mule's flanks. "Go on!"

They plunged down the bank, slipping and sliding in the thawed earth, crashing through the willows and into the water. He felt no shock, no cold, he on one side of the swimming mule, grasping the pommel with one hand and holding his gun above the water with the other, Boon opposite him. Sam was behind them somewhere, and then the river, the water about them, was full of dogs. They swam faster than the mules; they were scrabbling up the bank before the mules touched bottom. Major de Spain was whooping from the bank they had just left and, looking back, he saw Tennie's Jim and the horse as they went into the water.

Now the woods ahead of them and the rain-heavy air were one uproar. It rang and clamored; it echoed and broke against the bank behind them and reformed and clamored and rang until it seemed to the boy that all the hounds which had ever bayed game in this land were yelling down at him. He got his leg over the mule as it came up out of the water. Boon didn't try to mount again. He grasped one stirrup as they went up the bank and crashed through the undergrowth which fringed the bluff and saw the bear, on its hind feet, its back against a tree while the bellowing hounds swirled around it and once more Lion drove in, leaping clear of the ground.

This time the bear didn't strike him down. It caught the dog in both arms, almost loverlike, and they both went down. He was off the mule now. He drew back both hammers of the gun but he could see nothing but moiling spotted houndbodies until the bear surged up again. Boon was yelling something, he could not tell what; he could see Lion still clinging to the bear's throat and he saw the bear, half erect, strike one of the hounds with one paw and hurl it five or six feet and then, rising and rising as though it would never stop, stand erect again and begin to rake at Lion's belly with its forepaws. Then Boon was running. The boy saw the gleam of the blade in his hand and watched him leap among the hounds, hurdling them, kicking them aside as he ran, and fling himself astride the bear as he had hurled himself onto the mule, his legs locked around the bear's belly, his left arm under the bear's throat where Lion clung, and the glint of the knife as it rose and fell.

It fell just once. For an instant they almost resembled a piece of statuary: the clinging dog, the bear, the man stride its back, working and probing the buried blade. Then they went down, pulled over backward by Boon's weight, Boon under-neath. It was the bear's back which reappeared first but at once Boon was astride it again. He had never released the knife and again the boy saw the almost infinitesimal move-ment of his arm and shoulder as he probed and sought; then the bear surged erect, raising with it the man and the dog too, and turned and still carrying the man and the dog it took two or three steps toward the woods on its hind feet as a man would have walked and crashed down. It didn't collapse, crumple. It fell all of a piece, as a tree falls, so that all three of them, man dog and bear, seemed to bounce once.

He and Tennie's Jim ran forward. Boon was kneeling at the bear's head. His left ear was shredded, his left coat sleeve was completely gone, his right boot had been ripped from knee to instep; the bright blood thinned in the thin rain down his leg and hand and arm and down the side of his face which was no longer wild but was quite calm. Together they prized Lion's jaws from the bear's throat. "Easy, goddamn it," Boon said. "Cant you see his guts are all out of him?" He began to remove his coat. He spoke to Tennie's Jim in that calm voice: "Bring the boat up. It's about a hundred yards down the bank there. I saw it." Tennie's Jim rose and went away. Then, and he could not remember if it had been a call or an exclamation from Tennie's Jim or if he had glanced up by chance, he saw Tennie's Jim stooping and saw Sam Fathers lying motionless on his face in the trampled mud.

The mule had not thrown him. He remembered that Sam was down too even before Boon began to run. There was no mark on him whatever and when he and Boon turned him over, his eyes were open and he said something in that tongue which he and Joe Baker had used to speak together. But he couldn't move. Tennie's Jim brought the skiff up; they could hear him shouting to Major de Spain across the river. Boon wrapped Lion in his hunting coat and carried him down to the skiff and they carried Sam down and returned and hitched the bear to the one-eyed mule's saddle-bow with Tennie's Jim's leash-thong and dragged him down to the skiff and got him into it and left Tennie's Jim to swim the horse and the two mules back across. Major de Spain caught the bow of the skiff as Boon jumped out and past him before it touched the bank. He looked at Old Ben and said quietly: "Well." Then he walked into the water and leaned down and touched Sam and Sam looked up at him and said something in that old tongue he and Joe Baker spoke. "You dont know what happened?" Major de Spain said.

"No, sir," the boy said. "It wasn't the mule. It wasn't anything. He was off the mule when Boon ran in on the bear. Then we looked up and he was lying on the ground." Boon was shouting at Tennie's Jim, still in the middle of the river.

"Come on, goddamn it!" he said. "Bring me that mule!"

"What do you want with a mule?" Major de Spain said.

Boon didn't even look at him. "I'm going to Hoke's to get the doctor," he said in that calm voice, his face quite calm beneath the steady thinning of the bright blood.

"You need a doctor yourself," Major de Spain said. "Tennie's Jim——"

"Damn that," Boon said. He turned on Major de Spain.

His face was still calm, only his voice was a pitch higher. "Cant you see his goddamn guts are all out of him?"

"Boon!" Major de Spain said. They looked at one another. Boon was a good head taller than Major de Spain; even the boy was taller now than Major de Spain.

"I've got to get the doctor," Boon said. "His goddamn guts——"

"All right," Major de Spain said. Tennie's Jim came up out of the water. The horse and the sound mule had already scented Old Ben; they surged and plunged all the way up to the top of the bluff, dragging Tennie's Jim with them, before he could stop them and tie them and come back. Major de Spain unlooped the leather thong of his compass from his buttonhole and gave it to Tennie's Jim. "Go straight to Hoke's," he said. "Bring Doctor Crawford back with you. Tell him there are two men to be looked at. Take my mare. Can you find the road from here?"

"Yes, sir," Tennie's Jim said.

"All right," Major de Spain said. "Go on." He turned to the boy. "Take the mules and the horse and go back and get the wagon. We'll go on down the river in the boat to Coon bridge. Meet us there. Can you find it again?"

"Yes, sir," the boy said.

"All right. Get started."

He went back to the wagon. He realised then how far they had run. It was already afternoon when he put the mules into the traces and tied the horse's lead-rope to the tail-gate. He reached Coon bridge at dusk. The skiff was already there. Before he could see it and almost before he could see the water he had to leap from the tilting wagon, still holding the reins, and work around to where he could grasp the bit and then the ear of the plunging sound mule and dig his heels and hold it until Boon came up the bank. The rope of the led horse had already snapped and it had already disappeared up the road toward camp. They turned the wagon around and took the mules out and he led the sound mule a hundred yards up the road and tied it. Boon had already brought Lion up to the wagon and Sam was sitting up in the skiff now and when they raised him he tried to walk, up the bank and to the wagon and he tried to climb into the wagon but Boon did not wait; he picked Sam up bodily and set him on the seat. Then they hitched Old Ben to the one-eyed mule's saddle again and dragged him up the bank and set two skid-poles into the open tail-gate and got him into the wagon and he went and got the sound mule and Boon fought it into the traces, striking it across its hard hollow-sounding face until it came into position and stood trembling. Then the rain came down, as though it had held off all day waiting on them.

They returned to camp through it, through the streaming and sightless dark, hearing long before they saw any light the horn and the spaced shots to guide them. When they came to Sam's dark little hut he tried to stand up. He spoke again in the tongue of the old fathers; then he said clearly: "Let me out. Let me out."

"He hasn't got any fire," Major said. "Go on!" he said sharply.

But Sam was struggling now, trying to stand up. "Let me out, master," he said. "Let me go home."

So he stopped the wagon and Boon got down and lifted Sam out. He did not wait to let Sam try to walk this time. He carried him into the hut and Major de Spain got light on a paper spill from the buried embers on the hearth and lit the lamp and Boon put Sam on his bunk and drew off his boots and Major de Spain covered him and the boy was not there, he was holding the mules, the sound one which was trying again to bolt since when the wagon stopped Old Ben's scent drifted forward again along the streaming blackness of air, but Sam's eyes were probably open again on that profound look which saw further than them or the hut, further than the death of a bear and the dying of a dog. Then they went on, toward the long wailing of the horn and the shots which seemed each to linger intact somewhere in the thick streaming air until the next spaced report joined and blended with it, to the lighted house, the bright streaming windows, the quiet faces as Boon entered, bloody and quite calm, carrying the bundled coat. He laid Lion, blood coat and all, on his stale sheetless pallet bed which not even Ash, as deft in the house as a woman, could ever make smooth.

The sawmill doctor from Hoke's was already there. Boon would not let the doctor touch him until he had seen to Lion. He wouldn't risk giving Lion chloroform. He put the entrails back and sewed him up without it while Major de Spain held his head and Boon his feet. But he never tried to move. He lay there, the yellow eyes open upon nothing while the quiet men in the new hunting clothes and in the old ones crowded into the little airless room rank with the smell of Boon's body and garments, and watched. Then the doctor cleaned and disinfected Boon's face and arm and leg and bandaged them and, the boy in front with a lantern and the doctor and McCaslin and Major de Spain and General Compson following, they went to Sam Fathers' hut. Tennie's Jim had built up the fire; he squatted before it, dozing. Sam had not moved since Boon had put him in the bunk and Major de Spain had covered him with the blankets, yet he opened his eyes and looked from one to another of the faces and when McCaslin touched his shoulder and said, "Sam. The doctor wants to look at you," he even drew his hands out of the blanket and began to fumble at his shirt buttons until McCaslin said, "Wait. We'll do it." They undressed him. He lay there—the copper-brown, almost hairless body, the old man's body, the old man, the wild man not even one generation from the woods, childless, kinless, peopleless—motionless, his eyes open but no longer looking at any of them, while the doctor examined him and drew the blankets up and put the stethoscope back into his bag and snapped the bag and only the boy knew that Sam too was going to die.

"Exhaustion," the doctor said. "Shock maybe. A man his age swimming rivers in December. He'll be all right. Just make him stay in bed for a day or two. Will there be somebody here with him?"

"There will be somebody here," Major de Spain said.

They went back to the house, to the rank little room where Boon still sat on the pallet bed with Lion's head under his hand while the men, the ones who had hunted behind Lion and the ones who had never seen him before today, came quietly in to look at him and went away. Then it was dawn and they all went out into the yard to look at Old Ben, with his eyes open too and his lips snarled back from his worn teeth and his mutilated foot and the little hard lumps under his skin which were the old bullets (there were fifty-two of them, buckshot rifle and ball) and the single almost invisible slit under his left shoulder where Boon's blade had finally found his life. Then Ash began to beat on the bottom of the dishpan with a heavy spoon to call them to breakfast and it was the first time he could remember hearing no sound from the dogs under the kitchen while they were eating. It was as if the

old bear, even dead there in the yard, was a more potent terror
still than they could face without Lion between them.

The rain had stopped during the night. By midmorning
the thin sun appeared, rapidly burning away mist and cloud,
warming the air and the earth; it would be one of those windless Mississippi December days which are a sort of Indian
summer's Indian summer. They moved Lion out to the front
gallery, into the sun. It was Boon's idea. "Goddamn it," he
said, "he never did want to stay in the house until I made him.
You know that." He took a crowbar and loosened the floor
boards under his pallet bed so it could be raised, mattress and
all, without disturbing Lion's position, and they carried him
out to the gallery and put him down facing the woods.

Then he and the doctor and McCaslin and Major de
Spain went to Sam's hut. This time Sam didn't open his eyes
and his breathing was so quiet, so peaceful that they could
hardly see that he breathed. The doctor didn't even take out
his stethoscope nor even touch him. "He's all right," the doctor said. "He didn't even catch cold. He just quit."

"Quit?" McCaslin said.

"Yes. Old people do that sometimes. Then they get a good
night's sleep or maybe it's just a drink of whisky, and they
change their minds."

They returned to the house. And then they began to
arrive—the swamp-dwellers, the gaunt men who ran traplines
and lived on quinine and coons and river water, the farmers of
little corn- and cotton-patches along the bottom's edge whose
fields and cribs and pig-pens the old bear had rifled, the loggers from the camp and the sawmill men from Hoke's and the
town men from further away than that, whose hounds the old
bear had slain and traps and deadfalls he had wrecked and

whose lead he carried. They came up mounted and on foot and in wagons, to enter the yard and look at him and then go on to the front where Lion lay, filling the little yard and overflowing it until there were almost a hundred of them squatting and standing in the warm and drowsing sunlight, talking quietly of hunting, of the game and the dogs which ran it, of hounds and bear and deer and men of yesterday vanished from the earth, while from time to time the great blue dog would open his eyes, not as if he were listening to them but as though to look at the woods for a moment before closing his eyes again, to remember the woods or to see that they were still there. He died at sundown.

Major de Spain broke camp that night. They carried Lion into the woods, or Boon carried him that is, wrapped in a quilt from his bed, just as he had refused to let anyone else touch Lion yesterday until the doctor got there; Boon carrying Lion, and the boy and General Compson and Walter and still almost fifty of them following with lanterns and lighted pineknots—men from Hoke's and even further, who would have to ride out of the bottom in the dark, and swampers and trappers who would have to walk even, scattering toward the little hidden huts where they lived. And Boon would let nobody else dig the grave either and lay Lion in it and cover him and then General Compson stood at the head of it while the blaze and smoke of the pine-knots streamed away among the winter branches and spoke as he would have spoken over a man. Then they returned to camp. Major de Spain and McCaslin and Ash had rolled and tied all the bedding. The mules were hitched to the wagon and pointed out of the bottom and the wagon was already loaded and the stove in the kitchen was cold and the table was set with scraps of cold food and bread and only the coffee was hot when the boy ran into the kitchen where Major de Spain and McCaslin had already eaten. "What?" he cried. "What? I'm not going."

"Yes," McCaslin said, "we're going out tonight. Major wants to get on back home."

"No!" he said. "I'm going to stay."

"You've got to be back in school Monday. You've already missed a week more than I intended. It will take you from now until Monday to catch up. Sam's all right. You heard Doctor Crawford. I'm going to leave Boon and Tennie's Jim both to stay with him until he feels like getting up."

He was panting. The others had come in. He looked rapidly and almost frantically around at the other faces. Boon had a fresh bottle. He upended it and started the cork by striking the bottom of the bottle with the heel of his hand and drew the cork with his teeth and spat it out and drank. "You're damn right you're going back to school," Boon said. "Or I'll burn the tail off of you myself if Cass dont, whether you are sixteen or sixty. Where in hell do you expect to get without education? Where would Cass be? Where in hell would I be if I hadn't never went to school?"

He looked at McCaslin again. He could feel his breath coming shorter and shorter and shallower and shallower, as if there were not enough air in the kitchen for that many to breathe. "This is just Thursday. I'll come home Sunday night on one of the horses. I'll come home Sunday, then. I'll make up the time I lost studying Sunday night. McCaslin," he said, without even despair.

"No, I tell you," McCaslin said. "Sit down here and eat your supper. We're going out to——"

"Hold up, Cass," General Compson said. The boy did not know General Compson had moved until he put his hand on his shoulder. "What is it, bud?" he said.

"I've got to stay," he said. "I've got to."

"All right," General Compson said. "You can stay. If missing an extra week of school is going to throw you so far behind you'll have to sweat to find out what some hired pedagogue put between the covers of a book, you better quit altogether.— And you shut up, Cass," he said, though McCaslin had not spoken. "You've got one foot straddled into a farm and the other foot straddled into a bank; you aint even got a good hand-hold where this boy was already an old man long before you damned Sartorises and Edmondses invented farms and banks to keep yourselves from having to find out what this boy was born knowing and fearing too maybe but without being afraid, that could go ten miles on a compass because he wanted to look at a bear none of us had ever got near enough to put a bullet in and looked at the bear and came the ten miles back on the compass in the dark; maybe by God that's the why and the wherefore of farms and banks.— I reckon you still aint going to tell what it is?"

But still he could not. "I've got to stay," he said.

"All right," General Compson said. "There's plenty of grub left. And you'll come home Sunday, like you promised McCaslin? Not Sunday night: Sunday."

"Yes, sir," he said.

"All right," General Compson said. "Sit down and eat, boys," he said. "Let's get started. It's going to be cold before we get home."

They ate. The wagon was already loaded and ready to depart; all they had to do was to get into it. Boon would drive them out to the road, to the farmer's stable where the surrey had been left. He stood beside the wagon, in silhouette on the sky, turbaned like a Paythan and taller than any there, the bottle tilted. Then he flung the bottle from his lips without even lowering it, spinning and glinting in the faint starlight, empty. "Them that's going," he said, "get in the goddamn wagon. Them that aint, get out of the goddamn way." The others got in. Boon mounted to the seat beside General Compson and the wagon moved, on into the obscurity until the boy could no longer see it, even the moving density of it amid the greater night. But he could still hear it, for a long while: the slow, deliberate banging of the wooden frame as it lurched from rut to rut. And he could hear Boon even when he could no longer hear the wagon. He was singing, harsh, tuneless, loud.

That was Thursday. On Saturday morning Tennie's Jim left on McCaslin's woods-horse which had not been out of the bottom one time now in six years, and late that afternoon rode through the gate on the spent horse and on to the commissary where McCaslin was rationing the tenants and the wage-hands for the coming week, and this time McCaslin fore-stalled any necessity or risk of having to wait while Major de Spain's surrey was being horsed and harnessed. He took their own, and with Tennie's Jim already asleep in the back seat he drove in to Jefferson and waited while Major de Spain changed to boots and put on his overcoat, and they drove the thirty miles in the dark of that night and at daybreak on Sun-day morning they swapped to the waiting mare and mule and as the sun rose they rode out of the jungle and onto the low ridge where they had buried Lion: the low mound of unan-nealed earth where Boon's spade-marks still showed and beyond the grave the platform of freshly cut saplings bound between four posts and the blanket-wrapped bundle upon the platform and Boon and the boy squatting between the plat-form and the grave until Boon, the bandage removed, ripped, from his head so that the long scoriations of Old Ben's claws resembled crusted tar in the sunlight, sprang up and threw down upon them with the old gun with which he had never been known to hit anything although McCaslin was already off the mule, kicked both feet free of the irons and vaulted down before the mule had stopped, walking toward Boon.

"Stand back," Boon said. "By God, you wont touch him. Stand back, McCaslin." Still McCaslin came on, fast yet without haste.

"Cass!" Major de Spain said. Then he said "Boon! You, Boon!" and he was down too and the boy rose too, quickly, and still McCaslin came on not fast but steady and walked up to the grave and reached his hand steadily out, quickly yet still not fast, and took hold the gun by the middle so that he and Boon faced one another across Lion's grave, both holding the gun, Boon's spent indomitable amazed and frantic face almost a head higher than McCaslin's beneath the black scoriations of beast's claws and then Boon's chest began to heave as though there were not enough air in all the woods, in all the wilderness, for all of them, for him and anyone else, even for him alone.

"Turn it loose, Boon," McCaslin said.

"You damn little spindling—" Boon said. "Dont you know I can take it away from you? Dont you know I can tie it around your neck like a damn cravat?"

"Yes," McCaslin said. "Turn it loose, Boon."

"This is the way he wanted it. He told us. He told us exactly how to do it. And by God you aint going to move him. So we did it like he said, and I been sitting here ever since to keep the damn wildcats and varmints away from him and by God—" Then McCaslin had the gun, downslanted while he pumped the slide, the five shells snicking out of it so fast that the last one was almost out before the first one touched the ground and McCaslin dropped the gun behind him without once having taken his eyes from Boon's.

"Did you kill him, Boon?" he said. Then Boon moved. He turned, he moved like he was still drunk and then for a moment blind too, one hand out as he blundered toward the big tree and seemed to stop walking before he reached the tree so that he plunged, fell toward it, flinging up both hands and catching himself against the tree and turning until his back was against it, backing with the tree's trunk his wild spent scoriated face and the tremendous heave and collapse of his chest, McCaslin following, facing him again, never once having moved his eyes from Boon's eyes. "Did you kill him, Boon?"

"No!" Boon said. "No!"

"Tell the truth," McCaslin said. "I would have done it if he had asked me to." Then the boy moved. He was between them, facing McCaslin; the water felt as if it had burst and sprung not from his eyes alone but from his whole face, like sweat.

"Leave him alone!" he cried. "Goddamn it! Leave him alone!"

4

then he was twenty-one. He could say it, himself and his cousin juxtaposed not against the wilderness but against the tamed land which was to have been his heritage, the land which old Carothers McCaslin his grandfather had bought with white man's money from the wild men whose grandfathers without guns hunted it, and tamed and ordered or believed he had tamed and ordered it for the reason that the human beings he held in bondage and in the power of life and death had removed the forest from it and in their sweat scratched the surface of it to a depth of perhaps fourteen inches in order to grow something out of it which had not been there before and which could be translated back into the money he who believed he had bought it had had to pay to get it and hold it and a reasonable profit too: and for which reason old Carothers McCaslin, knowing better, could raise his children, his descendants and heirs, to believe the land was his to hold and bequeath since the strong and ruthless man has a cynical foreknowledge of his own vanity and pride and strength and a contempt for all his get: just as, knowing better, Major de Spain and his fragment of that wilderness which was bigger and older than any recorded deed: just as, knowing better, old Thomas Sutpen, from whom Major de Spain had had his fragment for money: just as Ikkemotubbe, the Chickasaw chief, from whom Thomas Sutpen had had the fragment for money or rum or whatever it was, knew in his turn that not even a fragment of it had been his to relinquish or sell

not against the wilderness but against the land, not in pursuit and lust but in relinquishment, and in the commissary as it should have been, not the heart perhaps but certainly the solar-plexus of the repudiated and relinquished: the square, galleried, wooden building squatting like a portent above the fields whose laborers it still held in thrall '65 or no and placarded over with advertisements for snuff and cures for chills and salves and potions manufactured and sold by white men to bleach the pigment and straighten the hair of negroes that they might resemble the very race which for two hundred years had held them in bondage and from which for another

hundred years not even a bloody civil war would have set
them completely free

himself and his cousin amid the old smells of cheese and
salt meat and kerosene and harness, the ranked shelves of
tobacco and overalls and bottled medicine and thread and
plow-bolts, the barrels and kegs of flour and meal and
molasses and nails, the wall pegs dependant with plowlines
and plow-collars and hames and trace-chains, and the desk
and the shelf above it on which rested the ledgers in which
McCaslin recorded the slow outward trickle of food and sup-
plies and equipment which returned each fall as cotton made
and ginned and sold (two threads frail as truth and impalpable
as equators yet cable-strong to bind for life them who made
the cotton to the land their sweat fell on), and the older
ledgers clumsy and archaic in size and shape, on the yellowed
pages of which were recorded in the faded hand of his father
Theophilus and his uncle Amodeus during the two decades
before the Civil War, the manumission in title at least of
Carothers McCaslin's slaves:

"Relinquish," McCaslin said. "Relinquish. You, the direct
male descendant of him who saw the opportunity and took it,
bought the land, took the land, got the land no matter how,
held it to bequeath, no matter how, out of the old grant, the
first patent, when it was a wilderness of wild beasts and wilder
men, and cleared it, translated it into something to bequeath
to his children, worthy of bequeathment for his descendants'
ease and security and pride and to perpetuate his name and
accomplishments. Not only the male descendant but the only
and last descendant in the male line and in the third generation, while I am not only four generations from old Carothers,
I derived through a woman and the very McCaslin in my

name is mine only by sufferance and courtesy and my grand-mother's pride in what that man accomplished whose legacy and monument you think you can repudiate." and he

"I cant repudiate it. It was never mine to repudiate. It was never Father's and Uncle Buddy's to bequeath me to repudiate because it was never Grandfather's to bequeath them to bequeath me to repudiate because it was never old Ikkemo-tubbe's to sell to Grandfather for bequeathment and repudia-tion. Because it was never Ikkemotubbe's fathers' fathers' to bequeath Ikkemotubbe to sell to Grandfather or any man because on the instant when Ikkemotubbe discovered, realised, that he could sell it for money, on that instant it ceased ever to have been his forever, father to father to father, and the man who bought it bought nothing."

"Bought nothing?" and he

"Bought nothing. Because He told in the Book how He created the earth, made it and looked at it and said it was all right, and then He made man. He made the earth first and peopled it with dumb creatures, and then He created man to be His overseer on the earth and to hold suzerainty over the earth and the animals on it in His name, not to hold for him-self and his descendants inviolable title forever, generation after generation, to the oblongs and squares of the earth, but to hold the earth mutual and intact in the communal anonymity of brotherhood, and all the fee He asked was pity and humility and sufferance and endurance and the sweat of his face for bread. And I know what you are going to say," he said: "That nevertheless Grandfather—" and McCaslin

"—did own it. And not the first. Not alone and not the first since, as your Authority states, man was dispossessed of Eden. Nor yet the second and still not alone, on down through the tedious and shabby chronicle of His chosen sprung from Abraham, and of the sons of them who dispossessed Abraham, and of the five hundred years during which half the known world and all it contained was chattel to one city as this plantation and all the life it contained was chattel and revokeless thrall to this commissary store and those ledgers yonder during your grandfather's life, and the next thousand years while men fought over the fragments of that collapse until at last even the fragments were exhausted and men snarled over the gnawed bones of the old world's worthless evening until an accidental egg discovered to them a new hemisphere. So let me say it: That nevertheless and notwithstanding old Carothers did own it. Bought it, got it, no matter; kept it, held it, no matter; bequeathed it: else why do you stand here relinquishing and repudiating? Held it, kept it for fifty years until you could repudiate it, while He—this Arbiter, this Architect, this Umpire— condoned—or did He? looked down and saw—or did He? Or at least did nothing: saw, and could not, or did not see; saw, and would not, or perhaps He would not see—perverse, impotent, or blind: which?" and he

"Dispossessed." and McCaslin

"What?" and he

"Dispossessed. Not impotent: He didn't condone; not blind, because He watched it. And let me say it. Dispossessed of Eden. Dispossessed of Canaan, and those who dispossessed him dispossessed him dispossessed, and the five hundred years of absentee landlords in the Roman bagnios, and the thousand years of wild men from the northern woods who dispossessed them and devoured their ravished substance ravished in turn again and then snarled in what you call the old world's worthless twilight over the old world's gnawed bones, blasphemous in His name until He used a simple egg to discover to them a new world where a nation of people could be

founded in humility and pity and sufferance and pride of one
to another. And Grandfather did own the land nevertheless
and notwithstanding because He permitted it, not impotent
and not condoning and not blind because He ordered and
watched it. He saw the land already accursed even as Ikkemotubbe and Ikkemotubbe's father old Issetibbeha and old
Issetibbeha's fathers too held it, already tainted even before
any white man owned it by what Grandfather and his kind, his
fathers, had brought into the new land which He had vouch-
safed them out of pity and sufferance, on condition of pity and
humility and sufferance and endurance, from that old world's
corrupt and worthless twilight as though in the sailfuls of the
old world's tainted wind which drove the ships—" and
McCaslin

"Ah."

"—and no hope for the land anywhere so long as Ikkemotubbe and Ikkemotubbe's descendants held it in unbroken
succession. Maybe He saw that only by voiding the land for a
time of Ikkemotubbe's blood and substituting for it another
blood, could He accomplish His purpose. Maybe He knew
already what that other blood would be, maybe it was more
than justice that only the white man's blood was available and
capable to raise the white man's curse, more than vengeance
when—" and McCaslin

"Ah."

"—when He used the blood which had brought in the
evil to destroy the evil as doctors use fever to burn up fever,
poison to slay poison. Maybe He chose Grandfather out of all
of them He might have picked. Maybe He knew that Grandfather himself would not serve His purpose because Grandfather was born too soon too, but that Grandfather would have
descendants, the right descendants; maybe He had foreseen

already the descendants Grandfather would have, maybe He saw already in Grandfather the seed progenitive of the three generations He saw it would take to set at least some of His lowly people free—" and McCaslin

"The sons of Ham. You who quote the Book: the sons of Ham." and he

"There are some things He said in the Book, and some things reported of Him that He did not say. And I know what you will say now: That if truth is one thing to me and another thing to you, how will we choose which is truth? You dont need to choose. The heart already knows. He didn't have His Book written to be read by what must elect and choose, but by the heart, not by the wise of the earth because maybe they dont need it or maybe the wise no longer have any heart, but by the doomed and lowly of the earth who have nothing else to read with but the heart. Because the men who wrote his Book for Him were writing about truth and there is only one truth and it covers all things that touch the heart." and McCaslin

"So these men who transcribed His Book for Him were sometime liars." and he

"Yes. Because they were human men. They were trying to write down the heart's truth out of the heart's driving complexity, for all the complex and troubled hearts which would beat after them. What they were trying to tell, what He wanted said, was too simple. Those for whom they transcribed His words could not have believed them. It had to be expounded in the everyday terms which they were familiar with and could comprehend, not only those who listened but those who told it too, because if they who were that near to Him as to have been elected from among all who breathed and spoke language to transcribe and relay His words, could comprehend truth only through the complexity of passion and lust and hate and fear which drives the heart, what distance back to truth must they traverse whom truth could only reach by word-of-mouth?" and McCaslin

"I might answer that, since you have taken to proving your points and disproving mine by the same text, I dont know. But I dont say that, because you have answered yourself: No time at all if, as you say, the heart knows truth, the infallible and unerring heart. And perhaps you are right, since although you admitted three generations from old Carothers to you, there were not three. There were not even completely two. Uncle Buck and Uncle Buddy. And they not the first and not alone. A thousand other Bucks and Buddies in less than two generations and sometimes less than one in this land which so you claim God created and man himself cursed and tainted. Not to mention 1865." and he

"Yes. More men than Father and Uncle Buddy," not even glancing toward the shelf above the desk, nor did McCaslin. They did not need to. To him it was as though the ledgers in their scarred cracked leather bindings were being lifted down one by one in their fading sequence and spread open on the desk or perhaps upon some apocryphal Bench or even Altar or perhaps before the Throne Itself for a last perusal and contemplation and refreshment of the Allknowledgeable before the yellowed pages and the brown thin ink in which was recorded the injustice and a little at least of its amelioration and restitution faded back forever into the anonymous communal original dust

the yellowed pages scrawled in fading ink by the hand first of his grandfather and then of his father and uncle, bachelors up to and past fifty and then sixty, the one who ran the plantation and the farming of it and the other who did the house-

work and the cooking and continued to do it even after his
twin married and the boy himself was born

the two brothers who as soon as their father was buried
moved out of the tremendously-conceived, the almost barn-
like edifice which he had not even completed, into a one-
room log cabin which the two of them built themselves and
added other rooms to while they lived in it, refusing to allow
any slave to touch any timber of it other than the actual raising
into place the logs which two men alone could not handle,
and domiciled all the slaves in the big house some of the windows of which were still merely boarded up with odds and
ends of plank or with the skins of bear and deer nailed over the
empty frames: each sundown the brother who superintended
the farming would parade the negroes as a first sergeant dis-
misses a company, and herd them willynilly, man woman and
child, without question protest or recourse, into the tremendous abortive edifice scarcely yet out of embryo, as if even old
Carothers McCaslin had paused aghast at the concrete indi-
cation of his own vanity's boundless conceiving: he would call
his mental roll and herd them in and with a hand-wrought
nail as long as a flenching-knife and suspended from a short
deer-hide thong attached to the door-jamb for that purpose,
he would nail to the door of that house which lacked half its
windows and had no hinged back door at all, so that presently
and for fifty years afterward, when the boy himself was big to
hear and remember it, there was in the land a sort of folk-tale:
of the countryside all night long full of skulking McCaslin
slaves dodging the moonlit roads and the Patrol-riders to visit
other plantations, and of the unspoken gentlemen's agreement between the two white men and the two dozen black
ones that, after the white man had counted them and driven
the home-made nail into the front door at sundown, neither

of the white men would go around behind the house and look
at the back door, provided that all the negroes were behind
the front one when the brother who drove it drew out the nail
again at daybreak

the twins who were identical even in their handwriting,
unless you had specimens side by side to compare, and even
when both hands appeared on the same page (as often happened, as if, long since past any oral intercourse, they had
used the diurnally advancing pages to conduct the unavoid-
able business of the compulsion which had traversed all the
waste wilderness of North Mississippi in 1830 and '40 and sin-
gled them out to drive) they both looked as though they had
been written by the same perfectly normal ten-year-old boy,
even to the spelling, except that the spelling did not improve
as one by one the slaves which Carothers McCaslin had
inherited and purchased—Roscius and Phoebe and Thucy-
dides and Eunice and their descendants, and Sam Fathers and
his mother for both of whom he had swapped an underbred
trotting gelding to old Ikkemotubbe, the Chickasaw chief
from whom he had likewise bought the land, and Tennie
Beauchamp whom the twin Amodeus had won from a neighbor in a poker-game, and the anomaly calling itself Percival
Brownlee which the twin Theophilus had purchased, neither
he nor his brother ever knew why apparently, from Bedford
Forrest while he was still only a slave-dealer and not yet a general (It was a single page, not long and covering less than a
year, not seven months in fact, begun in the hand which the
boy had learned to distinguish as that of his father:

*Percavil Brownly 26yr Old. cleark @ Bookepper. bought from
N.B.Forest at Cold Water 3 Mar 1856 $265. dolars*

and beneath that, in the same hand:

> 5 mar 1856 No bookepper any way Cant read. Can write his Name but I already put that down My self Says he can Plough but dont look like it to Me. sent to Feild to day Mar 5 1856

and the same hand:

> 6 Mar 1856 Cant plough either Says he aims to be a Precher so may be he can lead live stock to Crick to Drink

and this time it was the other, the hand which he now recognised as his uncle's when he could see them both on the same page:

> Mar 23th 1856 Cant do that either Except one at a Time Get shut of him

then the first again:

> 24 Mar 1856 Who in hell would buy him

then the second:

> 19th of Apr 1856 Nobody You put yourself out of Market at Cold Water two months ago I never said sell him Free him

the first:

> 22 Apr 1856 Ill get it out of him

the second:

> *Jun 13th 1856 How $1 per yr 265$ 265 yrs Wholl sign his Free*
> *paper*

then the first again:

> *1 Oct 1856 Mule josephine Broke Leg @ shot Wrong stall*
> *wrong niger wrong everything $100. dolars*

and the same:

> *2 Oct 1856 Freed Debit McCaslin @ McCaslin $265. dolars*

then the second again:

> *Oct 3th Debit Theophilus McCaslin Niger 265$ Mule 100$*
> *365$ He hasnt gone yet Father should be here*

then the first:

> *3 Oct 1856 Son of a bitch wont leave What would father*
> *done*

the second:

> *29th of Oct 1856 Renamed him*

the first:

> *31 Oct 1856 Renamed him what*

the second:

> *Chrstms 1856 Spintrius*

) took substance and even a sort of shadowy life with their passions and complexities too as page followed page and year year; all there, not only the general and condoned injustice and its slow amortization but the specific tragedy which had not been condoned and could never be amortized, the new page and the new ledger, the hand which he could now recognise at first glance as his father's:

> *Father dide Lucius Quintus Carothers McCaslin, Callina 1772 Missippy 1837. Dide and burid 27 June 1837*
> *Roskus. rased by Granfather in Callina Dont know how old. Freed 27 June 1837 Dont want to leave. Dide and Burid 12 Jan 1841*
> *Fibby Roskus Wife. bought by granfather in Callina says Fifty Freed 27 June 1837 Dont want to leave. Dide and burd 1 Aug 1849*
> *Thucydus Roskus @ Fibby Son born in Callina 1779. Refused 10acre peace fathers Will 28 Jun 1837 Refused Cash offer $200. dolars from A. @ T. McCaslin 28 Jun 1837 Wants to stay and work it out*

and beneath this and covering the next five pages and almost that many years, the slow, day-by-day accrument of the wages allowed him and the food and clothing—the molasses and meat and meal, the cheap durable shirts and jeans and shoes and now and then a coat against rain and cold—charged against the slowly yet steadily mounting sum of balance (and it would seem to the boy that he could actually see the black man, the slave whom his white owner had forever manumitted by the very act from which the black man could never be free so long as memory lasted, entering the commissary, asking permission perhaps of the white man's son to see the ledger-page which he could not even read, not even asking for the white man's word, which he would have had to accept for the reason that there was absolutely no way under the sun for him to test it, as to how the account stood, how much longer before he could go and never return, even if only as far as Jefferson seventeen miles away) on to the double pen-stroke closing the final entry:

3 Nov 1841 By Cash to Thucydus McCaslin $200. dolars Set Up blaksmith in J. Dec 1841 Dide and burid in J. 17 feb 1854 Eunice Bought by Father in New Orleans 1807 $650. dolars. Marrid to Thucydus 1809 Drownd in Crick Cristmas Day 1832

and then the other hand appeared, the first time he had seen it in the ledger to distinguish it as his uncle's, the cook and housekeeper whom even McCaslin, who had known him and the boy's father for sixteen years before the boy was born, remembered as sitting all day long in the rocking chair from which he cooked the food, before the kitchen fire on which he cooked it:

June 21th 1833 Drownd herself

and the first:

23 Jun 1833 Who in hell ever heard of a niger drownding him self

and the second, unhurried, with a complete finality; the two
identical entries might have been made with a rubber stamp
save for the date:

Aug 13th 1833 Drownd herself

and he thought *But why? But why?* He was sixteen then. It was
neither the first time he had been alone in the commissary nor
the first time he had taken down the old ledgers familiar on
their shelf above the desk ever since he could remember. As a
child and even after nine and ten and eleven, when he had
learned to read, he would look up at the scarred and cracked
backs and ends but with no particular desire to open them,
and though he intended to examine them someday because
he realised that they probably contained a chronological and
much more comprehensive though doubtless tedious record
than he would ever get from any other source, not alone of his
own flesh and blood but of all his people, not only the whites
but the black one too, who were as much a part of his ancestry
as his white progenitors, and of the land which they had all
held and used in common and fed from and on and would
continue to use in common without regard to color or titular
ownership, it would only be on some idle day when he was old
and perhaps even bored a little since what the old books contained would be after all these years fixed immutably, finished, unalterable, harmless. Then he was sixteen. He knew
what he was going to find before he found it. He got the commissary key from McCaslin's room after midnight while
McCaslin was asleep and with the commissary door shut and
locked behind him and the forgotten lantern stinking anew
the rank dead icy air, he leaned above the yellowed page and
thought not Why drowned herself, but thinking what he

believed his father had thought when he found his brother's
first comment: Why did Uncle Buddy think she had drowned
herself? finding, beginning to find on the next succeeding
page what he knew he would find, only this was still not it
because he already knew this:

> *Tomasina called Tomy Daughter of Thucydus @ Eunice*
> *Born 1810 dide in Child bed June 1833 and Burd. Yr stars fell*

nor the next:

> *Turl Son of Thucydus @ Eunice Tomy born Jun 1833 yr stars*
> *fell Fathers will*

and nothing more, no tedious recording filling this page of
wages day by day and food and clothing charged against them,
no entry of his death and burial because he had outlived his
white half-brothers and the books which McCaslin kept did
not include obituaries: just *Fathers will* and he had seen that
too: old Carothers' bold cramped hand far less legible than his
sons' even and not much better in spelling, who while capital-
ising almost every noun and verb, made no effort to punctuate
or construct whatever, just as he made no effort either to
explain or obfuscate the thousand-dollar legacy to the son of
an unmarried slave-girl, to be paid only at the child's coming-
of-age, bearing the consequence of the act of which there was
still no definite incontrovertible proof that he acknowledged,
not out of his own substance but penalising his sons with it,
charging them a cash forfeit on the accident of their own
paternity; not even a bribe for silence toward his own fame
since his fame would suffer only after he was no longer present to defend it, flinging almost contemptuously, as he might

a cast-off hat or pair of shoes, the thousand dollars which could have had no more reality to him under those conditions than it would have to the negro, the slave who would not even see it until he came of age, twenty-one years too late to begin to learn what money was. *So I reckon that was cheaper than saying My son to a nigger* he thought. *Even if My son wasn't but just two words. But there must have been love* he thought. *Some sort of love. Even what he would have called love: not just an afternoon's or a night's spittoon* There was the old man, old, within five years of his life's end, long a widower and, since his sons were not only bachelors but were approaching middle-age, lonely in the house and doubtless even bored since his plantation was established now and functioning and there was enough money now, too much of it probably for a man whose vices even apparently remained below his means; there was the girl, husbandless and young, only twenty-three when the child was born: perhaps he had sent for her at first out of lone-liness, to have a young voice and movement in the house, summoned her, bade her mother send her each morning to sweep the floors and make the beds and the mother acquiesc-ing since that was probably already understood, already planned: the only child of a couple who were not field hands and who held themselves something above the other slaves not alone for that reason but because the husband and his father and mother too had been inherited by the white man from his father, and the white man himself had travelled three hundred miles and better to New Orleans in a day when men travelled by horseback or steamboat, and bought the girl's mother as a wife for

and that was all. The old frail pages seemed to turn of their own accord even while he thought *His own daughter His own daughter. No No Not even him* back to that one where the

white man (not even a widower then) who never went anywhere any more than his sons in their time ever did and who
did not need another slave, had gone all the way to New
Orleans and bought one. And Tomey's Terrel was still alive
when the boy was ten years old and he knew from his own
observation and memory that there had already been some
white in Tomey's Terrel's blood before his father gave him the
rest of it; and looking down at the yellowed page spread
beneath the yellow glow of the lantern smoking and stinking
in that rank chill midnight room fifty years later, he seemed to
see her actually walking into the icy creek on that Christmas
day six months before her daughter's and her lover's (*Her first
lover's* he thought. *Her first*) child was born, solitary, inflexi-
ble, griefless, ceremonial, in formal and succinct repudiation
of grief and despair who had already had to repudiate belief
and hope

that was all. He would never need look at the ledgers
again nor did he; the yellowed pages in their fading and
implacable succession were as much a part of his consciousness and would remain so forever, as the fact of his own nativ-
ity:

*Tennie Beauchamp 21yrs Won by Amodeus McCaslin from
Hubert Beauchamp Esqre Possible Strait against three Treys
in sigt Not called 1859 Marrid to Tomys Turl 1859*

and no date of freedom because her freedom, as well as that of
her first surviving child, derived not from Buck and Buddy
McCaslin in the commissary but from a stranger in Washington and no date of death and burial, not only because
McCaslin kept no obituaries in his books, but because in this

year 1883 she was still alive and would remain so to see a grandson by her last surviving child:

> *Amodeus McCaslin Beauchamp Son of tomys Turl @ Tennie Beauchamp 1859 dide 1859*

then his uncle's hand entire, because his father was now a member of the cavalry command of that man whose name as a slave-dealer he could not even spell: and not even a page and not even a full line:

> *Dauter Tomes Turl and tenny 1862*

and not even a line and not even a sex and no cause given though the boy could guess it because McCaslin was thirteen then and he remembered how there was not always enough to eat in more places than Vicksburg:

> *Child of tomes Turl and Tenny 1863*

and the same hand again and this one lived, as though Tennie's perseverance and the fading and diluted ghost of old Carothers' ruthlessness had at last conquered even starvation: and clearer, fuller, more carefully written and spelled than the boy had yet seen it, as if the old man, who should have been a woman to begin with, trying to run what was left of the plantation in his brother's absence in the intervals of cooking and caring for himself and the fourteen-year-old orphan, had taken as an omen for renewed hope the fact that this nameless inheritor of slaves was at least remaining alive long enough to receive a name:

*James Thucydus Beauchamp Son of Tomes Turl and Tenny
Beauchamp Born 29th december 1864 and both Well
Wanted to call him Theophilus but Tride Amodeus
McCaslin and Callina McCaslin and both dide so Diss-
waded Them Born at Two clock A,m, both Well*

but no more, nothing; it would be another two years yet before
the boy, almost a man now, would return from the abortive
trip into Tennessee with the still-intact third of old Carothers'
legacy to his Negro son and his descendants, which as the
three surviving children established at last one by one their
apparent intention of surviving, their white half-uncles had
increased to a thousand dollars each, conditions permitting, as
they came of age, and completed the page himself as far as it
would ever be completed when that day was long passed
beyond which a man born in 1864 (or 1867 either, when he
himself saw light) could have expected or himself hoped or
even wanted to be still alive; his own hand now, queerly
enough resembling neither his father's nor his uncle's nor
even McCaslin's, but like that of his grandfather's save for the
spelling:

*Vanished sometime on night of his twenty-first birthday Dec
29 1885. Traced by Isaac McCaslin to Jackson Tenn. and
there lost. His third of legacy $1000.00 returned to McCaslin
Edmonds Trustee this day Jan 12 1886*

but not yet: that would be two years yet, and now his father's
again, whose old commander was now quit of soldiering and
slave-trading both; once more in the ledger and then not again
and more illegible than ever, almost indecipherable at all
from the rheumatism which now crippled him and almost

completely innocent now even of any sort of spelling as well as
punctuation, as if the four years during which he had followed
the sword of the only man ever breathing who ever sold him a
negro, let alone beat him in a trade, had convinced him not
only of the vanity of faith and hope but of orthography too:

Miss sophonsiba b dtr t t @ t 1869

but not of belief and will because it was there, written, as
McCaslin had told him, with the left hand, but there in the
ledger one time more and then not again, for the boy himself
was a year old, and when Lucas was born six years later, his
father and uncle had been dead inside the same twelve-
months almost five years; his own hand again, who was there
and saw it, 1886, she was just seventeen, two years younger
than himself, and he was in the commissary when McCaslin
entered out of the first of dusk and said, "He wants to marry
Fonsiba," like that: and he looked past McCaslin and saw the
man, the stranger, taller than McCaslin and wearing better
clothes than McCaslin and most of the other white men the
boy knew habitually wore, who entered the room like a white
man and stood in it like a white man, as though he had let
McCaslin precede him into it not because McCaslin's skin
was white but simply because McCaslin lived there and knew
the way, and who talked like a white man too, looking at him
past McCaslin's shoulder rapidly and keenly once and then
no more, without further interest, as a mature and contained
white man not impatient but just pressed for time might have
looked. "Marry Fonsiba?" he cried. "Marry Fonsiba?" and
then no more either, just watching and listening while
McCaslin and the Negro talked:

"To live in Arkansas, I believe you said."

"Yes. I have property there. A farm."

"Property? A farm? You own it?"

"Yes."

"You dont say Sir, do you?"

"To my elders, yes."

"I see. You are from the North."

"Yes. Since a child."

"Then your father was a slave."

"Yes. Once."

"Then how do you own a farm in Arkansas?"

"I have a grant. It was my father's. From the United States. For military service."

"I see," McCaslin said. "The Yankee army."

"The United States army," the stranger said; and then himself again, crying it at McCaslin's back:

"Call aunt Tennie! I'll go get her! I'll—" But McCaslin was not even including him; the stranger did not even glance back toward his voice, the two of them speaking to one another again as if he were not even there:

"Since you seem to have it all settled," McCaslin said, "why have you bothered to consult my authority at all?"

"I dont," the stranger said. "I acknowledge your authority only so far as you admit your responsibility toward her as a female member of the family of which you are the head. I dont ask your permission. I——"

"That will do!" McCaslin said. But the stranger did not falter. It was neither as if he were ignoring McCaslin nor as if he had failed to hear him. It was as though he were making, not at all an excuse and not exactly a justification, but simply a statement which the situation absolutely required and demanded should be made in McCaslin's hearing whether McCaslin listened to it or not. It was as if he were talking to himself, for himself to hear the words spoken aloud. They faced one another, not close yet at slightly less than foils' distance, erect, their voices not raised, not impactive, just succinct:

"—I inform you, notify you in advance as chief of her family. No man of honor could do less. Besides, you have, in your way, according to your lights and upbringing——"

"That's enough, I said," McCaslin said. "Be off this place by full dark. Go." But for another moment the other did not move, contemplating McCaslin with that detached and heatless look, as if he were watching reflected in McCaslin's pupils the tiny image of the figure he was sustaining.

"Yes," he said. "After all, this is your house. And in your fashion you have. . . . But no matter. You are right. This is enough." He turned back toward the door; he paused again but only for a second, already moving while he spoke: "Be easy. I will be good to her." Then he was gone.

"But how did she ever know him?" the boy cried. "I never even heard of him before! And Fonsiba, that's never been off this place except to go to church since she was born——"

"Ha," McCaslin said. "Even their parents dont know until too late how seventeen-year-old girls ever met the men who marry them too, if they are lucky." And the next morning they were both gone, Fonsiba too. McCaslin never saw her again, nor did he, because the woman he found at last five months later was no one he had ever known. He carried a third of the three-thousand-dollar fund in gold in a money-belt, as when he had vainly traced Tennie's Jim into Tennessee a year ago. They—the man—had left an address of some sort with Tennie, and three months later a letter came, written by the man although McCaslin's wife Alice had taught Fonsiba to read and write too a little. But it bore a different postmark from the address the man had left with Tennie, and he travelled by rail as far as he could and then by contracted stage and then by a hired livery rig and then by rail again for a distance: an experienced traveller by now and an experienced bloodhound too and a successful one this time because he would have to be; as the slow interminable empty muddy December miles crawled and crawled and night followed night in hotels, in roadside taverns of rough logs and containing little else but a bar, and in the cabins of strangers and the hay of lonely barns, in none of which he dared undress because of his secret golden girdle like that of a disguised one of the Magi travelling incognito and not even hope to draw him but only determination and desperation, he would tell himself: *I will have to find her. I will have to. We have already lost one of them. I will have to find her this time.* He did. Hunched in the slow and icy rain, on a spent hired horse splashed to the chest and higher, he saw it—a single log edifice with a clay chimney which seemed in process of being flattened by the rain to a nameless and valueless rubble of dissolution in that roadless and even pathless waste of unfenced fallow and wilderness jungle—no barn, no stable, not so much as a hen-coop: just a log cabin built by hand and no clever hand either, a meagre pile of clumsily-cut firewood sufficient for about one day and not even a gaunt hound to come bellowing out from under the house when he rode up— a farm only in embryo, perhaps a good farm, maybe even a plantation someday, but not now, not for years yet and only then with labor, hard and enduring and unflagging work and sacrifice; he shoved open the crazy kitchen door in its awry frame and entered an icy gloom where not even a fire for cooking burned and after another moment saw, crouched into the wall's angle behind a crude table, the coffee-colored face which he had known all his life but knew no more, the body which had been born within a hundred yards of the room that he was born in and in which some of his own blood ran but which was now completely inheritor of generation after generation to whom an unannounced white man on a horse was a white man's hired Patroller wearing a pistol sometimes and a blacksnake whip always; he entered the next room, the only other room the cabin owned, and found, sitting in a rocking chair before the hearth, the man himself, reading—sitting there in the only chair in the house, before that miserable fire for which there was not wood sufficient to last twenty-four hours, in the same ministerial clothing in which he had entered the commissary five months ago and a pair of gold-framed spectacles which, when he looked up and then rose to his feet, the boy saw did not even contain lenses, reading a book in the midst of that desolation, that muddy waste fenceless and even pathless and without even a walled shed for stock to stand beneath: and over all, permeant, clinging to the man's very clothing and exuding from his skin itself, that rank stink of baseless and imbecile delusion, that boundless rapacity and folly, of the carpetbagger followers of victorious armies.

"Dont you see?" he cried. "Dont you see? This whole land, the whole South, is cursed, and all of us who derive from it, whom it ever suckled, white and black both, lie under the curse? Granted that my people brought the curse onto the land: maybe for that reason their descendants alone can—not resist it, not combat it—maybe just endure and outlast it until the curse is lifted. Then your peoples' turn will come because we have forfeited ours. But not now. Not yet. Dont you see?"

The other stood now, the unfrayed garments still ministerial even if not quite so fine, the book closed upon one finger to keep the place, the lenseless spectacles held like a music master's wand in the other workless hand while the owner of it spoke his measured and sonorous imbecility of the boundless folly and the baseless hope: "You're wrong. The curse you whites brought into this land has been lifted. It has been voided and discharged. We are seeing a new era, an era dedicated, as our founders intended it, to freedom, liberty and equality for all, to which this country will be the new Canaan——"

"Freedom from what? From work? Canaan?" He jerked his arm, comprehensive, almost violent: whereupon it all seemed to stand there about them, intact and complete and visible in the drafty, damp, heatless, negro-stale negro-rank sorry room—the empty fields without plow or seed to work them, fenceless against the stock which did not exist within or without the walled stable which likewise was not there. "What corner of Canaan is this?"

"You are seeing it at a bad time. This is winter. No man farms this time of year."

"I see. And of course her need for food and clothing will stand still while the land lies fallow."

"I have a pension," the other said. He said it as a man might say *I have grace* or *I own a gold mine.* "I have my father's pension too. It will arrive on the first of the month. What day is this?"

"The eleventh," he said. "Twenty days more. And until then?"

"I have a few groceries in the house from my credit account with the merchant in Midnight who banks my pension check for me. I have executed to him a power of attorney to handle it for me as a matter of mutual——"

"I see. And if the groceries dont last the twenty days?"

"I still have one more hog."

"Where?"

"Outside," the other said. "It is customary in this country to allow stock to range free during the winter for food. It comes up from time to time. But no matter if it doesn't; I can probably trace its footprints when the need——"

"Yes!" he cried. "Because no matter: you still have the pension check. And the man in Midnight will cash it and pay himself out of it for what you have already eaten and if there is any left over, it is yours. And the hog will be eaten by then or you still cant catch it, and then what will you do?"

"It will be almost spring then," the other said. "I am planning in the spring——"

"It will be January," he said. "And then February. And then more than half of March—" and when he stopped again in the kitchen she had not moved, she did not even seem to breathe or to be alive except her eyes watching him; when he took a step toward her it was still not movement because she could have retreated no further: only the tremendous fathomless ink-colored eyes in the narrow, thin, too thin coffee-colored face watching him without alarm, without recognition, without hope. "Fonsiba," he said. "Fonsiba. Are you all right?"

"I'm free," she said. Midnight was a tavern, a livery stable, a big store (that would be where the pension check banked itself as a matter of mutual elimination of bother and fret, he thought) and a little one, a saloon and a blacksmith shop. But there was a bank there too. The president (the owner, for all practical purposes) of it was a translated Mississippian who had been one of Forrest's men too: and his body lightened of the golden belt for the first time since he left home eight days ago, with pencil and paper he multiplied three dollars by twelve months and divided it into one thousand dollars; it would stretch that way over almost twenty-eight years and for twenty-eight years at least she would not starve, the banker promising to send the three dollars himself by a trusty messenger on the fifteenth of each month and put it into her actual hand, and he returned home and that was all because in 1874 his father and his uncle were both dead and the old ledgers never again came down from the shelf above the desk to which his father had returned them for the last time that day in 1869. But he could have completed it:

> *Lucas Quintus Carothers McCaslin Beauchamp. Last surviving son and child of Tomey's Terrel and Tennie Beauchamp. March 17, 1874*

except that there was no need: not *Lucius Quintus @c @c @c*, but *Lucas Quintus*, not refusing to be called Lucius, because he simply eliminated that word from the name; not denying, declining the name itself, because he used three quarters of it; but simply taking the name and changing, altering it, making it no longer the white man's but his own, by himself composed, himself selfprogenitive and nominate, by himself ancestored, as, for all the old ledgers recorded to the contrary, old Carothers himself was

and that was all: 1874 the boy; 1888 the man, repudiated denied and free; 1895 and husband but no father, unwidowered but without a wife, and found long since that no man is ever free and probably could not bear it if he were; married then and living in Jefferson in the little new jerrybuilt bungalow which his wife's father had given them: and one morning Lucas stood suddenly in the doorway of the room where he was reading the Memphis paper and he looked at the paper's dateline and thought *It's his birthday. He's twenty-one today* and Lucas said: "Whar's the rest of that money old Carothers left? I wants it. All of it."

that was all: and McCaslin

"More men than that one Buck and Buddy to fumble-heed that truth so mazed for them that spoke it and so confused for them that heard yet still there was 1865": and he

"But not enough. Not enough of even Father and Uncle Buddy to fumble-heed in even three generations not even three generations fathered by Grandfather not even if there had been nowhere beneath His sight any but Grandfather and so He would not even have needed to elect and choose. But He tried and I know what you will say. That having Himself created them He could have known no more of hope than He could have pride and grief but He didn't hope He just waited because He had made them: not just because He had set them alive and in motion but because He had already worried with them so long: worried with them so long because He had seen how in individual cases they were capable of anything any height or depth remembered in mazed incomprehension out of heaven where hell was created too and so He must admit them or else admit His equal somewhere and so be no longer God and therefore must accept responsibility for what He Himself had done in order to live with Himself in His lonely and paramount heaven. And He probably knew it was vain but He had created them and knew them capable of all things because He had shaped them out of the primal Absolute which contained all and had watched them since in their individual exaltation and baseness and they themselves not knowing why nor how nor even when: until at last He saw that they were all Grandfather all of them and that even from them the elected and chosen the best the very best He could expect (not hope mind; not hope) would be Bucks and Buddies and not even enough of them and in the third generation not even Bucks and Buddies but—" and McCaslin

"Ah": and he

"Yes. If He could see Father and Uncle Buddy in Grand-father He must have seen me too.—an Isaac born into a later life than Abraham's and repudiating immolation: fatherless and therefore safe declining the altar because maybe this time the exasperated Hand might not supply the kid—" and McCaslin

"Escape": and he

"All right. Escape.—Until one day He said what you told Fonsiba's husband that afternoon here in this room: *This will do. This is enough*: not in exasperation or rage or even just sick to death as you were sick that day: just *This is enough* and looked about for one last time, for one time more since He had created them, upon this land this South for which He had done so much with woods for game and streams for fish and deep rich soil for seed and lush springs to sprout it and long summers to mature it and serene falls to harvest it and short mild winters for men and animals and saw no hope anywhere and looked beyond it where hope should have been, where to East North and West lay illimitable that whole hopeful conti-nent dedicated as a refuge and sanctuary of liberty and free-dom from what you called the old world's worthless evening and saw the rich descendants of slavers, females of both sexes, to whom the black they shrieked of was another specimen another example like the Brazilian macaw brought home in a cage by a traveller, passing resolutions about horror and out-rage in warm and air-proof halls: and the thundering cannon-ade of politicians earning votes and the medicine-shows of pulpiteers earning Chatauqua fees, to whom the outrage and the injustice were as much abstractions as Tariff or Silver or Immortality and who employed the very shackles of its servi-tude and the sorry rags of its regalia as they did the other beer and banners and mottoes redfire and brimstone and sleight-of-hand and musical handsaws: and the whirling wheels which manufactured for a profit the pristine replacements of the shackles and shoddy garments as they wore out and spun the cotton and made the gins which ginned it and the cars and ships which hauled it, and the men who ran the wheels for that profit and established and collected the taxes it was taxed with and the rates for hauling it and the commissions for selling it: and He could have repudiated them since they were his creation now and forever more throughout all their generations until not only that old world from which He had rescued them but this new one too which He had revealed and led them to as a sanctuary and refuge were become the same worthless tideless rock cooling in the last crimson evening except that out of all that empty sound and bootless fury one silence, among that loud and moiling all of them just one simple enough to believe that horror and outrage were first and last simply horror and outrage and was crude enough to act upon that, illiterate and had no words for talking or perhaps was just busy and had no time to, one out of them all who did not bother Him with cajolery and adjuration then pleading then threat and had not even bothered to inform Him in advance what he was about so that a lesser than He might have even missed the simple act of lifting the long ancestral musket down from the deer-horns above the door, whereupon He said *My name is Brown too* and the other *So is mine* and He *Then mine or yours cant be because I am against it* and the other *So am I* and He triumphantly *Then where are you going with that gun?* and the other told him in one sentence one word and He: amazed: Who knew neither hope nor pride nor grief *But your Association, your Committee, your Officers. Where are your Minutes, your Motions, your Parliamentary Procedures?*

and the other *I aint against them. They are all right I reckon for them that have the time. I am just against the weak because they are niggers being held in bondage by the strong just because they are white.* So He turned once more to this land which He still intended to save because He had done so much for it—" and McCaslin

"What?" and he

"—to these people He was still committed to because they were his creations—" and McCaslin

"Turned back to us? His face to us?" and he

"—whose wives and daughters at least made soups and jellies for them when they were sick and carried the trays through the mud and the winter too into the stinking cabins and sat in the stinking cabins and kept fires going until crises came and passed but that was not enough: and when they were very sick had them carried into the big house itself into the company room itself maybe and nursed them there which the white man would have done too for any other of his cattle that was sick but at least the man who hired one from a livery wouldn't have and still that was not enough: so that He said and not in grief either Who had made them and so could know no more of grief than He could of pride or hope: *Apparently they can learn nothing save through suffering, remember nothing save when underlined in blood*—" and McCaslin

"Ashby on an afternoon's ride, to call on some remote maiden cousins of his mother or maybe just acquaintances of hers, comes by chance upon a minor engagement of outposts and dismounts and with his crimson-lined cloak for target leads a handful of troops he never saw before against an entrenched position of backwoods-trained riflemen. Lee's battle-order, wrapped maybe about a handful of cigars and doubtless thrown away when the last cigar was smoked, found by a

Yankee Intelligence officer on the floor of a saloon behind the
Yankee lines after Lee had already divided his forces before
Sharpsburg. Jackson on the Plank Road, already rolled up the
flank which Hooker believed could not be turned and, waiting only for night to pass to continue the brutal and incessant
slogging which would fling that whole wing back into
Hooker's lap where he sat on a front gallery in Chancel-
lorsville drinking rum toddies and telegraphing Lincoln that
he had defeated Lee, is shot from among a whole covey of
minor officers and in the blind night by one of his own patrols,
leaving as next by seniority Stuart that gallant man born apparently already horsed and sabred and already knowing all there
was to know about war except the slogging and brutal stupidity
of it: and that same Stuart off raiding Pennsylvania hen-roosts
when Lee should have known of all of Meade just where Han-
cock was on Cemetery Ridge: and Longstreet too at Gettys-
burg and that same Longstreet shot out of saddle by his own
men in the dark by mistake just as Jackson was. His face to us?
His face to us?" and he

"How else have made them fight? Who else but Jacksons
and Stuarts and Ashbys and Morgans and Forrests?—the farmers of the central and middle-west, holding land by the acre
instead of the tens or maybe even the hundreds, farming it
themselves and to no single crop of cotton or tobacco or cane,
owning no slaves and needing and wanting none and already
looking toward the Pacific coast, not always as long as two generations there and having stopped where they did stop only
through the fortuitous mischance that an ox died or a wagon-
axle broke. And the New England mechanics who didn't even
own land and measured all things by the weight of water and
the cost of turning wheels and the narrow fringe of traders
and ship-owners still looking backward across the Atlantic and

attached to the continent only by their counting-houses. And those who should have had the alertness to see: the wildcat manipulators of mythical wilderness townsites; and the astuteness to rationalise: the bankers who held the mortgages on the land which the first were only waiting to abandon and on the railroads and steamboats to carry them still further west, and on the factories and the wheels and the rented tenements those who ran them lived in; and the leisure and scope to comprehend and fear in time and even anticipate: the Boston-bred (even when not born in Boston) spinster descendants of long lines of similarly-bred and likewise spinster aunts and uncles whose hands knew no callus except that of the indicting pen, to whom the wilderness itself began at the top of tide and who looked, if at anything other than Beacon Hill, only toward heaven—not to mention all the loud rabble of the camp-followers of pioneers: the bellowing of politicians, the mellifluous choiring of self-styled men of God, the—" and McCaslin

"Here, here. Wait a minute": and he

"Let me talk now. I'm trying to explain to the head of my family something which I have got to do which I dont quite understand myself, not in justification of it but to explain it if I can. I could say I dont know why I must do it but that I do know I have got to because I have got myself to have to live with for the rest of my life and all I want is peace to do it in. But you are the head of my family. More. I knew a long time ago that I would never have to miss my father, even if you are just finding out that you have missed your son.—the drawers of bills and the shavers of notes and the schoolmasters and the self-ordained to teach and lead and all that horde of the semi-literate with a white shirt but no change for it, with one eye on themselves and watching each other with the other one. Who

else could have made them fight: could have struck them so
aghast with fear and dread as to turn shoulder to shoulder and
face one way and even stop talking for a while and even after
two years of it keep them still so wrung with terror that some
among them would seriously propose moving their very capi-
tal into a foreign country lest it be ravaged and pillaged by a
people whose entire white male population would have little
more than filled any one of their larger cities: except Jackson
in the Valley and three separate armies trying to catch him
and none of them ever knowing whether they were just
retreating from a battle or just running into one and Stuart riding his whole command entirely around the biggest single
armed force this continent ever saw in order to see what it
looked like from behind and Morgan leading a cavalry charge
against a stranded man-of-war. Who else could have declared
a war against a power with ten times the area and a hundred
times the men and a thousand times the resources, except
men who could believe that all necessary to conduct a successful war was not acumen nor shrewdness nor politics nor
diplomacy nor money nor even integrity and simple arith-
metic but just love of land and courage——"

"And an unblemished and gallant ancestry and the ability
to ride a horse," McCaslin said. "Dont leave that out." It was
evening now, the tranquil sunset of October mazy with windless woodsmoke. The cotton was long since picked and
ginned, and all day now the wagons loaded with gathered
corn moved between field and crib, processional across the
enduring land. "Well, maybe that's what He wanted. At least,
that's what He got." This time there was no yellowed proces-
sion of fading and harmless ledger-pages. This was chronicled
in a harsher book and McCaslin, fourteen and fifteen and sixteen, had seen it and the boy himself had inherited it as

Noah's grandchildren had inherited the Flood although they had not been there to see the deluge: that dark corrupt and bloody time while three separate peoples had tried to adjust not only to one another but to the new land which they had created and inherited too and must live in for the reason that those who had lost it were no less free to quit it than those who had gained it were: — those upon whom freedom and equality had been dumped overnight and without warning or preparation or any training in how to employ it or even just endure it and who misused it not as children would nor yet because they had been so long in bondage and then so suddenly freed, but misused it as human beings always misuse freedom, so that he thought *Apparently there is a wisdom beyond even that learned through suffering necessary for a man to distinguish between liberty and license*; those who had fought for four years and lost to preserve a condition under which that franchisement was anomaly and paradox, not because they were opposed to freedom as freedom but for the old reasons for which man (not the generals and politicians but man) has always fought and died in wars: to preserve a status quo or to establish a better future one to endure for his children; and lastly, as if that were not enough for bitterness and hatred and fear, that third race even more alien to the people whom they resembled in pigment and in whom even the same blood ran, than to the people whom they did not, — that race threefold in one and alien even among themselves save for a single fierce will for rapine and pillage, composed of the sons of middle-aged Quartermaster lieutenants and Army sutlers and contractors in military blankets and shoes and transport mules, who followed the battles they themselves had not fought and inherited the conquest they themselves had not helped to gain, sanctioned and protected even if not blessed, and left their

bones and in another generation would be engaged in a fierce
economic competition of small sloven farms with the black
men they were supposed to have freed and the white descendants of fathers who had owned no slaves anyway whom they
were supposed to have disinherited and in the third generation would be back once more in the little lost county seats as
barbers and garage mechanics and deputy sheriffs and mill-
and gin-hands and power-plant firemen, leading, first in mufti
then later in an actual formalised regalia of hooded sheets and
passwords and fiery christian symbols, lynching mobs against
the race their ancestors had come to save: and of all that other
nameless horde of speculators in human misery, manipulators
of money and politics and land, who follow catastrophe and
are their own protection as grasshoppers are and need no
blessing and sweat no plow or axe-helve and batten and vanish
and leave no bones, just as they derived apparently from no
ancestry, no mortal flesh, no act even of passion or even of
lust: and the Jew who came without protection too since after
two thousand years he had got out of the habit of being or
needing it, and solitary, without even the solidarity of the
locusts and in this a sort of courage since he had come thinking not in terms of simple pillage but in terms of his great-
grandchildren, seeking yet some place to establish them to
endure even though forever alien: and unblessed: a pariah
about the face of the Western earth which twenty centuries
later was still taking revenge on him for the fairy tale with
which he had conquered it. McCaslin had actually seen it,
and the boy even at almost eighty would never be able to distinguish certainly between what he had seen and what had
been told him: a lightless and gutted and empty land where
women crouched with the huddled children behind locked
doors and men armed in sheets and masks rode the silent

roads and the bodies of white and black both, victims not so much of hate as of desperation and despair, swung from lonely limbs: and men shot dead in polling-booths with the still wet pen in one hand and the unblotted ballot in the other: and a United States marshal in Jefferson who signed his official papers with a crude cross, an ex-slave called Sickymo, not at all because his ex-owner was a doctor and apothecary but because, still a slave, he would steal his master's grain alcohol and dilute it with water and peddle it in pint bottles from a cache beneath the roots of a big sycamore tree behind the drug store, who had attained his high office because his half-white sister was the concubine of the Federal A.P.M.: and this time McCaslin did not even say Look but merely lifted one hand, not even pointing, not even specifically toward the shelf of ledgers but toward the desk, toward the corner where it sat beside the scuffed patch on the floor where two decades of heavy shoes had stood while the white man at the desk added and multiplied and subtracted. And again he did not need to look because he had seen this himself and, twenty-three years after the Surrender and twenty-four after the Proclamation, was still watching it: the ledgers, new ones now and filled rapidly, succeeding one another rapidly and containing more names than old Carothers or even his father and Uncle Buddy had ever dreamed of; new names and new faces to go with them, among which the old names and faces that even his father and uncle would have recognised, were lost, vanished—Tomey's Terrel dead, and even the tragic and miscast Percival Brownlee, who couldn't keep books and couldn't farm either, found his true niche at last, reappeared in 1862 during the boy's father's absence and had apparently been living on the plantation for at least a month before his uncle found out about it, conducting impromptu revival meetings among negroes, preaching and leading the singing also in his high sweet true soprano voice and disappeared again on foot and at top speed, not behind but ahead of a body of raiding Federal horse and reappeared for the third and last time in the entourage of a travelling Army paymaster, the two of them passing through Jefferson in a surrey at the exact moment when the boy's father (it was 1866) also happened to be cross- ing the Square, the surry and its occupants traversing rapidly that quiet and bucolic scene and even in that fleeting moment and to others beside the boy's father giving an illusion of flight and illicit holiday like a man on an excursion during his wife's absence with his wife's personal maid, until Brownlee glanced up and saw his late co-master and gave him one defiant female glance and then broke again, leaped from the surrey and dis- appeared this time for good and it was only by chance that McCaslin, twenty years later, heard of him again, an old man now and quite fat, as the well-to-do proprietor of a select New Orleans brothel; and Tennie's Jim gone, nobody knew where, and Fonsiba in Arkansas with her three dollars each month and the scholar-husband with his lenseless spectacles and frock coat and his plans for the spring; and only Lucas was left, the baby, the last save himself of old Carothers' doomed and fatal blood which in the male derivation seemed to destroy all it touched, and even he was repudiating and at least hoping to escape it;—Lucas, the boy of fourteen whose name would not even appear for six years yet among those rapid pages in the bindings new and dustless too since McCaslin lifted them down daily now to write into them the continuation of that record which two hundred years had not been enough to complete and another hundred would not be enough to dis- charge; that chronicle which was a whole land in miniature, which multiplied and compounded was the entire South,

twenty-three years after surrender and twenty-four from eman-
cipation—that slow trickle of molasses and meal and meat, of
shoes and straw hats and overalls, of plowlines and collars and
heelbolts and buckheads and clevises, which returned each
fall as cotton—the two threads frail as truth and impalpable as
equators yet cable-strong to bind for life them who made the
cotton to the land their sweat fell on: and he

"Yes. Binding them for a while yet, a little while yet.
Through and beyond that life and maybe through and beyond
the life of that life's sons and maybe even through and beyond
that of the sons of those sons. But not always, because they will
endure. They will outlast us because they are—" it was not a
pause, barely a falter even, possibly appreciable only to himself, as if he couldn't speak even to McCaslin, even to explain
his repudiation, that which to him too, even in the act of
escaping (and maybe this was the reality and the truth of his
need to escape) was heresy: so that even in escaping he was
taking with him more of that evil and unregenerate old man
who could summon, because she was his property, a human
being because she was old enough and female, to his widower's house and get a child on her and then dismiss her
because she was of an inferior race, and then bequeath a thousand dollars to the infant because he would be dead then and
wouldn't have to pay it, than even he had feared. "Yes. He
didn't want to. He had to. Because they will endure. They are
better than we are. Stronger than we are. Their vices are vices
aped from white men or that white men and bondage have
taught them: improvidence and intemperance and evasion—
not laziness: evasion: of what white men had set them to, not
for their aggrandisement or even comfort but his own—" and
McCaslin

"All right. Go on: Promiscuity. Violence. Instability and

lack of control. Inability to distinguish between mine and thine—" and he

"How distinguish, when for two hundred years mine did not even exist for them?" and McCaslin

"All right. Go on. And their virtues—" and he

"Yes. Their own. Endurance—" and McCaslin

"So have mules": and he

"—and pity and tolerance and forbearance and fidelity and love of children—" and McCaslin

"So have dogs": and he

"—whether their own or not or black or not. And more: what they got not only not from white people but not even despite white people because they had it already from the old free fathers a longer time free than us because we have never been free—" and it was in McCaslin's eyes too, he had only to look at McCaslin's eyes and it was there, that summer twilight seven years ago, almost a week after they had returned from the camp before he discovered that Sam Fathers had told McCaslin: an old bear, fierce and ruthless not just to stay alive but ruthless with the fierce pride of liberty and freedom, jealous and proud enough of liberty and freedom to see it threatened not with fear nor even alarm but almost with joy, seeming deliberately to put it into jeopardy in order to savor it and keep his old strong bones and flesh supple and quick to defend and preserve it; an old man, son of a Negro slave and an Indian king, inheritor on the one hand of the long chronicle of a people who had learned humility through suffering and learned pride through the endurance which survived the suffering, and on the other side the chronicle of a people even longer in the land than the first, yet who now existed there only in the solitary brotherhood of an old and childless Negro's alien blood and the wild and invincible spirit of an old bear; a boy who wished to learn humility and pride in order to become skillful and worthy in the woods but found himself becoming so skillful so fast that he feared he would never become worthy because he had not learned humility and pride though he had tried, until one day an old man who could not have defined either led him as though by the hand to where an old bear and a little mongrel dog showed him that, by possessing one thing other, he would possess them both; and a little dog, nameless and mongrel and many-fathered, grown yet weighing less than six pounds, who couldn't be dangerous because there was nothing anywhere much smaller, not fierce because that would have been called just noise, not humble because it was already too near the ground to genuflect, and not proud because it would not have been close enough for anyone to discern what was casting that shadow and which didn't even know it was not going to heaven since they had already decided it had no immortal soul, so that all it could be was brave even though they would probably call that too just noise. "*And you didn't shoot,*" McCaslin said. "*How close were you?*"

"*I dont know,*" he said. "*There was a big wood tick just inside his off hind leg. I saw that. But I didn't have the gun then.*"

"*But you didn't shoot when you had the gun,*" McCaslin said. "*Why?*" But McCaslin didn't wait, rising and crossing the room, across the pelt of the bear he had killed two years ago and the bigger one McCaslin had killed before he was born, to the bookcase beneath the mounted head of his first buck, and returned with the book and sat down again and opened it. "Listen," he said. He read the five stanzas aloud and closed the book on his finger and looked up. "All right," he said. "Listen," and*

*read again, but only one stanza this time and closed the book
and laid it on the table.* "She cannot fade, though thou hast not
thy bliss," *McCaslin said:* "Forever wilt thou love, and she be
fair."

"He's talking about a girl," *he said.*

"He had to talk about something," *McCaslin said. Then he
said,* "He was talking about truth. Truth is one. It doesn't
change. It covers all things which touch the heart—honor and
pride and pity and justice and courage and love. Do you see
now?" *He didn't know. Somehow it had seemed simpler than
that, simpler than somebody talking in a book about a young
man and a girl he would never need to grieve over because he
could never approach any nearer and would never have to get
any further away. He had heard about an old bear and finally
got big enough to hunt it and he hunted it four years and at last
met it with a gun in his hands and he didn't shoot. Because a
little dog—But he could have shot long before the fyce covered
the twenty yards to where the bear waited, and Sam Fathers
could have shot at any time during the interminable minute
while Old Ben stood on his hind legs over them. . . . He ceased.
McCaslin watched him, still speaking, the voice, the words as
quiet as the twilight itself was:* "Courage and honor and pride,
and pity and love of justice and of liberty. They all touch the
heart, and what the heart holds to becomes truth, as far as we
know truth. Do you see now?" and he could still hear them,
intact in this twilight as in that one seven years ago, no louder
still because they did not need to be because they would
endure: and he had only to look at McCaslin's eyes beyond
the thin and bitter smiling, the faint lip-lift which would have
had to be called smiling;—his kinsman, his father almost, who
had been born too late into the old time and too soon for the

new, the two of them juxtaposed and alien now to each other against their ravaged patrimony, the dark and ravaged fatherland still prone and panting from its etherless operation:

"Habet then.—So this land is, indubitably, of and by itself cursed": and he

"Cursed": and again McCaslin merely lifted one hand, not even speaking and not even toward the ledgers: so that, as the stereopticon condenses into one instantaneous field the myriad minutia of its scope, so did that slight and rapid gesture establish in the small cramped and cluttered twilit room not only the ledgers but the whole plantation in its mazed and intricate entirety—the land, the fields and what they represented in terms of cotton ginned and sold, the men and women whom they fed and clothed and even paid a little cash money at Christmas-time in return for the labor which planted and raised and picked and ginned the cotton, the machinery and mules and gear with which they raised it and their cost and upkeep and replacement—that whole edifice intricate and complex and founded upon injustice and erected by ruthless rapacity and carried on even yet with at times downright savagery not only to the human beings but the valuable animals too, yet solvent and efficient and, more than that: not only still intact but enlarged, increased; brought still intact by McCaslin, himself little more than a child then, through and out of the debacle and chaos of twenty years ago where hardly one in ten survived, and enlarged and increased and would continue so, solvent and efficient and intact and still increasing so long as McCaslin and his McCaslin successors lasted, even though their surnames might not even be Edmonds then: and he: "Habet too. Because that's it: not the land, but us. Not only the blood, but the name too; not only its color but its designation: Edmonds, white, but, a female line, could have no other but the name his father bore; Beauchamp, the elder line and the male one, but, black, could have had any name he liked and no man would have cared, except the name his father bore who had no name—" and McCaslin

"And since I know too what you know I will say now, once more let me say it: And one other, and in the third generation too, and the male, the eldest, the direct and sole and white and still McCaslin even, father to son to son—" and he

"I am free": and this time McCaslin did not even gesture, no inference of fading pages, no postulation of the stereoptic whole, but the frail and iron thread strong as truth and impervious as evil and longer than life itself and reaching beyond record and patrimony both to join him with the lusts and passions, the hopes and dreams and griefs, of bones whose names while still fleshed and capable even old Carothers' grandfather had never heard: and he: "And of that too": and McCaslin

"Chosen, I suppose (I will concede it) out of all your time by Him as you say Buck and Buddy were from theirs. And it took Him a bear and an old man and four years just for you. And it took you fourteen years to reach that point and about that many, maybe more, for Old Ben, and more than seventy for Sam Fathers. And you are just one. How long then? How long?" and he

"It will be long. I have never said otherwise. But it will be all right because they will endure—" and McCaslin

"And anyway, you will be free.—No, not now nor ever, we from them nor they from us. So I repudiate too. I would deny even if I knew it were true. I would have to. Even you can see that I could do no else. I am what I am; I will be always what I was born and have always been. And more than me. More than me, just as there were more than Buck and Buddy in what you called His first plan which failed": and he

"And more than me": and McCaslin

"No. Not even you. Because mark. You said how on that instant when Ikkemotubbe realised that he could sell the land to Grandfather, it ceased forever to have been his. All right; go on: Then it belonged to Sam Fathers, old Ikkemotubbe's son. And who inherited from Sam Fathers, if not you? co-heir perhaps with Boon, if not of his life maybe, at least of his quitting it?" and he

"Yes. Sam Fathers set me free." And Isaac McCaslin, not yet Uncle Ike, a long time yet before he would be uncle to half a county and still father to none, living in one small cramped fireless rented room in a Jefferson boarding-house where petit juries were domiciled during court terms and itinerant horse- and mule-traders stayed, with his kit of brand-new carpenter's tools and the shotgun McCaslin had given him with his name engraved in silver and old General Compson's compass (and, when the General died, his silver-mounted horn too) and the iron cot and mattress and the blankets which he would take each fall into the woods for more than sixty years and the bright tin coffee-pot

there had been a legacy, from his Uncle Hubert Beauchamp, his godfather, that bluff burly roaring childlike man from whom Uncle Buddy had won Tomey's Terrel's wife Tennie in the poker-game in 1859—"possible strait against three Treys in sigt Not called"—; no pale sentence or paragraph scrawled in cringing fear of death by a weak and trembling hand as a last desperate sop flung backward at retribution, but a Legacy, a Thing, possessing weight to the hand and bulk to the eye and even audible: a silver cup filled with gold pieces and wrapped in burlap and sealed with his godfather's ring

in the hot wax, which (intact still) even before his Uncle
Hubert's death and long before his own majority, when it
would be his, had become not only a legend but one of the
family lares. After his father's and his Uncle Hubert's sister's
marriage they moved back into the big house, the tremendous
cavern which old Carothers had started and never finished,
cleared the remaining negroes out of it and with his mother's
dowry completed it, at least the rest of the windows and doors
and moved into it, all of them save Uncle Buddy who declined
to leave the cabin he and his twin had built, the move being
the bride's notion and more than just a notion and none ever
to know if she really wanted to live in the big house or if she
knew before hand that Uncle Buddy would refuse to move:
and two weeks after his birth in 1867, the first time he and his
mother came down stairs, one night and the silver cup sitting
on the cleared dining-room table beneath the bright lamp
and while his mother and his father and McCaslin and Tennie (his nurse: carrying him)—all of them again but Uncle
Buddy—watched, his Uncle Hubert rang one by one into the
cup the bright and glinting mintage and wrapped it into the
burlap envelope and heated the wax and sealed it and carried
it back home with him where he lived alone now without
even his sister either to hold him down as McCaslin said or to
try to raise him up as Uncle Buddy said, and (dark times then
in Mississippi) Uncle Buddy said most of the niggers gone and
the ones that didn't go even Hub Beauchamp could not have
wanted: but the dogs remained and Uncle Buddy said Beauchamp fiddled while Nero fox-hunted

they would go and see it there; at last his mother would
prevail and they would depart in the surrey, once more all save
Uncle Buddy and McCaslin to keep Uncle Buddy company
until one winter Uncle Buddy began to fail and from then on

it was himself, beginning to remember now, and his mother and Tennie and Tomey's Terrel to drive: the twenty-two miles into the next county, the twin gateposts on one of which McCaslin could remember the half-grown boy blowing a fox-horn at breakfast dinner and supper-time and jumping down to open to any passer who happened to hear it but where there were no gates at all now, the shabby and overgrown entrance to what his mother still insisted that people call Warwick because her brother was if truth but triumphed and justice but prevailed the rightful earl of it, the paintless house which out-wardly did not change but which on the inside seemed each time larger because he was too little to realise then that there was less and less in it of the fine furnishings, the rosewood and mahogany and walnut which for him had never existed any-where anyway save in his mother's tearful lamentations and the occasional piece small enough to be roped somehow onto the rear or the top of the carriage on their return (And he remembered this, he had seen it: an instant, a flash, his mother's soprano "Even my dress! Even my dress!" loud and outraged in the barren unswept hall; a face young and female and even lighter in color than Tomey's Terrel's for an instant in a closing door; a swirl, a glimpse of the silk gown and the flick and glint of an ear-ring: an apparition rapid and tawdry and illicit yet somehow even to the child, the infant still almost, breathless and exciting and evocative: as though, like two limpid and pellucid streams meeting, the child which he still was had made serene and absolute and perfect rapport and contact through that glimpsed nameless illicit hybrid female flesh with the boy which had existed at that stage of inviolable and immortal adolescence in his uncle for almost sixty years; the dress, the face, the ear-rings gone in that same aghast flash and his uncle's voice: "She's my cook! She's my

new cook! I had to have a cook, didn't I?" then the uncle himself, the face alarmed and aghast too yet still innocently and
somehow even indomitably of a boy, they retreating in their
turn now, back to the front gallery, and his uncle again,
pained and still amazed, in a sort of desperate resurgence if
not of courage at least of self-assertion: "They're free now!
They're folks too just like we are!" and his mother: "That's
why! That's why! My mother's house! Defiled! Defiled!" and
his uncle: "Damn it, Sibbey, at least give her time to pack her
grip": then over, finished, the loud uproar and all, himself and
Tennie and he remembered Tennie's inscrutable face at the
broken shutterless window of the bare room which had once
been the parlor while they watched, hurrying down the lane at
a stumbling trot, the routed compounder of his uncle's uxory:
the back, the nameless face which he had seen only for a
moment, the once-hooped dress ballooning and flapping
below a man's overcoat, the worn heavy carpet-bag jouncing
and banging against her knee, routed and in retreat true
enough and in the empty lane solitary young-looking and forlorn yet withal still exciting and evocative and wearing still the
silken banner captured inside the very citadel of respectabil-
ity, and unforgettable.)

the cup, the sealed inscrutable burlap, sitting on the shelf
in the locked closet, Uncle Hubert unlocking the door and
lifting it down and passing it from hand to hand: his mother,
his father, McCaslin and even Tennie, insisting that each take
it in turn and heft it for weight and shake it again to prove the
sound, Uncle Hubert himself standing spraddled before the
cold unswept hearth in which the very bricks themselves were
crumbling into a litter of soot and dust and mortar and the
droppings of chimneysweeps, still roaring and still innocent
and still indomitable: and for a long time he believed nobody

but himself had noticed that his uncle now put the cup only
into his hands, unlocked the door and lifted it down and put it
into his hands and stood over him until he had shaken it obediently until it sounded then took it from him and locked it
back into the closet before anyone else could have offered to
touch it, and even later, when competent not only to remember but to rationalise, he could not say what it was or even if it
had been anything because the parcel was still heavy and still
rattled, not even when, Uncle Buddy dead and his father, at
last and after almost seventy-five years in bed after the sun
rose, said: "Go get that damn cup. Bring that damn Hub
Beauchamp too if you have to": because it still rattled though
his uncle no longer put it even into his hands now but carried
it himself from one to the other, his mother, McCaslin, Tennie, shaking it before each in turn, saying: "Hear it? Hear it?"
his face still innocent, not quite baffled but only amazed and
not very amazed and still indomitable: and, his father and
Uncle Buddy both gone now, one day without reason or any
warning the almost completely empty house in which his
uncle and Tennie's ancient and quarrelsome great-grandfather
(who claimed to have seen Lafayette and McCaslin said in
another ten years would be remembering God) lived, cooked
and slept in one single room, burst into peaceful conflagra-
tion, a tranquil instantaneous sourceless unanimity of com-
bustion, walls floors and roof: at sunup it stood where his
uncle's father had built it sixty years ago, at sundown the four
blackened and smokeless chimneys rose from a light white
powder of ashes and a few charred ends of planks which did
not even appear to have been very hot: and out of the last of
evening, the last one of the twenty-two miles, on the old white
mare which was the last of that stable which McCaslin
remembered, the two old men riding double up to the sister's

door, the one wearing his fox-horn on its braided deerhide thong and the other carrying the burlap parcel wrapped in a shirt, the tawny wax-daubed shapeless lump sitting again and on an almost identical shelf and his uncle holding the half-opened door now, his hand not only on the knob but one foot against it and the key waiting in the other hand, the face urgent and still not baffled but still and even indomitably not very amazed and himself standing in the half-opened door looking quietly up at the burlap shape become almost three times its original height and a good half less than its original thickness and turning away and he would remember not his mother's look this time nor yet Tennie's inscrutable expression but McCaslin's dark and aquiline face grave insufferable and bemused: then one night they waked him and fetched him still half-asleep into the lamp light, the smell of medicine which was familiar by now in that room and the smell of something else which he had not smelled before and knew at once and would never forget, the pillow, the worn and ravaged face from which looked out still the boy innocent and immortal and amazed and urgent, looking at him and trying to tell him until McCaslin moved and leaned over the bed and drew from the top of the night shirt the big iron key on the greasy cord which suspended it, the eyes saying Yes Yes Yes now, and cut the cord and unlocked the closet and brought the parcel to the bed, the eyes still trying to tell him even when he took the parcel so that was still not it, the hands still clinging to the parcel even while relinquishing it, the eyes more urgent than ever trying to tell him but they never did; and he was ten and his mother was dead too and McCaslin said, "You are almost halfway now. You might as well open it": and he: "No. He said twenty-one": and he was twenty-one and McCaslin shifted the bright lamp to the center of the cleared dining-room table and

set the parcel beside it and laid his open knife beside the parcel and stood back with that expression of old grave intolerant
and repudiating and he lifted it, the burlap lump which fifteen years ago had changed its shape completely overnight,
which shaken gave forth a thin weightless not-quite-musical
curiously muffled clatter, the bright knife-blade hunting amid
the mazed intricacy of string, the knobby gouts of wax bearing
his uncle's Beauchamp seal rattling onto the table's polished
top and, standing amid the collapse of burlap folds, the
unstained tin coffee-pot still brand new, the handful of copper
coins and now he knew what had given them the muffled
sound: a collection of minutely-folded scraps of paper sufficient almost for a rat's nest, of good linen bond, of the crude
ruled paper such as negroes use, of raggedly-torn ledger-pages
and the margins of newspapers and once the paper label from
a new pair of overalls, all dated and all signed, beginning with
the first one not six months after they had watched him seal
the silver cup into the burlap on this same table in this same
room by the light even of this same lamp almost twenty-one
years ago:

*I owe my Nephew Isaac Beauchamp McCaslin five (5)
pieces Gold which I,O.U constitutes My note of hand with
Interest at 5 percent.*
                        Hubert Fitz-Hubert Beauchamp
at Warwick 27 Nov 1867

and he: "Anyway he called it Warwick": once at least, even if
no more. But there was more:

*Isaac 24 Dec 1867 I.O.U. 2 pieces Gold H.Fh.B. I.O.U.
Isaac 1 piece Gold 1 Jan 1868 H.Fh.B.*

then five again then three then one then one then a long time
and what dream, what dreamed splendid recoup, not of any
injury or betrayal of trust because it had been merely a loan:
nay, a partnership:

I.O.U. Beauchamp McCaslin or his heirs twenty-five (25)
pieces Gold This & All preceeding constituting My notes of
hand at twenty (20) percentum compounded annually. This
date of 19th January 1873

Beauchamp

no location save that in time and signed by the single not
name but word as the old proud earl himself might have
scrawled Nevile: and that made forty-three and he could not
remember himself of course but the legend had it at fifty,
which balanced: one: then one: then one: then one and then
the last three and then the last chit, dated after he came to live
in the house with them and written in the shaky hand not of a
beaten old man because he had never been beaten to know it
but of a tired old man maybe and even at that tired only on the
outside and still indomitable, the simplicity of the last one the
simplicity not of resignation but merely of amazement, like a
simple comment or remark, and not very much of that:

One silver cup. Hubert Beauchamp

and McCaslin: "So you have plenty of coppers anyway. But
they are still not old enough yet to be either rarities or heir-
looms. So you will have to take the money": except that he
didn't hear McCaslin, standing quietly beside the table and
looking peacefully at the coffee-pot and the pot sitting one
night later on the mantel above what was not even a fireplace

in the little cramped icelike room in Jefferson as McCaslin tossed the folded banknotes onto the bed and, still standing (there was nowhere to sit save on the bed) did not even remove his hat and overcoat: and he

"As a loan. From you. This one": and McCaslin

"You cant. I have no money that I can lend to you. And you will have to go to the bank and get it next month because I wont bring it to you": and he could not hear McCaslin now either, looking peacefully at McCaslin, his kinsman, his father almost yet no kin now as, at the last, even fathers and sons are no kin: and he

"It's seventeen miles, horseback and in the cold. We could both sleep here": and McCaslin

"Why should I sleep here in my house when you wont sleep yonder in yours?" and gone, and he looking at the bright rustless unstained tin and thinking and not for the first time how much it takes to compound a man (Isaac McCaslin for instance) and of the devious intricate choosing yet unerring path that man's (Isaac McCaslin's for instance) spirit takes among all that mass to make him at last what he is to be, not only to the astonishment of them (the ones who sired the McCaslin who sired his father and Uncle Buddy and their sister, and the ones who sired the Beauchamp who sired his Uncle Hubert and his Uncle Hubert's sister) who believed they had shaped him, but to Isaac McCaslin too

as a loan and used it though he would not have had to: Major de Spain offered him a room in his house as long as he wanted it and asked nor would ever ask any question, and old General Compson more than that, to take him into his own room, to sleep in half of his own bed and more than Major de Spain because he told him baldly why: "You sleep with me and before this winter is out, I'll know the reason. You'll tell me. Because I dont believe you just quit. It looks like you just quit but I have watched you in the woods too much and I dont believe you just quit even if it does look damn like it": using it as a loan, paid his board and rent for a month and bought the tools, not simply because he was good with his hands because he had intended to use his hands and it could have been with horses, and not in mere static and hopeful emulation of the Nazarene as the young gambler buys a spotted shirt because the old gambler won in one yesterday, but (without the arrogance of false humility and without the false humbleness of pride, who intended to earn his bread, didn't especially want to earn it but had to earn it and for more than just bread) because if the Nazarene had found carpentering good for the life and ends He had assumed and elected to serve, it would be all right too for Isaac McCaslin even though Isaac McCaslin's ends, although simple enough in their apparent motivation, were and would be always incomprehensible to him, and his life, invincible enough in its needs, if he could have helped himself, not being the Nazarene, he would not have chosen it: and paid it back. He had forgotten the thirty dollars which McCaslin would put into the bank in his name each month, fetched it in to him and flung it onto the bed that first one time but no more; he had a partner now or rather he was the partner: a blasphemous profane clever old dipsomaniac who had built blockade-runners in Charleston in '62 and '3 and had been a ship's carpenter since and appeared in Jefferson two years ago nobody knew from where nor why and spent a good part of his time since recovering from delirium tremens in the jail; they had put a new roof on the stable of the bank's president and (the old man in jail again still celebrating that job) he went to the bank to collect for it and the president said, "I should borrow from you instead of paying you": and it had been seven months now and he remembered for the first time, two-hundred-and-ten dollars, and this was the first job of any size and when he left the bank the account stood at two-twenty, two-forty to balance, only twenty dollars more to go, then it did balance though by then the total had increased to three hundred and thirty and he said, "I will transfer it now": and the president said, "I cant do that. McCaslin told me not to. Haven't you got another initial you could use and open another account?" but that was all right, the coins the silver and the bills as they accumulated knotted into a handkerchief and the coffee-pot wrapped in an old shirt as when Tennie's great-grandfather had fetched it from Warwick eighteen years ago, in the bottom of the iron-bound trunk which old Carothers had brought from Carolina and his landlady said, "Not even a lock! And you dont even lock your door, not even when you leave!" and himself looking at her as peacefully as he had looked at McCaslin that first night in this same room, no kin to him at all yet more than kin as those who serve you even for pay are your kin and those who injure you are more than brother or wife

and had the wife now, got the old man out of jail and fetched him to the rented room and sobered him by superior strength, did not even remove his own shoes for twenty-four hours, got him up and got food into him and they built the barn this time from the ground up and he married her: an only child, a small girl yet curiously bigger than she seemed at first, solider perhaps, with dark eyes and a passionate heart-shaped face, who had time even on that farm to watch most of the day while he sawed timbers to the old man's measurements: and she: "Papa told me about you. That farm is really yours, isn't it?" and he

"And McCaslin's": and she

"Was there a will leaving half of it to him?" and he

"There didn't need to be a will. His grandmother was my father's sister. We were the same as brothers": and she

"You are the same as second cousins and that's all you ever will be. But I dont suppose it matters": and they were married, they were married and it was the new country, his heritage too as it was the heritage of all, out of the earth, beyond the earth yet of the earth because his too was of the earth's long chronicle, his too because each must share with another in order to come into it and in the sharing they become one: for that while, one: for that little while at least, one: indivisible, that while at least irrevocable and unrecoverable, living in a rented room still but for just a little while and that room wall-less and topless and floorless in glory for him to leave each morning and return to at night; her father already owned the lot in town and furnished the material and he and his partner would build it, her dowry from one: her wedding-present from three, she not to know it until the bungalow was finished and ready to be moved into and he never knew who told her, not her father and not his partner and not even in drink though for a while he believed that, himself coming home from work and just time to wash and rest a moment before going down to supper, entering no rented cubicle since it would still partake of glory even after they would have grown old and lost it: and he saw her face then, just before she spoke: "Sit down": the two of them sitting on the bed's edge, not even touching yet, her face strained and terrible, her voice a passionate and expiring whisper of immeasurable promise: "I love you. You know I love you. When are we going to move?" and he

"I didn't—I didn't know—Who told you—" the hot fierce

palm clapped over his mouth, crushing his lips into his teeth, the fierce curve of fingers digging into his cheek and only the palm slacked off enough for him to answer:

"The farm. Our farm. Your farm": and he

"I—" then the hand again, finger and palm, the whole enveloping weight of her although she still was not touching him save the hand, the voice: "No! No!" and the fingers themselves seeming to follow through the cheek the impulse to speech as it died in his mouth, then the whisper, the breath again, of love and of incredible promise, the palm slackening again to let him answer:

"When?" and he

"I—" then she was gone, the hand too, standing, her back to him and her head bent, the voice so calm now that for an instant it seemed no voice of hers that he ever remembered: "Stand up and turn your back and shut your eyes": and repeated before he understood and stood himself with his eyes shut and heard the bell ring for supper below stairs and the calm voice again: "Lock the door": and he did so and leaned his forehead against the cold wood, his eyes closed, hearing his heart and the sound he had begun to hear before he moved until it ceased and the bell rang again below stairs and he knew it was for them this time and he heard the bed and turned and he had never seen her naked before, he had asked her to once, and why: that he wanted to see her naked because he loved her and he wanted to see her looking at him naked because he loved her but after that he never mentioned it again, even turning his face when she put the nightgown on over her dress to undress at night and putting the dress on over the gown to remove it in the morning and she would not let him get into bed beside her until the lamp was out and even in the heat of summer she would draw the sheet up over them

both before she would let him turn to her: and the landlady
came up the stairs up the hall and rapped on the door and
then called their names but she didn't move, lying still on the
bed outside the covers, her face turned away on the pillow, listening to nothing, thinking of nothing, not of him anyway he
thought then the landlady went away and she said, "Take off
your clothes": her head still turned away, looking at nothing,
thinking of nothing, waiting for nothing, not even him, her
hand moving as though with volition and vision of its own,
catching his wrist at the exact moment when he paused beside
the bed so that he never paused but merely changed the direction of moving, downward now, the hand drawing him and
she moved at last, shifted, a movement one single complete
inherent not practiced and one time older than man, looking
at him now, drawing him still downward with the one hand
down and down and he neither saw nor felt it shift, palm flat
against his chest now and holding him away with the same
apparent lack of any effort or any need for strength, and not
looking at him now, she didn't need to, the chaste woman, the
wife, already looked upon all the men who ever rutted and
now her whole body had changed, altered, he had never seen
it but once and now it was not even the one he had seen but
composite of all woman-flesh since man that ever of its own
will reclined on its back and opened, and out of it somewhere,
without any movement of lips even, the dying and invincible
whisper: "Promise": and he

"Promise?"

"The farm." He moved. He had moved, the hand shifting
from his chest once more to his wrist, grasping it, the arm still
lax and only the light increasing pressure of the fingers as
though arm and hand were a piece of wire cable with one
looped end, only the hand tightening as he pulled against it.

"No," he said. "No": and she was not looking at him still but not like the other but still the hand: "No, I tell you. I wont. I cant. Never": and still the hand and he said, for the last time, he tried to speak clearly and he knew it was still gently and he thought, *She already knows more than I with all the man-listening in camps where there was nothing to read ever even heard of. They are born already bored with what a boy approaches only at fourteen and fifteen with blundering and aghast trembling:* "I cant. Not ever. Remember": and still the steady and invincible hand and he said Yes and he thought, *She is lost. She was born lost. We were all born lost* then he stopped thinking and even saying Yes, it was like nothing he had ever dreamed, let alone heard in mere man-talking until after a no-time he returned and lay spent on the insatiate immemorial beach and again with a movement one time more older than man she turned and freed herself and on their wedding night she had cried and he thought she was crying now at first, into the tossed and wadded pillow, the voice coming from somewhere between the pillow and the cachinnation: "And that's all. That's all from me. If this dont get you that son you talk about, it wont be mine": lying on her side, her back to the empty rented room, laughing and laughing

5

He went back to the camp one more time before the lumber company moved in and began to cut the timber. Major de Spain himself never saw it again. But he made them welcome to use the house and hunt the land whenever they liked, and in the winter following the last hunt when Sam Fathers and Lion died, General Compson and Walter Ewell invented a

plan to corporate themselves, the old group, into a club and
lease the camp and the hunting privileges of the woods—an
invention doubtless of the somewhat childish old General but
actually worthy of Boon Hogganbeck himself. Even the boy,
listening, recognised it for the subterfuge it was: to change the
leopard's spots when they could not alter the leopard, a baseless and illusory hope to which even McCaslin seemed to sub-
scribe for a while, that once they had persuaded Major de
Spain to return to the camp he might revoke himself, which
even the boy knew he would not do. And he did not. The boy
never knew what occurred when Major de Spain declined.
He was not present when the subject was broached and
McCaslin never told him. But when June came and the time
for the double birthday celebration there was no mention of it
and when November came no one spoke of using Major de
Spain's house and he never knew whether or not Major de
Spain knew they were going on the hunt though without
doubt old Ash probably told him: he and McCaslin and General Compson (and that one was the General's last hunt too)
and Walter and Boon and Tennie's Jim and old Ash loaded
two wagons and drove two days and almost forty miles beyond
any country the boy had ever seen before and lived in tents for
the two weeks. And the next spring they heard (not from
Major de Spain) that he had sold the timber-rights to a Memphis lumber company and in June the boy came to town with
McCaslin one Saturday and went to Major de Spain's office—
the big, airy, book-lined second-storey room with windows at
one end opening upon the shabby hinder purlieus of stores
and at the other a door giving onto the railed balcony above
the Square, with its curtained alcove where sat a cedar water-
bucket and a sugar-bowl and spoon and tumbler and a wicker-
covered demijohn of whiskey, and the bamboo-and-paper

punkah swinging back and forth above the desk while old Ash in a tilted chair beside the entrance pulled the cord.

"Of course," Major de Spain said. "Ash will probably like to get off in the woods himself for a while, where he wont have to eat Daisy's cooking. Complain about it, anyway. Are you going to take anybody with you?"

"No sir," he said. "I thought that maybe Boon—" For six months now Boon had been town-marshal at Hoke's; Major de Spain had compounded with the lumber company—or perhaps compromised was closer, since it was the lumber company who had decided that Boon might be better as a town-marshal than head of a logging gang.

"Yes," Major de Spain said. "I'll wire him today. He can meet you at Hoke's. I'll send Ash on by the train and they can take some food in and all you will have to do will be to mount your horse and ride over."

"Yes sir," he said. "Thank you." And he heard his voice again. He didn't know he was going to say it yet he did know, he had known it all the time: "Maybe if you . . ." His voice died. It was stopped, he never knew how because Major de Spain did not speak and it was not until his voice ceased that Major de Spain moved, turned back to the desk and the papers spread on it and even that without moving because he was sitting at the desk with a paper in his hand when the boy entered, the boy standing there looking down at the short plumpish grey-haired man in sober fine broadcloth and an immaculate glazed shirt whom he was used to seeing in boots and muddy corduroy; unshaven, sitting the shaggy powerful long-hocked mare with the worn Winchester carbine across the saddlebow and the great blue dog standing motionless as bronze at the stirrup, the two of them in that last year and to the boy anyway coming to resemble one another somehow as

two people competent for love or for business who have been
in love or in business together for a long time sometimes do.
Major de Spain did not look up again.

"No. I will be too busy. But good luck to you. If you have
it, you might bring me a young squirrel."

"Yes sir," he said. "I will."

He rode his mare, the three-year-old filly he had bred and
raised and broken himself. He left home a little after midnight
and six hours later, without even having sweated her, he rode
into Hoke's, the tiny log-line junction which he had always
thought of as Major de Spain's property too although Major
de Spain had merely sold the company (and that many years
ago) the land on which the sidetracks and loading-platforms
and the commissary store stood, and looked about in shocked
and grieved amazement even though he had had forewarn-
ing and had believed himself prepared: a new planing-mill
already half completed which would cover two or three acres
and what looked like miles and miles of stacked steel rails red
with the light bright rust of newness and of piled crossties
sharp with creosote, and wire corrals and feeding-troughs for
two hundred mules at least and the tents for the men who
drove them; so that he arranged for the care and stabling of his
mare as rapidly as he could and did not look any more,
mounted into the log-train caboose with his gun and climbed
into the cupola and looked no more save toward the wall of
wilderness ahead within which he would be able to hide himself from it once more anyway.

Then the little locomotive shrieked and began to move: a
rapid churning of exhaust, a lethargic deliberate clashing of
slack couplings traveling backward along the train, the
exhaust changing to the deep slow clapping bites of power as
the caboose too began to move and from the cupola he

watched the train's head complete the first and only curve in the entire line's length and vanish into the wilderness, dragging its length of train behind it so that it resembled a small dingy harmless snake vanishing into weeds, drawing him with it too until soon it ran once more at its maximum clattering speed between the twin walls of unaxed wilderness as of old. It had been harmless once. Not five years ago Walter Ewell had shot a six-point buck from this same moving caboose, and there was the story of the half-grown bear: the train's first trip in to the cutting thirty miles away, the bear between the rails, its rear end elevated like that of a playing puppy while it dug to see what sort of ants or bugs they might contain or perhaps just to examine the curious symmetrical squared barkless logs which had appeared apparently from nowhere in one endless mathematical line overnight, still digging until the driver on the braked engine not fifty feet away blew the whistle at it, whereupon it broke frantically and took the first tree it came to: an ash sapling not much bigger than a man's thigh and climbed as high as it could and clung there, its head ducked between its arms as a man (a woman perhaps) might have done while the brakeman threw chunks of ballast at it, and when the engine returned three hours later with the first load of outbound logs the bear was halfway down the tree and once more scrambled back up as high as it could and clung again while the train passed and was still there when the engine went in again in the afternoon and still there when it came back out at dusk; and Boon had been in Hoke's with the wagon after a barrel of flour that noon when the train-crew told about it and Boon and Ash, both twenty years younger then, sat under the tree all that night to keep anybody from shooting it and the next morning Major de Spain had the log-train held at Hoke's and just before sundown on the second

day, with not only Boon and Ash but Major de Spain and
General Compson and Walter and McCaslin, twelve then,
watching, it came down the tree after almost thirty-six hours
without even water and McCaslin told him how for a minute
they thought it was going to stop right there at the barrow-pit
where they were standing and drink, how it looked at the
water and paused and looked at them and at the water again,
but did not, gone, running, as bears run, the two sets of feet,
front and back, tracking two separate though parallel courses.

It had been harmless then. They would hear the passing
log-train sometimes from the camp; sometimes, because
nobody bothered to listen for it or not. They would hear it
going in, running light and fast, the light clatter of the trucks,
the exhaust of the diminutive locomotive and its shrill peanut-
parcher whistle flung for one petty moment and absorbed by
the brooding and inattentive wilderness without even an echo.
They would hear it going out, loaded, not quite so fast now yet
giving its frantic and toylike illusion of crawling speed, not
whistling now to conserve steam, flinging its bitten laboring
miniature puffing into the immemorial woodsface with frantic and bootless vainglory, empty and noisy and puerile, carrying to no destination or purpose sticks which left nowhere any
scar or stump as the child's toy loads and transports and
unloads its dead sand and rushes back for more, tireless and
unceasing and rapid yet never quite so fast as the Hand which
plays with it moves the toy burden back to load the toy again.
But it was different now. It was the same train, engine cars and
caboose, even the same enginemen brake-man and conductor
to whom Boon, drunk then sober then drunk again then fairly
sober once more all in the space of fourteen hours, had
bragged that day two years ago about what they were going to
do to Old Ben tomorrow, running with its same illusion of

frantic rapidity between the same twin walls of impenetrable and impervious woods, passing the old landmarks, the old game crossings over which he had trailed bucks wounded and not wounded and more than once seen them, anything but wounded, bolt out of the woods and up and across the embankment which bore the rails and ties then down and into the woods again as the earth-bound supposedly move but crossing as arrows travel, groundless, elongated, three times its actual length and even paler, different in color, as if there were a point between immobility and absolute motion where even mass chemically altered, changing without pain or agony not only in bulk and shape but in color too, approaching the color of wind, yet this time it was as though the train (and not only the train but himself, not only his vision which had seen it and his memory which remembered it but his clothes too, as garments carry back into the clean edgeless blowing of air the lingering effluvium of a sick-room or of death) had brought with it into the doomed wilderness even before the actual axe the shadow and portent of the new mill not even finished yet and the rails and ties which were not even laid; and he knew now what he had known as soon as he saw Hoke's this morning but had not yet thought into words: why Major de Spain had not come back, and that after this time he himself, who had had to see it one time other, would return no more.

Now they were near. He knew it before the engine-driver whistled to warn him. Then he saw Ash and the wagon, the reins without doubt wrapped once more about the brake-lever as within the boy's own memory Major de Spain had been forbidding him for eight years to do, the train slowing, the slackened couplings jolting and clashing again from car to car, the caboose slowing past the wagon as he swung down with his gun, the conductor leaning out above him to signal the engine, the caboose still slowing, creeping, although the engine's exhaust was already slatting in mounting tempo against the unechoing wilderness, the crashing of draw-bars once more travelling backward along the train, the caboose picking up speed at last. Then it was gone. It had not been. He could no longer hear it. The wilderness soared, musing, inattentive, myriad, eternal, green; older than any mill-shed, longer than any spurline. "Mr Boon here yet?" he said.

"He beat me in," Ash said. "Had the wagon loaded and ready for me at Hoke's yistiddy when I got there and setting on the front steps at camp last night when I got in. He already been in the woods since fo daylight this morning. Said he gwine up to the Gum Tree and for you to hunt up that way and meet him." He knew where that was: a single big sweet-gum just outside the woods, in an old clearing; if you crept up to it very quietly this time of year and then ran suddenly into the clearing, sometimes you caught as many as a dozen squirrels in it, trapped, since there was no other tree near they could jump to. So he didn't get into the wagon at all.

"I will," he said.

"I figured you would," Ash said, "I fotch you a box of shells." He passed the shells down and began to unwrap the lines from the brake-pole.

"How many times up to now do you reckon Major has told you not to do that?" the boy said.

"Do which?" Ash said. Then he said: "And tell Boon Hogganbeck dinner gonter be on the table in a hour and if yawl want any to come on and eat it."

"In an hour?" he said. "It aint nine oclock yet." He drew out his watch and extended it face-toward Ash. "Look." Ash didn't even look at the watch.

"That's town time. You aint in town now. You in the woods."

"Look at the sun then."

"Nemmine the sun too," Ash said. "If you and Boon Hogganbeck want any dinner, you better come on in and get it when I tole you. I aim to get done in that kitchen because I got my wood to chop. And watch your feet. They're crawling."

"I will," he said.

Then he was in the woods, not alone but solitary; the solitude closed about him, green with summer. They did not change, and, timeless, would not, anymore than would the green of summer and the fire and rain of fall and the iron cold and sometimes even snow

the day, the morning when he killed the buck and Sam marked his face with its hot blood, they returned to camp and he remembered old Ash's blinking and disgruntled and even outraged disbelief until at last McCaslin had had to affirm the fact that he had really killed it: and that night Ash sat snarling and unapproachable behind the stove so that Tennie's Jim had to serve the supper and waked them with breakfast already on the table the next morning and it was only half-past one oclock and at last out of Major de Spain's angry cursing and Ash's snarling and sullen rejoinders the fact emerged that Ash not only wanted to go into the woods and shoot a deer also but he intended to and Major de Spain said, "By God, if we dont let him we will probably have to do the cooking from now on": and Walter Ewell said, "Or get up at midnight to eat what Ash cooks": and since he had already killed his buck for this hunt and was not to shoot again unless they needed meat, he offered his gun to Ash until Major de Spain took command and allotted that gun to Boon for the day and gave Boon's unpredictable pump gun to Ash, with two buckshot shells but Ash said, "I got

shells": and showed them, four: one buck, one of number three
shot for rabbits, two of bird-shot and told one by one their history and their origin and he remembered not Ash's face alone
but Major de Spain's and Walter's and General Compson's too,
and Ash's voice: "Shoot? In course they'll shoot! Genl Cawmp-
son guv me this un"—the buckshot—"right outen the same gun
he kilt that big buck with eight years ago. And this un"—it was
the rabbit shell: triumphantly—"is oldern thisyer boy!" And
that morning he loaded the gun himself, reversing the order: the
bird-shot, the rabbit, then the buck so that the buckshot would
feed first into the chamber, and himself without a gun, he and
Ash walked beside Major de Spain's and Tennie's Jim's horses
and the dogs (that was the snow) until they cast and struck, the
sweet strong cries ringing away into the muffled falling air and
gone almost immediately, as if the constant and unmurmuring
flakes had already buried even the unformed echoes beneath
their myriad and weightless falling, Major de Spain and Tennie's Jim gone too, whooping on into the woods; and then it was
all right, he knew as plainly as if Ash had told him that Ash had
now hunted his deer and that even his tender years had been
forgiven for having killed one, and they turned back toward
home through the falling snow—that is, Ash said, "Now whut?"
and he said, "This way"—himself in front because, although
they were less than a mile from camp, he knew that Ash, who
had spent two weeks of his life in the camp each year for the last
twenty, had no idea whatever where they were, until quite soon
the manner in which Ash carried Boon's gun was making him a
good deal more than just nervous and he made Ash walk in
front, striding on, talking now, an old man's garrulous mono-
logue beginning with where he was at the moment then of the
woods and of camping in the woods and of eating in camps
then of eating then of cooking it and of his wife's cooking then

briefly of his old wife and almost at once and at length of a new light-colored woman who nursed next door to Major de Spain's and if she didn't watch out who she was switching her tail at he would show her how old was an old man or not if his wife just didn't watch him all the time, the two of them in a game trail through a dense brake of cane and brier which would bring them out within a quarter-mile of camp, approaching a big fallen tree-trunk lying athwart the path and just as Ash, still talking, was about to step over it the bear, the yearling, rose suddenly beyond the log, sitting up, its forearms against its chest and its wrists limply arrested as if it had been surprised in the act of covering its face to pray: and after a certain time Ash's gun yawed jerkily up and he said, "You haven't got a shell in the barrel yet. Pump it": but the gun already snicked and he said, "Pump it. You haven't got a shell in the barrel yet": and Ash pumped the action and in a certain time the gun steadied again and snicked and he said, "Pump it": and watched the buckshot shell jerk, spinning heavily, into the cane. This is the rabbit shot: he thought and the gun snicked and he thought: The next is bird-shot: and he didn't have to say Pump it; he cried, "Dont shoot! Dont shoot!" but that was already too late too, the light dry vicious snick! before he could speak and the bear turned and dropped to all-fours and then was gone and there was only the log, the cane, the velvet and constant snow and Ash said, "Now whut?" and he said, "This way. Come on": and began to back away down the path and Ash said, "I got to find my shells": and he said, "Goddamn it, goddamn it, come on": but Ash leaned the gun against the log and returned and stooped and fumbled among the cane roots until he came back and stooped and found the shells and they rose and at that moment the gun, untouched, leaning against the log six feet away and for that while even forgotten by both of them, roared, bellowed and flamed, and ceased: and he carried it now, pumped out the last mummified shell and gave that one also to Ash and, the action still open, himself carried the gun until he stood it in the corner behind Boon's bed at the camp

—; summer, and fall, and snow, and wet and saprife spring in their ordered immortal sequence, the deathless and immemorial phases of the mother who had shaped him if any had toward the man he almost was, mother and father both to the old man born of a Negro slave and a Chickasaw chief who had been his spirit's father if any had, whom he had revered and harkened to and loved and lost and grieved: and he would marry someday and they too would own for their brief while that brief unsubstanced glory which inherently of itself cannot last and hence why glory: and they would, might, carry even the remembrance of it into the time when flesh no longer talks to flesh because memory at least does last: but still the woods would be his mistress and his wife.

He was not going toward the Gum Tree. Actually he was getting farther from it. Time was and not so long ago either when he would not have been allowed here without someone with him, and a little later, when he had begun to learn how much he did not know, he would not have dared be here without someone with him, and later still, beginning to ascertain, even if only dimly, the limits of what he did not know, he could have attempted and carried it through with a compass, not because of any increased belief in himself but because McCaslin and Major de Spain and Walter and General Compson too had taught him at last to believe the compass regardless of what it seemed to state. Now he did not even use the compass but merely the sun and that only subconsciously, yet he could have taken a scaled map and plotted at any time to within a hundred feet of where he actually was; and sure enough, at almost the exact moment when he expected it, the earth began to rise faintly, he passed one of the four concrete markers set down by the lumber company's surveyor to establish the four corners of the plot which Major de Spain had reserved out of the sale, then he stood on the crest of the knoll itself, the four corner-markers all visible now, blanched still even beneath the winter's weathering, lifeless and shockingly alien in that place where dissolution itself was a seething turmoil of ejaculation tumescence conception and birth, and death did not even exist. After two winters' blanketings of leaves and the flood-waters of two springs, there was no trace of the two graves anymore at all. But those who would have come this far to find them would not need headstones but would have found them as Sam Fathers himself had taught him to find such: by bearings on trees: and did, almost the first thrust of the hunting knife finding (but only to see if it was still there) the round tin box manufactured for axle-grease and containing now Old Ben's dried mutilated paw, resting above Lion's bones.

He didn't disturb it. He didn't even look for the other grave where he and McCaslin and Major de Spain and Boon had laid Sam's body, along with his hunting horn and his knife and his tobacco-pipe, that Sunday morning two years ago; he didn't have to. He had stepped over it, perhaps on it. But that was all right. *He probably knew I was in the woods this morning long before I got here,* he thought, going on to the tree which had supported one end of the platform where Sam lay when McCaslin and Major de Spain found them—the tree, the other axle-grease tin nailed to the trunk, but weathered, rusted, alien too yet healed already into the wilderness' concordant generality, raising no tuneless note, and empty, long since empty of the food and tobacco he had put into it that

day, as empty of that as it would presently be of this which he
drew from his pocket—the twist of tobacco, the new ban-
danna handkerchief, the small paper sack of the peppermint
candy which Sam had used to love; that gone too, almost
before he had turned his back, not vanished but merely translated into the myriad life which printed the dark mold of these
secret and sunless places with delicate fairy tracks, which,
breathing and biding and immobile, watched him from
beyond every twig and leaf until he moved, moving again,
walking on; he had not stopped, he had only paused, quitting
the knoll which was no abode of the dead because there was
no death, not Lion and not Sam: not held fast in earth but free
in earth and not in earth but of earth, myriad yet undiffused of
every myriad part, leaf and twig and particle, air and sun and
rain and dew and night, acorn oak and leaf and acorn again,
dark and dawn and dark and dawn again in their immutable
progression and, being myriad, one: and Old Ben too, Old
Ben too; they would give him his paw back even, certainly
they would give him his paw back: then the long challenge
and the long chase, no heart to be driven and outraged, no
flesh to be mauled and bled—Even as he froze himself, he
seemed to hear Ash's parting admonition. He could even hear
the voice as he froze, immobile, one foot just taking his
weight, the toe of the other just lifted behind him, not breathing, feeling again and as always the sharp shocking inrush
from when Isaac McCaslin long yet was not, and so it was fear
all right but not fright as he looked down at it. It had not coiled
yet and the buzzer had not sounded either, only one thick
rapid contraction, one loop cast sideways as though merely for
purchase from which the raised head might start slightly backward, not in fright either, not in threat quite yet, more than six
feet of it, the head raised higher than his knee and less than

his knee's length away, and old, the once-bright markings of its youth dulled now to a monotone concordant too with the wilderness it crawled and lurked: the old one, the ancient and accursed about the earth, fatal and solitary and he could smell it now: the thin sick smell of rotting cucumbers and something else which had no name, evocative of all knowledge and an old weariness and of pariah-hood and of death. At last it moved. Not the head. The elevation of the head did not change as it began to glide away from him, moving erect yet off the perpendicular as if the head and that elevated third were complete and all: an entity walking on two feet and free of all laws of mass and balance and should have been because even now he could not quite believe that all that shift and flow of shadow behind that walking head could have been one snake: going and then gone; he put the other foot down at last and didn't know it, standing with one hand raised as Sam had stood that afternoon six years ago when Sam led him into the wilderness and showed him and he ceased to be a child, speaking the old tongue which Sam had spoken that day without premeditation either: "Chief," he said: "Grandfather."

He couldn't tell when he first began to hear the sound, because when he became aware of it, it seemed to him that he had been already hearing it for several seconds—a sound as though someone were hammering a gun-barrel against a piece of railroad iron, a sound loud and heavy and not rapid yet with something frenzied about it, as the hammerer were not only a strong man and an earnest one but a little hysterical too. Yet it couldn't be on the log-line because, although the track lay in that direction, it was at least two miles from him and this sound was not three hundred yards away. But even as he thought that, he realised where the sound must be coming from: whoever the man was and whatever he was doing, he was somewhere near the edge of the clearing where the Gum Tree was and where he was to meet Boon. So far, he had been hunting as he advanced, moving slowly and quietly and watching the ground and the trees both. Now he went on, his gun unloaded and the barrel slanted up and back to facilitate its passage through brier and undergrowth, approaching as it grew louder and louder that steady savage somehow queerly hysterical beating of metal on metal, emerging from the woods, into the old clearing, with the solitary gum tree directly before him. At first glance the tree seemed to be alive with frantic squirrels. There appeared to be forty or fifty of them leaping and darting from branch to branch until the whole tree had become one green maelstrom of mad leaves, while from time to time, singly or in twos and threes, squirrels would dart down the trunk then whirl without stopping and rush back up again as though sucked violently back by the vacuum of their fellows' frenzied vortex. Then he saw Boon, sitting, his back against the trunk, his head bent, hammering furiously at something on his lap. What he hammered with was the barrel of his dismembered gun, what he hammered at was the breech of it. The rest of the gun lay scattered about him in a half-dozen pieces while he bent over the piece on his lap his scarlet and streaming walnut face, hammering the disjointed barrel against the gunbreech with the frantic abandon of a madman. He didn't even look up to see who it was. Still hammering, he merely shouted back at the boy in a hoarse strangled voice:

"Get out of here! Dont touch them! Dont touch a one of them! They're mine!"

EDITORS' NOTE

"Spotted Horses," is taken from *The Hamlet*, which began as a group of sketches and fragments about the Snopes clan written early in Faulkner's career (probably the mid-1920s) and elaborated in a series of short stories over the next decade or so. First begun by Faulkner in 1927, various versions of "Spotted Horses" were entitled "As I Lay Dying," "Aria con Amore," and "The Peasants." *The Hamlet* was eventually published by Random House on April 1, 1940. Although the editors did not make the kind of revisions they had made in other works by Faulkner, the text was marred by many typographical and compositional errors. Copy-text for "Spotted Horses" is the ribbon typescript setting copy at the Alderman Library of the University of Virginia (other relevant documents consulted were the holograph manuscript, also at the University of Virginia, and two sets of uncorrected galleys, one privately owned and the other at the Mississippi Department of Archives and History in Jackson).

"Old Man" was originally published as alternating sections with "The Wild Palms" in the novel *The Wild Palms* (and subsequently republished by The Library of America as *If I Forget Thee, Jerusalem*, Faulkner's original title). All evidence from the typescripts and manuscripts in the Alderman Library of the University of Virginia, from which the current text is derived, indicates that Faulkner did not take two separate stories and interweave them, but rather, wrote, in alternating stints, for a "Wild Palms" section, then an "Old Man" section.

"The Bear" first originated as a 1935 short story, "Lion," about a dog who tracked a bear. The central character of "Lion," however is not Isaac McCaslin, but Quentin Compson, who had committed suicide in *The Sound and the Fury* (1929), and whom Faulkner was resurrecting at the same time he was writing "Lion," for his role in *Absalom, Absalom.* "Lion" was the central story around which he collected a number of stories he had been working on since the 1930s, which he incorporated into *Go Down, Moses.* Throughout 1940, Faulkner apparently worked on revising this story into the long complicated chapter that eventually became "The Bear," though it was still called "Lion" on the typescript he submitted to Random House. In the fall of 1941, needing money as usual, Faulkner reduced the narrative materials of "Lion" to a twenty-page version (published in *The Saturday Evening Post,* May 4, 1942). Faulkner then carefully revised each story in *Go Down, Moses* and sent to Random House a completely revised and retyped typescript, which the editors pushed through with a minimum of intervention that amounted to virtual indifference. The problems are mostly typographical errors, things that should have been caught by a careful proofreader. The typescript submitted by Faulkner is the copy-text for this edition.

American English continues to fluctuate; for example, a word may be spelled more than one way, even in the same work.

Commas are sometimes used expressively to suggest the movements of the voice, and capitals are sometimes meant to give significances to a word beyond those it might have in its uncapitalized form. Since standardization would remove such effects, this volume preserves the spelling, punctuation, capitalization, and wording of the text as established by Noel Polk, which strives to be as faithful to Faulkner's usage as surviving evidence permits.

The following notes were prepared by Joseph Blotner and are reprinted with permission from *Novels 1936–1940*, (1985) and *Novels 1942–1954* (1994) in the edition of Faulkner's collected works published by The Library of America. Numbers refer to page and line of the present volume (the line count includes chapter headings). No note is made for material included in the eleventh edition of *Merriam-Webster's Collegiate Dictionary*. For further information on these three works, consult the appropriate portions of Joseph Blotner, *Faulkner, A Biography*, 2 vols. (New York: Random House, 1974); Joseph Blotner, *Faulkner, A Biography, One- Volume Edition* (New York: Random House, 1984); *Selected Letters of William Faulkner* (New York: Random House, 1977), edited by Joseph Blotner; and Calvin S. Brown, *A Glossary of Faulkner's South* (New Haven: Yale University Press, 1976).

Spotted Horses
18.24 frail] Variant of flail.

Old Man
86.7 sandboils] Places where water mixed with sand comes up though the landward side of a levee, forced up by the pressure of water contained in the levee.

86.23 Ahenobarbus'] The paternal name of Nero (A.D. 37–68), first called Lucius Domitius Ahenobarbus, later Nero Claudius Caesar.

87.31 Mound's Landing] Two miles west of Scott, Mississippi, and 14 miles north of Greenville.

142.3 Carnarvon] Carnarvon, on the eastern bank of the Mississippi, 14 miles south of New Orleans, where the levee was dynamited on April 29, 1927, to ease the strain on the levee at New Orleans.

The Bear
202.13 frail] Variant of flail.